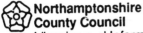

RED CARD

Also by Mel Stein

Fiction
Danger Zone
Rags to Riches
McGovern's Horses (as Tim Elsen)
The White Corridors
Race Against Time
Marked Man

Non-Fiction
Waddle: the Authorised Biography
Gazza: My Life in Pictures
Gazza's Football Year
Soccer Skills with Gazza
Ha'Way The Lad (the authorised biography of Paul Gascoigne)

RED CARD

Mel Stein

HEADLINE

First published in 1996 by
HEADLINE BOOK PUBLISHING

10 9 8 7 6 5 4 3 2 1

British Library Cataloguing in Publication Data

Stein, Mel
Red Card
1. English fiction - 20th century
I. Title
823.9'14 [F]

ISBN 0 7472 1393 3

Typeset by Avon Dataset Ltd, Bidford-on-Avon, Warks

Printed and bound in Great Britain by
Mackays of Chatham PLC, Chatham, Kent

HEADLINE BOOK PUBLISHING
A division of Hodder Headline PLC
338 Euston Road
London NW1 3BH

For those who've not yet finished *Marked Man,*
Nicky's left foot, Paul's right
and especially the cat who prowls at two in the morning

PROLOGUE

It was another hot summer's day in Tel Aviv. The grey-haired man playing a flute at the entrance to the high-rise beach hotel seemed oblivious to the sweltering sun. He wore thick dark trousers falling over heavy black shoes, and his white shirt and stained tie were topped by a shapeless cardigan of an anonymous colour. He barely looked up as the hundred-shekel note fell into his beret, and in a scarcely audible whisper he said, 'Room 814' to its donor, the language of his home familiar to them both.

It was the fifth time that morning he had gone through the same ritual, and each time he had removed the note from the hat at the end of the tune and slipped it into his inside pocket, concerned lest somebody should wonder why his music might command such a high price. He sensed rather than heard the revolving doors of the hotel swing smoothly around to allow the man entrance, then began another plaintive melody, knowing that there was one more visitor to arrive.

He did not have long to wait. A shadow fell across him, and this time he broke off in mid-tune. This man was large and, despite the wealth of those who had gone before, far more smartly dressed. The lightweight suit needed no label to confirm it was designer-made, and the silk tie that adorned the initial-embossed cotton shirt had obviously emanated from the same exclusive source.

'Room 814,' the musician said in the same language he had used to the others. The big man, who had already placed the

1

hundred-shekel note in the beret, looked bemused. The musician realised that he was not Russian and repeated the message in English. The man frowned, as if the delay had interfered with his plans, then moved on into the foyer, walking fast towards the bank of elevators to ensure nobody disturbed him further.

By the time he reached the eighth floor he felt more relaxed. The air-conditioning in the hotel and in the lift itself was working efficiently, and for the first time that day he actually felt cool and in control. These people might think they were efficient, with their look-outs and passwords, but he came from a race with thousands of years of plotting and planning behind them. He knew he would be outnumbered this morning, but it no longer concerned him. He did not think they would dare to trick him – but if they did he would be ready.

He knocked at the door, the double knock followed by the single as he had been told. More games – but for the moment it suited him to play along with them. When the time came for him to change the rules, then he would know. He always knew. That was what had kept him alive for so long; that was what had made him seriously rich. This new project was not about the money – he was beyond that – but still he loved the challenge, the excitement, and at the end of the day if it made him richer still then he had no objection to that.

The five men were seated at the table already, one at the head and two to each side. A sixth man stood alone at the window, gazing out at the panoramic view of the Mediterranean, the rocky outlet that was Jaffa just visible to the left. He had black curly hair, a dark complexion, and with his T-shirt, jeans and trainers stood out from the older group at the table. The last entrant looked around him, then, catching sight of the younger man, asked in English, 'Who is he?'

'An interpreter,' the man at the table's head replied. 'Our discussions may be complicated. We thought we might need him.'

'Can we trust him?'

The young man turned around slowly, as if he had only just realised that he was the subject of the conversation. 'I hear, I translate, I forget,' he said, his teeth flashing white as he smiled.

'Very well. Then let us get to work. Can somebody get me a drink?'

The young man looked towards the chairman, reluctant to obey any request without his authority.

'Of course. You've come a long way. Vodka, Scotch, wine, coffee? We have whatever you want.'

'If you did not have what I want then I would not have come. Water, please, with gas.'

'Alas. It is not a popular drink in this country. They seem to have other use for their water than to pump it full of bubbles. Club soda is the best we can do.'

The young man translated as he poured the drink, assuming the other man would accept. The chairman made a gesture of looking impatiently at his watch and soon everybody was seated. Nobody produced pen or paper – this was not a meeting to be minuted. Whatever would be agreed would be agreed. Nobody would forget.

The swarm of locals and tourists, who would spend hours walking back and forth along the sea-front, had already gathered. By the beach, on a raised platform, a live band broke into rock and roll in Ivrit. The sound reached the room despite the double-glazing and the absence of any open window.

The chairman shrugged. 'Young people . . .'

The interpreter did not bother to translate.

The discussions continued long after the music had faded into the night. Finally, the chairman spoke. 'So it is agreed then. The first one is ready to be brought out.'

'It's agreed,' replied the last man to arrive. Again, the interpreter did not translate.

'So we are finished then,' the chairman said.

3

They shook hands, and then the big man shook hands with the other four men at the table. One of them, with a broken nose and eyes that almost disappeared beneath bushy white eyebrows, rose and gestured to the interpreter that it was time he was paid. The young man followed him to the bedroom. The man with the eyebrows bent over a case, as if looking for money, then removed a gun with a silencer and shot him twice: once in the head and once in the heart. He returned to the room and lifted the phone, speaking rapidly in his native tongue.

'Yes, the parcel is ready for collection and delivery.'

The chairman turned towards the man who had been the last to arrive. 'You see? You had no need to worry. We are very careful about security.'

The interpreter did not translate.

CHAPTER 1

Mark Rossetti sat opposite his daughter in the late September sunshine, oblivious to the Sunday tourists wandering in droves around the Covent Garden piazza. He had not yet spent sufficient time with her to take her for granted, and he was watching every movement of her body like an artist whose subject might disappear at any moment.

Emma Rossetti, at eleven years old, nearly twelve, but at times going on twenty, was more interested in her Hägen-Dazs ice cream with its three-scoop contents – chocolate, strawberry and pistachio – topped off with Smarties. She ate with the fierce concentration of somebody who is not yet concerned with what calories might do to her figure; although looking at her slight, street-urchin frame, she did not look as if she would ever be bothered with such problems.

Yet, her father knew, you could not take such things for granted. As a professional footballer over ten years ago, with an international career beginning to flourish, he could not have forseen that he would be banned from the game for a decade, for something of which he was entirely innocent. That was all behind him now, and those who had set him up had received their own punishment. If he could not have forseen his exit from the game then, even less predictable was his leading out Hertsmere United (as manager) to victory at Wembley in the FA Cup Final. That had been just over four months ago, and since his decision to resign almost immediately thereafter he had been concentrating on taking some time to smell the flowers – to smell the flowers and get to know the daughter whom his wife had taken away some eight years ago, and to whom he had only recently been granted access. Now he could not get enough of her. He was hooked on her as surely as any addict. She was his heroine, and he had to convince her that he should be her hero; but first he had to persuade her that *he* was really her father, not his one-time team-mate Stuart Macdonald, with whom his wife, Sally, had been living since she left him, and with whom she'd been having an affair before she departed. It had not been easy having Macdonald as the captain of Hertsmere, but since the player had pointed Mark and the police in the direction of those guilty of depriving him of the best years of his playing career, he was able to regard him almost as a friend. Whatever he had felt for Sally was long dead, but what he felt for his daughter was a burning life-force that threatened to consume him every time he had to say goodbye to her. He looked at his watch; three in the afternoon already, and he had promised to return her by five. She was back at school now and, according to Sally, had to finish a history project before she went to bed. A year before he would have asked belligerently why she could not have done it on the Saturday, but experience had taught him to take the softly, softly approach.

Emma finished the ice cream and took up the menu again as if she had just arrived.

'Surely you've had enough. I don't want you up all night being sick; your mother will kill me.'

'I won't be sick.'

He waited for the word 'dad', but it did not come. Some things would take time.

'Can I have a chocolate milk-shake?' she persisted. 'Please.' She looked at him, her head dropped to one side, towards her left shoulder. He had seen that mannerism before on her mother, and he had not been able to resist then either. He caught the eye of a passing waitress. She looked too young to be working, or perhaps it was just him getting older. Policemen, waitresses and footballers: when they started looking like your own children, then it was time to get worried.

The milk-shake duly arrived in all its enormity, and Mark breathed an inward sigh of relief. It would take her at least a quarter of an hour to plough through that – another fifteen minutes of time with her when he need not struggle to make conversation, when he could just look and, as Leopold Schneider would say, 'enjoy'. He was worried about Leo. The old man had rushed himself out of hospital after his heart attack, and was still dragging himself around his innumerable properties collecting his own rents. With his frail frame draped in the inevitable ankle-length cashmere overcoat it was a miracle that nobody had mugged him for the cash that bulged out his inside pockets. On reflection, it was surprising that he defied gravity by keeping upright with the weight of the money that grew with each visit. Leo had believed in Mark when it seemed nobody else did, and as an only child, with his own mother and father dead, Leo was the nearest thing he had to a relation. He would never forget the weeks and months that had passed without him paying any rent to Leo, who was then his landlord.

It was odd the way families disintegrated. He had photographs at home of himself with his parents at the seaside, them sitting in deck-chairs at Bournemouth, him making a sand castle, all three smiling smiles that he thought at the time would last for ever. He had only a few snaps of Emma with Sally and himself. The pair of them had left before the child was really old enough to enjoy herself with her mother and father. It was yet another thing that had been stolen from him. Death and divorce – they both had the same effect; they created history, freeze-framed the past in a cold, merciless time-warp.

He surreptitiously looked again at his watch, hoping she

would not notice and think he was bored with her company. He was merely ensuring he got her home on time and avoided any unpleasant confrontations with Sally. The brief truce that she'd called, when Stuart Macdonald had persuaded her that Mark should have access, had been broken off within a month when he'd delivered Emma back an hour late.

'It's bloody typical of you, Mark. You'll never change. You think that nobody else in the world has any arrangements except you. We're supposed to be going out to the pictures with friends, and now I've got to feed Emma and get her sorted out all in half an hour. I'm warning you, if you mess me about again like this, then whatever my soft-hearted husband might say I'll force you through the courts to get to see her.'

He'd had enough of all that. He was tired and all he wanted was a quiet life. Or did he? Three or four months of doing virtually nothing had taken their toll on him. Even his mind was reluctant to wake up in the mornings. Thinking was an effort, and it was far easier to let each day slide by at its own pace. He could understand why people were becoming irritated by him, but was helpless to do anything about it. It was his attitude that had fouled up his relationship with Patti Delaney. He'd known before he got involved with her that she was an ambitious young journalist, but somehow before the relationship exploded into a full-scale affair she had always found time for him. In his more cynical moments he half convinced himself that it was because she saw him as a potential story, but the thought never stayed for too long. She had genuinely cared, and he had also cared for her – but once again he seemed to have screwed up another opportunity in his life.

She had made all the right excuses. 'Mark, it's not about you, but I've lived alone for too long. I'm getting a reputation now for someone who delivers the goods, and somehow or other when I'm around you I just can't write.'

He'd tried to argue with her, but she had been adamant.

'Take it as a compliment. You've got the power to distract me; there's not many people I'd say that about.'

And then there had been her mother. In all the time he'd known Patti she'd hardly mentioned her family, and he'd had no idea whether her parents were even alive. It had come out one night after they'd taken Leo out to eat at a Kosher restaurant in Golders Green. He'd eaten sparingly, as if the effort of lifting the fork to his mouth was just too much, while Patti had tucked in with a confidence that suggested she was familiar with the culinary delights of kreplach, kneidlech, latkas and lockshen pudding. He'd asked her how she knew her way so well around the menu, while he'd settled for an unappetising bloodless steak and chips.

'Irish father, Jewish mother,' she'd replied. 'Her family wrote her off, but it didn't stop me getting invited to all sorts of weddings and bar mitzvahs. I couldn't eat this sort of stuff every day, but if you wait long enough between meals you almost get the taste for it.'

The Irish father – whose sole contribution to her life seemed to have been the name Delaney – had long gone, but the mother, Valerie, was still there – and she was not a well person. The first time Mark realised that was when he'd lain beside Patti in her West Hampstead flat, that they'd named 'The Burrow' for the sense of warmth and security it gave them both. She was asleep, but as he listened to her regular deep breathing after a bout of lovemaking that should have exhausted them both, he found it impossible to become unconscious. He had to make a decision about which way he and Patti should proceed. As the phone rang he did not realise that the decision was about to be made for him.

The receiver was on his side of the bed, and he picked it up before Patti was fully awake.

'I'm phoning in relation to Mrs Conway, Mrs Valerie Conway...' The voice on the other end of the line was cool and professional, a voice that seemed well experienced in imparting bad tidings.

'You've got the wrong number; there's no Mrs Conway here . . .' It was at that moment that Patti rolled across and grabbed the receiver from his hand.

'Yes, yes, this is her daughter speaking. She has? Again? Yes, I'm sorry. I'll be straight down.'

She was out of bed before she'd finished the final sentence, madly pulling on clothes as if she was changing costumes backstage between scenes. 'I'm going to have to go to the Whittington Hospital. My mother's OD'd.'

'Is she OK? Do you want me to come with you?' Mark asked.

'Yes . . . and no. I'd rather deal with her myself . . . on my own. She's done this before. I'm going to need to spend some time with her. I think it might be best if you went home for a while. I'll call you, don't worry.'

That had been the start of things. When he'd accused her of striking the first blow in demolishing whatever it was they had, she'd denied it.

'It's you, Mark. You're the one that's changed. When you were trying to clear your name, to fight your way back, you had a sense of direction, but now you're drifting and I'm not the desert island you're going to be washed up on.'

When Valerie had been discharged from the hospital, Patti had arranged for her to enter a private psychiatric clinic in North London.

'It's bloody expensive. I'm going to have to work even harder. It's better if we don't see each other for a while. It'll give us both time to get ourselves sorted out.'

He still spoke to her on the phone, but there was a distance between them that went further than the few miles between Barnet and Hampstead. Maybe he'd call her tonight after he'd taken Emma home. She was alternately scooping up the last dregs of the milk-shake with her spoon and sucking the straw with noisy enthusiasm. If she was going to be sick at least she would have enjoyed the causes of it.

They walked back to where he'd parked the car near the river, and gradually the sounds of the entertainers in the Garden faded behind them. As they crossed Aldwych she put her hand into his and he felt a terrible responsibility, not just for seeing her across the road, but for her future happiness. He had to do something with his life. The money he'd earned from his brief but glorious flirtation with fame would not last for ever and, although he'd been advised he might well have a claim for damages against those who had prevented him from earning his livelihood, he did not think he had either the energy or the desire for the publicity such an action would bring.

He let her into the car, politely opening the door for her, and she curtsied her thanks, bringing a smile to his face. Maybe he shouldn't take her home; maybe he should simply drive until they arrived where nobody knew them and live the sort of life yearned for by Little Nell and her grandfather. Instead, he headed north towards St Albans, kissed her gently on the forehead when they arrived, and watched her run up the drive into the waiting arms of Stuart Macdonald. He raised one arm in greeting, relieved that it had been him rather than Sally who had come to the door. He realised as he turned for home that he had absolutely nothing to do, and that the week stretched endlessly before him with very little to offer.

CHAPTER 2

He had to buy a new car. The Escort GTi had been fine when he'd been twenty-one, but now that Daniel Lewis was pushing thirty it was simply not good enough. Neither was it good enough for The Bishop's Avenue, North London's most prestigious road, stretching from Kenwood at one end (the good end) to East Finchley at the other (the cheap end). Here, the worst cars in the drives were BMWs and the lower end of the Mercedes scale, and these were probably seventeenth birthday presents to the younger sons of property owners.

Daniel Lewis had not had that sort of start in life. Back in 1965, when he was born, his parents were one of the last families of their social circle to move out of Stamford Hill. Even then they'd not made the usual leap to Finchley or Ilford, but had settled for a flat that he, as an estate agent, would now describe as being in Highgate, but was in truth in Archway. Not that truth had very much to do with his chosen profession. Once the punter finds out about the various lies that induced him to buy the property it is usually too late, and by the time the next transaction involving them comes around they have usually forgotten.

His mum and dad were still alive, still in their Archway flat, his dad still dragging himself off to work as a despatch manager with a West End fashion company, his mother still enjoying her afternoon Kalooki sessions with her well-preserved cronies. Whether or not he had lived up to their expectations he did not know. He did know, however, that he

13

had not fulfilled the hopes of his wife, Elaine. When she had married him some eight years before, the property market was still enjoying its boom, although history shows that the slump was not far behind. And so the three-bedroomed semi-detached house in Mill Hill, which had been regarded as merely a stepping stone to something far more impressive, was still their home – only now they shared it with two children, Sam and Lisa, who seemed to be taking up more space with every passing day.

'I don't know why we don't just give up our room to the kids and move into the attic. I have to put on mountaineering equipment to climb over the pile of toys they leave there every day.'

She had a nice line in sarcasm, did Elaine. Looking back on their relationship, Daniel supposed she had always possessed it. Only now she had more cause and more opportunity to use it. She used it about his spreading waistline, and his hair-line which seemed to be receding in inverse proportion.

He'd found her the previous weekend poring over their wedding album. At first he'd been touched by that, but then she'd shaken her head and closed the book with a decisive thump. 'I only wanted to know if I was certifiable when I married you – or merely short-sighted.' He hadn't bothered to ask her what conclusion she had reached.

There wasn't much he could do about his hair. All the dark curls that had made him so adorable at his bar mitzvah had surrendered under the constant onslaught of elderly aunts running their fingers through it, just after or just before pinching his cheeks and bestowing some incomprehensible Yiddish blessing upon him. His father had been bald by the time he was forty, and Daniel was well on the way to emulating him. After a day without shaving he had more stubble on his cheeks than on the top of his head, while at the sides the curls still grew in an abandoned frenzy that mourned

14

the loss of their connecting comrades and necessitated fortnightly visits to the hairdresser. The cheeks were still pinchable, but then so was so much else on his body. He wished he could have joined a health club like many of his contemporaries, but the membership fees did not fall within his budget. He had to settle for the odd visit when he was signed in as a guest in order to see exactly what it was he was missing.

Things could change, though. If he could pull off this deal there would be a commission of some £25,000. Although he would have to split that with the main agent, the man he was meeting this morning had promised that if they were happy with his work on the property there would be many more of the same type and price range in the future. He would be back in the big time. He couldn't remember when he had last been involved in a transaction that large, but once he had this one under his belt then his whole profile would be changed. He was not going to miss this opportunity; there had been too many missed opportunities in the past. When the building societies were buying up estate agents with rapacious glee in the early eighties he had held firm, whilst friends and associates were happily banking their cheques and buying their holiday homes in Marbella and Florida.

'I don't know how you can think of working for somebody,' he'd said to Richard Cowans when he'd sold out for one and a half million.

'For that sort of money I'd empty waste-paper baskets,' Richard had said, and then five years later when the bottom had fallen out of the market he'd bought back his company for a mere two hundred grand, stuck a manager in to run it and carried on living in the sunshine, returning to England only to show off his tan.

There had been times over the last few years when Daniel Lewis had not needed to empty waste-paper baskets, because they were never full. All he ever seemed to put in them were the envelopes from bills that came in with more frequency than clients. No, this time he was going to get it right and stop the whining of his wife – and her dear mother, with her 'told you so; why didn't you marry Henry Goldstone who's such a successful accountant?' look.

The principal agent pulled up in the drive of the house and stepped out of his Alfa-Romeo sports car. He looked about sixteen years old to Lewis, with his short hair style and Ray-Ban shades, light cotton suit and floral tie. He spoke with an affected accent that suggested a minor public school where he had obviously not proceeded to A levels.

'Morning. Simon Marchbanks. You must be Danny Lewis. We've spoken on the phone.'

'Yes, we have,' Lewis said, taking the extended hand and experiencing the firm, practised handshake. 'And it's Daniel, not Danny.'

'Right,' the young man said without any great interest. He looked around him. 'Your man not here yet? Sure this isn't a bit out of his class? I suppose you don't deal with many punters in this sort of price range.'

It was a statement, not a question, but before Lewis could think of a suitable response a large, black car drew up behind them. At the wheel was a chauffeur, grim-faced and dressed in matching black, a man who would have been more in place at a funeral than a house purchase. Neither Lewis nor Marchbanks could see who was in the back of the car, as the tinted windows revealed neither the number nor sex of the passengers. The chauffeur climbed down from his seat and opened the rear door as reverentially as if he were carrying royalty. A small man stepped out and looked around him, blinking like a potholer who had just been rescued and was seeing the light and breathing the fresh air as if they were something novel.

The first thing Lewis noticed about him were his eyes. They were ebony black, dark precious stones that pierced through everything they regarded and seemed to take in the whole scene in one glance. It took a while to get past the gaze, and then Daniel saw that the rest of him was no more than five feet tall and pencil thin, the line of the hand-made suit making him seem even slimmer. He was so cleanly shaven that it was hard to believe any hair would dare to grow on his face. Lewis did not think he had ever seen a man so linear, so pared to the bone.

He seemed to be confused by the fact that he was being met by two people who had obviously come separately. 'Which is Mr Lewis?' he asked, as if he were regarding two specimens of insect. The voice was melodious, almost too high to be masculine, the accent definitely there, but seemingly regarded by the speaker as a mild irritation rather than an impediment.

'I am,' Daniel said.

'And this . . . ?' A dismissive gesture of the hand accompanied the question.

Simon Marchbanks moved confidently forward, his hand extended, only to find his path blocked by the chauffeur, who had received the slightest signal to intercept the agent.

'You were not invited to the meeting. Perhaps you would leave now. My business is with Mr Lewis.'

Daniel Lewis did not know whether he should take that as a compliment or a threat but, whatever came from the day, the look on Marchbank's face had to be worth it. If Lewis ended up face-down in a gutter he could remember that scene and die with a smile on his face.

'Yes, well, as you wish, although it is our property,' Marchbanks said, backing towards his car, followed by the ominous shadow of the chauffeur. 'You'll let me know what happens then, Lewis, although I must say, he doesn't look like our sort of client.' The last was tossed back over his shoulder as he virtually leapt into the driver's seat of his car and roared away.

With his departure the man's whole attitude changed. 'I do

17

not like surprises. In my country we were for many years suspicious of surprises or change. Now, Mr Lewis, we can get down to business. My name is Nikolei Yevneko and I have, I think, come to buy this property.'

Lewis led the way into the house, his shoes noisily disturbing the gravel.

'We will hear if anybody should decide to visit us unexpectedly,' Yevneko said.

Lewis could not tell if this was a serious observation. 'What part of Russia are you from?' he asked. He found himself struggling with the key in the lock of the empty house and was surprised to see that it was because his hand was shaking.

'Does it matter?' Yevneko replied. He signalled to the driver that his opinion would not be required over the matter of the house and the man returned to the car, his movements swift and cat-like for such a big man.

'Yuri has his uses, but interior design is not one of them. Yuri has uses. I think that is an English pun.'

'Yes, yes it is,' Lewis replied, laughing nervously. He had the distinct impression that Yevneko did not make too many jokes, and that when he did he expected a positive reaction.

They stood in the vast hall, looking up at a minstrel gallery. 'Where would you like to start?' Lewis asked.

'Here is as good a place as any,' Yevneko said with a thin smile that melted before it had settled on his features. 'You like football, I see.'

'Yes I do. How did you know?'

'I saw the sign . . . No, that is wrong.' He furrowed his brow and Lewis guessed correctly that he would not welcome any assistance. 'I saw the sticker on the back of your car. Your team is Hertsmere.'

Lewis was impressed by how much the Russian had taken in during the few moments they had spent outside.

'I've supported them since they got into the league.'

'Not Tottenham or Arsenal?'

18

'No. I got tired of the big boys. And they priced their tickets out of the market for people like me.'

'But now your Hertsmere are big boys I think. They have won the cup and they are in Europe. Perhaps they too will price themselves out of the market. We must see what we can do to ensure that you move up into the same market as them.'

'You obviously follow English football,' Lewis said, hoping the man meant what he said. 'Are your kids interested?'

'Did I say I had children?'

'No, but I thought . . . a big house like this. That you must have a family. There are so many bedrooms to fill.'

'It is unwise to leap to conclusions – unwise and dangerous. Later, perhaps, we shall talk some more about football, but now you will allow me to see the rest of the house.' Yevneko's voice rose inquiringly, but as he moved towards the stairs as if he were showing Lewis around, the estate agent realised that it was not a question, but an order.

CHAPTER 3

There were times when Mark knew it was going to be bad news from the way the telephone rang. Everybody to whom he had tried to explain this phenomenon thought him crazy, but he was sure it was so. There was a slow, solemn pace about the ring, as if the telephone was warning him that he should not pick it up, if he did not want his day to be ruined. He looked at the clock by the side of his bed. It was seven a.m. and the alarm had not been set to go off for another hour and a half. He fumbled for the receiver and cursed as he knocked over the glass of water he'd placed there the night before to swallow the paracetamol he'd needed for a headache. He'd got accustomed to headaches when he was drinking, but now they crept up on him by surprise, beginning as a dull ache that he felt would go away, then digging in like First World War frontliners. He ought to see an optician. '. . . While you can still see your way there,' Patti had said when he'd last mentioned it to her. That had been a couple of weeks before, when she'd told him she was going away for a holiday. She'd not said where and she'd not invited him along, and he was still awaiting the postcard she'd promised him.

At first he thought it was her on the line. The only other woman who called him was Sally, and he could never forget her voice with its endless demands and ultimatums.

'Hello, Mark Rossetti?' The speaker had only got as far as 'Mark' when he realised it was a total stranger. A total stranger calling at seven in the morning. That normally meant bad news about somebody he did know. 'I'm sorry to call you so early, but Mr Schneider was very specific about it.'

'Mr Schneider – Leo. What's happened?'

He'd grown to love the old refugee over the last few years. Leo had started out as his landlord, but had ended as his friend. He'd spent hours with Mark, eating the biscuits he'd brought with him, waiting resignedly for the rent that he knew the younger man did not have. After his first heart attack Mark had actually helped to collect the rents for the innumerable properties he owned, but when Mark took over the mantle of Manager at Hertsmere he hardly thought it appropriate to persuade tenants to part with their money when they might well be paying customers on a Saturday afternoon.

He'd neglected Leo lately, and he felt badly about that. As far as he knew he had nobody else to visit him, no relations, no friends; no one was invited to the decaying house that he called home.

The voice continued, cool, professional. 'I'm afraid Mr Schneider passed away an hour ago.'

Mark was fully awake by now. It was impossible; Leo was indestructible. He'd survived the camps, he'd survived his heart attack – he'd survive this. The woman had got it wrong. He wanted to tell her to go back and check. He couldn't conceive of Leo's body, thin and naked in a mortuary with a label on his toe. That wasn't Leo. He'd be cold without the huge cashmere overcoat he'd worn for the last thirty years; he'd be hungry without the biscuits he seemed to buy daily from the Kosher bakers.

'Mr Schneider said you would make all the arrangements,' the woman said.

Mark thought, Did he indeed? But all he said was, 'Yes. Yes, of course.'

'He said that you knew the name of his solicitor and that you and a lady, Miss Delaney, would know what to do.'

'I'll be down there as soon as I can,' Mark replied, then

realising he did not know where 'there' was, asked and was told Leo had died at the North Middlesex Hospital in Edmonton.

He pulled on his clothes automatically. Although he'd experienced the death of loved ones before – his mother and his father – and despite the tragic nature of his father's death – he'd suffered a heart attack while watching his café burn down after an arson attack – Leo's passing was in its way much worse. At his father's funeral, Mark had realised that he'd not known the man well enough. He was well into his alcoholic haze by then, and even the happier memories of his childhood were blurred; the earlier days of success on the field were blotted out by the disgrace it appeared he had brought upon his family. Leo had been with him on his clearer days, had seen the transformation from all-time loser to all-conquering winner. Leo had seen the relationship with Patti develop. There had not been much that Leo had missed, and now he would see no more.

The old man had not believed it ended like that.

'How can you have any sort of faith, Leo, after what happened to your people in the camps?' Mark had asked one wet afternoon as they sat in his dingy flat.

'How can you not?' Leo had answered. He'd always had that annoying habit of answering a question with a question; but he'd made Mark think and he'd made Mark believe – if not in a divine force then at least in himself.

He was fully dressed and ready to leave in twenty minutes, but he had no idea of what he would do once the body passed into his possession. Did they just give you the corpse and let you put it in the boot of your car? He doubted it. And this was a Jewish corpse. If his vague knowledge of the religion was anything to go by, there would be all sorts of rituals to go through before they could finally lay the body to rest. He lifted the phone and began to dial Patti's number. There was no real reason to believe that she would have returned overnight, but

23

if he could only contact her he was confident that she would know what to do. She had a Jewish mother, and even though he knew the family had never practised or professed to be Jewish, as a journalist she would have the right contacts to guide them through.

Normally Patti's answerphone cut in after half a dozen rings, but today it just rang and rang. He was about to assume the tape was full when a sleepy voice answered faintly, the words obviously coming from some distance away from the mouthpiece.

'Patti, is that you? It's Mark.'

'Too loud, too loud. Mark, call me back next year when I've woken up.' He could visualise her staring blearily at the clock. 'Jesus, it's seven o'clock. Is it night-time? Did I miss a day?'

'Look, I'm sorry. It's just that Leo's died. He wants me . . . us . . . to make the arrangements for the funeral.'

Suddenly she was awake. 'Oh no. Give me ten minutes. No, get in your car. But the time you get here, I'll be ready.'

It took him nearly three quarters of an hour to get from Barnet to West Hampstead. The holiday season was now fully over, the schools were back, and the rush hour had returned as if it had never been away. The morning was bright, but with that indefinable scent in the air that said, Don't be fooled. This is Autumn, not Summer. Today will do nothing to help you preserve that suntan on which you worked so hard. A few drivers had their windows down, bare brown arms dangling out, telling the rest of the road that they'd been away somewhere so expensive that the weather had been good all the time. Oblivious to the rude gestures the tanned hands gave him, Mark drove as fast as he could, weaving in and out of the slow-moving lanes. It was only when he got to Patti at 'The Burrow' that he realised there had been no rush. Leopold Schneider was not going anywhere other than a hole in the ground. He was dead and Mark Rossetti would miss him.

CHAPTER 4

Mark had been right in thinking that Patti would sort things out. The hospital gave them the name of a local Rabbi who arrived a short time afterwards. His generous black beard and black coat contrasted sharply with his gentle brown eyes that had a permanent twinkle even the sympathetic voice could not subdue. As he drew closer, Mark was surprised at how young he was, no more than twenty-five – yet, as he learned after half an hour in his company, he already had four children and his American wife was expecting their fifth. His name was Abelson and he came from New York where, without being from a particularly orthodox background, he'd got himself involved with the Lubavitch movement as a child and had never looked back.

As soon as the various offices were open Abelson arranged for somebody to come and wash the body in the traditional manner and sit with it until the funeral. The Rabbi accompanied Mark and Patti to the registry office to get the death certificate, and then to the United Synagogue Burial Service to acquire a plot. Leo had not been a member of any synagogue. Mark had spoken to Leo's solicitor, Arnold Leigh, who had assured him that Leo wanted an orthodox service and that there was ample money to pay for it.

'Strange really,' Leigh had mused. 'He wasn't what you'd call an orthodox man. Ring me back when you've made the arrangements because I'd like to come to pay my respects. He could be a miserable old bastard when it came to paying fees, but he was loyal and I got a lot of work out of him over the years.'

Mark made a mental note not to ask the lawyer to give a eulogy at the funeral – if in fact eulogies played any part in them.

The cost of the land for the burial was exorbitant and the lady behind the desk shrugged apologetically, pointing out by way of consolation that if Leo had paid Synagogue and Burial Rights fees while he was alive they would have cost him far more than his estate was now being asked to contribute. Mark knew that Leo would not have been happy with the deal. He was always very particular about his property transactions and this was one from which he would get no returns.

Incredibly enough, by four in the afternoon they were gathered at Waltham Abbey Cemetery in Essex. Leo's body lay in the middle of the hall in a simple pine coffin, covered by a black cloth and lying on a wagon with mud-stained wheels. Flowers were frowned upon at Jewish funerals, but there was a stark simplicity about the room and the grounds beyond that had a beauty of its own. Abelson was officiating. He had arranged for a few strangers to be present so that with him and Leigh there were ten adult Jewish males, a *minyan* without which it would not have been possible to recite the Mourner's *Kaddish* for the repose of Leo's soul.

Only Rabbi Abelson was permitted to speak, and what he said was brief and to the point.

'I never knew Leopold Schneider, and I believe that was my loss not his. I have met his friends only today, and their devotion pays tribute to the sort of man he must have been. He was one of the few to survive for more than five years in the horror camps of Germany, and his survival is a testimony to the strength and courage of human nature, the triumph of man over animal. He was not a religious man in the accepted definition of the word, but he was a man who believed. He believed in G-d and he believed in good, and you who have

26

come here today without having known him are all the poorer for that.'

Abelson signalled to Mark to take one handle of the wagon, and Leigh took the other. The Rabbi led them out into the sunshine, through two huge doors which opened like gates leading to heaven. He intoned prayers that were meaningless to Mark and Patti, walking several paces behind, the only woman at the ceremony. They finally came to the graveside, the earth freshly dug, giving out its own unique scent – at once welcoming and suffocating. Without undue ceremony the grave-diggers lowered the coffin into the ground, the box swinging unsteadily from side to side, Leo's weight inside, covered with a *tallit*, a prayer shawl provided by Abelson, barely enough to give it any ballast.

Again Abelson's mournful tones rose into the sky. Mark read the English translation: 'A man, whether he be a year old, or whether he lives a thousand years, what does it profit him? As if he has never been shall he be . . .' He couldn't agree with that; there had to be a way to leave a permanent legacy on the face of the world. He had Emma. She would be there long after he had been consigned to the same earth as Leo. But then there would come a time when she too would be buried. He shivered. He longed to be away from this place, back somewhere that had light and laughter, noise and smell. He wanted a drink, and if there had been one on hand he had no doubt he could have downed it there and then and asked for another, despite all the vows and promises he had made in the past. Dogs in the kennels that backed onto the cemetery began to howl, their sounds following them all the way back to the hall for the rest of the ceremony. It was odd, the prayers being recited when the reason for them being there had been left behind in the grave. They'd all had to fill in the clods of earth, each person having thrown three shovel-loads upon the coffin. The first three had landed with a hollow sound on the lid, but then they became progressively quieter as the wood gradually disappeared from sight. Earth upon earth, consigning what lay beneath to the worms. Then finally it was over. Abelson instructed them that they should pick some blades of grass on their way out and toss them over their right shoulders, saying, 'May they blossom forth from the city like the grass of the earth. Remember that we are but dust.'

'I'll say a prayer for him every day,' the Rabbi said. 'There doesn't seem to be anybody else.' And then he was gone, and the other mourners were gone, and Patti and Mark were left alone with Arnold Leigh.

The lawyer was a bulky man in his mid-fifties, well wrapped in a heavy raincoat despite the warmth of the day and the blue of the sky. 'Here's my card. I wonder if the two of you could come into my office, perhaps tomorrow. There are some matters to do with Leopold's estate that I need to discuss with you –' he hesitated, and then went for the cliché – 'that will be to your advantage. Give my secretary a ring in the morning and she'll tell you what time would be convenient. Now, if you'll excuse me, I have to get back to the office. Life goes on, life goes on . . .'

Although Mark and Patti had been together since early morning, there had been little opportunity to talk. She looked tanned, but beneath the surface she also looked tired and drawn. He could put part of it down to the traumatic day, but not all of it. Some of the strain was more deeply engrained than that.

'Drink?' he asked.

'Sure. Whisky for me, water for you.'

'I wouldn't have it any other way.'

He drove back along the M25, then turned off at Potters Bar, driving down through Southgate, past his old flat and office, the main shopping street now filled with charity shops and the windows of abandoned premises covered by posters. He pulled in opposite the Cherry Tree pub at the Green. The bar was filled with foreign students and au pairs who had just arrived from all over Europe, and had discovered that this was where they had the best chance of hearing their own language. They might have come to learn English, but they didn't have to speak it all the time.

'I didn't get the postcard,' Mark said, when he'd bought the drinks and they'd moved out to the rear garden.

'I didn't send one,' she said.

'Thanks,' he said, in a tone that could have been interpreted as hurt if she chose to take him seriously.

She did. 'There's no need to sulk. I was going to phone you today anyway. I thought you'd prefer me to the card. For a journalist I'm a lousy correspondent.'

He sipped his sparkling water, watching the slice of lemon and the cube of ice chasing each other round as he swirled the glass. She looked as good as ever. She'd had her hair cut very short yet again, and had abandoned her normal T-shirt in favour of a tightly cut dark suit that made her seem taller and slimmer by flattening her generous breasts that he had so loved. She lit up a cigarette. He had been counting and knew it was her twentieth of the day, but he also knew there was nothing he could say or do to persuade her to give up.

'I have to be honest,' she said, 'it wasn't only because of you that I came back. The hospital said they felt my mother needed to see me more regularly as part of her treatment.'

'You've not been very lucky with your parents,' Mark said, knowing what had happened to her father.

'It's not a question of luck. My dad succeeded in topping himself, and my mother keeps failing. One of the doctors told me that if someone really wants to do it then they make sure, otherwise it's a cry for help. I thought by going away I could get out of earshot, but I was wrong.'

'You thought by going away that you could get out of range of me as well,' Mark said.

She lifted her hand and ran the back of it down the side of his face. 'Maybe I was wrong about that as well.'

She pushed her empty glass towards Mark. 'I could do with another. A double, I think.'

He rose to go to the bar, but she pulled him back into his seat.

'Forget the drink. Why don't we buy a bottle at an off-licence and go back to the Burrow?'

'Are you sure?' Mark asked.

'Not when you ask that sort of stupid question. Let's make it your place, though. At least my mother and the doctors won't be able to get hold of me there.'

This time Mark said nothing. He walked back to the car with Patti's arm linked with his. Leo was gone and she was back. One door closed and another opened. As she leant across the front seat to kiss him, he felt an awful need for her, a desire to have her there and then; but then the thought returned that she'd left him once – and he did not think he could take the pain of her leaving again. There were too few people in his life that he truly cared for. Now only Emma and Patti were left. He had to be careful; he knew from his own past that he trod a delicate line. As he drove towards Hampstead she ran her hand across his groin and he felt himself stumble on the tightrope that was his life – and he knew for certain that before the night was out he would fall, regardless of what lay below.

CHAPTER 5

The season had not gone well for Hertsmere United. With the FA Cup in their trophy cupboard they had every reason to look forward to the new campaign, but it had started badly and got progressively worse. Four league games played and all they had to show for it was one point from a home draw. There were all sorts of excuses: Tommy Wallace, the teenage prodigy, had been injured in a pre-season friendly; Liam O'Donnell was a long-term casualty with an Achilles problem; and Nicky Collier, the big, aggressive centre-forward, had got himself sent off in the Charity Shield at Wembley and was only one game into a three-match ban. And that wasn't the whole story. Ray Fowler, the manager, undoubtedly a good coach, was too naive, too trusting to be a real success in the transfer market.

For the first time in the history of the club there was money to be spent. They had earned a couple of million pounds already from their Cup win, and there was more to come if they progressed further in the Cup Winners' Cup. However, with the tie against Berlin in the first round there was no guarantee of that in their present form. Claudio Barlucci, the Italian millionaire, had done as he had promised and joined the board of Hertsmere. The first thing he did was to visit the bank, and when the manager, Frank Marsden, had hesitated over granting new facilities, Barlucci paid them off the next day with a transfer from his own corporate account. All too late Marsden had tried to change his mind, phoning the chairman, David Sinclair, with a barrage of metaphors. 'The grass is always greener, David. Better the devil you know. Old friends are best friends . . .'

'It's funny you should say that Mr Marsden,' Sinclair had replied, 'because I don't recall that we were friends, and I don't recall you calling me anything but Mr Sinclair when our overdraft was at its peak.'

Prices in England had gone crazy, and as soon as a club knew that Hertsmere were interested they went even crazier. It had happened with Blackburn Rovers and Newcastle United when Jack Walker and Sir John Hall opened their purses to the clubs, and it was happening again with Barlucci and Hertsmere. Before the Premier League had agreed to his appointment they had insisted he resign as president of Roma Cinquante, his first love; and to everybody's surprise, not least of all Sinclair's, he had agreed.

'I am developing interests in England . . . and I want to speak English better.'

There was room for improvement, but Sinclair did not feel it prudent to point that out to a man who was about to remove from his shoulders the unbearable weight of financial pressures. In fact, Barlucci had taken positive steps to improve his grasp of the language and had come on by such leaps and bounds that it was hard to believe he had not understood far more than he had let on during his negotiations with the club for their former player Mickey Wayne.

With Barlucci's arrival there had been a general clear-out of the existing board. Richard Lee, Sinclair's former solicitor, was still facing disciplinary action from the Law Society and had not been difficult to see off. Tom Kerr had been an appointee of the Bank and with the end of their relationship with the club came the end of his tenure as finance director. Freddie Scott, Sinclair's long-time friend and supporter, had died. As Helen Davies, the chief executive officer, had said, looking around the board room before the first meeting, 'It seems it's a matter of survivors of the plague.'

Helen had received her reward for both loyalty and intelligence. As Helen Archer she had been secretary of the club, a position that involved the ability to juggle financial and political balls in the air with a dexterity that any of the players might have envied. Now, married to Detective Sergeant Rob Davies, she had grasped the opportunity offered to her by Sinclair with both hands. Marriage and responsibility had combined to improve her appearance. Nothing could make her shorter than her five feet and ten inches, but the jolly-hockey-stick look had been replaced by a sleekness and sophistication that only her husband could have forseen just a few months ago. Her taste in clothing had shifted from Marks & Spencer separates to a Frank Usher suit, set off by a string of pearls that looked genuine. In fact her grandmother had given them to her as a wedding present, and not only were they genuine but nobody with whom she worked knew that they were the only item of jewellery she possessed. In the past she had been an object of derision to the younger players, but now she was a person to respect and fear.

Apart from Helen and Sinclair the other survivors were Ben Porter, seemingly less doddery this year despite having celebrated his eighty-fifth birthday, and Jonathan Black, the architect. To Sinclair, Black's face looked redder than ever and he could only think that either his blood pressure was rising or else he was drinking more heavily to forget it. Sinclair would have liked to have seen the back of Black as well, but despite Barlucci's more than generous offer for his shares he was sitting tight. Still, as a force on the board there was little he could do in the face of Sinclair and Barlucci. Sinclair wanted new faces, and certainly needed to appoint a new finance director, but he was not going to be rushed into anything. Whoever he invited had to have the club at heart; their money was now a secondary consideration. Yet, with the one new face on the board in the shape of Savvas Constantinou, he seemed to have satisfied the criteria.

Constantinou, or Savvas, as he liked to be called, was the UK general manager of the Cyprus Cooperative Bank. In the wake of the turmoil that followed the loss of the club's managerial predecessor to Mark Rossetti, Phil Reynolds, the departure of Wayne and the unexpected success at Wembley, he had appeared like a genie from the lamp. Yes, he had supported Hertsmere for many years; yes, he had his bank's authority to make available facilities of which the club could never have dreamed during its sojourn in the lower ranks of the league pyramid; yes, nothing was too much trouble. Mortgages for players, commitments to private boxes at the new stadium, even a long-term funding package for the new stadium itself. Barlucci on his own was good news, a guardian angel, but Savvas could offer the keys to the Kingdom of Heaven itself. He was a friendly little man, rarely without a smile on his face, revealing teeth irretrievably stained by nicotine from the cigarettes he endlessly chain-smoked with a cavalier disregard for any objections. His thick, wavy hair was interrupted by an odd bald spot that sprang up like an island on the crown of his head. Whatever the weather he wore a formal three-piece suit, the shirt always crisp and white in sharp contrast to his Mediterranean complexion. He was clearly comfortably off himself, yet there was no pretension in the man who favoured a Mini rather than a luxury saloon or sports car, his only concession to vanity being the personalised number plate, SAV 1.

Now, like everybody else in the room he listened carefully to what Ray Fowler had to say.

'It's not so much the prices, it's the quality – and even when I've had the club on the hook I've heard what the player wanted and nearly had a heart attack. If I recommended that you agree some of those wage demands we'd have a riot on our hands from those players we've got.'

Fowler, however, was no tactician when it came to making signings. He made no secret of his interest in a player, nor did he attempt to conceal any checks Hertsmere made on a

34

player's ability. If Hertsmere wanted a player, the tabloids knew about it almost before they did themselves. Today's match was crucial in more ways than one. The crowd was far healthier than it had been the previous season, but it was not the capacity they'd enjoyed for the first two home matches. If they lost, then doubtless the gate for the home leg of the Coca-Cola Cup match against First Division Barston City would be even less. The new stadium would not be ready for another twelve months, but they had to be sure they would have enough supporters to fill it for it to be a viable proposition. Yes, Barlucci's money and the support from Savvas' bank were there today, but who could say whether or not they would be there tomorrow?

Hertsmere ran out in the new blue and white halves, a kit they had adopted this season instead of the traditional stripes. That had been Barlucci's idea, as had the deal he had struck with Verde, the Italian kit manufacturers.

'We have an Italian director, we need Italian shirts,' he had said, or at least that was what Sinclair thought he had said. It wasn't always easy to make out the broken English amid the broad Italian accent. The fans had brought the replicas of the new shirts without complaint. Unlike most other clubs, Hertsmere had worn the same design for as long as Sinclair could remember. Indeed, the shirt given to him by his Uncle Tim – who'd played for the club some thirty years before – would not have looked out of place on the terraces today. It was another source of income, and working with Barlucci made Sinclair realise just how badly he had fared in bringing his own business acumen into the boardroom. He could not understand how it could be that a successful property developer such as himself, a man who was reputed to strike a hard bargain even in an industry infamous for the hard men who operated within it, could have allowed all his good commercial habits to fly out of the window seconds before the boardroom door opened.

Sinclair was amazed at how well he got on with Barlucci. During the transfer negotiations for Mickey Wayne, which had ended in tragedy, he had felt the man to be obstructive. When Barlucci had first shown an interest in Hertsmere, Sinclair had thought that to be a gimmick to distract the fans back home in Rome from the fact that he had not delivered the English player he had promised; but now he seemed to be a genuine supporter, who spent more time at the club than on his own multi-national business interests.

Today, the two of them sat in the front row of the Directors' Box, an oddly matched couple: Sinclair, tall and lean, with his grey hair and rugged good looks; Barlucci with his dark Mediterranean complexion and tangled curly hair, his bulky, bear-like frame uncomfortably squeezed into the standard-size seat. The Italian put his hand on Sinclair's arm, and the chairman leaned forward in his usual tense pose, his chin almost resting on the shelf in front of him.

Stuart Macdonald, the Hertsmere captain, won the toss. As a matter of superstition he chose to attack the River End, making it necessary for their visitors, Farningham Albion, to race down to defend the opposite goal to that in which they had been kicking. Yet for the first twenty minutes they had little or no defending to do. A terrible error by Hertsmere's Serbian goalkeeper, Greg Sergovich, allowed a harmless cross to fall at the feet of a Farningham forward, and from ten yards he could hardly miss. It got worse a couple of minutes later when a ball bobbled awkwardly in the penalty area, hitting Darren Braithwaite on the arm. Everybody on the pitch except the referee thought it was accidental, but the penalty was given. Before it could be taken, Braithwaite had argued his case so vehemently that he earned a red card for his troubles. Down to ten men, the penalty converted, Hertsmere were rocked back on their heels. To their credit the crowd did not turn on them or the chairman, as they might have done a year ago, and with them urging their team on, Hertsmere reduced

36

the arrears on the stroke of half-time, with a solo effort from the young Geordie, Barry Reed, who'd done so well when he'd come on as substitute in the Cup Final.

Sinclair had to restrain Barlucci physically from going down to the dressing room at the interval.

'In Italy I always give the team talk.' Barlucci beat his breast. 'I give them heart. No heart, no player.'

'I think we'll leave it to Ray,' Sinclair said, knowing full well, from watching Fowler on the training ground, that it wouldn't be the heart that the manager was talking about, though certain other parts of the human anatomy would certainly enter the equation. Whatever Fowler said, it seemed to work for some forty-four minutes of the second half. Hertsmere battled like demons, tackling back, covering the gaps that Braithwaite's dismissal had left. It was odd the way a team reduced in this way stepped up their game, making the opposition's extra man an irrelevance, an advantage they never worked out quite what to do with. Within five minutes of the restart Macdonald had scored from a corner, and after that it was Hertsmere who did all the attacking. With their winner just eluding them time after time, the wilful g-d of football tossed his dice. With only a minute left and their only serious shot of the half, Farningham saw the ball loop over the head of Sergovich, who had wandered off his line, hit the crossbar, drop down on the line, then creep almost apologetically into the net. The small travelling group of Farningham fans who had come down from the Black Country celebrated with triumphant war whoops. The only sound that could be heard from the Hertsmere stands was the clanging of the seats against back rests as they were vacated in unison by discontented supporters, sufficiently confident of defeat not to wait for the final whistle.

Sinclair and Barlucci stood tight-lipped to applaud the players off the field, Savvas at their side, for once the smile wiped from his round face.

'We need new players,' the Italian said.

'I know,' Sinclair replied grimly, 'but where do we find them?'

'Not in England. Too much money,' the Italian replied.

'My bank will supply the money,' Savvas said confidently.

Barlucci dismissed the offer with a wave of his hand. He had an idea and he was determined to pursue it.

'We look abroad. We look East. We will find.'

He sounded supremely confident, but Sinclair did not know where they would discover this hidden talent, nor indeed who would look for it.

CHAPTER 6

If it had felt strange when Mark Rossetti had arrived back at Hertsmere as manager after ten years away, it felt even more curious to return as a mere spectator. He'd promised himself when he resigned that he would not watch the team again until he was specifically invited. To have imposed his presence on Ray Fowler would have been unfair even though the two men had got along so well. There was room for only one cook in the kitchen, only one coach in the dressing room. He'd had to wait until mid-September for the invitation to arrive. David Sinclair had phoned.

'Mark. I finally got you rather than your answerphone.'

'You could have left a message.'

'I could, but I never do. It's one of my hang-ups, if you'll excuse the pun.'

'Can't help in your sort of business,' Mark said, ignoring the attempt at a joke and wondering where the conversation was leading.

'It doesn't, but with the property market like it is not a lot helps anyway. I didn't call to talk about answerphones though. I rang to see if you'd like to come to the Coca-Cola Cup-Tie on Tuesday – against Barston.'

'I do know who you're playing,' Mark said, surprised at how annoyed he sounded. He had not realised just how much he missed being at the heart of things.

The chairman was taken aback. 'Sorry. When you've led a team to a Cup Final at Wembley and then don't bother to come and watch them, we thought—'

'What did you think, David?'

'Well, we thought, perhaps, you weren't interested.'

Mark said nothing. Whatever he might say would only appear childish, petulant, even conceited. Waiting for an invitation. He was like the kid at school who'd been inadvertently omitted from the party list and preferred to sulk rather than point it out to the birthday boy.

'So, you'll come then?' Sinclair continued eagerly, taking the silence for acquiescence. 'Claudio and I, we'd both like to talk to you.'

'Yes, I'll come,' Mark said, trying desperately to be at least civil to a man to whom he owed so much.

'Good.' There was a note of relief in Sinclair's voice, as if he'd just closed a beneficial property deal. 'We'll leave your tickets at the Directors' entrance.' Sinclair hesitated. 'Should that be two?' he asked.

'Why, do you think I may have put on as much weight as Barlucci?'

'No, I thought maybe you'd like to bring Patti.'

It was Mark's turn to pause before his reply. 'I'll ask her. And let you know.'

The conversation threatened to stumble to an end. Sinclair could not help but be struck by how much Mark had changed. There was not a hint of the nervous individual who'd come to see him the previous season, desperate for a job – any job – to get a wedge to open the door that led to the privileged and private world of professional football. It wasn't ingratitude he was showing, it was a kind of indifference, an ennui that Sinclair felt hard to understand. It was like listening to a character from a nineteenth-century Russian play, the languor of Chekov or Turgenev. It was odd. Putting down the phone, David Sinclair felt that Mark needed his help more now than he had when he'd first interviewed him.

In a way he was right. Leopold Schneider's death had

changed Mark's life in several ways. He and Patti had duly gone to the lawyer's office the day after the funeral, and what they heard had astonished them both.

Arnold Leigh had seated them in two high-backed chairs that gave no opportunity to the occupants to make themselves too comfortable. There was very little that was comfortable about Leigh's offices, or his room in particular. They'd already kicked their heels for half an hour in a waiting room they'd shared with his receptionist. The girl with heavily peroxided hair had spent a good twenty minutes talking to somebody called Debbie who appeared to be on the verge of a nervous breakdown if another individual by the name of Terry did not ask her to the wine bar that evening. So enwrapped was she in this conversation that the main incoming line was allowed to ring incessantly without distracting her enough to consider answering it, while Mark and Patti were not even offered a drink.

When they were finally ushered into Leigh's office he was clearly pressurised. 'Sorry to keep you. I shouldn't have taken the time off to go to the funeral yesterday. Price you pay for being a one man band. It's the clients who are driving me crazy. I've just had a woman on the phone for thirty minutes complaining that the vendors of her house removed all the light bulbs. And, if you don't mind, this is my fault. Why didn't I get them to confirm they'd leave the bulbs? I asked her how many light bulbs we were talking about in a three-bedroomed house. About ten, she said. I offered to buy her ten bulbs; I said I'd have them delivered. No, that's not good enough. She wants me to knock a hundred quid off my bill. A tenner a light bulb. I ask you – clients! Who'd be with them and who'd be without them? I tell you sometimes I go home nowadays and I say to my wife I've had enough. I'll pack it in. Sell up, buy a place in the country. The days of the sole practitioner are numbered. All the youngsters are specialists. In my day only doctors were specialists, and then they had to

have a Harley Street address to prove it. I see the letters from
these little *pishers*, they all want to show off how much they
know. Well, they may know a bit more law than Arnold Leigh,
but you can't learn experience from books.'

Mark and Patti sat quietly through the soliloquy, waiting for
Leigh to wind himself down gradually.

'A drink. Did Lisa make you a drink? No, she didn't. The
kettle broke this morning. We've been too busy to get it
mended. If not, then it's a new kettle. One expense after
another in this business.' He took out a handkerchief and
sneezed noisily, disturbing piles of paper and dust on his desk.
'I think I caught a cold at the cemetery yesterday. Can't be too
careful with this autumnal weather. You never know what to
expect. Still, must get on. Time's money, nothing else to sell
but your time. Fellow I was articled to always used to say that
and I've never forgotten it. Most important thing I ever learned
– that and how to make a cup of tea.' He rustled among the
edifices of files on his desk, then rose and began destroying
the piles, scattering them file by file at random. Unable to
locate what he wanted, he moved on to the volumes strewn
around the floor. Mark looked around the room, trying to
focus away from the lawyer who seemed to be getting out of
breath from the exercise. On the desk there were family
photographs, a gentle-faced wife, round and pleasant, a boy at
a degree ceremony, a wedding photo of a girl – his son and
daughter, Mark guessed. The walls sported a few pictures that
seemed to bear no relation to each other in either content or
position: an old print of blind justice; a watercolour of Swiss
lakes; a map of Jerusalem; and an oil painting of a cat with a
particularly malevolent expression. It was not the sort of
exhibition that would have encouraged him to pay for
admission.

'There we are.' Leigh emerged triumphantly with a file in
his hand that seemed to have been used a dozen times before.
'I had it all ready for you this morning and then my articled

clerk comes in to look for something and starts making a mess.' He swept around the room with a grand gesture of his hand, as if it had been a suitable subject for a feature in a glossy magazine before the clerk had entered and caused chaos.

'Right, let's get down to business. I don't want you getting bills from me and then complaining because you don't feel you've had your money's worth. Leo always made a fuss about that. Said I charged him for talking about my lumbago.'

'I'm sure you didn't,' Patti said, struggling to keep a straight face, but relieved to be able finally to get a word in edgeways.

'No, of course I didn't. Never had lumbago in my life. Asthma, that's the bane of my life. Doctor once told me that as long as I worked with paper there'll be dust, and as long as there was dust there'd be asthma. How did he expect a solicitor to work without paper? I've been in some of these modern offices in the City. All red braces, machinery and silences. I can't work like that. Do you know how much a word-processor costs? Try and pass that on to my sort of clients and they'd have a heart attack.'

'Like Leo,' Patti said, trying gently to guide him back to the reason for their visit.

'Poor Leo. May he rest in peace. When I started up here over thirty years ago he was one of my first clients. He'd fallen out with his old solicitor. Said the man was anti-semitic. How could he be anti-semitic when he was a Jewish lawyer with an office in Golders Green? But that was Leo for you – he had some funny ways about him. Once he got an idea into his mind there wasn't a soul who could budge it, not even the Archangel Gabriel himself.'

'Did he ever talk to you about his past, about his years in the camps?' Mark asked, thinking that perhaps he was about to discover more about the man with whom he'd spent so much time over the years, yet about whom he'd learned so little.

'No, we never had time to talk. Too much business to deal

43

with. When he came here, he came for a purpose.'

Despite the solemnity of the situation Mark and Patti could hardly refrain from laughing. The previous day's funeral was forgotten. Arnold Leigh had unintentionally brought Leo back to life for them. At long last he opened the file and cleared his throat. Mark shook his head in disbelief. He was actually going to read the will. He thought that sort of thing only happened in books and movies, but clearly when it came to the aftermath of death Leigh was accustomed to treating it with all due ceremony.

The lawyer began to read, slowly and carefully, as if dictating English to a couple of foreigners about to take an exam.

'This is the last will and testament of me, Leopold Abraham Schneider . . .'

'I didn't know he had a middle name,' Mark said, still surprised by just how much he had not known about the man.

Leigh began again, reciting Schneider's address. This time it was Patti who interrupted him. 'Look, Mr Leigh, can we take all the formal stuff as read?'

Leigh appeared mildly irritated, as if he had been deprived of a treat that did not come his way every day. 'Very well. Leo did ask that arrangements be made for prayers to be said for the repose of his soul. I assume you do not regard that as a formality, Miss Delaney.'

'Well, no – but what's that got to do with us? I mean, we're not even Jewish.' She hesitated. 'I suppose I am, technically, but I wouldn't know where to start. Can't you deal with all of that?'

Leigh adjusted his spectacles and peered over them in a way that he might well have rehearsed in front of a mirror to give him a legally prepossessing appearance. 'Yes, I can deal with all of that. But please allow me to continue. Leo specifically requested that efforts be made to trace his family's property in Russia.'

'Russia!' Patti exclaimed. 'But he came from Austria.'

'Yes . . . and no. He was a refugee from the Nazis, but he was born in Russia. The family moved to Germany and then to Austria when he was a young man. It was, I fear, out of the frying pan and into the fire, not just once, but twice.' He did not seem to realise that what he had said could have been taken as a very sick joke.

'Prayers, property in Russia. I still don't understand how we're involved.'

Leigh permitted himself the smile of a parent producing a surprise present from his coat pocket. 'It's really quite simple, my dear. Your involvement is that Leopold Schneider in his wisdom has left his entire estate to you and Mr Rossetti.'

CHAPTER 7

Mark had not taken Patti with him to see Hertsmere play although his offer had originally been accepted. She'd phoned just before he was due to leave home to pick her up, making an urgent and surprise commission her excuse. He was not sure that he believed her, but the empty seat in the Directors' Box saddened him every time he looked at it. To his left in the front row sat David Sinclair, whilst on his left was Claudio Barlucci, wrapped in a thick winter coat despite the mildness of the Autumn evening. Beside him was Savvas Constantinou, to whom Mark had been introduced for the first time that evening. He'd immediately liked the plump Cypriot. It amazed him that it was possible to tell whether somebody was really a football person just from the first few moments of speaking to them; and if they were a football person then the likelihood was that everything else would fall into place. Cultural, financial, physical and intellectual differences all counted for nothing. The common language made up for everything, and there could be no doubting that Savvas spoke the common language.

'It is my honour, Mark, to meet you. I was one of the lucky ones who saw you play and it was when you left that my love affair with Hertsmere began to turn sour. Now the romance is back on again. I am only sorry you sit with us and you're not out on the field.'

In the mouth of another man the words would have sounded insincere, but Savvas looked him straight in the eye as he

47

spoke, and Mark was left in no doubt that he meant everything he said.

Mark had declined the chairman's offer to go into the home dressing room to wish the team good luck.

'It's OK. I've spoken to Ray. He said that he and the boys would be pleased to see you.'

'Let's leave it until after the match. Then I can toast them with Perrier while they have the champagne,' Mark had replied – but ten minutes into the game it did not look as if there were going to be too many corks being popped. Barston had come to Park Crescent without any great reputation. They lay mid-table in the First Division, having gained more points than they'd scored goals. Even as they'd run out on to the pitch they'd looked what they were; a team without any great charisma, without any individual flair. Any one of the defence could have played Goliath in a Hollywood epic, while the forwards were all knotted muscles rather than lean athleticism. Their kit of a plain white shirt and black shorts spoke of the no-nonsense approach of the team, an attitude of Yorkshire grit, outdoor toilets and Hovis for tea. If he'd not discovered Barnsley first, then Michael Parkinson would have followed Barston with the same devotion.

At one point in the first half, when the Northern centre-forward charged up for a ball in the Hertsmere penalty area, the referee had been on the blind side of his flailing elbow, which left Darren Braithwaite, the home defender, writhing on the ground with a broken nose. All the referee had seen was the ball fly into the net as it took a cruel diversion to escape Sergovich's desperate dive. Down to ten men while Braithwaite received emergency repairs to staunch the flow of blood, the Hertsmere defence was pulled out of shape again a few minutes later. This time Barston were able to tap the ball into the net from five yards.

Barlucci leaned across Sinclair, the material from his coat virtually smothering the chairman. He gripped Mark's arm tightly. Whatever improvement there had been in his English seemed to fail him in the emotion of the moment. 'You must come back, Marco. Money is not the object,' he shouted in guttural Italian.

Money was no longer the object for Mark either, after he and Patti had learned that the value of Schneider's estate was over a million pounds – but he did not think that now was the appropriate moment to tell that to the excitable Italian. Instead he tried to explain to him that the first goal had been a blatant foul, that the second had only been scored because of the deficiency in numbers, and that all the football had actually been played by Hertsmere. Barlucci, though, was not listening.

By half-time he was still not listening, although Mark was telling him in both English and Italian. Sinclair was looking embarrassed, trying his best to be hospitable to the visiting directors while attempting to keep Barlucci quiet, so that anybody else in the cramped and crowded boardroom could conduct a conversation.

'Claudio, don't push him. He's done enough for the club already,' Sinclair said, trying to get his body between the two men to defuse the situation.

'If you don't come back as manager, then you have to help us find some new players. You will be our scout. You will travel.' Barlucci waved his arms around as if he had just discovered a new concept in football.

'I don't even know about that, Claudio. There's my daughter, you see. I want to spend as much time with her as I can.'

'So you take her with you. Travel is good for the young. When I was her age I thought it an adventure to ride on a horse and cart. You must give her the opportunity.'

To give himself some breathing space Mark translated for Sinclair and Savvas.

'He's not wrong, you know,' Sinclair said. 'If you really

want to get to know your daughter, there'd be nothing like taking her on holiday. The two of you together without her having the chance to run back to mother if things go wrong. You know, when Holly was her age . . .' He stopped in midstream, suddenly remembering that his own daughter was dead – a death too recent for him to be able to talk of his own memories of her.

Mark tried to change the subject quickly. 'And then there's Patti. I thought that maybe there was a future there, but it all seems to have gone terribly wrong. The only time I've felt close to her recently was at Leo's funeral.'

Had the old man been trying to send them a message from the grave? What was he doing asking them to arrange prayers when he'd never shown any interest in organised religion during his life? But then there was so much about his life that did not add up, that made little or no sense. A millionaire who lived like a tramp, a loveable man with no friends, and now a Russian past of which he'd made no mention in his lifetime. It was too late to ask Leo anything now, and Mark regretted that; regretted that he'd been too firmly entrapped in his own problems to take enough interest in the man who was now his benefactor.

He had asked Leigh whether or not there was any legal obligation to try and trace the property in the country of Schneider's birth. The solicitor had shrugged and given him a typical lawyer's reply. 'It depends what you mean by obligation. If you're asking if you still get all of his money and property whether you do anything about the property or not, then the answer is yes, you do. But then you have to ask yourself why he put that request in the will. That's the moral side of things, and that's up to you.'

By the end of the match it was Barlucci of all people who helped him make up his mind. Hertsmere pulled a goal back through Pat Devine, a stunning twenty-five-yard volley from the midfielder, but Barston held out, booting the ball into the

crowd, over the stand, wherever they might gain a few
moments' respite from the non-stop Hertsmere onslaught. The
crowd booed the players off the pitch, the same players whose
names they had chanted with such fervour and joy at Wembley
just a few months before.

'Long memories, eh?' Sinclair said. 'It won't be long before
they get after me again. And as for Claudio here, I reckon he'll
be glad to get back to Rome.'

The Italian seemed thoroughly dejected by the evening's
entertainment, as if it had been a personal affront to his own
honour and dignity. He put his arm around Mark's shoulder
and pulled him into a corner to give the conversation some
semblance of privacy. He spoke in Italian, his thick accent
making it difficult for even Mark to understand. The former
manager thought Barlucci was erring on the side of caution.

'They are not bad, this team, but they have no heart.' He
placed his right hand over his own vital organ, underlining that
he wanted for nothing in that department. 'When you were in
charge they played for you not just with their heads and their
feet, but with their—'

'Don't tell me, Claudio – they played with their hearts,'
Mark said. If he'd hoped to slow him down or divert him from
his task, then he was to be disappointed.

'You see, you do understand. You understand immediately
what I am trying to say. You are sympathetic. I accept you do
not want to be manager again; they are like goalkeepers,
managers, all of them are crazy.'

'A bit like club chairmen,' Mark added.

Barlucci did not smile, perhaps he did not even hear, he was
totally caught up with his own train of thought. 'You know a
good player when you see one. I saw what you did with the
youngsters you brought into the team. Nowadays all the good
players in England think they are better than they are; they are
pricing themselves out of their own market. I have seen it all
before in Italy. But there we have stadiums that hold a hundred

thousand, we have fans who will pay millions of lira for tickets. Here . . .' He swept his arm with disgust around the room, taking in the stained wallpaper, the well-worn carpets, the debris of pies and chicken legs on the table. 'So, I have told David and Savvas and Helen—'

'. . . and anybody else who will listen,' Sinclair interrupted. 'No wonder old Ben pretends to be asleep.'

Barlucci was in full flow and was not to be stopped. 'We must broaden our horizons. We have Sergovich in goal, but he has been here so long he is practically English. Where was he found? I asked. In the wilds of Serbia, I am told. What did he cost? I ask. Ten thousand pounds, they tell me. I ask about his wages when he came and I learn that he earned less than the boys who sweep the terraces at my old club in Rome. Maybe now they are wiser in Serbia, yes, I think so, but still there are bargains to be had. I ask people who know the Eastern bloc. Already I have a few names, but names are no good without first-hand reports.'

At last he allowed Mark to take over the conversation. 'And you want me to prepare the reports?'

'You see?' Barlucci said, becoming even more animated and excited if that was at all possible. 'You are already with me. We think alike, you and I. David Sinclair, he is a nice man, but in football he is just a choirboy. We need people like him, but also the club needs people like you and me. Savvas here is a banker, but even he is too nice.'

Barlucci squeezed Mark so tightly that the recipient of the embrace thought his shoulder would give way under the pressure. Mark tried to tell him that the question of scouting had already been raised at half-time – and the fact that he had been able to retain the suggestion in his memory for forty-five minutes was not definitive proof of any great empathy – but he could not produce the breath to say anything.

'So it is agreed,' Barlucci said, not releasing his grip in the slightest. 'I will find the players and you will approve them.

Already I have a list. I have some of the best contacts in the world. This will be a labour of love, a holiday for you. And, as we said, for your daughter.' He began to fish in the pockets of his overcoat, that he still wore despite the fug and heat of the crowded boardroom. Eventually he produced a piece of crumpled paper, covered with a spiderish scrawl in a language that Mark did not recognise as Italian or any other tongue known to man.

Barlucci peered at it, turned it ninety degrees, then held it up to the light as if to reveal some hidden code. 'Ah, here we are. Dimitri Murganev. He's with Lokomotiv Moscow. Top scorer in the Russian second division last season, and he's already scored enough in the top flight this year to suggest he has—'

'Heart?' Mark asked, suddenly feeling weary, lonely, wanting to talk to Patti. He had never wanted to visit Russia, never considered it a holiday resort, but in the space of a couple of days two people had asked him go. It was as if somebody was trying very hard to send him a message, and the only question was whether or not he would respond.

CHAPTER 8

Emma Rossetti lay on her bed, hands behind her head. She was undergoing one of the daily tests of discipline she had decided to impose upon herself. This particular one involved keeping totally silent and still for fifteen minutes. Only her eyes were permitted to move and then just to check the time on the clock that stood on her bookcase. She'd had that particular object since she was three and she made a mental note for the umpteenth time that Noddy and Big Ears had to go, despite the fact that they had been a gift from her father.

She allowed herself the luxury and distraction of music during these thinking sessions. Take That warbled on about wanting somebody back for good, and she tried, as she always did when she listened to this sort of music, to understand why all the romance in every pop song counted for nothing when it came to real life. It wasn't that her mother had remarried badly. In fact, most of the time Emma preferred Stuart Macdonald, her stepfather, to her mother. But she didn't prefer him to her father, that was for sure.

She had been deprived of Mark's company for so much of her life that now she felt like a child given the freedom of a sweet shop. She wanted to gorge herself until she felt sick and because of that desire she had to back off, had to demonstrate a discipline and instinct far beyond her years. There were times when she felt a million light-miles away from her classmates at school. It wasn't that she was the only product of a broken marriage. Her best friend, Becky, her parents had just split up and Emma had found herself in the role of the older, wiser and more experienced woman, even though Becky was two months her senior. In her class alone she'd worked out that forty per cent of the pupils had parents who were either divorced or separated. And that didn't take into account poor Lucy Wainwright whose father had been killed in a skiing accident and whose mother had gone off her trolley.

Yet, somehow, Emma's story was different. No one else had a father whose name appeared so often in the papers. Lucy Wainwright had had her fifteen minutes of fame, of course, but for the most part that had been only in the local rags. No one else could be asked for tickets for football matches against Manchester United or Liverpool by pupils and teachers alike. No one else seemed to be at the epicentre of the sort of burning hatred that her mother still seemed to feel for her father. It wasn't her imagination. She *was* different.

Even at the age of nearly twelve Emma had been able to figure out that, sometimes, love and hate were almost indistinguishable. Some days she and Becky would sit in the corner of the school dining room with their sandwiches, discussing such matters, and Emma would feel she was really twelve going on forty. Just the other day she'd said, as if declaiming a line from a play, 'You know, Beck, I don't think you can truly hate somebody unless you've loved them.'

Becky had looked at her uncomprehendingly. 'I hate Miss Van Roost,' she said, referring to their maths teacher, 'and I can honestly say, I've never loved her.'

'That's not the sort of love and hate I'm talking about,' Emma had replied, with a huge sigh to indicate that she didn't know why she bothered to discuss such momentous matters with so insensitive a friend. To keep her quiet, Becky had said she understood, but Emma knew that she hadn't. Nobody understood her, that was the problem; although she thought her father might in time if he worked at it – if she allowed him to get near to her. The only trouble was that if you allowed people to get too near then you ran the risk of getting hurt.

Six minutes to go of her thinking time. None of her contemporaries would or could do this. They lived with phones in their hands, their lives filled with 'Neighbours' and 'Home and Away', the latest gossip about their favourite pop group, and all the rest of the junk media and junk food that they could swallow. She, on the other hand, was growing up too fast, force-feeding herself with a kind of emotional compost to accelerate her growth. Everything seemed to happen to her too early. She'd been the first of her friends to have a period, the first to need a bra, the first to know the facts of life, courtesy of Sally, who at least in that respect seemed to have no hang-ups.

Then there was that nice-looking lad who helped out in the pizza place at weekends. He couldn't be more than sixteen and she could tell by the way he looked at her that he fancied her. If she put on make-up, wore those tight blue jeans, the shrunken T-shirt and the baseball cap, she could get away with looking like a teenager herself. She wondered how old she'd have to be before she could persuade Sally to let her go on the Pill. She could hardly see it happening, but you never knew. That thirteen-year-old had got married in Turkey. Now, to do that you had to be crazy. She was never going to get married. She'd seen what it had done to her parents.

The alarm rang and, almost reluctantly, she sat up and dragged herself back to the present. She had homework to do; French and Geography. She quite liked both subjects, but now she just wasn't in the mood. She was still thinking, not about her school work, but about her father. She needed to get closer to him, to spend more time with him, but the only problem was persuading her mother that it was a good idea. It would have to be a carefully approached campaign. She knew her mother well enough to know that she would have to think it was her own idea, rather than her daughter's.

She tiptoed out of her room and into her mother's bedroom.

She could hear her downstairs in the kitchen getting the supper ready and calculated that she had about ten minutes before being disturbed. She lifted the phone and quickly dialled her father's number. She wasn't sure if he'd be there, was sure that he wouldn't be expecting the call, but it made no difference. She had to make the effort. She needed to know what sort of man Mark Rossetti was. Not through old newspaper clippings, not through today's columns and not through the eyes of her mother. She had to make her own personal voyage of discovery, whatever might lie at the end of it. She heard his voice at the other end of the line. There, in person, not a recorded message.

'Hi, Dad, it's me. Have you got a few minutes to talk?'

CHAPTER 9

Two people might be telling Mark Rossetti to go to Russia, but the scales were balanced. He felt that he was getting closer to his daughter for the first time in her life, and neither of the companions he would have chosen to accompany him on the trip were able to go. Patti Delaney was the first to decline. It had taken him three days after the Barston match to persuade her to meet him for dinner. In his more optimistic moments he thought her refusal was because she was frightened to get too involved with him, but in the dark hours of the night, when he awoke with worrying regularity, he came to believe that she simply no longer wanted him to be an integral part of her life.

On the evening of their dinner, he tried to do everything right, tried perhaps a little too hard, and it showed in the strained silences between them which in the past both had accepted as companionable. He had bought her an orchid rather than a bunch of flowers, but she had nowhere to fasten it on the cashmere top of the two-piece suit she was wearing. He preferred her in the T-shirts and jeans that she seemed to live in when he had first known her. The formal clothing she now chose was further evidence of the widening gap between them that he was now fighting to close.

The orchid lay neglected by the side of her plate as she toyed with a desert of Pear Hélène that she had not really wanted. She had also played with the pâté that had started the meal and the Dover Sole that had followed. The restaurant had several rosettes and prices to match. They could both afford

59

those now, though Patti's menu gave no clue what the final bill might be. That had annoyed her feminist instincts and she demanded a duplicate of the menu that had been handed to Mark. The waiter, a young Italian, had looked to Mark for guidance and that had whipped her into an even greater fury; 'You don't have to ask him for permission. Just do it.' There was a pause, then 'Please', which struck greater terror down the waiter's spine than the order that had preceded it.

'You didn't have to speak to him like that. He's not the one who makes the rules here,' Mark said, and immediately regretted it, just as he was now regretting not simply taking her to the deli they had patronised when things had not been so easy for them.

'Don't tell me what to do or not to do. I'm not your wife or daughter.'

He looked closely at her, trying to peer behind the tight lines of anger that creased her forehead. They gave her the appearance of premature age, the dark shadows beneath her eyes cruelly mocking the hit-or-miss shadow make-up she had used when he first knew her. She was there somewhere, the person he thought he could have loved if she had only given him the chance. He had to find her, whatever risks the voyage of discovery might entail.

It had taken him until the coffee and the two brandies Patti had consumed for him to get around to broaching the question of the trip. He had thought she would be pleased by the invitation. The Russian property, wherever and whatever it was, like everything else of Leo's, belonged to them both equally. It would be an adventure, and she was being invited to join in from the beginning.

Her response was anything but positive. 'It's easy to ask, isn't it, when you know I can't come?'

'I don't understand.' It was lame, but it was also true.

'There are times, Mark, when you are really stupid. How can I just swan off and leave my mother? And I know you don't think so, but I do have a job. If I don't write, I don't eat.'

He began to point out to her that Schneider's inheritance meant that she did not need to work, that she could be independent, that she could get the best treatment for her mother – but all to no avail. Eventually he shrugged. 'OK. I'll just take Emma . . .'

'Why do you have to go right now? Why can't you wait until things are a bit easier for me? Leo had this property for donkey's years without doing anything about it. I can't believe it's reached critical point since his death.'

Mark sighed. There was no pleasing her. He was damned if he went, and damned if he stayed. He drove her home and she fell asleep in the car, snoring gently, her face finally at rest after the potent cocktail of wine, brandy and exhaustion. He didn't ask to come in for coffee. It wasn't that he didn't want her; he did, with an aching longing that began in his groin and ended in his head. But if they slept together it would be for all the wrong reasons. It would be because he was there, and she was available with her barriers of resistance lowered for the night. He kissed her gently on the cheek as he reached across her to open the car door, watched as she struggled to fit the key into the lock, and then drove away too quickly to look back.

Patti's refusal had been quiet, calm and polite compared to Sally's reaction when he suggested he take Emma with him for the week of her half-term.

'Russia! Russia!' The double exclamation made it sound as if they were just about to invade. 'With you in charge of her for a week the pair of you would probably end up in some Siberian prison camp.'

'I'm not sure they actually have those any more, since Glasnost.'

'Oh, so all of a sudden you're an expert on Soviet affairs. We've been a footballer, we've played at being a private detective, we've had our fling as a football manager, so now it's time to join the Foreign Office.'

Mark tried to speak, but was given no opportunity once she was in full flight. All he could do was wonder why every woman who entered his life had to use him as the personal chopping block for their axe-sharp tongues.

'When you take her out for an ice cream you bring her back late, so tired that she's in no fit state to do her homework. And you expect me to let her go with you thousands of miles away, on some wild goose chase? You know nothing about property law in Russia—'

'I'll find a lawyer there.'

'Oh, and I'm sure all the lawyers there speak perfect English! So you really think that even if you make a proper claim for this property they won't try and cheat you? You've been taken for a mug in England, and now you want to try your luck the other side of the world.'

'So the answer's no?' he said with heavy sarcasm, knowing that he should have stayed silent and bided his time.

'It's more than no, it's never – and if you start filling my daughter's head with nonsense about travel, then whatever your little friend Stuart might say I'll stop access in this country let alone the Soviet Union or whatever it's calling itself this week.'

He found himself in the hall, and before he knew it he was in the street, the echo of the door being slammed attracting the attention of passers-by and neighbours alike. When it came to making a statement there was nobody quite like Sally.

And so that left him, alone. Dejectedly, Mark Rossetti made his arrangements to travel to Russia, to seek out Leopold Schneider's property, and to see just how good a player was Dimitri Murganev.

CHAPTER 10

The child did not seem to stop crying nowadays. There had always been an excuse; Sonya would never accept that the girl cried because she was downright miserable. In her first year it had been wind, in the second it was teething, in the third bed-wetting, at four there had been bad dreams, and when she was five she had been bullied at school. And now – at six – he was waiting. Perhaps she was reaching puberty some six years early. It would be nice to think she was ahead in something, because there was certainly no indication of that in her schoolwork.

Dimitri Murganev put down his glass of lemon tea and wandered slowly towards Katiana's tiny bedroom. Not even a real room, more a broom cupboard, but he could not complain. They lived better than most people in Moscow, although nowhere near as well as the privileged minority, with their huge apartments and summer dachas in the forests or by the sea. Their apartment was within walking distance of Kursk Station, the vast steel and glass shed, modernised in the 1970s, though intended some forty years before to be a focal mega-terminal serving every serviceable point in Russia. As was so often the case in Russia, the intention did not give birth to the deed, and the station today consisted of a dark and dank labyrinth of underpasses, with beggars indistinguishable from travellers waiting for trains that might or might not come.

Slotted into the backstreets between the Garden and Boulevard Rings, the Murganevs' communal flat formed part

63

of a building that had once been an elegant mansion in pre-Bolshevik days. Now only the outside facade gave any hint of what might once have been. The paint was a faded deep red, there were carved cornices, and a tired marble angel that looked towards the station, wondering when the train would finally arrive to take him away from the decay.

Dimitri Murganev was also waiting for the departing train. Twenty-five years old, in his first season in the Russian First Division with Lokomotiv Moscow, he was full of ambition – not just for himself, but also for his family. First he would get Sonya and Katriana out of this dull flat, and then he would try to do something for his parents before it was too late. He had not seen them for a couple of months. It was nearly a thousand miles to Arkhangel where he had been born and, unlike Mussolini, Yeltsin had not been able to make the trains run on time.

By the time he opened the hardboard door to her room, Katriana was merely whimpering in her sleep. She lay with one arm clinging to her favourite toy, a miserable-looking stuffed penguin called Peter, the other arm lolling out of the bed in a parody of death rather than sleep. He kissed her dark hair which smelt of sweat, wondering how she could keep so warm when the heating in the building was so inadequate. The very young had their own methods of self-preservation, and almost certainly she would survive the tears that had so far been an integral part of her short life.

Not for the first time that evening he looked at his watch, hoping nothing had befallen Sonya. He did not like her to be out on her own after ten at night. Moscow had become a city of gangsters, and it was not just foreign tourists who were their targets. Sonya was a pretty girl. Even though she was only a few months younger than him he still could not think of her as anything other than a girl. She looked like a teenager, with her petite figure, the tight jeans she always wore and the hair tied in a ponytail that he kept telling her was no longer fashionable.

He wished he could tell her that there was no longer any need for her to work, that her place was here with her daughter, but the time was not yet ready for that. Yes, he was earning more here in Moscow than he had with his old club, Krasnador, but he was still light years behind his European compatriots. In football, as in everything else, Russia was the poor relation. And so Sonya had kept her job at the bar. It was secure, it was regular, and their old friend Lev ran a tight ship – no drugs, no fighting. It was a place where the world-weary went to drink, to talk about old times that had assumed a distant distortion, like a photograph of a moving subject. By rights her shift finished at eight. When travelling back on the tightly packed subway from Tverskaya Metro there was safety in numbers, where the worst damage she could suffer would be a bruised backside from an admiring pinch. Tonight, though, her replacement had not arrived and Lev had asked if she would stay an hour or so until business died down. Dimitri had not been happy about it, but, as ever, she had had her way.

'Don't be so fussy. I'm not a baby. Lev's isn't like Night Life or Alexander Blok.' She referred to two of the less salubrious night spots in Moscow. 'We're not talking hookers and Mafia. He's strictly local. You're just upset because you have to put Katyia to bed.'

'It's not that. And her name's Katriana. If you treat her like a baby then she'll never grow up. I may be in bed when you get back. I'm very tired. Training was terrible today. When that East German arrived nobody told us we were getting the coach from hell.' He liked that phrase. He'd heard it in an American movie and it had been he who had given the trainer his nick-name. The other players had liked it and it had helped him to be accepted within the club. No longer was he regarded as the boy from the sticks, a threat to those who had played up front before his arrival. It had made his goal-scoring more of a success than an embarrassment, which was fortunate because he had now found the net five times in four matches.

He heard a car door slam outside, followed by the sound of a woman's footsteps, high-heeled boots he guessed, ringing resonantly on the rain-soaked pavement. He looked out of the window, but the vehicle was already no more than a distant tail-light. The elevator stopped on their floor. They were five flights up and the efficacy of the lift – or lack of it – was a constant source of disagreement between Dimitri and the janitor. 'You're a trained athlete. What are five flights of steps to you?' The man supported Moscow Dynamo and had never had a civil word to say to the Lokomotiv player since he had arrived in the city and been allocated this apartment by his team as part of his contract.

'It's not me. It's my wife and daughter. It's difficult for them, particularly when she's been shopping.'

'She's lucky to find something to buy. Glasnost.' The man spat forcibly on the ground as he said the word. 'What's Glasnost brought us that we didn't have under Bulganin and Kruschev? To me it's just another word for surrender.'

He was an unprepossessing individual, who appeared to sleep in the basement where there was little or no washing facilities. It was as if he deliberately made himself unbearable to be near, so that nobody would trouble him with such petty problems as the failing lift. He had a shock of white hair which stopped suddenly in the middle of his scalp without the courage to make it to the back of his head. A self-rolled cigarette was permanently in his hand, which had discoloured his teeth to a deep orange that gave him an ape-like appearance when he smiled, which was not often. Dimitri did not like the smirk that came to his face when he watched Sonya struggle up the stairs, his eyes, with the slight cast in the left one, taking in every rhythmic movement of her buttocks.

He heard the key turn in the lock and Sonya entered through the hall that barely took two steps to cover before she was in the living room.

'Hello. I thought you were going to bed.'

'I was. Katriana was restless. I couldn't sleep.' He recalled the slamming car door, his eyes dropping to his wife's calf-length leather boots of which she was so proud. 'How did you get home?'

She looked up at him sharply, realising that he knew she had not travelled by public transport. 'Lev got me a taxi. He's as bad as you when it comes to worrying about me. How can a girl go wrong in this town when she's got two big strong minders to look after her?' She threw her bag down on the settee and collapsed alongside it, lifting her feet up in the air. 'Be a dear. Pull my boots off, my feet are agony.'

He knelt at her feet, never ceasing to wonder at the sheer sexuality of the woman who was his wife. He knew others felt it too, yet he never doubted her fidelity. She was his and his alone. He gently massaged her feet, then reached up to pull down her tights, taking care not to tear them, knowing how difficult they were to replace. He took her little toe between his teeth and slowly sucked it, enjoying the taste, a mixture of her talcum powder, sweat and the scent that moved down her body from her most secret parts. She leaned back luxuriously against the cheap leather, her eyes closed, her breath held after the first sharp intake. He noticed she had adopted the western habit of shaving her armpits. It was another move away from the old ideas. He moved his tongue up her thigh, seeking the white flesh that led toward the dark shadows. She suddenly threw herself forward and grabbed him around the neck. He reacted by lifting her bodily in one smooth motion, wondering at her lightness of being, then, with his hand across her mouth to stifle any noise that might wake his daughter, he carried her to the bedroom. There it no longer mattered where they were. She was his, he was hers and they were together.

CHAPTER 11

Daniel Lewis was feeling pleased with himself. Not only had he just concluded the third sale of the week to a Russian-speaking buyer, but his agency was about to be featured in London's *Evening Chronicle*. He didn't know where the reporter had got his name from, but in any event he was not too bothered about that. As long as she spelled his name right and the photographer made sure he had film in his camera, then he was in for a free burst of publicity that would normally have cost him a five-figure sum.

Even Elaine was a bit more pleasant to live with. They'd sat together the night before, looking over glossy holiday catalogues that promised them the excitement of real lion kills on safari, the delights of a Nile cruise, or the sun and sand of beautiful Hawaii. She'd even held his hand, and for a while he'd been able to see the girl he'd fancied so much that he had to marry her once he realised that was the only way he was going to get her into bed. She'd liked the new car he'd bought as well. A Mercedes soft-top with a personalised number plate, DL 1. At last her husband was beginning to be someone, someone who could be recognised by the status symbols with which he surrounded himself.

The Russians were perfect clients. They spoke little English, but they knew exactly what they wanted in terms of property, and paid cash to complete as soon as they possibly could. He'd tried to persuade them to use one of his tame solicitors, who would always give him back a percentage of

69

his legal fees in return for the introduction. However, it was as if they had not heard him. That was exactly how they reacted to anything they did not wish to agree.

Each transaction was conducted by the same lawyer, a humourless (and faceless) individual called Nicholas Spence. Spence ran a one-man practice in an area that might be part of the City if you were feeling generous, but as that was an emotion Lewis did not feel towards him, the estate agent always described him as an 'East End spiv'. Given Daniel's own roots there was, in that, an element of the pot calling the kettle black – particularly given the fact that Spence's cold tones, whilst having a slightly clipped foreign accent, in no way carried any cockney undertones.

The man was efficient, though. If you called him in the morning you received an answerphone message from a female voice that said simply, 'Mr Spence does not accept calls before midday. Please call back after noon.' No offer to leave a message; nor was Mr Spence prepared to undertake the financial burden of calling anybody back. Yet, if you did call after twelve you got through, not just to the number, but to Spence himself, and it occurred to Daniel on more than one occasion that the line never seemed to be engaged. Was it that Spence had no other clients, or was it simply that he managed to organise himself better than anybody else he had ever met? Whichever might be the case, there was no way of asking the lawyer, who seemed never to have learned the niceties of small talk. Nor was the faceless girl of the recorded message ever there to provide any information. If Spence had been more amenable, then Daniel might have felt inclined to give him a plug in the *Chronicle* interview, but as it was he had kept the interviewer's spotlight of attention firmly fixed on himself.

Mitchell Sachs, Lewis's young assistant, came through the door at the strike of twelve, the paper in his hand already folded to reveal Danny's smiling face posing in front of the office window, the name on the fascia clear for all to see.

Danny had ordered Mitchell to wait by the news-stand at the entrance to Hampstead station until the first edition was delivered, and the boy had hardly noticed the chill of the morning in his eagerness to please his boss.

'It looks really good, Danny,' he said.

His employer, who had encouraged him to be informal, looked mildly peeved – not merely by the abhorrent use of the diminutive form of his name, but also that the paper had not been presented to him in a pristine condition, that he had not been the first to read all about himself. However, he said nothing, but opened the newspaper on the desk in front of him and read the article first with relish, then with the satisfaction of the cat who had not only got the cream, but had caught the mouse as well.

The journalist had done a good job for him. She'd been a good-looking girl and he'd felt he'd turned his full charm on her. She was interested in foreigners buying into London. The Arabs were gone and she wanted to know who was replacing them. She'd expressed surprise and then interest in the fact that so many Russians seemed to have substantial funds available.

'Not bad for a communist state,' she'd said as Danny showed her the photographs of the sort of properties his clients were buying. She's encouraged him to reminisce about the golden days of London's property boom, and now in the article he came across as a professional with experience who knew exactly what he was doing, just the sort of man you'd want on your side if you were a foreigner buying your first property in England.

'So, what do you think, Danny?' Mitchell asked, taking a proprietary interest in the article. He'd only been with the company six weeks. It was his first job after leaving school with five very ordinary GCSE passes. He'd not intended to stay too long, just long enough to be able to tell a future employer that he had some experience, but now it looked as if there might be a future both for him and the firm.

'I think . . .' Daniel hesitated, and Mitchell leaned forward as if he were waiting for the man from Del Monte to say 'yes'. 'I think it's fucking fantastic. Go down to the station. Buy a dozen copies. No, buy two dozen copies. Then ring the paper and see if you can get the originals of the photos and have them blown up for the window.' He fished in his pocket for a twenty-pound note. 'And keep the change,' he added expansively, knowing he was underpaying the young man. Those times were fast fading. He'd taken on Mitchell because he was all he could afford. Now he could envisage row upon row of desks filled with eager negotiators holding a phone in each hand. The shop next door had been empty for months and he could knock straight through. For the first time in years he felt optimistic about the future, felt glad that he had not sold out, that he had kept his independence. The phone rang and he picked it up quickly and confidently, sure it was a friend calling to congratulate him.

It was Nikolei Yevneko. Daniel greeted him warmly. It was since he had met with him that things had looked up. 'Mr Yevneko, good to hear from you. How are you? I've been meaning to call. I think I owe you lunch.'

Yevneko did not seem to respond. Suddenly Daniel was reminded of Spence as the frost permeated down the line. 'Mr Lewis, I think we should talk.'

'Yes, yes, that's what I was suggesting. Lunch? Or maybe dinner. Perhaps next week, if you've got your diary handy.'

'No, you misunderstand me. I think we should talk right now. I will expect you in ten minutes.'

As Daniel Lewis replaced the receiver his own photograph in the newspaper on the desk seemed to be telling him that he had made a terrible mistake.

CHAPTER 12

Mark Rossetti collapsed on to the hotel bed. He had been told that this was the place to stay for a visitor with a bit of money, if you couldn't get into the Metropol. And he hadn't been able to get into the Metropol. But if this was the next best, then he hated to think what it would be like to travel to Moscow on a tight budget. There was a bed which meant there was no misdescription in calling it a bedroom. However, there was little or nothing else. A cheap plywood wardrobe which looked as if it had been assembled that very day by a do-it-yourself novice; what appeared to be an overturned orange box serving as a bedside table, and a dark green phone that seemed unconnected to anything except a cross-sounding woman who spoke no English. No fridge, no mini-bar, no guide books or information about the hotel. He knew there was a shower-room attached because he could hear the steady drip of a leaking fawcet and see a trail of water creeping under the stained carpet. Closer investigation revealed one very thin towel that did not wrap around his waist, and a bar of soap that had the hairs of the previous occupant still attached. From his west-facing room he could at least look out onto the Kremlin with its towers jabbing their way aggressively into the sky, its cathedrals and palaces laid out in a vague symmetry above the Moskva River. He had not come here as a tourist; indeed, he almost hoped he would have no time for sight-seeing. He wanted to get back to England, to Patti and, most of all, to Emma.

He wandered down to the bar and ordered a glass of orange juice. When it arrived it had clearly travelled some way in inefficient packaging, as it fizzed miserably in the glass, denied the company of even one ice cube.

'You should have the vodka, it's cheaper,' the barman said, his English heavily weighted by an American accent.

'No thanks. I don't drink,' Mark replied.

'You'll start pretty soon if you have to spend any time around here,' the barman said, in the same sort of world-weary tone that Mark had heard in a thousand different bars from Torquay to Torremolinos.

The man was the first friendly face that Mark had seen or spoken to since he arrived in the country. If the authorities were trying to develop a tourist trade then they were not trying very hard. 'I need to make a phone call, but I don't seem to be having much luck with the phone in my room.'

The barman smiled, his hand moving forward in the age-old gesture of somebody who can do something for somebody else as long as his palm is crossed with silver. Mark brought out a five-dollar bill, having been warned that roubles were unlikely to impress.

The barman pocketed the note neatly, and almost in the same motion produced a phone from beneath his counter. 'My name's Rudi. Tell me the number and I will get it for you.'

Mark fished into his pocket for his diary and gave him the number of Dimitri Murganev.

Rudi whistled. 'Good player. Are you taking him away from us?'

'Maybe,' Mark replied.

'Not giving too much away. That's wise in this city. You look as if you play yourself.'

'I did once. Now I just watch.'

'Me too. Lokomotiv's my team. Perhaps you can get Murganev to sign something for me.'

Mark nodded. He would have agreed to anything to finish

his business and get home. He never thought he would have admitted it to himself, but he was lonely. All those years spent on his own in Schneider's beat-up flat, and now he was lonely. Was that an emotion only felt by people who had money?

The phone was answered at the other end and Mark waited patiently. Listening to one end of a conversation in Russian was not his idea of a fun evening, and Rudi seemed to be replaying every Lokomotiv match of the season with his hero.

Finally he paused for breath. 'Dimitri speaks very little English.'

'I'm pleased you've got on first name terms with him,' Mark said.

The barman was oblivious to the sarcasm. 'We Russians can be very warm and friendly people once you get to know us. A few vodkas and you'd be singing of Volga boatmen and dancing the kazutsky. Come, my friend. Have a drink. It will be on the house, as I think you say.'

Mark refrained from pointing out that he very much doubted if the house was Rudi's upon which to place the liability of the drink; instead he politely declined.

'Dimitri was expecting your call. He would like to meet with you, but first he wants you to see him play. He thinks you'll want to meet him even more once you have watched a match.'

'There's a game tomorrow night, isn't there?' Mark asked, hoping that the vague programme information he'd obtained in England was reliable.

'Yes. We play Rostov. I will arrange a ticket for you. I have a night off. Perhaps Dimitri will leave us both tickets.'

Mark was half expecting Rudi to offer to act as an interpreter, but if the barman had any ambitions in that quarter they had already been quashed by the player.

'There is something he asked me to tell you,' Rudi said, for the moment his mask of self-confidence slightly slipping. 'He has an adviser. A man who will translate and conduct the negotiations.'

Mark sighed. He had wondered whether he would be able to strike a deal with the player without the intervention of any agents. 'This adviser. Does he represent many players in Russia?' Mark asked.

Rudi shook his head. 'No, I do not think so. You see, he is English.'

Mark swore quietly to himself. As he drained the last drop of the undrinkable orange juice, he asked himself how many English agents had learned of Hertsmere's interest, and, perhaps even more curiously, which agent spoke sufficiently fluent Russian to negotiate the deal.

CHAPTER 13

The stadium, out near the Leningradsky prospekt, was the biggest Mark had ever seen, its high banking of uncomfortable stone seats giving it the look of the ancient Colosseum. Quite how anybody seated in the very back row could have distinguished one player from another defied comprehension, and Mark did not suppose the spectators were likely to get opera glasses thrown in with the price of a ticket.

The Englishman sat in what was obviously the privileged part of the ground. He had a proper seat, albeit wooden, but it did have a back to it and he was near enough to the pitch to be able to see the numbers on the backs of the players' shirts. It came as no surprise to him that Dimitri Murganev was number eleven. That number seemed to haunt him – first Mickey Wayne, who had caused him so many problems when he had returned to Hertsmere, and now the Russian. Rudi, the barman, sat by his side in a thick sheepskin coat. He had smiled when he saw what Mark was proposing to wear to keep out the cold of a Moscow evening. Every so often he produced a bottle of cheap brandy that, he explained, he had 'borrowed' from the hotel bar, although how he intended to return it Mark did not know.

'You're allowed to bring alcohol into the ground?' Mark asked naively, making comparisons with the English regulations and restrictions.

'My friend, here in Moscow, you are not allowed into the

ground without alcohol,' Rudi replied with a broad smile.

'And there's no trouble?'

'You must be joking,' the barman replied. 'Of course there is trouble. When TsKA play Dynamo it is usual for the riot police to be called to break up the fights.'

'And yet they don't do anything about banning the booze?'

'No. If they did that there would be even bigger riots!'

There were only about thirty thousand spectators, and Mark could not help noticing the vast empty spaces dotted with small clusters of visiting fans. At first there was little singing from the home supporters, despite their superior number. What noise there was rose and disappeared into the chilly night air. A few efforts to copy their Western counterparts, a guttural chanting that came from the stomach – and then a kind of silent fascination at the movement of ball and players.

There was no missing Murganev wherever you were seated. He was like a human amongst automatons. The other twenty-one players were all fit, all workmanlike, well trained, well programmed, but Murganev thought for himself. After a quarter of an hour he came back to his defence to collect a short pass and hit a perfectly judged long ball with his left foot. He watched the number nine seize upon it, pushing it ahead, by which time Murganev had made enough ground down the left to receive a return pass. Mark's eyes were fixed on the Russian as he waited for the opposition full-back to come to him, then taunted him into a tackle which left the defender sliding along the floor in embarrassment. Even from a distance Mark could clearly see Murganev's head go up for a second, the arrogant gesture of the natural-born striker giving the goalkeeper the eye, before clinically striking the ball into the corner of the net.

Now the crowd erupted. Although the words of the chant were unrecognisable, Mark could tell they were aimed at Murganev.

'What are they saying?' he asked Rudi.

'They are calling his name, Dimitri. They are saying he is the Messiah. They love him.'

'I can tell. Will they still love him if he goes to England?'

'They will understand. Everybody here would leave the Mother Country for such an opportunity.'

Mark refocused on the field of play. Murganev had the ball again, this time just inside his own half. There was no denying his skill, his enthusiasm and energy. There was no such thing as a lost cause for him. On the rare occasions he lost possession he would be biting at the heels of whoever had robbed him, urging them on to make a mistake, yet never committing himself to a rash tackle that might concede a free-kick.

There was an arrogance about him that Mark had seen previously in the likes of Best, Marsh, Law and Gascoigne. If a team-mate did not keep up with the play, if he did not interpret correctly the complicated script Murganev had written for him, then the creator would stand, arms akimbo in disbelief, amazed that others could not rise to his own heights. Mark wondered what that did to the atmosphere in the dressing room, and whether the Russian would adopt the same attitude if he came to England. He would discover all too soon the limitations of some of the present Hertsmere team. It had been bad enough when Mickey Wayne had shouted at them; Mark could hardly imagine what they would feel at being cursed in a foreign language.

Half-time came with the home side two-nil ahead. Mark waited for the normal rush from the terraces to the comparative comfort of bars and indoor toilets, but nobody in the crowd moved. He could see a few in the seats around unwrapping packaged sandwiches made with huge chunks of black bread. Almost to a man they produced bottles that he assumed contained alcohol of uncertain strength. Rudi took a swig from a bottle that he produced from the voluminous pockets of his coat. He wiped the rim of the neck with the back of his hand and offered it to his English companion. Mark controlled his thirst and shook his head. There would be no returning to that slippery path for him.

'You are odd, an Englishman who does not drink. It is like a fish who does not swim. All the others I meet are drunk from the moment they arrive to the moment they leave. They enjoy our cheap vodka. It gives value for money.'

'Yeah, I used to enjoy it too,' Mark replied, remembering all too clearly the inability to remember. Rudi shot him an odd sidelong look, but did not question him further. Like most barmen, he sensed when a man wanted to talk and when he wanted to keep his own counsel. Any further conversation was interrupted by a huge roar that greeted the teams as they returned to the pitch. Mark was immediately captivated again, his own past an irrelevancy as the technical battle unfolded before him. It had always been this way for him at matches; the ability to block out anything extraneous. All he could see was the thrust and counter-thrust of the twenty-two players, with even the noise of the crowd relegated to the background. Rudi asked him a question, but Mark did not respond. It was not that he wanted to be rude, he simply did not hear. As Murganev went on yet another mazy run, selling dummy after dummy, slaloming his way between players like an expert skier, Mark knew with all the certainty of a child picking a present from a toy-shop window that he could not return to Hertsmere without him. Whatever the price might be, he had to persuade his old club to pay it, and he had to persuade the Russian to accept it.

This time he heard Rudi. 'You are impressed, I think.'

'Yes, I'm impressed. When do we meet him?'

'Straight after the match. We will go to a little drinking club I know. It will be good, yes?'

'Yes, Rudi, it will be good,' and Mark turned his concentration back to the game just in time to see his target score his hat-trick. There were still twenty minutes of the match to go and for once he could not wait for a game of football to come to its end.

CHAPTER 14

Rudi's little drinking club was like no club Mark had ever visited before. He wasn't sure exactly where he had been taken, but he thought Rudi had muttered something about Okhotniy Ryad, which at least gave him some bearings if he were to be abandoned. Rudi had led them down some steeply winding stairs to what appeared to be a solid brick wall. The barman had placed his right elbow on a metal plaque and, as if in a gangster B-movie, a section of the wall moved away to reveal a face that was barely improved by being half glimpsed in the dark. Mark recognised the word 'Rudi' and then, to his astonishment, the whole wall swung inwards and they were ushered into a room so filled with smoke that he could not gauge its size.

Rudi confidently led them through the smog towards a table in a corner. He seemed to be known to everybody, as he responded to waves from men and kisses blown by women.

Above them, two naked women who looked in need of a good meal gyrated in a bored fashion that passed for eroticism, within a huge globe that hung perilously from the ceiling.

'I know what you are thinking,' Rudi said. 'They are kept thin so as not to put any strain on the cord.' Apart from that comment he ignored the sex show and continued to battle through to the far corner.

'Here,' he said finally, 'you sit beside me, and you two, over there. It is easier for negotiation, I think.'

The two other men took their seats a little nervously. The player, Dimitri Murganev, seemed smaller off the field than on it, his charisma concealed beneath his silence. He had a thin, pale face, grey eyes with a gentle, distant expression that gave him the look of an artist desperately seeking the perfect subject. His high cheekbones and fair hair confirmed his Slavic roots, and a nervous, hesitant smile suggested that this was not the sort of place in which he really wanted to be seen.

His companion had been waiting with the player when Mark and Rudi had met them outside the stadium and, apart from a desultory greeting, had not said a word directly to them since, although he had spoken in Russian to Murganev throughout the cab ride to the club. The man was so small as almost to be considered a dwarf – certainly under five feet tall – but with a head in proportion to the rest of his body, a head that he carried bird-like, tilted slightly towards his right shoulder. It was difficult to guess at his age, which could have been anything between the late twenties and early forties. His hair was thick and straight, cut short at the front but surprisingly tied into a pigtail at the back. His skin was badly scarred with pock-marks that suggested something worse than childhood chicken-pox. When he finally spoke his voice was rich and mellow, seemingly belonging to another person.

'We've not been formally introduced,' he said to Mark, belatedly extending his hand. 'The name is Jennings, Alex Jennings. As in *Jennings at School*.' He saw the puzzled look on Mark's face. 'Jennings, Jennings and Darbyshire. No? Sorry, wrong generation. Or maybe it was me in the wrong generation. My parents preferred the schoolboy classics to *Star Trek* and *Dr Who*. That's why I chose to support Wolverhampton. There was something classical about the old gold. I was always sorry I never saw Cullis's Cubs. The black and white flicker of the films doesn't do them justice. Then, of course, there was that first floodlit match . . .' It was almost as if he had become unaware of the noise in the room. His voice had dropped to a whisper and Mark found himself leaning forward so as not to miss a word. There was something mesmeric about Jennings' delivery. He was a natural-born lecturer, a man unlike any other Mark had met in the world of football in England.

Rudi ordered drinks with a wave of his hand, shouting a reminder at the retreating back of a broken-nosed waiter. 'I've told him whiskey for three and tea for you, Mark. You don't know what you are missing. This is one of the few places in our city that you can get real American rye without having to sell your home or your body.' As if she'd heard his last word, a slim girl in a low-cut, figure-hugging dress stopped by their table and leaned across to light a cigarette for Jennings. Mark looked down and saw her nipples clearly revealed. She sensed he was looking and stroked the side of his face gently with the back of her hand. Rudi slapped her backside with a hint of more than familiarity and sent her packing with a couple of words and a smile.

'I think she likes you, Mark. I told her to come back when we have finished our business. She is very cheap if you have dollars.'

'She could be very expensive if she's got AIDS,' Mark replied, knowing in his present state that he was tempted and aroused by the very sexuality of the girl who could be bought, yet at the same time mindful of what the disease had done to another player in his life.

'No. I don't think so. They run a good clean ship here. Stefan –' and here he pointed towards a man who was built like a mountain, standing with arms folded, reviewing the whole scene from behind the bar – 'Stefan does not accept any trouble. And nobody wishes to run foul of Stefan – at least not more than once.'

'I can understand that,' Mark said, noting that the tea which had mysteriously appeared by his side was in a glass with only a twist of lemon and a long spoon for company. He tried to turn the conversation around to the real point of their meeting, but found himself having to wait until the three other men had paid their due respects to the whiskey with various comments of admiration. He had not been in the country long, but he could see already that doing business here was going to make Italian negotiations seem a piece of cake.

It was Jennings who set the wheels in motion first. 'I understand you want to take Dimitri here back to England with you.'

'Yes, that's right,' Mark replied, relieved that discussions seemed to be finally underway while everybody was still sober.

'Well, Dimitri would like to go, so at least we have a mutual aim. As you have probably gathered he has authorised me to conduct the negotiations for him. I am afraid he speaks no English so you will just have to take my word for that.'

Mark nodded. He could hardly believe that the man would have the nerve to conduct these discussions in the player's presence unless he really did represent him. 'You don't strike me as a typical agent. Have you done anything like this before?'

Jennings emptied his glass, then slowly refilled it as if the answer lay in the drink. 'Now, if I say I haven't will you take advantage of me, and if I say I have will you think any the less of me?'

Mark said nothing. He was trying to place the man's accent. There was a hint of Irish, a suggestion of Welsh, both hidden beneath tones that had education stamped all over them.

'A man who keeps his own counsel is a wise man indeed,' Jennings said in response to Mark's silence.

'We'll see,' Mark said, 'but you've not answered my question.'

'Well, it might be the drink, and then again it might not, but I feel I can trust you. No, I've not done anything like this before. I work for the Anglo-Soviet Trade Development

Corporation here in Moscow. Or ASTRID as its known to its close friends. I read about the interest in Dimitri going to England in the papers. I was here, I love football, I speak Russian. Some people seem to think I speak English passably well. So I got in touch with him and here I am and here we are.'

Throughout the speech Rudi had been speaking to the player. Without any indication that he had been doing anything other than concentrate on Mark, Jennings suddenly turned to the barman and gripped his arm tightly. 'Dimitri doesn't need any women from you. He's a happily married man. Now I've no objection to you continuing to buy us drinks, but pretty soon we're going to be talking about money, and as, I suspect, you've a few friends here, can I suggest that it might be in your interest to renew their acquaintances until it's time for us to leave?'

Rudi was well over six feet tall, with huge hands that could hold a couple of bottles by their bases in each of them; but there was something about Jennings' tone, a note not just of authority, but of potential retribution, that stopped his protests before they could even form on his lips. He rose, giving Jennings a long hard look, which the Englishman returned unwaveringly with a smile on his lips and what appeared to be a twinkle in his eyes.

'I'll see you later then, my friend. If you need anything, or if anybody gives you any trouble, just shout. I'm more likely to hear you than see you in all this mist,' Rudi said, then spoke rapidly in Russian to Murganev, gripping his shoulder, and disappeared into the crowd.

'Cheeky devil,' Jennings said, with a crooked but attractive smile. 'He said that if I don't work out for our friend here, then he's always available.'

Both Jennings and Murganev refilled their glasses and Mark saw that the bottle was nearly empty. His own glass of tea was also diminished and the smoke was beginning to affect his throat. He traced a finger around the label on the whiskey bottle, half reflectively, half longingly, then with a sigh asked Jennings to order him another tea. It was clearly going to be a long and thirsty night.

CHAPTER 15

Daniel Lewis was beginning to wish he'd never set his eyes upon any Russians, that the iron curtain had remained firmly in place. Nikolei Yevneko had been waiting for him with ill-concealed impatience, and when he arrived he had been virtually dragged into the room. On his previous visit, after the house had been bought, he had been offered champagne and caviar, but now he was not even given the chance of a cup of tea. The man who had escorted him into the room – and escorted was a mild description, frog-marched might have been better – stood behind him, one hand locking him into the chair. Another man, in a dark suit, who Daniel recognised as Yuri from his first visit, leaned against the door-jamb, as if daring the estate agent to make one move in his direction.

Yevneko waved a copy of the newspaper in his face, then said in a voice that could have frozen Mars, 'You are pleased with your publicity?'

Lewis did not know what to say. Yes, of course he'd been pleased with the publicity, he'd been delighted with it, but somehow he did not think that was the answer for which Yevneko was looking. He did not need to worry, at least not about that particular enquiry, because Yevneko gave him no time to reply.

'I am not pleased with it, I am not pleased at all. I deal with my lawyer; I know I can rely upon lawyer-client confidentiality. I deal with my banker; I know I can rely on banker-client confidentiality. I deal with my estate agent . . . I think I can rely on his client confidentiality. And I am wrong. I think you are part of my team. I think you want to be part of my team, but perhaps you are not a team player. An Englishman letting the side down. It is not cricket, but . . .' the Russian took a long hard look at Lewis. 'I am not sure you are really English.'

There was a silence. Lewis wondered whether he should say something, make an apology, but he did not think it was likely to have any effect. It would be best to let Yevneko have his say. Sooner or later he would run out of steam, although Lewis had not realised the man had such a strong grasp of the language. And when he did finally come to the end of the tirade, they would let him go and the worst that would happen would be that he had lost a client. The fact that it was such an important client, and one who had promised to lead to so much, did not seem to be the main issue at the moment. Daniel Lewis just wanted things to be the way they were. He would be quite content to be sitting in his office waiting for the phone to ring, wondering what sort of mood his wife would be in when he got home. He would settle for the glossy car magazines with their models as remote for him as those who posed on Page Three of the *Sun*. He would settle for anything to be out of here.

Yevneko snapped his fingers and the man by the door moved rapidly forward. Lewis took a sharp intake of breath as he saw the man's hand move towards his pocket and produce something metal that glinted beneath the artificial light. A click, a flame, and then Lewis's anxiety drained away as he saw it was just a cigarette lighter.

Yevneko took a drag on his cigarette. 'That is how I like things. I snap my fingers and those who work for me obey. They do it quickly and quietly. They ask no questions and they do no more nor less than I ask. Now, is that how you will behave in the future?'

Lewis almost cried with relief. This was to be it. This was

the warning. He had stepped out of line, and now Yevneko had given him his warning he was back on the team. 'I'm grateful to you for being so understanding,' he said, his voice sounding distant to his own ears. He took the absence of a response as encouragement to continue. 'I don't know how it came out in the interview . . .'

'Journalists can be very persuasive. They are the same the world over,' Yevneko said.

'Yes, yes, you're so right,' Daniel added, pleased to be made to feel a man of the world.

'But I do not think you will make the same mistake again.'

'No, I won't. You have my word on that.'

Yevneko nodded. His associates nodded in sympathy. Lewis hesitated, rose an inch or two from his chair, then paused in mid-air as if caught in some child's game of statues. Nobody pushed him down, so he awkwardly completed his movement to his feet and began backing towards the door, half bowing to a minor royalty.

'So, I'll be in touch then,' he said, unthinking of what he was actually saying. The men in the room were ignoring him, talking rapidly amongst themselves in Russian. Daniel was reminded of his grandparents when they had looked after him, using Yiddish to conceal anything that they considered too grown-up for his infantile ears. Yuri, the large man by the door, laughed crudely. Daniel's ears reddened as he sensed he was the subject of the joke, but he was at the door now and he was not going to hang around for the translation. He stumbled into the light, feeling he had been imprisoned underground for days, then blinked and blinked again at the sight that met his eyes.

His car was exactly where he had left it, or at least what remained of it was where he had parked it. The roof was in shreds, as if it had just been subjected to the full violence of a tropical storm. The windows were gone, smashed by what must have been a sledge-hammer. Whoever had wielded it had taken the time and trouble to sweep all the shattered glass into a pile, perhaps to ensure it did not damage the tyres of any other vehicle. However, once they had finished with the windows they had turned their attention to the bonnet, which resembled a V-sign made from twisted metal. The wheels had not escaped either. All four were totally flat, the rubber flowing from them like streamers from a kite. The house must have been most efficiently soundproofed, because he had not heard a thing from inside.

Daniel tried to speak, but the words would not come out. He stood there for fully five minutes, making noises that somehow expressed the gut-wrenching sensation he felt far more than any coherent curses. He turned back to the door to ring the bell. Surely they would at least allow him to call a taxi. Nobody answered, although he thought he glimpsed a blind being momentarily lifted, somebody satisfying themselves he was still there. Finally, he pulled the car-keys from his pocket and tossed them on to what was left of the back seat. He walked slowly and unsteadily up the drive and towards public transport. He did not know whether Yevneko and his associates watched him disappear, and he did not care. Whatever lesson they had wanted to teach him, he had learned and would never forget it.

CHAPTER 16

Mark Rossetti sat on the bed in the hotel bedroom. He had tried the chair, but it had not been designed for relaxation – indeed, it was hard to believe it had been designed for sitting. It was after two in the morning but he did not feel tired, although he knew he should have been exhausted. Rudi had ensured he made it to the hotel foyer, then, as if embarrassed to be seen with a guest within his own working environment, he had disappeared without even saying goodnight.

Mark's clothes stank of cigarette smoke and he could sense the acrid taste of alcohol on his lips even though he had not drunk a drop. It had been like sitting in a room permeated with rising damp – you did not need to place your mouth against the wall to experience the problem. And what had he got to show for it? He hoped he had got the services of Dimitri Murganev for Hertsmere United, but he knew too much about footballers to be certain of that until the man had signed on the dotted line.

He tried to put the evening's events in order, his mind as muddled as if he, himself, had shared every drink with Murganev and Alex Jennings. Jennings. As the night had worn on he had found himself more and more fascinated by the other Englishman. After a while his odd appearance had become an irrelevancy, as the strange, mesmeric voice had insinuated itself into his head. The man knew his football, there was no doubt of that, but the way he spoke of it made it seem an operatic art form rather than a sport. Yet, when it had come to the terms he had wanted for the player, there had been nothing lyrical. He had produced a slip of paper from his pocket and had read to Mark as coolly and calmly as if he were reciting a shopping list.

'We're looking for a three-year contract, with a break clause on our side at any time after the first year if Hertsmere aren't in the top six in the Premier. Similarly, if they're knocked out in the third round of the FA Cup or the second round of the Coca-Cola, we have the right to leave unless the club is in the top three . . .'

It had not escaped Mark's attention that Jennings had begun with matters of ambition rather than money, but when he got to the cash element it was clear he had been merely orchestrating the introduction to the main act.

'I'd be setting up an off-shore trust for Dimitri and we'd be looking to the club to make a substantial payment into that for marketing rights.'

'What's a substantial payment?' Mark had asked, wondering how Sinclair and Barlucci, and indeed Savvas and the bank, would react to the principal. What was more to the point was how the Premier League would react. Mark had studied enough reports on the game, seen enough disciplinary punishments handed out, to know that nobody was going to want to risk breaching the rules, even for a player of Murganev's talents.

Jennings anticipated him. 'Don't worry. We've no problem about you disclosing the payment on the face of the contract. This is tax planning, not rule-busting as far as we're concerned. I'll be taking Dimitri into the UK through a tax haven, and after that it'll be a matter of arguing with my old friends the Inland Revenue as to whether or not it's taxable. Anyway, I'm not sure how I want the sums split, but the total over three years has to be a million . . .'

Mark took a deep breath. He should have checked it out before he came – this was outside of Hertsmere's capabilities

– but he ploughed on, hoping that this was just an opening position and that everything was negotiable. 'I assume that the million would include the salary as well.'

'Wrong assumption,' Jennings had said, with a winning smile that made Mark think he could forgive him anything. 'The salary would be whatever is the top salary at the club now plus ten per cent, and would be geared to rise every year to exceed what was then the top salary —'

'Plus ten per cent?' Mark had asked resignedly.

'You read my mind.'

'And that's it?' Mark had asked, hoping the sardonic tone had got across.

'Not quite. If the club wins a major trophy in the three years, then Dimitri gets a half-million-pound bonus.'

'There are club bonuses already. There's no way they'll single out one player for a team effort.'

Jennings shrugged. 'If you didn't think you needed Dimitri to win something, then you wouldn't be here trying to sign him. You can reduce your risk by placing a bet on yourselves to win things, or maybe take out some insurance at Lloyds against the event. Then we'll want full removal expenses, a house, a car, private health insurance . . .' He looked closely at the scrawled notes on the paper. 'Oh, and a percentage of any profit the club makes if it sells him on.'

'A percentage,' Mark echoed, wondering when the next plane back to England was.

'Yes, say fifty per cent,' Jennings added, thinking he had been asked a question.

'Why not?' Mark said. 'Why not say seventy-five per cent, or a hundred per cent? Maybe a hundred and fifty per cent, in case you think you've sold your man a bit short. Look, Alex, this is Hertsmere United you're talking to, not Manchester United or Juventus.'

Jennings was in no way concerned. 'I know. I know all about Hertsmere. I've done my homework, believe me, and if you ever want to be a really big club, then you have to find a way to do this deal. Where Dimitri leads, others will follow. You can't carry on picking up the crumbs from rich clubs' tables.'

'It's just not possible with our attendances. Have you ever seen our ground?'

'I've seen every ground in the league, and a fair number that aren't as well. Before I met Dimitri, I was planning a holiday to see Ross County and Caledonian Thistle play in Scotland. You have to move, and it's players like Dimitri who will give you the credibility to do it. Also you're in the Cup-Winners' Cup. You're sure to make a fair bit of money out of that.'

Mark leaned back in his seat, and nearly fell before he realised it had no back. Rudi had returned to see if they were ready to go, but Jennings had waved him airily away.

'You've done this before, haven't you?' Mark asked.

'Negotiated? Yes, I've done that before. A football transfer? No. But at the end of the day, one piece of negotiation is very much like another. I have a commodity to sell, you want to buy the same commodity. It's what we in the West are accustomed to call market forces. Here in Russia they are just learning to recognise that such things exist.'

'And you're helping with the lessons.'

'In a modest way, yes.'

They had gone round and round in circles for the next hour or so, the discussions punctuated by Jennings' bursts of Russian as he explained to Murganev exactly what was happening. The player seemed remarkably uninterested in his fate, his expression not changing, nor the steady pace at which he drank whatever was put before him. Somehow or other Mark did not see Ray Fowler allowing him to have a bottle of vodka on the touchline. At the end of the evening it was Mark who felt he had made all the concessions – and he had no idea whether or not he had the authority to make them. It had been a mutually warm parting, the drink finally having had sufficient effect on both Jennings and Murganev to encourage them to take Mark in bear-like embraces, the hint of tears in their eyes. Now he had to wait.

Jennings had said he had to talk to Murganev's present club to see if they would give him anything from the fee to be paid by Hertsmere. 'I could hide it from you, but I prefer to talk openly. Secrets that become no longer secrets often leave a nasty taste in the mouth.'

There was a knock on the bedroom door. Mark hesitated. He had heard all the horror stories about visitors to Moscow being mugged in their hotel bedrooms for nothing more valuable than a pair of Levis. He tried to peer through the spyhole, but whoever was outside was out of vision.

'Who is it?' he asked in a semi-whisper, not sure who he might be frightened of awakening.

'My name's Sophia. Rudi sent me.'

'There must be some mistake. It's two-fifteen in the morning.'

'No, no mistake. Just open the door and I will explain. You have no need to be afraid. I will stand back and you will see I am alone.'

Mark's room was in the middle of a long narrow corridor, and as far as he could recall there were no alcoves which could be used for concealment. He was probably being neurotic, but still he opened the door slowly and cautiously, ever ready to pull it shut if the woman or anybody with her made a sudden movement. Nobody did. His visitor leaned back against the wall, seemingly trying to create as much distance between herself and the door as was humanly possible.

It was her eyes that first caught his attention, huge blue saucers, that made the rest of her face an irrelevancy. She was small, and he guessed by the size of her breasts that regular good meals might have given her a weight problem; but she clearly had not been getting four courses a day, because her clothes hung loosely on her, while a bangle swung around her wrist as she span it with her finger.

She threw her arms open wide. 'You see? Only me. I can come in? They do not like these scenes in this hotel.'

'What scenes?' Mark asked, but by then she had already pushed past him with surprising speed and strength and, almost before he was beside her, she had produced a bottle from her bag and poured two drinks. She pushed a glass into his hand and clinked her own against it, then knocked it back in one movement. She refilled it, then put it down carefully and began to undress. She removed a dark waistcoat and then unbuttoned the blouse to confirm Mark's first views on the ampleness of her bosom. She was about to unfasten her belt when Mark took her hand and held it firmly for a moment. It felt cold to his touch and she looked up at him in a silent apology that she should have brought any discomfort, however slight, to his own skin.

'Look, Sophie, or whatever your name is, it's late and I'm tired and, while I think you're the prettiest thing I've seen since I arrived in Moscow, I just want to go to bed.'

'Yes, that is fine. We go to bed. I can keep my boots on if you like.' She pointed down to the thigh-length black leather into which her trousers had been tucked. They looked genuine and, knowing the price of ordinary shoes, Mark could well imagine what they had cost and how much she might cherish them. He could also imagine how she had got the money together to buy them in the first place.

'Please, keep your boots on. And put your clothes back on. Take your bottle back to Rudi. Tell him I said thanks, but no thanks.'

She pouted. 'You prefer a boy. I think the English like boys better than girls. I can get you a boy. Very young, very pretty. Not so pretty as me, I think. You give me money?' She held out her hand.

'No, no boy. No you. Nobody. Just me.'

She looked at him, her eyes opening impossibly wider. 'I

98

see. OK. But maybe you give me a little money. The man who sends me, he will be upset if I do not give him any money.'

'You mean Rudi? Don't worry, I'll handle him in the morning. I have a thing or two to tell him about this little effort.'

'No, not Rudi. Rudi is funny. This is the man who sends me to Rudi. Not nice, not funny.'

Mark bit his lower lip. A part of him told him this was a shake-down, that this girl had done this with success a thousand times before. But those eyes bored into him, mining his inner resources, convincing him that she was in real danger if he gave her nothing.

'How much would it have cost me to sleep with you?'

'A hundred dollars.'

'I don't think so,' he said with a smile, at once embarrassed and amused by the conversation. He needed Alex Jennings here to conclude these negotiations. 'Fifty, I think, would have bought me a day in this city, even with somebody as pretty as you. I should just give you twenty, but here's fifty, so maybe you can have a night off tomorrow –' he looked down at the rings on her fingers – 'to spend with your family.'

He had not meant to be cruel, but she gave a howl, plucked the note from his fingers and was gone before he could apologise.

Suddenly he felt terribly weary – weary with this country, weary with football, with women, with life. He picked up the glass the woman had poured, brought it half-way to his lips, then with a distinct effort took it into the tiny bathroom and emptied it into the stained sink. He washed it slowly, rubbing his fingers to smear and then remove the lipstick. Its touch to his skin gave him a vicarious sense of excitement and he momentarily regretted sending the woman away. He returned to the bedroom. Without removing any of his clothes he tossed himself down on the bed. He caught a brief hint of her perfume and then, before he knew it, he was asleep, dreaming of

Dimitri Murganev scoring a hat-trick on his Hertsmere debut against a beautiful woman, naked but for a pair of fine, thigh-length, black leather boots.

CHAPTER 17

Mark did not know what had made him trust Alex Jennings. They had agreed to meet for lunch the following day, and by then he had decided to tell him everything about the Schneider inheritance. He seemed the sort of man who would know somebody who could help, even if he were unable to do so himself. As far as Murganev was concerned, after the hard bargaining of the previous night, they seemed to have reached an accord. It was almost as if, having knocked Mark around, Jennings wanted to prove he could be magnanimous in victory, and as part of that generosity he had booked them a table at the Grand Imperial. Mark did not need to be told that this was one of Moscow's most exclusive restaurants. The antique silver cutlery, the crisp linen tablecloths, the silent but expert service and the extraordinary wine list all made their own announcements. Sitting there, with music gently playing in the background, he felt at once a part of the old Russian nobility, felt it difficult to believe that the revolution had ever happened.

'So you'll report back to your board,' Jennings said, swirling a huge brandy glass in his tiny hand. 'I've already had a preliminary chat with the local Lokomotiv lads here and I think I can put together a decent package. I can't see you'll have a work permit problem back home, given the number of international caps Dimitri has got. I've had a look at your fixture list. You're at home to Camfleet the second week of October. I think that would make a good debut game.

101

Indifferent opposition with a slow central defender, but unlikely to roll over and play dead. You can never guarantee a goal, but he's got as good a chance as any against a team like that. Nothing like a goal first time out in front of your own fans to endear you to them.'

Mark smiled and took a mouthful of coffee. It had a burnt, acrid taste which was concealed by the heat, but the overall effect was not unpleasant. 'Are you sure you don't want a seat on the board as part of the overall deal?'

'It would be nice,' Jennings said a little wistfully. 'You know, Mark, when I was young I wanted nothing else but to be involved in football. I lived it, I breathed it. My parents would go crazy with me when I filled my room with programmes and magazines and statistics. Always statistics. The snobs say that cricket is the real game for statisticians, but they're wrong. It's only now that television is beginning to realise what I have always known, that football is a game of percentages. How much control, how many shots, how much possession, how many corners, how many accurate passes. All you see in the paper is the goals, but what about the saves, the "assists", as our American friends like to call them? I have no time for the Yanks generally, nor for what they laughingly call sports, but they do understand the fascination of figures – even if, in their case, it is preferable to watch the figures rather than the matches themselves.'

'So what happened? How did you end up out here, rather than at Lancaster Gate?'

Jennings sighed. 'That's a long story. Another time, perhaps. Save to say it did not take long to discover that I was best with the theory rather than the practice of the game. Always the last to be picked in the playground games. Sometimes a one-goal inducement would be offered to take me. I had my revenge when I reported on school matches for the magazine. People soon realised that my pen was more effective than my feet.' He waved to a hovering waiter for more coffee. 'That's the thing about Russian coffee. It leaves you wanting more in the vain hope that the next cup will be better than the last. It is like supporting an unsuccessful team. You know in your heart of hearts that they are poor, but you never surrender the fantasy that one day, just one day, they will play like worldbeaters. But I'm sorry, you get me on to football, I can't stop. When are you going home? I know Dimitri wants to get the wheels in motion.'

'What about his family?' Mark asked. 'Will they be travelling with him? That's going to be relevant in the accommodation.'

'Ah, so you thought I missed something. Yes, you will have to apply for visas for the family as well. A wife and a small child. But you didn't answer my question about going home.'

'That's because I'm not sure; it rather depends on you. Do you have time for a story?'

'Time is the one commodity it is easy to acquire in Russia.'

It occurred to Mark that so far Jennings had disclosed no necessity to be at any particular place of work at any particular moment, but he felt he had asked enough questions. If the man wanted to tell him anything about his real job then doubtless he would.

'So tell me the story,' Jennings said, and Mark found himself telling not just about Leopold Schneider, but also about Patti Delaney and then about himself and the long lonely years of exile. Jennings sat and listened, asking the odd question, but basically letting Mark tell it in his own way and in his own time. By the time Mark had finished they were the only two customers in the restaurant and outside the clear blue sky had turned to the grey of dusk.

'I wonder if they intended closing between lunch and supper,' Jennings said, signalling for yet another coffee. 'I don't know what this stuff does to my stomach, but it sure as hell keeps my brain working.' He paused. 'Quite a story, quite a story; but you've survived and poor old Leopold has not. And you want me to help you find and sell his property.' He nodded as if this were the sort of thing he were asked to do every day of the week.

'Can you?' Mark asked.

'Who knows? I can try. That's the least you can do in this country is try. They try to earn a living, try to feed themselves, clothe themselves, better themselves.'

'And do they succeed?'

'Success is an odd equation. By our standards I suppose you would say they do not; but somehow or other they muddle through. People are born, people die, and generally in between it sort of works. You have to live here for a while to understand what I mean. Anyway – your property. I'll ask some questions. If I get the right answers quickly, then perhaps we'll make a trip.'

'I'm grateful to you.' Mark hesitated, not knowing if the other man would be offended if he offered him some financial incentive. Having seen him in action on behalf of Murganev the night before, he doubted if it were possible to offend Jennings when it came to money. 'If you can pull the pieces together I'm sure Patti would be happy to agree with me that you should get something out of it.'

Jennings was unpredictable. He waved a hand. 'Don't worry. A few calls won't cost. If I can help, then I'll help.'

They shook hands and Jennings insisted on giving Mark a lift back to the hotel. 'I want you to get back in one piece. One of our fellow countrymen got mugged this side of the swing doors last week. It's become real terrorist country round here. Shoot-outs are almost the norm. I'll be in touch.'

Mark looked back once from the steps, and saw Jennings wait with the engine running until he was back inside the lobby. He made his way through to the bar. Rudi was busy polishing glasses, but looked up and smiled when he saw Mark.

'Hello. I thought you had gone on the missing list.'

'No. I've just been with Alex Jennings.'

104

Rudi screwed up his face. 'I think maybe you should be careful of that one. I asked a few questions in the bar when you were having your private talks. Nobody knows him.'

'And that makes you think I should be careful?'

'Sure. This is a big city, but it is a bit like a village. We gossip. We know the good guys and we know the bad guys; and we know which bad guys are good and which good guys are bad. But when somebody is not known, then that is not good. You understand?'

'Not really, but I can look after myself, that much I've learned over the last few years. At least Alex hasn't sent me any night-time visitors.'

The barman appeared puzzled. 'What do you mean?'

'The girl, the present. Sophie or whatever her name was.'

Rudi's face showed nothing but a blank. 'I don't know what you mean.'

'Last night, or rather early this morning, I got a visit from a hooker. She said you'd sent her . . .'

Rudi shook his head. 'No. You are a friend. If I think you need a girl I can get you one, but I ask first. I sent nobody. You allowed her in?'

'She was on her own. We talked. I gave her fifty dollars and she left.'

'You were lucky. It was cheap insurance. Even if she'd not robbed you while you were asleep she may have left you a more permanent reminder of Moscow, if you understand what I mean.'

Mark knew exactly what he meant. 'She seemed a nice type of person. I felt sorry for her.'

Rudi held a glass up to the light and polished it until it shone. 'Never forget, my friend, that in this country nothing is what it seems.' And then he added, as an after-thought, 'Nothing, and nobody.'

CHAPTER 18

Back in England, the trip to Russia seemed like a dream – although as far as David Sinclair, Claudio Barlucci and Savva Constantinou were concerned it was more like a nightmare.

'I can't believe you ever thought we could afford these sorts of terms. He's a good player, but he's not Pele,' Sinclair said. 'And Lokomotiv are being greedy as well. I thought we had a deal with them, and they've suddenly pushed up the ante by two hundred grand. Whatever happened to communism?'

'Well done, Alex Jennings,' Mark muttered to himself. It was clear that whatever he had beaten out of the Russian club they in turn were seeking from Hertsmere. 'I think you could stand firm on your original offer,' Mark said, 'and if you look at what Murganev wants compared to what some of the so-called superstars are earning in this country, it's not outrageous.'

'But he's got it all to prove in the Premier. We'll offer him half of what he's asking, and if he's doing the business after a dozen games then we'll double it,' Sinclair said firmly.

Mark sighed. It was almost the first time he'd come into conflict with David Sinclair, but then it was David's money and not his own on the line. 'Look, you sent me out there, you relied on my judgement – isn't that good enough?'

'I sent you out there to bring us back a player, not to pay off the Russian National Debt. Be reasonable, Mark. You know how much I care about this club. I've put myself on the line time and time again, but somehow or other at the end of the

107

day we have to balance the books. We've no idea if the insurers are going to pay out on Mickey Wayne. If we'd got the Italian money from him then there'd be no problem.'

'No, it would be me who would have the problem.' Barlucci spoke for the first time.

Mark turned his powers of persuasion on the Italian. 'Claudio, you know what it takes to turn a small club into a big one. How long did your team live in the shadows of Roma and Lazio? If we don't take a flyer sooner or later we'll go down the leagues as quickly as we came up. Sure you can go out and buy a player for half of what Murganev wants, but he'll be half the player as well. I've seen this boy play. Believe me, he's good.'

'I believe you; but we went to look abroad because we thought we'd pick up bargains there.'

'And he is a bargain. Once he's played half a dozen games for us he'll have doubled in value,' Mark persisted.

'And I suppose we sell him then, make a nice profit, and you go out and find another one. Football doesn't work like that. If we could sell all our players and put out our youth team we'd be a very rich club indeed.'

'OK, OK. I get the message. You think I'm a lousy negotiator. I wasn't dealing with some peasant who counted in apples, you know. This guy Jennings was just about the most switched-on individual I've ever met. Not only could he have won Mastermind on football, but he made all the figures make sense. Why can't we try and get a sponsor for the player, perhaps some company that wants to do business in Russia?'

Sinclair shook his head. 'We're talking long shots. A brewery might have taken Keegan to Newcastle all those years ago, but I don't see a vodka company bringing Murganev to Hertsmere.'

'A vodka company, no, but a crazy Italian, maybe.'

Both Mark and Sinclair turned towards Barlucci, who had the satisfied look on his huge face of a man who had just given an expensive present to a favourite mistress.

'What have you got up your sleeve, Claudio?' Sinclair asked.

The Italian made an exaggerated gesture of peering up the arm of his jacket. 'Sleeve. You see, I know the word. My English is improving by jumps and springs.'

'Leaps and bounds,' Mark corrected with a smile, but Barlucci merely shrugged and continued.

'This is what I will do. Whatever is the best salary at the club at the moment the club pays to this Russian. The difference I pay. As far as the extra transfer money is concerned, if we can't get it down, and our friend Savvas's bank will not produce it, then I pay that as well.'

Sinclair looked at Barlucci in astonishment. 'You're really serious about Hertsmere, aren't you, Claudio?'

'If I do something then I am always serious. If you are not serious about something then you do not bother. So, Mark, you go back to this Jennings and you conclude the deal. And you do it quickly.'

Savvas had said little during the discussion, but now brought both hands down firmly on the table. 'I will see what we can do. I can't let you think Italians are more generous than Greeks.'

'More generous, no; better footballers, I think so,' Barlucci replied with a smile, and Mark was left with the warm feeling that for once Hertsmere was a family again, all pulling in the same direction.

'Can I use the phone?' he asked.

'Use the one in my office. There's a direct line,' Sinclair replied.

Mark almost ran into the other room before the Italian could change his mind, and dialled the number Jennings had given him for the direct contact. A recorded voice with a foreign accent asked him to leave a message, and he obeyed with a sense of disappointment. He wanted to talk to Jennings, not just about Murganev, but also about Schneider's property. He was due to meet Patti in an hour for lunch, and he did not believe the answers to his enquiries were likely to satisfy her.

His belief was well founded.

'We can't just leave it there. It's not the money, it's what Leo wanted.'

'Patti, you obviously don't believe me. I asked Alex Jennings to help us trace the property. He told me to accept that the property didn't exist, that it never had existed. He asked me if it would make a difference to my life if I accepted that, and I had to say it wouldn't. So he told me to go home and forget all about it. That some things are better left untouched in Russia, even in 1996. Perhaps particularly in 1996.'

'And you accepted that, from a man you've just met, a man you hardly know, whose only claim to credibility is that he ran rings around you when it came to negotiating a transfer?'

Mark played with the pasta on his plate. He had let it get cold while they talked and he had lost his appetite. He wanted to turn back the clock to the time when he and Patti had none of the pressures of money and success, when all they had was a will to survive, a desire to overcome the odds that eventually became a desire for each other. Now they seemed to have no time for each other. Patti was in regular demand as a freelancer and, as she'd already told him over the soup, she'd been offered the post as features editor for one of the leading quality Sundays. Yet he could not place all the blame on her. He, too, had veered away from commitment, not just to Patti, but even to Hertsmere. He'd led them to victory at Wembley, so why had he not stuck with it, taken them into Europe and taken his chances? He couldn't answer that, even today, any more than he could answer Patti when she asked him why he had accepted as gospel all that Jennings had told him.

'This man, Patti, he sounded genuinely worried. I didn't figure him as the sort of man who would worry over nothing.'

110

'But you didn't find out why he was concerned. I bet you didn't even ask him.'

'You're wrong there. I did ask. He sort of clammed up. Said there were some people it was best not to mention, let alone deal with.'

'And these people are interested in a property that he tells you doesn't exist? Come on, what are we talking about here, Mafia?'

Mark pushed the plate away, tired of making patterns with the cold food. 'Maybe we are. Why can't you accept for once that you're on a loser?'

It was the wrong thing to say. Patti had been simmering quietly for no apparent reason since they'd met. Now she exploded. 'And if I'd accepted I was on a loser with you, where would you be today? When we first met you were a broken-down not-so-ex-drunk. You were chasing rainbows and at the same time you were running away from your wife.'

'Ex-wife,' Mark interrupted, then, receiving a look that would have frozen molten lava, wished he hadn't.

'Whatever. All I wanted from you was an interview, but I saw something else there and I went for it.'

'Did you get it?' he asked, his eyes fixed on her.

'For a while I thought I had.'

'And now?'

'Now I'm not so sure. Fuck it, Mark, we've changed. We're in too much of a hurry to even stop and look at ourselves, and if we did I'm not sure we'd like what we saw. When we do sit down, what do we have to say to each other?'

Mark felt a sense of hopelessness. 'Are you saying it's over between us?'

'Over? For something to be over it has to begin. Did we ever really start?'

He reeled back at that, taking the blow from the words fairly and squarely in his lower abdomen. He did not know why she was so angry with him; or maybe she was just angry.

111

'Don't look at me like a hurt puppy. You're over thirty years old, you're not a kid any more. You have to listen to what people are telling you even if it hurts. Just because we slept together doesn't make it the grand love affair of the twentieth century.'

'This isn't you talking,' Mark said, knowing it was a feeble response to an all-out bombardment.

She rattled her wine glass against the half-empty bottle which only she had consumed. 'What is it then, the booze? You should know all about that.'

She lit a cigarette, knowing how much he disliked smoking, daring him to criticise, the anger rising when he refused to rise to the bait.

'Why are you like this?' Mark asked.

Just for a second she let slip her guard and he thought she was going to cry, but then the shutters were firmly slammed down once again. 'Like what? Like me? This is what I am, Mark. I don't know what rosy, romantic, picture you've been painting of me for yourself while you've been joyriding around the globe. We're not teenagers, we're all grown up.'

He clenched his fists so tightly that he could feel the nails digging into his flesh. He wanted the sensation of physical pain to drive away the emotional agony that was threatening to overwhelm him. 'So what do you want to do?' he asked finally, the words sounding to him as though they were being forced out staccato between his teeth.

She put her glass down on the table and looked him straight in the eyes until it was he who had to break away and stare downwards as if he had something of which to be ashamed.

'Do about what, Mark?' Again she posed the question as if it were rhetorical.

'About us.'

'I'm not sure there is an us. Sometimes I'm not even sure there's a me. I'm sorry.'

'It's your call,' he said slowly, realising as he spoke that once again he was passing his destiny from his own control.

She framed her face in her hands, testing its shape, then, seemingly satisfied, said, 'I'll tell you what I want to do. I want to go to Russia to find Leo's property. I want to set my mother up in the best rest home in the South East and head for Moscow. Now do I do that on my own or are you coming back for a second try?'

'I'm coming back,' he said, knowing that what he had been offered was not really a choice.

CHAPTER 19

It had all gone smoothly, too smoothly. With the financial backing of Barlucci and the speedy co-operation of Savvas in setting up the off-shore financial and corporate arrangements, the finalisation of the contract with Dimitri Murganev had been concluded in a matter of days. There had been a series of faxes and telephone calls to Alex Jennings, and then the work permit had been granted remarkably rapidly after the intervention of the local MP Gary Noakes, who had always regarded the fact that he stood on the terraces of Hertsmere as a boy, to be a relevant vote-getter.

In fact, Murganev's arrival came not a moment too soon. The goals which had come so freely for the club the previous season had dramatically and suddenly dried up. A goalless draw, followed by a one-nil defeat, had virtually ended any realistic chance of keeping up with the leaders in the championship chase. By luck rather than judgement, they had progressed past Berlin in the Cup-Winners' Cup, although one scrappy goal after one hundred and eighty minutes' football had failed to warm the cockles of the hearts of the loyal travelling Hertsmere fans.

There had not been any organised demonstrations for the head of Ray Fowler, the manager, but there had been rumblings of discontent as the crowds filed out of the ground. There had been a marked drop in attendances as well. Notwithstanding the promise of further dramatic European ties, the natives were getting restless. The season needed to be kick-started, and the signing of the Russian was just the thing to do it.

Claudio Barlucci had insisted that they hire a smarter venue for the press conference than Hertsmere's own impoverished stadium could offer, which was why a horde of journalists had gathered at the West Lodge Hotel in Hadley Wood, just south of the M25.

All morning they had been streaming in, as anxious to set up for photos of his arrival as they were to ensure they got to the free drink and food that had been provided for them. Charlie Woods of the *Dispatch* got Mark into a corner, his piggy eyes showing little or no expression as he fired question after question, his speech already slurred at midday after the white wines he'd tossed down his throat.

'I don't know why you fucking packed it in, Markie. Fowler's not a bad coach, but he knows fuck all about managing.'

Mark hated to be called Markie, and he remembered all too clearly some of the things Woods had written when he had been suspended ten years before.

'I packed it in to avoid having to talk to bastards like you,' he replied, without any hint of a smile.

Woods either did not hear or else chose not to understand. 'This Russki. Got a pretty wife, I hear. Do you think she'd give us some exclusives? We pick the clothes and she gets to keep them. Bit of tit showing, bit of thigh. These Russian women would screw their own grandfathers for a pair of Levis.'

'Well, you'd better ask her. I'm sure with your charm she couldn't refuse you.'

Mark drifted back towards the white-clothed table upon which were rapidly diminishing wine bottles and plates, the patterns of which were now being revealed as the locusts consumed the food. He took a deep breath and inhaled clouds of cigarette smoke into his lungs. Then he looked at his watch. It was already a quarter after noon and there was no sign of

Murganev or Jennings. He idly wondered how Jennings had managed to get the time off work to accompany the player to England, and how he would explain to his employers his picture which would doubtless appear in most of the English dailies.

Suddenly there was a buzz from outside, and to a man the journalists flocked towards the entrance in case their rivals should get a story or a picture they might miss. Mark stayed behind, at the top table erected on a dais at the far side of the room. Although it was only Murganev and Jennings who arrived, it seemed like a procession as the press and television crews followed behind them, rushing to grab the best seats and viewing positions. There was a non-stop click of cameras as David Sinclair ushered the two men into the couple of vacant seats to his right, so that Mark was positioned on their left.

Jennings put a hand on his shoulder, gripped it tightly and said, 'Good to see you again.'

'And you,' Mark replied. 'Listen, Alex, when this circus is over I need to talk to you again about the property in Russia.'

'Certainly, Mark. I told you already there are problems, but whatever I can do to help . . .'

The tone was calm and polite, but Mark could not help but think he saw a shadow of avoidance flit across the other man's face, as if he hoped that whatever it was Mark wanted to ask would vanish from his mind before he had the chance to raise the question.

Murganev looked thinner and paler than he had appeared either on the field or in the drinking club in Moscow. He leaned across Jennings and offered Mark his hand, seemingly pleased to see a familiar face amongst the throng of strangers.

'Is good,' he said, in what appeared to be the sum total of his English.

Not sure whether this was a question or a greeting, Mark just smiled, grasped his hand tightly and replied, 'Yes, it's good.'

117

David Sinclair rose to speak and a hush fell over the room, though the cameras never ceased clicking. Mark tried to recall what it had been like to be under the microscope twenty-four hours a day. It all seemed so far away that he could not even remember it being intrusive. Perhaps he had just been enjoying himself too much to care about anything. Dimitri Murganev did not look as if he was enjoying himself. He looked like a man under pressure, a man who was somewhere he did not want to be, and for the first time it occurred to Mark that he might have made a mistake taking this particular fish out of the Moscow pond into the shark-infested waters of English football. If it all went terribly wrong he had little doubt who would bear the blame.

Sinclair was finished and the audience gave him a reception of spattered and bored applause. He was not the reason they were here. They could talk to him any time. There'd been Russian players in England before, but none of them had been preceded by the reputation for flair and charisma that had trumpeted Murganev's entrance. It was not just on the field that he would have a lot to live up to.

The Russian rose to his feet and produced a piece of paper from which he read swiftly and fluently in his own language. The journalists looked blank, waiting for the translation, but Mark noticed a man at the back who seemed to be following every word. It was hard to say what an English reporter looked like, but this man did not look like one. He wore a dark blue suit, a dark blue tie and a white shirt with a collar that was slightly out of date in its shape and size. He could just as well have been dressed for a funeral as a conference of this nature. His hair was steely grey, slightly receding, but brushed straight back without any attempt to conceal the fact. He wore spectacles with steel frames that could have been chosen to match his hair, but more likely had been selected for utility rather than style. He was not particularly tall, but he presented a solid frame behind the ranks of seated journalists, and Mark realised that he had first assumed he was some kind of security man provided by the hotel. He did not know why, but he felt that he ought to discover who he was, and resolved to find out as soon as the formal part of the meeting was over. If he had something to do with Murganev then he should know. Dimitri belonged to Hertsmere now, and they had every right to understand everything about him.

Mark had been so intent on the man that he hardly noticed the diminutive figure of Alex Jennings getting to his feet. It did not surprise him that he had no use for notes, nor that his voice immediately caught the attention of the crowd, who had been threatening to react as one to demonstrate that they did not consider the food and drink sufficient compensation for a non-event.

'Dimitri Murganev has said that he does not consider it enough just to come and play in England. He wishes to show the supporters of Hertsmere and all English football fans that he is the best player in the world . . .'

Mark silently groaned to himself. He wished he'd had a chance to discuss with Jennings just what he was going to say. These words, 'The best player in the world', were going to be an albatross around his neck every time he made an error with his feet. The reporters were all now scribbling furiously, their stories and headlines already formulating in their narrow minds.

Jennings had not yet finished with his translation. 'He has joined Hertsmere because he is confident they will win a major trophy this season with his help, and because he was impressed with Mark Rossetti, who negotiated the deal . . .'

Thanks for that one, Mark thought, drag me into this story as well.

'He will make them a major force in this country and in Europe.'

'He's forgotten we're the bloody cup holders,' Sinclair whispered to Barlucci, who seemed oblivious to the sort of problems this opening speech could bring the player. Jennings finished off with more traditional greetings and thankyous, then sat down.

Sinclair rose again, this time more nervously. 'If there are any questions, Mr Jennings here had kindly offered to act as interpreter . . .'

Charlie Woods was the first to get to his feet, moving remarkably swiftly for a man of his bulk and age. 'How many times has Dimitri here seen Hertsmere play?' he asked, with a belligerence that those who knew him would have regarded as quite normal.

Jennings did not need to consult with the player. 'He saw them on television winning the Cup Final.'

'And that's it?' Woods pursued.

'Yes, that's it,' Jennings responded calmly.

'And on that basis he reckons he's going to bring a new dimension to the team and turn them around?'

This time Jennings spoke to the player. 'He says that he feels he can bring a new dimension to any team. If he did not feel that, then he would not bother to play football.'

Woods made to sit down, then, as an apparent afterthought, rose again to his full height. 'I think we'd all like to know about his family. When can we meet his beautiful wife?'

There was an animated exchange between Jennings and Murganev. By the time the Englishman rose to answer, Mark did not think the translation was going to be precise and literal.

'His wife had a few arrangements to make in Moscow. He will be delighted to introduce her to you all as soon as she arrives, and at the same time you can meet his daughter – if you promise not to propose marriage to her.'

'To his wife or his daughter?' Charlie said loudly and got a huge laugh. Murganev may or may not have understood, but he did not smile. Mark watched him closely, trying to understand whether what he had said was conceit or bravado.

He tried to convince himself that all the great players had a touch of arrogance. It was a necessary part of the formula. Yet there was something else in Murganev's face, a cadence in his voice he could interpret without the assistance of Alex Jennings. It was fear – not just nerves, but fear – and as Mark turned his attention back to the room he saw that the man in the grey suit had disappeared.

CHAPTER 20

David Sinclair was not a great believer in history repeating itself, but as his secretary ushered in Lennie Simons on a bleak November morning he could not help but feel he had been there before. There had been a time when Simons had represented many of the top players in the country, including Mickey Wayne; but the word was out on the football grapevine that he was past his sell-by date. Sinclair had thought for a while that the club was free of the man, that all the Hertsmere players had experienced a mass revelation and realised that for all his jokes, for all his confidence and bonhomie, he could no longer deliver what he so vociferously promised.

Simons, though, was nobody's fool. He'd realised just before it was too late that he needed a new image, and like Prince Hal turning into Henry the Fifth, he had cast off the cloak of his past in one grand gesture. Seated in the chair opposite Sinclair, the out-moded perm was gone, as was the moustache. His hair was cut short and he had even adopted a conservative pair of glasses that gave him a mildly academic appearance. The eyebrows no longer met in the middle, the cigars had been discarded together with at least a stone in weight, and anybody who had not met him in the past would have felt they were dealing with a respectable, intelligent businessman.

He had been creeping back into the club of late, like poison ivy. It had begun with one or two visits to the training ground and surreptitious, hurried conversations with a couple of the more promising young players. Then Tommy Wallace's contract had come up for renewal, and Ray Fowler had suddenly found himself confronted with the old enemy. Both manager and chairman had tried to persuade Wallace he was better off without Simons, that they would offer him the best deal possible in any event, and he would have no need to throw away ten per cent of his package; but the young Scot would have none of it. His friendly, freckled face simply looked puzzled at the warnings, and Sinclair had realised he was blank paper just waiting to be written upon by someone like Lennie Simons.

The agent had seemed to strike a hard bargain for his client, or at least he had adopted his old fighting pose when negotiating in Tommy's presence. It was no good telling the lad that at the end of the day Simons had not earned his commission. The agent had sold himself too well for that. Items that were trivia in the contract, vague dreams of bonuses to be won through hard work, became stone-cold certainties as he boasted of the breadth of his achievements to the young player. It did not bode well for the future. There were other kids coming through the club, and Lennie Simons now had a publicist in the shape of Tommy Wallace. He had made sure of that by promising the kid a kick-back for every player he introduced. It was an approach he'd adopted often in the past with managers – but with an honest man like Ray Fowler in charge at Hertsmere he had no chance. Using a young player was a fresh concept, and so far it had inveigled three of the most promising apprentices into Simons' net, including Matthew Mbute, the sixteen year old from South Africa. The club had paid for his fare, paid for his education, even paid to bring his parents over when he was homesick. Simons had used that last act of generosity as an opportunity to get the boy's father to endorse the contract, in case anybody tried to challenge its validity on the ground of the boy's tender age. Even assuming Mbute stayed loyal and signed professional terms for Hertsmere, Simons would earn his money without any need for the sort of investment the club had already made.

'Still no offer of coffee, eh, David?' Simons said, jerking Sinclair back to reality. 'Some things never change. I don't know what you've got against me. There's others out there far worse than me. They'd sell their own granny if it meant a player could be thrown in with the deal.'

'And because you'd hesitate over selling your own grandmother I'm supposed to trust you. I suppose some people think the Japs were worse than the Nazis. You'll be wanting an OBE for your services to football next.'

The agent smiled, with his teeth rather than his eyes. 'Nice one, David, but it's a knighthood I deserve. Maybe you are beginning to warm to me after all. I can't remember you cracking jokes with me in the past.'

Sinclair made a point of looking at his watch, then calling his secretary to see when his next appointment was, even though he was well aware of the contents of his diary.

Simons leaned back in his chair, crossed his legs and relaxed. 'You've got half an hour yet before you see the programme editor; I already checked.' He raised a hand to stifle Sinclair's objections at his nerve, then continued. 'Don't worry, what I've got to talk about won't take thirty minutes.'

Sinclair clenched his hands into fists before him on the desk. 'What is it, Simons? We've only just completed a new contract with Tommy Wallace, and if what I hear is true all your other clients need nappies and dummies rather than signing-on fees.'

Again Simons laughed, a short terse noise that was more punctuation than amusement. 'No, I'm not here to talk about Tommy – though I still think you got the best of the bargain . . .'

'Is that what you told him?' Sinclair interrupted.

'What do you think?' Simons replied, and this time the smile was genuine.

'Do you really care what I think? I think you and your fellow travellers are a disgrace to the game, but as you say you don't care and I doubt it would make any difference if you did.'

Simons nodded as if he could not agree more with what Sinclair was saying. 'I love it when you get emotional with me, David. Now, you're busy and I'm busy so let's get on. I hear your man Murganev has been a bit of a disappointment . . .'

'Hear? Haven't you seen?'

Simons made a face. 'As I said, I've been busy. Sometimes I'm just too busy to get to matches. Anyway, my reports are always accurate. That's part of my business, having informants who are reliable. I can't be everywhere at once. As I was saying, the Russian hasn't done a lot for the old entente cordial or whatever they call it . . .'

'Glasnost?'

'Yeah, whatever. Usually I have enough trouble remembering English names without getting involved in all this foreign nonsense. It was a bit of a mistake, all that big talk at the Press Conference. Best in the world – and he can't even score against Palace. What's going to happen when you try him out in Europe next month? Olympique Paris, isn't it? Tough draw.'

'So what do you suggest to help our beleaguered forces? I'm sure Ray Fowler can't wait to hear your advice,' Sinclair said sarcastically, although it hurt him to admit to himself that what Simons was saying about Murganev was true. Of course, he needed time to settle in, but he'd not asked for time and there were hints that the Hertsmere fans weren't going to grant him any. He seemed edgy, nervous, a far cry from the confident picture Mark had painted when he'd urged a signing, a world apart from the near-arrogance he'd demonstrated to the press.

They'd put him in a hotel at first, the same Hertfordshire hotel they used for all new signings until they'd had time to settle. One or two of the rest of the squad were still living there, waiting for houses to be bought or built, and Sinclair had thought they would be good company for the Russian despite the language problem. Yet within days Murganev had asked to be moved to a rented, furnished flat, and pursuant to the way Jennings had insisted the contract be drafted, there could be no objection from the club.

Considering he spoke little or no English he seemed to have arranged the move with considerable ease, telling the club which flat he wanted then simply moving all his stuff in the course of an afternoon. Fowler had visited him there with the language student, Jim Beckwith, whom they were using to translate, and reported back to Sinclair that it was small and cramped – one bedroom, a sitting room with a kitchenette off it, a combined toilet and shower room, and that was it. Murganev seemed to think he was living in the lap of luxury, but if he intended staying there when his wife and daughter arrived he was going to find things very cramped indeed. They'd got Jim to ask when the family might be arriving, but the answer had been vague and evasive, as if he had enough problems without these added complications and responsibilities.

On the pitch there had been the same hesitation, the same inconsistency. Passes that Mark had seen made with telling accuracy in Moscow were now either wildly overhit or simply given away to the opposition. Each mistake would be followed by a waving of arms, an anger with himself that he was not fulfilling his own potential.

Simons had an expression on his face that those familiar with him would have recognised as an intention to move in for the kill. 'So this is how I can help you. Our friend Dimitri doesn't want his family here for the moment, he doesn't appear to want to have his team-mates around, and he doesn't seem to welcome the attention of your young interpreter. So what I'm suggesting is that you bring over another Russian to keep him company...'

'This is a football club we're running, not Noah's Ark. If we sign players they come on their own merits, not two by two,' Sinclair said impatiently.

'Ah, but this one I'm representing *would* come on his own merits. Karpov. Anatol Karpov. The one and only Tolly. The nearest thing they've ever had to Gazza in the East.'

Sinclair suddenly sat bolt upright. He'd been about to tell Simons to leave. They already had Greg Sergovich, the Serb keeper, and if Murganev really wanted somebody to talk to then he was there. However, it had to be said that the two men had not shown any seeds of a flourishing friendship. Sergovich had dismissed the newcomer as a 'Bloody Muscovite', the description being accompanied by a spit on the turf. But Karpov... He was good. He'd been the star of the European Championships, and a host of foreign clubs, led by the Italian pack, had sought his signature. Yet he had elected to stay in Russia and had become a local hero for his sacrifice. The question had to be asked of how Lennie Simons had got hold of him. Simons responded by merely tapping the side of his nose with a finger of his right hand.

'Trade secrets, David, trade secrets. Do I take it that you're interested?'

'I'll have to talk to the rest of the board, and the manager . . .' He had great difficulty in forcing the words from his mouth. 'But, yes, you can take it that we're interested.'

Simons visibly relaxed and, smiling, rose to leave. 'So, it looks like we're back in business. I'll be in touch as soon as I can sort out some details.' He extended his hand, which the chairman took reluctantly. 'My pleasure, David, my pleasure.'

And for once David Sinclair could not help but agree with him.

CHAPTER 21

Life was suddenly moving fast for Mark Rossetti. Since their last meeting Patti's mood had changed dramatically, as if a high fever had broken the illness and purged her of all infection. Mark no longer questioned the irrationality of women and this woman in particular. Years of marriage to Sally had been excellent training. Patti had started to make plans for her mother, having decided that she was wasting her time hanging around looking sad, and had enthusiastically begun to look forward to an early return to Russia.

If Mark found it hard to believe her swings of emotion he found it even harder to accept the coincidence that Sinclair also wanted him to return to Moscow on behalf of the club, this time to try and sign Tolly Karpov.

'I'm beginning to feel like your Moscow correspondent,' he'd said jokingly, but the smile had been wiped off his face when he had found that Lennie Simons was involved. He'd tried to reason with Sinclair. 'However good Karpov is, he'd have to be Best, Matthews and Milburn all rolled into one to sign him from that man's books.'

'Look, Mark. Don't think I was happy about it. The first thing I did was get Jim to call Dynamo, to see if he was really for sale or if this was another one of Simons' efforts to pull both ends of a fictional deal together.'

'And?'

'And it was all kosher.'

'You're beginning to sound like Simons.'

'Say that in public and I'll sue you for slander,' Sinclair said with a weak smile.

'And where's the money coming from?' Mark asked practically.

'We've done some number crunching. With what we get from TV for the Paris game and the proceeds of sale from Ian Clark we're nearly there. Savvas has said that the bank will almost certainly bridge us. And Claudio's said he'll kick in whatever we're short.'

'He's really committed, isn't he, our Italian friend? I never thought he'd take to English football without the wine and half-time canapés.'

'He's even stopped wearing his jewellery and astrakhan coat to matches. Up at Manchester he actually produced a cloth cap from his pocket – Burberry, of course, but a cap for all that.'

The two men permitted themselves to laugh at Barlucci's expense. It was the comfortable laughter of people who had become friends through adversity. If anybody knew how precious Hertsmere United was to its chairman, then that man was Mark Rossetti.

'I'm sorry to lumber you again so soon, but I can't leave here, and I don't trust Simons running wild on his own. Can you leave before the end of the week? I think your visa's still in order.'

Mark hesitated. 'I have to talk to Patti. She wants to come with me.'

'No problem. We'll spring for her fare.'

Mark did not rush to accept the offer. 'I'm not so sure she'll want that. Listen, David, if you get Karpov, then with Murganev and Greg you'll have three foreigners in the team before you even start counting the Scots, Welsh and Irish.'

'I've thought of that and discussed it with Ray. If the Bosman decision holds good then we've not got a problem,' he said, referring to the judgement of the European Court which had not only signified the end of transfer fees for players moving from one country to another at the end of the contract, but had also ended the limitations on the number of foreign players that any side could field. 'Even if it doesn't we've got cover for Greg. No, the more I think of it, provided you're sure he'll fit in, then Tolly Karpov is the last piece of our jigsaw.'

'Why do they call him Tolly?'

'Just short for Anatol. Jim Beckwith found that out for me. I thought I might send him with you to translate.'

'I managed well enough last time.'

'Yes, but last time you had Alex Jennings.'

Mark looked up hopefully. 'Any objections if I use him again, provided he's ready and willing? This time he'll have no axe to grind and, quite frankly, nice lad that Jim is, I get the feeling he'll get eaten alive out there in the real world. Jennings won't just say what I want him to say, he'll put his own slant on it.'

'You like him, don't you?' Sinclair asked rhetorically.

'Yes, I do. He's got just about the best brain I've ever come across.'

Sinclair threw a friendly punch at Mark's shoulder. 'You've been around football people too long to make sensible judgements.'

'Maybe you're right. I'll be in touch.'

Mark found no resistance from Patti to their early departure.

'Suits me,' she'd said, when he'd told her on the phone. 'I've got a commission from the *Sunday Gazette* for an article. They liked an idea I floated by them about the importation of foreign players into the UK. How it affects home-grown players, the foreigners, their families, et cetera. I thought I'd start with Hertsmere and Murganev, but if you've another one coming then the more the merrier.'

He was puzzled by her sudden burst of enthusiasm, the return to the vivacious girl he'd first met. Although he'd not liked the world-weary woman with whom he'd had such a difficult dinner, it had not stopped him loving her. He knew with certainty now that he did love her, and he was angry with himself for once again allowing his emotions to take command. After Sally he'd promised himself there'd be no more involvements. Once he'd got over his love affair with the bottle, he vowed he'd save all his emotions for his daughter. Promises are made only to be broken, he tried to reassure himself. Leo had once explained to him how, on the Jewish Day of Atonement, all the congregation asked that all the vows they'd made in the last year or would make in the next year be annulled. Maybe they had the right idea, but he wasn't convinced.

He was worried about his daughter. To his delight he'd got the go-ahead to take her on this latest Russian trip but on the last couple of occasions he'd seen her she'd appeared quiet and withdrawn, as if she was deliberately erecting a screen between herself and her father to protect the modesty of her inner-self. He could not put his finger on the problem, or indeed confirm that there was a problem at all. Any questions she fielded with consummate ease, a skill that belied her age and made him wonder what secrets she could conceal if she ever put her mind to it. Although their time together recently had been minimal, he imagined that not many girls who had just turned twelve could have the intellect or ingenuity of his daughter.

There was no point in asking her mother if anything was wrong. Sally was of the firm belief that he had denied himself the right to have any input into her upbringing the first week he failed to bring home a wage-packet. He did not think she was being mistreated, nor even that she was particularly unhappy at home. It was as if her horizons were too narrow. She had friends at school, but not the particular friend that was so common amongst her contemporaries. She was invited to the average number of parties, was suitably fixated on a

132

merry-go-round of pop groups, and demonstrated an appalling dress sense of which she seemed totally unaware. To the casual observer she was the typical teenager, even before she had officially reached her teens; but Mark was not the casual observer, he was her father – and as such he knew something was wrong. He was not going to make the same mistakes as David Sinclair.

It had not been easy persuading Sally to let her daughter go with him, but help had come from an unexpected quarter. Her new husband, Stuart Macdonald, his old team-mate, had stepped in when his wife seemed immovable.

'How can you stand in her way, love? It's not every day of the week you get the chance to go to Russia.'

'It's not where she's going that worries me, it's who she's going with,' Sally had said, her face assuming the tight, grim expression that arrived whenever she had to speak to or of her ex-husband. 'It was bad enough when he was playing, worse when he took to drink – but now he seems to be a cross between a private eye, Superman, and a football agent. Christ knows what he's likely to get up to.'

Mark had stood quietly while Stuart had continued to fight his corner.

'Look, Mark's been as good as gold since he's been working. He proved his innocence to the world; it's not fair that you expect him still to prove it to you.'

Sally had stomped off into the kitchen then. Although Mark could hear the sound of china and cutlery being tossed about, no offer of tea or coffee was forthcoming. Macdonald had shrugged an apology, and while Mark knew Sally well enough to be assured of the grief she would cause her husband once he had gone, both men realised for the moment she had abandoned the field.

It was that victory that had carried Mark, Patti and Emma on board the British Airways flight to Moscow, and saw them side-by-side in three seats like any other family about to embark on holiday. The relationship between Patti and Emma was not, as yet, a comfortable one. Whereas the child had first regarded the journalist with some awe, rushing to read anything with her by-line, now, through some mixture of childish illogicality and perversity, she seemed merely jealous. If there was to be a competition for her father's emotions then she had no intention of coming second. As with most children her timing was perfect. Sensing that the relationship between her father and Patti Delaney was on the rocks, she was quite content to stand on the clifftop, not just watching, but actually waving a wrecker's torch.

She began almost from the first minute they boarded the plane.

Mark had offered to sit between them. 'What more could a man want than to sit between two beautiful women?' he'd joked, but Emma was neither flattered nor amused, merely insisting that he take the window seat, she sit beside him and Patti be relegated to the aisle. She did not even take the opportunity of talking to her father, placing the headphones firmly over her ears and rocking in time to whatever rhythm blasted from the pop channel. She took the airline food with bad grace, complained that he'd not ordered her a vegetarian meal, then lectured Patti about the conditions under which, she had little doubt, the chicken she was eating had been reared.

'That's what you should be writing about, not wasting your time on boring old footballers.'

'Your dad was a boring old footballer once,' Patti said.

The girl shot her father a side-long glance. 'He still is, if you ask me. The only difference is he doesn't play any more.'

And as she pulled her hand away from Mark's touch, he suspected she might be right.

CHAPTER 22

Daniel Lewis had abandoned all his dreams of early retirement. He was back to reality, back to persuading clients they should accept £100,000 for their three-bedroomed semi-detached houses in North-West London even though they were convinced they were palaces worth double that. 'Look at that kitchen. It's a feature. The conservatory cost us ten thousand. I can't believe anybody wouldn't fall in love with the tool shed at the bottom of the garden. I built it myself.' He'd heard it all, and for a few brief weeks he had hoped he would not need to hear it again. Even now he did not know quite what he had done wrong. Everybody knew that Russians were coming into the country in increasing numbers. It was not as if he had revealed names and figures. There were agents he knew who would have disclosed such information to the very last address and digit – although on reflection he thought it would be more than their cars that would have suffered had they done so to Yevneko and his associates. The insurers had found the story he had told them hard to swallow. Vandals in the more affluent parts of North-West London were not usually so thorough in their acts of destruction.

He went through his daily ritual of reading the property details in all the newspapers, then moving on to the freebies to see how many of the houses on his books were also be offered for sale by his competitors. There seemed to be an awful lot of competitors nowadays. Every shop in the street that became vacant was taken over either by a building society or estate agency. The retailers had surrendered the area, and on mornings like this he felt like doing the same thing himself. There were only so many houses and so many buyers; and the buyers seemed to be disappearing as speedily as the retailers.

He went to make a cup of coffee. He'd had to let Mitchell go and so he was back to square one. Just Daniel Lewis, a couple of telephones and an empty office. Mitchell had been curious about what had happened on the day of his boss's visit, but when he'd seen the photographs of the car provided by the insurers he had ceased to ask questions. Daniel had been left with the distinct impression that the boy had left with some relief, fully prepared to dine out for some time on the stories of his late lamented employer, Mr Danny – who liked to be called Daniel – Lewis, who had once thought he was going to get rich quick.

He poured his drink into a blue and white cup that bore the name and logo of the firm. He noticed the cup was chipped and the lettering was fading from its countless immersions in water. He wondered whether it was worthwhile getting another batch printed up. They'd been a popular promotional item for a while, but he desperately needed some clients to whom to promote them.

As he resumed his seat at his desk he wondered what sort of picture he presented to the world passing by. His grandfather had been a gents' barber in the days before unisex salons. All too often, when he'd visited the shop, his grandfather had been sitting staring out of the window, cigarette in mouth, willing customers to come in, even if only to shelter from the rain. Yes – his grandfather, an empty shop and the rain, they were the abiding images of his childhood. And now, as the rain lashed down outside and he sat with his head bowed over newsprint that blurred beneath his eyes, he felt that history was repeating itself. Then the telephone rang.

For a moment he stared at it in disbelief. He'd not effected an exchange of contracts for nearly a month, and the only call he'd had the whole of the previous day was from his bank manager reminding him, politely but firmly, that he needed a response to the two unanswered letters regarding his overdraft and mortgage. He had not yet had the courage to tell Elaine that they were two months in arrears with the payments on the house. Each day he had hung around until the post came at home, then quickly swept it up and opened it with trepidation at the office, returning the harmless communications to his domestic letter-rack at the end of the day. He knew exactly what her reaction would be. First of all tears, then rage, then a phone call to her mother, followed by a visit to her mother, followed, in turn, by a visit from her mother. He let the phone ring, mesmerised by the sound, wondering not for the first time since the car incident, if he had been so traumatised by it that he was having some kind of nervous breakdown. That was all he needed – no business, increasing debts and him confined to the funny farm.

Eventually, on the tenth ring, he picked up the phone. When he heard the voice on the other end he immediately wished he hadn't.

'Daniel.' The accent was unmistakeable. 'I hope you are well and that business is flourishing. It's been too long since we spoke.'

'Hello, Mr Yevneko,' Daniel said without enthusiasm. He didn't know what the Russian wanted, but he could not believe it was likely to bring any sunshine into his life.

'Nikolei, please. Why so formal? I thought we were friends.'

Daniel was about to point out that friends don't trash each other's brand new cars, but then he thought maybe friendship in the East had a whole different meaning. He suspected Nikolei Yevneko had not been the sort of child one invited round to play with a treasured toy and then fell out with. Daniel had experienced a friend like that when he was small. He'd got to the last twenty or so pieces of a thousand-piece jigsaw puzzle when the schoolmate had not liked something he'd said about West Ham and had thrown the whole tray on the floor. He didn't know where that particular friend was now, but if he could find out, then maybe he could introduce him to Yevneko. He figured they would get on well with each other.

'You don't sound too pleased to hear from me, Daniel. I do hope that the incident with your car did not force a permanent wedge between us. I am not one for bearing grudges. I have a temper, it blows up, I cool down, it is all forgotten.' Yevneko paused. 'It is forgotten, is it not?'

The estate agent decided there could only be one answer to the question – and that was the one that the Russian wanted. 'Oh, sure, it's forgotten. I opened my big mouth. It was unforgivable. And anyway the insurance company paid up.'

'Eventually', he muttered under his breath, thinking of the no-claims bonus he'd built up so carefully over the years and which had been blasted away.

'I am pleased. I do not enjoy the teacher–pupil relationship with those with whom I work. I like us to be equals, to be friends. So, now that the lesson has been taught and, I think, learned, I have some more business for you. That is unless you are too busy for us now?'

You bastard, Danny thought, you know bloody well I've got no business. You've checked that out. But all he said was, 'No, I'm pretty quiet at the moment.'

'Good. Not that you are quiet, but that you have time for us, that you are back on the team.'

And then Yevneko told the estate agent what he wanted, and Danny felt as if he were being sucked into a bottomless black pit.

CHAPTER 23

There had been little time for sightseeing or parent–daughter bonding since Mark and his small party had arrived in Moscow. They had stumbled off the plane feeling tired and dirty, and it was with some gratitude that Mark had spotted Alex Jennings waving to them beyond the luggage collection point. Somehow or other, despite all the security controls, Jennings had magicked himself to their side, and then wafted them through all the red tape that seemed likely to tie up the rest of their fellow passengers for a good part of the night.

'I've arranged for us to see Tolly Karpov tonight. I hope that is in order. If the two ladies would like I can have them driven around the city.'

The two ladies did not like, or at least one of them did not. Emma had become paler and paler during the flight and had finally greeted Moscow by vomiting into her sick-bag as the plane taxied to a halt. Throughout the ride to the hotel she was shivering and shaking and, in view of the efficient heating system in the vehicle, Mark did not think it was the city's cold that had got to her.

Jennings had been as efficient as ever. This time he'd had them booked into the Baltschug-Kempinski Hotel, and had even got them deluxe corner rooms with incredible views across the river into Red Square, not that Emma was in any condition to appreciate the Germanic efficiency of the establishment or the scenic qualities of the views. All she wanted was to feel better, and, if the truth be told, to have her

139

mother there to tuck her into bed. Mark sat with her while Jennings had a doctor summoned. Within fifteen minutes the doctor arrived. She was smartly dressed, spoke passable English and told Mark calmly that his daughter merely had a chill, should stay in bed for twenty-four hours and then, with all the remarkable powers of youth, she would be ready to enjoy the beautiful city. Patti had immediately insisted on looking after Emma while Mark went off to his meeting, but the child had given him a look as he left that suggested abandonment to the workhouse.

He had felt guilty for a while, but now, sitting in the smoky room with Jennings, Tolly Karpov and Lennie Simons, he was concentrating on the negotiations which had reached a critical stage. He had warned Jennings about Simons, but he need not have done so. The man had the agent's measure from the first handshake. He smiled at him, joked with him, but never took his eyes off him, as if he might do something underhand if left to his own devices.

Karpov was everything Murganev had seemed not to be on first meeting. He was brash, confident, and Mark could not help but think that he would not have needed the sort of script that Dimitri had read at his initial press conference, declaring himself to be the best in the world. He looked, at first sight, too stocky to be a footballer, built like a latter-day Maradona, but then the Argentinian had not managed too badly even in his twilight years. If Mark had not known he was only twenty-six he would have thought him well into his thirties. His hair was thinning, and he made no Bobby Charltonesque effort to conceal the fact. He had high Slavic cheekbones, with skin stretched taughtly over them in stark contrast to the lower part of his body. His eyes were the main feature of his face, making one forget the flattish nose, the slightly surly lips. The eyes were dark yet bright, like two polished stones glinting in the sunlight. They were everywhere, flitting from speaker to speaker, suggesting he understood everything that was being said, however rapidly and colloquially it was spoken.

In the first break in the discussions, when they had stepped outside for some fresh air, Alex said to Mark, 'You know, there's no real need for you to have me here. Karpov speaks English better than I speak Russian. Simons seems to have no problem in taking instructions, and in fact I'm not too sure that our little friend Tolly isn't a better negotiator than our big friend Simons.'

'Never underestimate Lennie. That's when he's at his most dangerous. Everybody at the club thought they'd seen the back of him, but now he's come bouncing back in a big way. By the way, have you found out how this unholy alliance of Karpov and Simons came about?'

'No, that's one little gem of information that's eluded even me. You don't like either of them, do you?'

'I can't say I've taken to Karpov. But then everybody tells me he's a genius, so who am I to argue? I'm just the messenger boy.'

Jennings grinned, and once again Mark felt himself warmed by his personality.

'So that makes me the messenger boy's messenger. Any chance of promotion in this town?'

'You wouldn't want this job. I'm just going to call Patti to make sure Emma's OK.'

She was.

'She's been sleeping like a babe since you left. She was tired already, she'd had her strop, and whatever the doctor gave her put her out like a light. I'll save a few of the tablets in case we have to kidnap your footballer in a crate.'

'I'd like to put Lennie Simons in a crate. He's being as obnoxious as usual, and I can't say this Karpov character is any more appealing. He'd better be good.'

'What time will you be back?'

When he heard the tone of her voice he wanted to say that he'd be right back and that she should be in bed waiting for him, but then he still never really knew with Patti how she would react. Whatever running needed to be made he felt it would be safer to let her make it.

'When we finish,' he said, and as she replaced the receiver he suspected it was not the answer she was seeking.

The figures that Simons was bandying about were beyond anything Hertsmere had ever paid before, and were certainly beyond any topping up that Claudio Barlucci might have in mind. Simons seemed disinclined to listen to reason, and Mark felt like tossing his hands in the air and returning to Patti to see what could be salvaged from the night. But Jennings was only just warming to his task.

'Lennie, let's be honest with each other. You know and I know that Hertsmere can't and won't pay the sort of monies you're talking about. If you're trying to impress your client then I suspect he's impressed, but he'll be less impressed if we go away from here without an agreement. We'll make sure the whole footballing world knows that the deal fell through because you and he were too greedy. He'll get branded as difficult and you'll be called incompetent. Now, none of us wants that, do we?'

'If we're being honest,' Simons said, although he seemed to have some difficulty with the phrase, 'I think you're a cunt who knows fuck all about football. But I'm not an unreasonable man, so try and persuade me.'

Mark thought it was time to intervene. He'd already discussed tactics with Jennings before they started and they'd agreed that as soon as Simons began to come down from whatever planet he was residing upon that Mark would put the best offer they had to him.

The package Mark put forward was little more than half of that suggested by Simons, but he was also offering the proceeds from a friendly to be arranged between the two clubs, as well as a double bonus for European success. The figures were batted back and forth, each side giving a little ground, each saying that the other's demands were impossible. Finally, although there was still a hundred thousand pounds between them, Mark got the impression that Simons was on the point of recommending the deal. Then Karpov suddenly spoke up for himself.

'Mr Rossetti.' He had resisted all efforts by Mark or Alex to persuade him to call either of them by their first names. 'I have heard all you have to say. I do not think you realise quite who I am or what I can do for your little team. There have been times when I could have joined any club in the world. Real Madrid, Barcelona, Juventus, Milan, Benfica, Ajax – all of them have approached me from time to time, but always I have been loyal to my mother country. Now I think it is time for me to move abroad. Do I contact any of the giants? No. I talk to the dwarf because I think with me they might become a giant. And all the while you insult me with your offers. You pick at a hundred pounds here, a thousand pounds there, and I let my agent here take your insults, because I think maybe he is used to them and that is the way you do business in your country. But please, do not insult me. This is what I say: tomorrow night I play. If I score or make three goals then you pay me the hundred thousand pounds over which we argue. If I do not, then I accept your terms even though they are too little. I will come cheap, but I will never mention it again. I am not Dimitri Murganev. I will come alone and I will star alone.'

'Sounds an expensive hat-trick to me,' Mark said. 'Who are you playing, anyway?'

'Volgograd. They are top of the league. I will earn my money.'

Mark exchanged glances with Alex. He did not know how he would explain it away to the Hertsmere board, but the gamble did appeal to him. Arriving at the agreement also meant he could get to bed. 'Very well, you have a deal.'

'And if I score or make more than three goals?' Karpov pursued.

'Then you get to keep the match ball,' Mark replied. He might not like the player but he could not help admiring his nerve.

'And maybe you'd like to buy the ball for another hundred grand,' Simons added, feeling his thunder had been stolen by his client.

'And maybe not,' Mark replied and, without shaking the agent's hand, rose and left.

CHAPTER 24

Seated high in the tiers of the stadium, Mark felt a certain unease at being there. Although Emma had faithfully taken the medication – for which he had paid a not inconsiderable amount of US dollars – the prognosis of her recovery within twenty-four hours had not proved correct. So far her total view of Moscow after the drive from the airport had been the inside of the hotel bedroom, and in particular the bathroom. He just hoped he could get her up and about soon, not just for her own sake, but also to be able to deal with the cross-examination that he would be sure to undergo from Sally.

He did not know how long he could rely on Patti's good offices. She had, after all, also come on business, and had already told him that she was going to have to be released from daughter-watching duties the following afternoon when she was due to interview Sonya Murganev, the player's wife. They had not even begun to make any progress on Schneider's property. Mark felt guilty that he had these concerns when his daughter was clearly so unwell. He did not feel too happy about his company either. Alex Jennings had told him he was likely to be late but had arranged transport, and Mark had been annoyed to find that his sole travelling companion – and, at present, viewing companion – was Lennie Simons.

The agent appeared totally oblivious to Mark's antipathy towards him – or if he was aware of it, it simply did not matter. He offered Mark an apple and a bar of chocolate, and when both were refused chatted away as if they went to matches together every week. Mark noticed that one thing Simons did not talk about was football, that the main subject of his conversation was himself and how he had made a success of his life from humble beginnings and in the face of overwhelming odds. He did not cease in his chatter and self-congratulatory recollections once the game was underway, and it was only after a full fifteen minutes of Mark ignoring him that he finally bit into his apple and began to focus on what was happening on the pitch.

What was occurring was a one-man exhibition of football the like of which Mark had never seen before in his life. Karpov was simply mesmeric, every so often looking up into the huge stand to ensure that his audience were appreciating him. He stood on the ball, taunted players to come at him like a Muhammed Ali of football, then arrogantly turned them inside out. After twenty minutes he seemed to tire of the game that he alone was playing, beat a man not twice, but once, then made for goal and scored as if it were a practice session. He turned towards Mark and Simons in the stand and extended the index finger of his left hand. Then, just before half-time, he broke down the left, put in a pin-point cross to the head of the tall centre-forward, who could not miss from six yards. Karpov did not run to congratulate him and, curiously, none of his team-mates approached him either. Karpov's focus was once more upon the men in the stand, and this time two fingers were raised, not in a gesture of disdain, but one of arithmetic.

At half-time, with no further scoring, Jennings arrived, actually looking hot and flustered despite the fact that the temperature had dropped below freezing.

'Missed anything, did I?' he asked, pulling a thermos flask from his capacious pocket and offering Mark a drink. 'Don't worry, it's only coffee, no booze. And it's not the local muck either. I have this specially delivered from Fortnums.'

Not knowing whether he was being serious or not about the source of the drink, Mark gratefully took a huge gulp, feeling an enormous pleasure as the scalding liquid burned the back of his throat (that he was sure had already been afflicted by frostbite). He hesitated before passing the flask to Simons, but Alex nodded.

'Don't worry, you won't catch anything,' Simons said. 'And as to what you've missed, I'd say two thirds of a hundred grand.'

He made it sound as if the final instalment was a mere formality, but it proved to be otherwise. Volgograd came out for the second half like a team possessed, determined to justify and retain their position at the top of the league. Suddenly Karpov found himself marked by at least two opponents every time he touched the ball, and if he had the skill to beat them both, a sweeper system found him running time and time into blind alleyways. Whether it was the lure of additional signing-on fees or not, he continued to run at the defence, demonstrating his stamina as well as his determination.

'Never gives up, that one,' Simons said with proprietary pride, as if he had brought him into the world and trained him from his birth for this very moment.

There was no surrender from Volgograd either. They found the net only for their effort to be ruled offside by what appeared to be an overeager linesman, then scored with a twenty-five-yard swirling shot that was undeniably a goal. Of the home side, only Karpov appeared willing to attack, and ten minutes from time they paid for their defensive approach when a Volgograd defender with nothing to lose was allowed to come forward, put in a spectacular cross which was caught by the cross-wind and taken straight into the top corner of the goal. Two all, and it was Volgograd pressing forward for the winner when with just a minute to go Karpov went on one last mazy run, only to be felled by a challenge some six feet outside of the penalty area. He rose to protest, but the referee had already taken the decision. A red card was in his hand and being shown to the defender, while almost with the same sweep of the hand he was pointing to the penalty spot. He was surrounded by protesting Volgograd players, and for a moment the whole match looked to be in doubt as at least one of them caught the man in black by the shoulders. But when he too was shown a dismissive card the steam seemed to go out of his team-mates and they bowed to the inevitable. It was clear from the arm-waving and arguments that were going on between Karpov and the rest of his team that he was not the usual penalty-taker, but that he was determined to take this particular spot-kick. He wrestled the ball out of the hands of the arm-banded captain, placed it on the white spot and signalled to the referee that he was ready to take the kick even if nobody else was. The official blasted his whistle, Karpov took just one step back, then side-footed the ball towards the left hand corner. If the keeper had gone the correct way he would certainly have saved it, but he tumbled awkwardly and prematurely to his right, and was just another spectator as the ball trickled over the goal-line.

Karpov turned and punched the air, then added two fingers to his thumb and gave a three-finger salute to the three men in the stand.

'A hundred thousand pounds, I think,' Simons said. 'I do believe we now have a deal.'

Mark watched the dying seconds of the match before the referee brought the contest to an end. He had seen enough to convince him of Karpov's talents, but his actions and attitudes on the field had not brought him any closer to liking him. Still, his first duty was to Hertsmere. There could be no doubting that this man would bring another dimension to the side. If at the same time he could bring out the best in Murganev, then it had to be right to sign him.

Yet, even as he confirmed to Simons reluctantly that they had a deal, even as he replayed the two pieces of action that had brought Karpov his first two credits, he wondered whether any English referee would have awarded such a penalty.

CHAPTER 25

After the match Simons left them to impart the good news to his client, while Jennings thoughtfully rushed Mark back to the hotel and his daughter. In the car their talk was not of Karpov, but of Schneider and his property.

'I've found it for you, Mark. It wasn't easy, believe me. I think this country's greatest gift to civilisation is red tape. Boundaries change, deeds disappear, even street names can vanish overnight – but I found it. At least, I think I have. Even when you think you're sure here, ideology can prove you wrong.'

'So when do we get to see it?' Mark asked, curious to see what Leopold Schneider had left behind.

'Not so easy. It's in a place called Pinsk. That's about six hundred and fifty miles from Moscow.'

'Considering how big this country is that doesn't sound too far – what, about an hour in a plane?'

Jennings laughed. 'Things are never what they seem or sound here. And yes, you're right, it would be about an hour's flight . . . if there was a flight. In fact, it's about a seven-hour rail journey, assuming the train has enough fuel to run and the tracks aren't up and there's actually somebody there to sober the driver up.'

'You make it sound like a real pleasure trip,' Mark said.

'Perhaps. Stalin at least made the trains run on time. The only problem was what they put in them and the fact that now Stalin is dead. The only certainty about the system is its uncertainty.'

For a while Jennings was silent, and Mark was sensitive enough to leave him to his own thoughts, whatever they might be. Then, as if shaking off a mild headache, Jennings was back in touch, his mind working as methodically as ever.

'Let's put the Karpov deal to bed first. I'll arrange to meet with your friend Simons and the player in the morning. You call England and tell them to confirm to you by fax that they agree the terms. They can send it through to my office; that's guaranteed to be confidential. I'll talk to the club, make sure they're not having second thoughts after tonight, and once we've got all that settled it's Pinsk here we come. I'll see if I can get us train tickets for Thursday morning.'

Mark hesitated. 'Don't get me wrong, Alex. I'd really like to go, and I'm grateful for all you've done, but I'm not sure Emma's up to all that travelling. The poor kid's all washed out. And I know Patti wants to go with us; it is her property as well, after all.'

'Sure. Kids – who'd be with them and who'd be without them?' Jennings replied wistfully as the car drew up outside the hotel. Patti was standing by the front door, a cigarette in her hand, being looked up and down by a couple of smartly dressed middle-aged businessmen, who were obviously discussing whether or not she was for hire. As Mark greeted her with a warm kiss, they gave one last disappointed stare and drifted off into the hotel in search of less exotic fare.

'How is she?'

'Asleep. That's all she seems to want to do – sleep,' Patti replied.

'Hey, I'm sorry about your trip so far. I know you didn't come all this way just to sit in a hotel bedroom with a sick kid who's not your own.'

She took him kindly by the hand and led him towards the bar with Jennings in tow. To his amazement, Rudi was there greeting them effusively.

'Ah, my good friend Mark. You come back for my cocktails.

And Mr Jennings too. So good to see you are still together,' he said without any great conviction. 'I can see you are wondering what I am doing here. Promotion, I think. This hotel, they also hear about my cocktails and offer me a job. I think you cannot blame me for accepting.'

He appeared to notice Patti for the first time, although his next comment made it clear he had been noticing her all evening. 'And this lovely lady is yours. She sits and drinks alone and I wonder what a woman like this is doing drinking by herself. So I make her my special cocktails and I talk to her. I practise my English. You do not mind, I hope, Mark. Between friends there is no jealousy.'

Mark smiled. He had forgotten how difficult it was to stop the barman from talking once he had started. 'No, there's no jealousy between friends. I'm grateful to you for looking after her.'

'Sure. In this city you have to look after a woman on her own, otherwise people get the wrong ideas. You know that, Mr Jennings, don't you?' He poured drinks as he spoke even though he had not taken any orders.

'Yes, Rudi, I know that. Now be a perfect barman and leave us alone. We've got some private business to discuss.'

'No problem. Okey dokey. You think maybe the rooms are bugged. Not in this hotel, I tell you. Maybe in the other place. A flea-pit. But Rudi, he understands. You have Murganev, maybe you want somebody else from this country. Maybe you want Yeltsin to play alongside him. Believe me, we are quite happy to agree to the transfer.' He moved out of earshot without seeming to take any offence at his dismissal and began to talk to a tired, faded woman at the end of the bar, who had in turn focused her attention on the two businessmen who had been hoping for some success with Patti. It was a sad picture, in what Mark perceived to be a sad city.

Mark quickly explained the position as far as the search for Leo's property was concerned, expecting a negative reaction

151

from Patti, but she never ceased to surprise him.

'I honestly don't think Emma's up to going. I'll stay with her, you go with Alex.'

'I feel bad about it.'

'Don't.' She took a sip of her drink. 'Wow. He may be a pain in the arse, but he sure makes a good cocktail. This one could be used as a Molotov without anybody noticing until it exploded.'

Mark swirled the fruit juice around in his glass, half-flattered that Rudi had remembered he was teetotal. 'How did your interview go with Sonya Murganev?'

'Good, really good. She's a nice lady. Her English isn't half bad. She brought along a friend, but I'm not sure we really needed her. When I told her about Emma she was quite happy to come along here. Your little barman mate, Rudi, seemed to know her quite well. He offered to translate as well, but I didn't know that you and he were a number at that stage.'

'We're not a number, and Rudi knows everybody, offers everything. As you probably gathered I met him last time around and he took me under his wing.'

'Some coincidence that he turns up at both hotels where you stay,' she said.

'Sure, some coincidence. I've got more on my mind than itinerant barmen. Did Sonya say anything about when she was coming to join her husband in England? Karpov or no Karpov, I still think we're going to see the best of Dimitri when he's living with his family.'

'No, but I can call her back tonight. I said I'd speak to her if you had anything to say.'

'Sure, why don't you do that? I think we're definitely going to get Karpov. Maybe we can arrange for him to travel over with Sonya and the kid. It'll make life easier for everybody.'

Patti drained her glass and lit another cigarette, pretending to be ashamed as she saw Mark's look of disapproval.

As if he had eyes in the back of his head, Rudi swivelled

around and moved over to fill her glass. 'You like my cocktails, I think. You are a woman of taste. Rudi's cocktails and Mr Mark, a great combination. You're a lucky girl. What can I possibly do for you to make you even happier?'

'You can get me a phone and you can dial me Sonya Murganev's number.'

The barman produced a telephone from beneath the counter with the panache and flourish of a magician conjuring a flock of doves from a top-hat, and duly obliged. The phone had an old-fashioned dial, and three time he had to replace the handset mid-session as he heard the line disconnect. 'Only the people work in Moscow, not the fucking telephone system. Sometimes I think it is better to use birds . . .' He looked to Patti hopefully for the word.

'Carrier pigeons?' she obliged.

'Sure, carrier pigeons, or an open window and a loudspeaker. Ah, we have a connection,' and he handed the receiver to Patti.

The two women spoke animatedly, despite the language differences, with Rudi standing close by in case his interpretative skills were likely to be required. Eventually Patti did hand back the phone, not wishing to disturb Mark and Alex who were deep in conversation, busy scribbling figures on a note-pad ready to transmit to David Sinclair. 'Can you speak to her, Rudi, please? I don't want there to be any misunderstandings as to what she's saying.'

The barman was delighted to be involved, spoke quickly, then listened intently, and repeated to Patti what he had been told.

'Good. Thank you. I thought that was what she was saying.' She took back the phone once again. 'Sonya? Yes, yes, I'm very grateful. I'll speak to Mark and let you know.'

She hurried over to the two men.

'Well, what did she say?' Mark asked.

'Soon, she says she's coming soon. Maybe she will be ready

to travel with Karpov. She didn't sound too keen on that, though.'

'No, I can't see anybody being too keen to travel with Karpov. Was that all she said? It took you a long time just to get that out of her.'

'No, she said something else. She said if I wanted to go with you on Thursday, that she'd look after Emma, either here if she wasn't well enough, or at her flat if she felt a bit better.'

'Come on, Patti, that's out of the question. I can't leave my daughter with a total stranger. Sally's going to blame me for her illness anyway; can you imagine what tortures she'd devise for my balls if she found out I'd left her with a total stranger?'

'She's not a total stranger.'

'Oh no. I was forgetting you spent most of yesterday afternoon with her. I suppose that practically makes her family.' He knew as soon as he said it that he had made a mistake. It had been a long tiring day for him and a long boring one for her; she needed reason and understanding rather than sarcasm.

'She seemed to me to be a hell of a lot more responsible than your family. You think you'd be grateful to me for looking after a part of it while you go gallivanting about with the soviet superstars. Look, Mark, when there was nobody else to look after Emma I was prepared to do it. But I think Sonya's offer is perfectly reasonable. If you want to reject it then that's your prerogative, but if you do then you can play wet-nurse and I'll go with Alex.'

Mark felt hopelessly drawn. He knew what Patti was saying was perfectly reasonable – that Emma was quite old enough to be left on her own with somebody trustworthy, that she might even enjoy the experience – but something still made him hesitate.

Patti rose defiantly. 'I'm going to bed. When you little schoolboys have finished your homework, maybe one of you will come and join me.' She paused. 'And quite frankly I'm not too bothered which one of you it is.' Then, with a dramatic flourish that would have done justice to Scarlett O'Hara, she was gone.

CHAPTER 26

Even as he sat on the train rolling through the dull Russian countryside Mark could not help feeling that he had given in too easily. Patti had that effect upon him. She had taught him to stand up to everyone but herself.

Eventually they had both calmed down after the confrontation in the hotel bar. It had been Mark who had joined her in the bedroom, now ready to listen, now reluctant to deal with an irate woman in what, for some reason, he already regarded as a hostile country.

'Mark, do you really think I'd put your daughter at risk? This woman's a reliable caring mother. If you don't believe me come and check her out for yourself.'

It was a challenge and a question. Did he trust her judgement? Did he trust her? He felt that there was much more to the situation than the question of whether or not Patti Delaney thought Sonya Murganev was a woman to whom he could entrust his daughter for a few days. In the end he neither took up the challenge nor answered the question, but slipped into his old ways and ducked them both.

'Let's let Emma decide. If she feels well enough to travel she comes with us. If not she says whether she goes to the beautiful Sonya or has me to baby-sit her.'

'How did you know she was beautiful?' Patti asked, trying manfully to restore some calm and humour to their relationship.

'I've already slept with her,' Mark said jokingly, grabbing the olive branch with relief.

'Yeah, she said.'

'How was I?'

'So-so.'

They put it to Emma.

'You go, dad. And you too, Patti. I feel fine, but I could do without the train-spotting exercise. Do you want me to buy you each an anorak?'

Maybe it was the quip that convinced Mark that she was well on the way to recovery; whatever it was that led to him giving in to her choice, he still did not have the guts to call Patti's bluff. He was not going to be checking up on Sonya Murganev. Whatever opinion Patti had formed of her, then he would rely on it.

Rudi had been reassuring. 'She's a nice lady. You've got no worries. Believe me, if you're going to Pinsk by rail, then she'll have a better time than you.'

And so he had left it to Patti to deliver Emma to Sonya's flat, with his sole contribution to the arrangement being an expensive bouquet of flowers to take with them as a token of gratitude. Emma had kissed him on the cheek, then almost rushed into the waiting cab with an overnight bag in hand.

'So much for loyalty,' Mark had said to Rudi, who had come to the front door to smoke a cigarette and chat with the doorman (who had until then appeared to be carved from granite). Rudi said something in Russian to the man who gave a deep resonant laugh without disturbing his rocky features. Mark had waited for a translation that did not come. There seemed to be all too many occasions nowadays when he did not understand what was being said around him – even when the language was English.

Jennings lit yet another cigarette in the already smoke-filled carriage and, much to Mark's annoyance, Patti accepted his offer and lit up herself. Mark tried hard to stifle a cough, not wanting to be accused of a dramatic protest. There had been no indication that Patti held any grudges over his objections to Emma being left behind, but still he felt as if he was walking on eggshells.

'How long to go?' he asked Alex.

'Another couple of hours, I guess. Depends how many unscheduled stops we have to make. Like right now,' he added as the train screeched to a halt. They sat for a few moments, the whole train reduced to the sort of silence that reminded Mark of a breakdown in a tunnel of the London Tube. The hard wooden seats bit into his buttocks, the smoke became a fug, and finally he could stand it no longer. He rose to a window, forced it open and leaned out, taking deep breaths of the cold, damp air. He could see fields, a farm that looked derelict until he spied a man tilling the earth with some equipment that would have found its way into a museum in England.

'And they put a man on the moon,' he muttered to himself, just before the world seemed to fall in just behind him.

Had he heard the footsteps running down the corridor, or had he merely imagined them? He had heard the shots, of that he was sure, but they were merged with confused screams that came from further down the train. When had he realised that the line had been deliberately blocked to bring the train to a halt? Had he seen that as he leaned out of the window and up towards the front of the train – or was it later? The door of the carriage, such as it was, was broken like matchwood, and three masked men suddenly stood there, firing their guns into the air. The canister rolled across the floor in slow motion and as the gas floated out of it in a noxious cloud Patti and Alex were immediately blinded. Mark instinctively pushed his head even further out of the window, at the same time fumbling for the door-handle. The door gave at once and Mark was able to roll out of the carriage on to the embankment, thanking heaven for the inadequacy of soviet safety procedures.

Concealed by the gas, the masked men did not even notice he had gone, but went about their work with a ruthless efficiency. First they went towards Jennings' inert figure, removing his wallet from his inside pocket and the watch from his wrist. His briefcase was swiftly emptied into a black refuse bag and then tossed away after a brief review of its potential value. Another man tugged a necklace from Patti's neck and added her watch to the collection, together with her handbag in its entirety.

They produced a torch and with its powerful beam swept the rest of the carriage to ensure that nothing else of value had eluded their efforts. Mark's bag was violently pulled down from the luggage rack and virtually ripped open. One of the men, clearly the leader, gesticulated to the others, holding up two fingers, then three. Another man shrugged, then pointed to his crutch, indicating that perhaps the third occupant of the carriage might be locked in a toilet. They flashed around the room once again, then moved on and joined up with other members of the gang who had dealt similarly with other carriages.

Rolling himself into a drainage ditch and hiding behind a clump of brave but relatively bare trees that bordered it, Mark could hear the sound of intermittent gunfire, the voices of the men, the odd hysterical cry of a woman passenger, quickly silenced by a dull thud. He rolled himself into a ball, thinking that somehow that made him more difficult to spot. He did not really care what they did with his baggage, but he had his wallet and his passport in his jacket pocket, as well as the papers relating to Schneider's property. The thought of losing all of those gave him a courage he did not really feel, allowed him to sit sufficiently upright to see exactly what was going on. They had blocked the line with a truck. The train-driver would clearly have had no choice but to stop, or risk a derailment with horrendous casualties. By the side there were parked two station-wagons, their tracks trailing behind them across the fields to show the route they had taken. Two wagons, and the truck – maybe a dozen of them. A serious and well-organised raid, but were they just into robbery or was murder also on their agenda?

Whatever might be the case there was no way that he alone could take them on, and there did not seem to be any noticeable support coming from any other passengers.

The men descended and, sure that no threat come from within the silent train, began to remove their masks. Mark took a sudden intake of breath as a thought dawned upon him – that even if they had not already killed anybody, they would have the perfect excuse to dispose of him, because he, and he alone, could identify them. The man tilling the field seemed oblivious to what was going on, as if an armed train robbery were an everyday occurrence in the neighbourhood. Indeed, who was to say it was not in this desolate landscape?

There was a lot of gesticulation going on amongst the group of men. Although Mark did not understand a word they were saying he gained the impression they had not found something they had expected to find – something or someone, he could not tell. Then the leader lost his temper and began to shout. One or two of his associates actually took a couple of steps backwards, revealing him fully to Mark, still cowering behind the slender protection of the dying trees. He was a big man, well over six feet tall, with the neck of a bull, the face of a concentration camp guard, his legs, inevitably encased in high leather boots, splayed apart in a pose of sheer aggression.

He was miming something to the others, and if Mark had been into party games at that moment he would have guessed he was pretending to play football. The boot drew back, and Mark could imagine the unstoppable shot bulging out of the back of the net behind a goalkeeper terrified by its sheer power. He shivered and then, hypnotised, tried to convince himself that it was pure fear and imagination that made him believe that what the huge, threatening man was now shouting was the name 'Rossetti'.

CHAPTER 27

He did not know how long he had lain there, hidden yet exposed. Time stood still in the surreal wasteland that was the Russian countryside. Eventually, the men began to move slowly towards their vehicles, letting off one final round of shots like outlaws leaving a Western town after they had robbed the bank. They need not have bothered; whatever life was reawakening on the train, none of it was bold enough to show itself even at a window.

Mark waited until the last station wagon had bumped its way out of sight, then rose unsteadily to his feet, only just becoming aware that he was bleeding. His leather jacket was ripped at the shoulder and the white shirt had been torn away, leaving raw exposed flesh where he had first rolled from the train. He did not stop to examine the damage, but ran towards the carriage in which he had been travelling, each bounding step sending a wave of pain through his body. As he pulled open the door the acrid smoke blew into his face until, coughing, he was forced to retreat. He ripped his shirt still further and wrapped it around his mouth and nose before making a further attempt, this time getting into the compartment itself.

Patti was lying across the seat, one arm lolling to the floor, the other tossed across her breast. He remembered the time in Italy, when he thought he'd lost her in an explosion – but then, within seconds he had realised she was alive. Now he could see no flicker of life as he dragged her inert body out into the fresh air, apologising as he bumped her head on the step, even though she showed no sign of pain or of hearing him say he was sorry. He got her under one of the trees and, desperately trying to recall his first aid, put her into what he believed was the recovery position.

Alex Jennings was easier. He was spluttering and vomiting by the time Mark got back to him, and was able to half walk, half crawl to the side of the train. Other passengers were tumbling out of their carriages, pale-faced, with the look of men and women who had survived a nuclear holocaust. A woman began to cry, and as Mark moved towards her she pointed to a man lying in a pool of blood. Perhaps he had been foolish enough to resist, or perhaps he had just been in the wrong place at the wrong time. Mark held her hand and sat her down gently. Neither had a word of the other's tongue, but she could sense that here was somebody who cared.

He found a couple with a basket of food and, after some gesturing, took some water and ran back towards Patti. Another segment of shirt passed as a flannel as very gently he began to wipe her forehead and wet her lips. After a few moments she began to groan. Jennings got unsteadily to his feet and pushed Mark aside with all the strength he could muster.

'I don't know what they threw but she took the full force of it. Give her a bit of air. I'm going to see if I can call for help.'

'Oh sure. There must be a phone-box just around the corner,' Mark said with a feeling of desperation. 'There is a farm over there, though,' he suddenly remembered as if it were from another life. 'I saw the farmer working on the fields.'

Somebody was bringing the body of the driver out of his cab. From the rag-doll look of him, and the bullet wound in his head, it did not appear that he would be driving this train or any other. Mark shook his head in disbelief. The attack must have occurred nearly half an hour ago and nobody had come to their aid. They might just as well have been on a desert island. He saw Alex weave his way across the fields like a crazy scarecrow and wondered if the farm was sophisticated enough to have a telephone. Clearly the driver had not had any form of communication in his cab, or somebody would have used it to call down the line. Mark just hoped that there were no other trains coming down the track, that the service was as infrequent and unreliable as he had been told. If another train came around the bend and went into the back of them, then whatever the armed robbers had achieved would be trivial in comparison.

For a moment he was torn between a sense of duty to the rest of the passengers and his feelings for Patti; then with some relief he saw a few of the male passengers making their way down the line to light a warning fire. Patti fluttered open her eyes and then was violently sick over what remained of his shirt. It seemed as if she might choke on her own vomit, but then she retched again and this time he was able to take evasive action.

'Missed,' he said, more lightheartedly than he felt.

She took in some deep gulps of air, filling her lungs to bursting point.

'Oh Mark, I'm sorry. Your poor shirt.'

'Don't worry. I wasn't going to be wearing it for best anyway.'

He stripped the cotton garment from his body and tossed it on the ground, looking around for the leather jacket he'd abandoned when he'd first attempted the rescue. He gathered it around him, shivering with a mixture of cold and shock as an icy wind chose that moment to blow from an easterly direction.

'You'll catch your death,' Patti said affectionately.

'You nearly did. I've played in colder weather than this when we were away to Sunderland. Hopefully Alex will be back soon with the cavalry.'

Patti eased herself into a sitting position and, picking up the wet cloth, began to sponge herself down as best she could until another coughing fit overtook her.

'Hey, take it easy.' Mark eased himself down to sit beside her.

For the first time, Patti began to take an interest in her surroundings and looked around her. 'Bleak, isn't it? People actually live here?'

'I hope so, otherwise Alex has had a long walk for nothing. Here he comes right now.'

Seemingly fully recovered from his ordeal, Jennings approached at what was almost a trot, his limp and lop-sided appearance giving him the look of a drunken tramp. 'We've got a call into the local police, although I think the old man up there bought his equipment straight from Alexander Graham Bell. We had to go through a switchboard in the nearest large town, so everybody in the vicinity knows what's happened, even if they didn't know beforehand.'

'What do you mean by that?' Patti asked, her journalist's nostrils sniffing a story.

Jennings merely shrugged. 'This is Russia. That's all I mean.'

He called out to a few of the other passengers in Russian, and they waved back at him gratefully.

'I was just telling them that help, such as it may be, is on its way. Goodness knows where the nearest hospital is. They say there are three dead, including our driver. Maybe half a dozen others who need some medical treatment – including you two, it seems to me.'

Mark looked at his shoulder as if he were seeing it for the first time. 'What sort of place is Pinsk?'

'Reasonable size,' Jennings replied.

'Then I'll just get this cleaned up with water and wait until I get there for treatment. I have the feeling that cottage hospital has a whole different meaning round here.'

'And I'm feeling better already,' Patti added. 'It takes more than a few Butch Cassidys to stop me.'

Jennings nodded. 'I wouldn't have expected anything else from you two little heroes. Just another day in Paradise as far as you're concerned. The only slight problem we have is how we're going to get to Pinsk. I guess we either wait until the authorities cut through enough red tape to send another driver down the line, or else I persuade the police when they come that it's in their interests to get you wherever you want to go in order to avoid an international incident. Or, of course, we can just turn back and all go home.'

'I think that's exactly what they, whoever they are, want us to do,' Mark said, explaining what he thought he had heard as he hid.

'Are you sure you're not letting your imagination run away with you?' Jennings asked, his tone now restored to its old calm cynicism.

'Perhaps Alex is right. It was all confusing; you were scared. It's understandable,' Patti added.

'Yes, it was confusing, yes, I was scared – but I know my own name. Now what I don't know is why there was the need to shoot up a train I'm on, why there was the need to involve innocent people to get what they were after. But somehow or other I have a feeling that the answer lies where we're going, and we're going where we set out for this morning.'

He paused as he heard the distant sound of sirens, then, leaning on Jennings for support, he added, 'Use your powers of persuasion, Alex. I want to be in Pinsk before it gets dark.'

CHAPTER 28

It had been a long hard journey to Pinsk, and there was no doubt they had had a cold coming of it. Alex had done his work with the police and the rest of their journey had been completed in a little under three hours in an unheated van whose driver obviously had greater faith in the ability of his vehicle than the designers ever intended. They had not meant to enjoy an extended stay in the city, and with their overnight bags stolen, they had even less incentive to change their minds. Pinsk was the last place one would consider a tourist city, and it had obviously long ago given up its own ambitions to become one. The hospital, where Mark's wounds were cleaned and dressed, was primitive to say the very least. The shops, such as they were, reluctantly yielded two very expensive pairs of pyjamas for Mark and Alex – but the best they could offer Patti was a T-shirt that Alex translated as welcoming its wearer to the Moscow Olympics of 1980.

'Are we paying for its antique value?' Patti asked, as she counted out the seemingly endless pile of notes.

'You're paying because you're foreign. Nobody Russian would buy it,' Jennings replied.

'If what we've seen so far is anything to go by, then they're more likely to steal it than pay good money,' Mark added ruefully.

They dragged themselves dejectedly from one empty dusty shop to another, with Alex negotiating at each establishment for some treasure they would have taken for granted at the local corner shop, let alone supermarket.

'The insurance company aren't going to believe this claim,' Mark said, 'it's going to be on par with Chernobyl.'

'Not funny,' Patti replied. 'Can we just get our business out of the way and get the hell out of this place? It depresses me.'

Mark shrugged, wincing as the pain ran down his side from the wound in his shoulder. 'I don't think it does a lot for the locals either, I must tell you.'

He laughed at his own joke, immediately regretting it as he screamed out in agony. A couple of passers-by, who already regarded the visitors as a curiosity, gave him a long, incomprehending look. Nobody came to Pinsk unless they had to, so why had these three Westerners arrived? Not to bring frankincense, myrrh and gold, that was for sure. If they had landed in the town square in a spaceship they could hardly have attracted more attention.

Mark's first concern was to get a message to Emma to tell her they were fine, but Alex had told him not to be worried.

'She won't even know. It was just another case of highway robbery, or railroad robbery in this case. I doubt it'll even make the papers – and if it does she won't be reading them.'

'What about TV?'

Alex gave him a look of sympathy. 'They stopped reporting bad news on the box. It upsets the tourists.'

Mark's next concern was the hotel in which they were going to have to spend at least one night. At first sight it could easily have been mistaken for an army barracks – although any troops stationed there for too long would certainly consider mass desertion.

'You mean we have to pay to stay here?' Mark asked incredulously.

'Through the nose,' Alex said.

The building squatted like a huge concrete toad, its windows narrow and ill fitted, a row of malevolent eyes, glaring and daring anybody to book into its dark and dank interior. Although there was no evidence of any other guests in what passed as the vestibule, the solitary old woman behind the desk made a great show of turning pages in her book, lifting keys and blowing away dust, as if to conjure up rooms for them would be a miracle worthy of a magnificent reward. When she finally told them the price, she clearly believed that her achievement was on a par with the transformation of water into wine. Alex did his best to beat her down but, simple as the old woman had first appeared, her lack of intellect did not extend to an inability to count. She was a seller in a market-place that was not conducive to buyers, and she knew it.

There were further problems when she asked for their passports. Mark's was in his pocket, together with the papers to the property, but both of the others had lost theirs in the raid. Alex had managed to get the police to fax the Embassy in Moscow, but Pinsk was unlikely to provide even an Honorary Consul to help any itinerant British subjects.

The old woman, until then, had been calm, even bored with her discussions, but now she became suddenly animated as if Jennings had said something irremediably offensive.

'What's going on, Alex? Did you ask her how much it would cost to sleep with her daughter?' Patti asked, wondering whether a tired female and an injured man could somehow or other melt this harridan's heart.

'She doesn't like the fact that we've only asked for two rooms; she's got no proof that you and Mark are married. She says if it's two rooms rather than three then I have to share with him and you sleep alone. She says that she may be old but she has very good hearing and if anybody has any ideas of swapping over in the night then she'll call the police.'

'Tell the old bag to fuck off and mind her own business,' Patti said without humour. It had been a long day and she wanted to go to bed. For the first time in many months she actually wanted Mark to hold her tight, to comfort her and then make love to her.

171

The woman turned her eyes on Patti, and for a moment the journalist thought that perhaps she had made a terrible mistake and her comments had been understood. She could smell the staleness of the woman's clothes, her breath stinking of garlic and tobacco, and all at once a terrible weariness engulfed her and she no longer cared if she slept alone or with Mark, just as long as she could sleep for ever.

The guardian of the hotel's moral values sensed she had won, and began to prepare forms for completion.

'Look, I'll tell her we'll take three rooms; maybe she'll give us a discount,' Alex said. He launched into another lengthy dialogue that threatened to turn into a Chekhov play on its own.

Mark felt his mind moving in and out of focus, the room slanting to the left, the smell of the woman and the old gas fire in the corner. He put his hand out to steady himself, but somebody had moved the wall and his fingers went through a misty nothingness. He fell to the floor in a crumpled heap, and the last thing he could remember hearing was Patti yelling at the old woman, 'There – see what you've done? You've killed him.'

CHAPTER 29

He had not believed he would ever have got as far as the lawyer's office. There had been times in the forty-eight hours following his collapse when he doubted he would see England or his daughter again. It sounded like a music-hall joke: 'Buried in Pinsk'. Tell that to David Sinclair, tell that to the papers, tell it to the marines and they'd all die laughing. It was Patti who told him about the doctor, but that was after a day of delirium, of drifting in and out of consciousness, of tossing and turning in the narrow, hard bed.

'You were lucky to find someone like Lamin here. He was really efficient. He was trained in East Berlin. I found out he was Jewish, and as soon as we get back to England I'm going to do my darndest to make sure we help him and his family come over. He told me he had the chance to get to Israel, but anywhere in Europe is out of the question.'

'So what did the amazing Dr Doolittle do for me?'

'He talked to the animals. What do you think he did? He said he couldn't believe they'd let you out of the hospital with just a patch-up. He reckoned you needed a complete overhaul. Another few hours and that wound would have become so infected that there was every chance of gangrene.'

'Come to sunny Russia and lose your arm. I must speak to the Tourist Office about the possibilities of that as a new slogan.'

'Hey, better your arm than your life,' Patti said soberly.

'Look, do me a favour. Get Alex to ring Mrs Murganev,

173

whatever her name is. Tell her we've been delayed for a couple of days and we'll be back for the weekend. Make some excuses as to why I can't get to the phone to speak to Emma myself.'

'Sure. At least I know you're well on the way to recovery if you're acting the worried parent again. Believe me, she's a lot better off than we are.'

It had been largely because of his desire to get back to Emma that he'd summoned up some hidden strength, pushed aside the objections of Doctor Lamin and Patti, and insisted on getting the earliest possible appointment with the lawyer that Alex had found for them. Like Dr Lamin, she was not what Mark had expected to find in a place like Pinsk.

Lydia Karlovich was a woman in her mid-thirties who, unlike most of the other females they had so far seen outside of Moscow, had made an effort with her appearance. Her hair was cut short at the front, but hung neatly to her collar at the back, the styling as good as anything Patti had seen in London. There were blonde streaks in the auburn colour, perhaps to hide the odd hint of grey, but more likely because they looked good. Her skin was clear and fresh, the skin of a teenager rather than – as they were to discover – that of a mother of a ten-year-old daughter. She was dressed smartly, if a little old fashioned, in a white blouse with a ruffled collar and a pencil-line black dress that perfectly showed off her slim, almost boyish figure. The desk behind which she sat seemed both too large for her and the office, as if it had been designed for another person in another place. She offered them freshly percolated coffee, and Mark felt for the first time since he'd been in the country that he was in the presence of somebody native he could truly trust. When she spoke she looked him straight in the face, and in her grey eyes he knew that, however painful it might be, this was a woman who would always tell her clients the truth. There was an oddly familiar look about those eyes, as if they had met before in another place in another country, but when she told him she had never been outside Russia he decided that his imagination was getting the better of him.

'You have had some unfortunate experiences since you have been in this country. I must apologise.' She sounded sincere, as if there might have been something she could have done to avoid it all. 'Still, with Dr Lamin, you are in safe hands. He delivered my daughter. He is an important part of our community here.' Her gaze shifted to Patti, as if she might have known about her plans to help him emigrate. 'Now, to business. While you have been recovering, Mr Rossetti, Mr Jennings here has told me the background to your inheritance. It is perhaps fitting that you should have come to me. Apart from my mother, who died ten years ago, I too lost all my family to the Germans in the war. Nowadays it is a little easier to be Jewish in Russia. Not a lot, but a little.'

'I thought things had improved under Yeltsin,' Patti said.

'Perhaps. Nobody has really bothered to tell us; only the Western world knows of these improvements.' She laughed and took a cigarette out of a silver box on the table. 'My inheritance. My father buried this before the Nazis took him away. Or rather, the collaborators who were only too pleased to work for the Nazis took him away. Once a Cossack always a Cossack, I think. You would like one?'

Only Patti accepted the offer. She felt that even a dedicated anti-smoker like Mark could not object after what she had been through.

'Anyway, your land. It was indeed fortunate that the deeds were not lost during the attack upon your train. Our land system here is not so sophisticated. In the old days if you were stronger than your neighbour you took his land. And then the State came along and it was bigger than all its neighbours, and so it took all its land and fed it back inch by inch to the new breed of Russians that they called peasants . . . or comrades, depending on your perspective. Nowadays the wheel has come full circle. If you are stronger than your neighbour and you want his land then you take it. And the Mafia is much stronger than all its neighbours. The Mafia is stronger than the State. Sometimes I think that the Mafia *is* the State.'

'The Mafia? This is Russia, not Italy,' Patti said.

'And I thought you were a journalist. Aren't journalists supposed to know everything, sometimes before it happens? And everything that happens today in Russia has something to do with the Mafia. Mothers can no longer frighten their children with stories of Stalin as the bogeyman. Now we have the Mafia. It is easier to be frightened of something that has no face.'

The whole conversation had been conducted by her in perfect English, and she pre-empted Mark and Patti's question by offering the answer. 'It is good to speak English again. In Pinsk there are not too many opportunities to speak. My husband worked in London for many years.'

'What does he do?' Patti asked politely.

'Does – did . . . Who knows? I've not seen him for six years.'

'I'm sorry,' Patti said with the tone of genuine sympathy she affected so well, and which made her the caring face of the tabloid for which she principally wrote.

'Don't be. He was a bastard. My mistake for marrying a Russian. And my punishment for marrying a non-Jewish one at that. As I said, they're all Cossacks at heart. I'm sorry, I talk too much. I get easily distracted. Don't worry, I will not charge for all this chatter.'

Jennings had sat there quietly in an armchair; Patti and Mark were positioned opposite Lydia, able to rest their arms on the desk. Now Alex leaned forward, his body looking even more twisted than usual as he contorted himself upwards.

'You mentioned the Mafia, Lydia – may I call you Lydia?' He did not wait for a reply. 'What have the Mafia to do with Leopold Schneider's land?'

'Did I say they had anything to do with it?' A spot of red appeared on each cheekbone. 'All I said was they are a problem in a country with too many problems already. Some people see them as the cure.'

'And you?' Jennings asked, oblivious to the audience of his two travelling companions.

'Me? I prefer not to see them at all.'

CHAPTER 30

It was not until the following day that they finally saw the plot of land that had brought them to this bleak part of the world, and it was Patti who summed up their feelings when she asked, 'Is this all there is?'

All there was consisted of what looked like a bomb-site, the buildings which had formerly stood upon it demolished, only a few broken bricks strewn about testifying to what once had been.

'Here, nothing goes to waste. We have human locusts. If it is there for the taking then they take it and worry about what they will do with it later on,' Lydia said.

'So what do we do with it?' Mark asked.

The lawyer shrugged. 'I think we have done well to find it. Now we have to prove you own it.'

'But we have the deeds,' Mark said, patting the inside pocket of his jacket. Somehow since the incident on the train he had become more protective of what had been left to him.

'Maybe other people also have the deeds,' Lydia said.

'You are joking,' Patti commented.

'Perhaps.'

'But surely it's not difficult to prove that something's a fake,' Patti persisted.

'And how do you know that what you received from your friend Mr Schneider was genuine?'

Mark produced the documents and held them reverently. 'Look at them. You can see how old they are. Look at the stamps.'

Lydia sighed. 'You told me Mr Schneider was a mere child when he left here. Yes, they are old. So was he when he died, I think. Who can say?'

'Lydia, has something happened that you're not telling us about?' Alex asked. 'You seem very downbeat today.'

The lawyer hesitated for a moment, as if trying to reach a decision. 'I have to be honest with you. Yes, something has happened. Yesterday, I spoke about the Mafia. I knew nothing, but perhaps I have a feeling. This morning I receive a phone call. It suggests that my practice would benefit if I lost two English clients. That I could find myself with many new valuable clients. That I could be involved as attorney to a group who will be building a new supermarket in this town. A corporation that is going places, that had access to Western goods. That my fees would not be limited to money.'

'And what did you say?' Mark asked.

'I said I would think about it. You have seen this place. You could imagine what a demand there would be for a business of this nature.'

'Let me have a guess,' Patti said. 'This supermarket will be built not a million miles from where we're standing.'

'You are a very astute woman,' Lydia said.

'And you, what sort of woman are you?' Mark asked.

'A foolish one, I think. I will tell them that I will keep my English clients.'

'Foolish no, brave yes,' Mark said.

'Perhaps foolhardy might be a better word,' Alex added. 'You have had the offer . . .'

'And now I get the threats,' Lydia interrupted.

'I can't believe this country,' Mark said, his hands outstretched wide. 'Whatever happened to law and order?'

'They died with Stalin, some people would say. He was the Law and he gave the orders,' Lydia replied with a cynical smile.

180

'I can't believe anybody would want Stalin back,' Patti said. 'All that killing . . .'

'Still there is killing. Maybe the poor had more to eat under the old guard.'

'Don't tell me you're a communist,' Patti pursued, forgetting for a moment that she was not conducting an interview.

'I still have my party card – my red card, as you might say in football,' she said, looking at Mark and this time giving an impish grin that wiped years from her age.

They stood for a moment in silence, each imagining the shining edifice that would be built upon this site in stark contrast to the dull grey industrial units that seemed to stretch for miles around it. It was Mark who finally broke the silence. He felt tired and aching. All he wanted to do was get back to the relative normality of Moscow. There had been something comforting about the crowds, the smell, the gridlocked traffic, the sheer pace of a city going about its business. He wanted to get back to Emma as well. He had tried to phone several times already, but as he listened to the phone ring on in the Murganevs' empty flat he could only presume that she, at least, was having a good time.

'So, where do we go from here?' he asked, the question addressed to nobody in particular.

It was Lydia who answered. 'I find out who exactly is laying claim to this land. I then file an application to the courts for verification of your deeds. We wait for a hearing and maybe then the land is yours, maybe it is not. All we can do is our best.'

She was right, Mark knew it – all anybody could do was their best – but all the way back to Moscow he felt an increasing sense of frustration and anger. It was not the money; he and Patti now had more than enough to live on even if they abandoned the Russian property. Yet Leopold Schneider had thought it worthwhile clinging to. He had survived the Nazi death camps and, miraculously, the deeds had also survived. Jennings and this bright lawyer had led them to the property, so why should he allow anybody else to seize it under the law of the frontier? Lydia Karlovich was prepared to stand up and be counted, and he would stand shoulder-to-shoulder with her at the barricades. Comrades. He was beginning to understand what had led this massive, ancient country towards revolution, towards comradeship. And right now it seemed as if there might be another battle to be fought against another enemy. If Lydia still had her red card, then he had no objection to becoming part of the club – only for him, this time around, the card meant he would stay on the field of play.

CHAPTER 31

The journey back to Moscow was speedy and trouble-free, and as they flashed through the scene of the hijack it was hard to believe it ever happened, that the soil was stained with blood. Both Alex and Patti wanted Mark to see another doctor as soon as they arrived. They could see he was in pain although he shrugged it off as a minor inconvenience. 'I played through ninety minutes once with a broken collar bone.' He sounded far more confident than he felt. His whole body throbbed with the pain and he knew he had a fever that might well signal an infection. But he wanted to get the business over with. In his mind he had the timetable all planned out. There was a structure and shape to his life which he was reluctant to abandon, despite – or perhaps because of – the chaos of the last few days.

He needed to get the Tolly Karpov deal finalised and see him on his way to Hertsmere; he wanted to get back to England and tie up the loose ends there; and then he would get back to Lydia, rather than leaving her to fight a lone battle. But most of all he wanted to see his daughter. Having been with her so much more recently, he could not believe that he had actually been able to survive those lonely years when his wife had denied him access. He just hoped that she had enjoyed herself so much while he'd been away that she would not think to reflect upon the possibility that he had abandoned her again.

'Alex, could we go straight to pick up Emma? After that, if you're all so worried about me, maybe you can get me to see

183

an English-speaking doctor. I'm sure that you can pull your Embassy strings to find me one.'

'Sure, Mark, no problem. I'll drop you off at the Murganevs', and then I've a few things to do.'

Mark would normally have wanted to know just what those other things were as he still could not work out exactly what it was Jennings did for a living that permitted him such flexibility. He had never met a man who seemed to have so little responsibility to others. Yet, he felt that making conversation was just too much for him. Instead he sat at the back of the Mercedes cab, willing it forward through the seemingly endless traffic jam that filled not only the main roads but even the side turnings that led to the apartment.

Outside the block Alex spoke quickly to the driver then made to leave them. 'I've told the cabbie to wait. I've also agreed that he turns off his meter. If he tries to charge you more than thirty dollars tell him to fuck off. You don't need any Russian for that. He'll get the message.'

Mark and Patti saw him walk away – an odd Chaplinesque figure, his limp more noticeable from the rear – then reach the corner and disappear.

'There's something very odd about Alex,' Patti said as they pressed the buzzer to gain admittance.

'I like him,' Mark said. 'You feel when you're with him that everything is possible.'

'I didn't say I didn't like him, I just said he was odd. And he is, believe me. I'm a woman and a journalist, and I know odd when I meet it.'

They received no response to the bell, and in frustration Mark began to kick the door. That produced an immediate response from the concierge, who threw the door open so quickly that his next kick landed on her boot. She screamed at him and for a moment Mark thought she was going to throw a punch. If she punched her weight it would have completed the job that the hijackers had started. She must have weighed at least twenty stone, all of which was pressured into a frame that could not have been more than five feet tall. She looked like a boulder dressed in a grimy apron, and as she approached, screaming and shouting, Mark and Patti recoiled from the smell of her. It was a mixture of boiled cabbages, sweat, tobacco and cheap alcohol.

It was the taxi driver who saved them from a full-frontal onslaught or the arrival of the police, when he suddenly awoke from his slumber and raced between the woman and the visitors. For a moment it looked as if she was about to flatten him, but gradually he calmed her down and whatever references he gave for them eventually satisfied her.

Mark gave her the sort of smile he normally reserved for the alsatians without leashes which cornered him in the park during his daily jogs. Cautiously he extended a hand, and when the woman took it and gripped it tightly he thanked his lucky stars that her fist had not connected with his chin. Still smiling, he carefully enunciated the word Murganev. The woman released his hand as if she had suddenly discovered that he had the plague and took several steps backwards. Mark looked from her to the taxi driver, who had clearly become interested at the mention of the famous player's name. The woman took the gesture to mean that the driver had been designated as the official interpreter to the exchange, not realising that his English was little more than her own. They spoke rapidly in Russian, arms flying in all directions, the woman animatedly indicating the stairs leading to the flat, then pointing at the door. The janitor also now shuffled towards them.

'What's going on?' Patti asked Mark in bewilderment.

'I'm not sure,' Mark muttered, 'but I'm going up to find out.

He began to climb the stairs and neither the concierge nor the janitor tried to stop him, but followed behind with the taxi driver like a tug in their wake. Patti indicated the correct door and Mark pressed the bell with all his failing strength. An overwhelming sense of panic began to sweep over him, making him forget the pain that had previously threatened to become the focal point of his life. The huge woman pushed him aside with a remarkable gentleness and produced a huge bunch of keys from around what should have been her waist. The door swung open and Mark jostled forward to be first into the room.

'Emma,' he called. 'Emma.' But even as he raced from room to room in the tiny apartment he knew it was useless. She was not there, and nor was Sonya Murganev or her daughter. Nobody was there and nothing was there, except the larger pieces of furniture. He pulled open the doors of wardrobes and cupboards but there was no trace of any clothing or personal possessions. He looked around for a note, a message, an explanation, but there was nothing. The Murganev family had vanished without trace, and with them they had his only child.

CHAPTER 32

Whatever had gone before could not have prepared him for any of this. Somehow or other Jennings had been summoned and – although he could not recall any part of the journey – Mark had arrived at the British Embassy. They had seated him a deep armchair and sent for a doctor. He had arrived within moments, young and London-trained.

'Mr Rossetti, you have had two traumas in a matter of days: one physical, one mental. The physical wound needs hospital treatment. I will clean it up for you, give you some shots, but you must have careful attention, rest, otherwise I cannot be responsible. As for the other, I can only imagine at what must be going on in your mind. I can give you something to sleep. They tell me they can find you a bed here at the Embassy. Take the tablets, crash out, as they say, for twelve hours. Perhaps by the time you wake she will have returned.'

Mark shook his head so violently that he almost cried out with the pain that shot down his body. 'No. Twelve hours asleep is twelve hours wasted, twelve hours we can spend looking for her.'

The consular official did his best to play down the situation, but Mark was by no means impressed with his best.

'I want some action and I want it now,' he almost screamed, irrational tears of despair and frustration coming to his eyes.

'Look, Mr Rossetti, we have absolute sympathy for your position. It is every parent's nightmare.'

'Are you a parent, whatever your name is?'

187

'I did attempt to introduce myself. I can quite understand your not wishing to listen. The name is Lytton, Anthony Lytton.'

Mark looked up at him as if seeing him for the first time, although the man had been trying to talk to him for the past twenty minutes. He was tall and thin, stooping down to speak to Mark, the eyes blank behind rimless spectacles. His fair hair was neatly parted and his smooth skin suggested that daily shaving was a burden he left to others. He did not appear to be the sort of man who encouraged anybody to call him Tony.

'I asked if you were a parent,' Mark persisted.

'I do not think my personal life has anything to do with your particular problem, Mr Rossetti.'

'So what *has* got to do with my problem, Mr Lytton?'

Throughout the doctor's visit and the exchanges between Mark and the diplomat Patti had sat in a silence that was so out of character as to border on the alarming. Now she spoke quietly, as if in a half-trance herself.

'Mark, I know how you're feeling, but there's no point in picking on Mr Lytton. Have a go at me if it makes you feel any better. I was the one who persuaded you to leave Emma behind. Believe me, I feel bad enough already, but fire away by all means.'

Mark looked at her despondently, all of his anger suddenly ebbing away. He put his head in his hands and began to cry, his whole body shaking in a mixture of pain and anguish. Lytton looked away in embarrassment, his gaze firmly fixed on the portrait of the Queen that hung above the ornately carved fireplace.

'Mr Rossetti, I do urge you to follow the doctor's advice. He's a sound fellow—'

'A sound fellow, is he? Public school chap and all that.' Mark raised his tear-stained face and wiped his nose on his sleeve without any worry for the niceties of polite behaviour, almost as if he was setting himself out to shock this urbane civil servant out of his complacency.

'I have no information as to his educational background. All I know is that he had treated many members of our staff and many of our visitors with success, and I have no reason to think that the course of conduct he suggests you follow would not meet with similar success. Believe me, this Embassy will do everything in its power to help track down your daughter, always assuming there is anything mysterious about her disappearance. We do not, as yet, know how long the Murganev family have been absent from their apartment, and it may be that we have jumped to conclusions, that there is a perfectly logical explanation for the vacation of the apartment. Our local friends here are notorious for not paying their rent. I'm not sure what is more hazardous in Moscow, being a landlord or a tenant.' He laughed at his own joke, then remembering Mark's tears tried, unsuccessfully, to convert the noise into a cough.

'I'm pleased you find things so amusing,' Patti said tartly.

'I do not. I really would not like you to get the wrong impression, Miss Delaney.'

'Is that because you really care, or is it because somebody has told you I'm a journalist?' she asked, a little of her old fire returning.

'If you are indeed a journalist, then I would hope that you realise we are trying to do our best in what is a very difficult situation. Nothing is easy in this country, and believe me it gets harder by the day. Now I do not expect you to care or understand, but kidnapping in Moscow, if indeed Miss Rossetti had been kidnapped, is not uncommon. What we have to establish is whether or not she has been removed and is being held against her wishes, and if so by whom.'

'Does any of that matter?' Patti asked, her irritation with the man and his attitude increasing with every word he so carefully pronounced.

'Yes, I am afraid that the whom definitely does matter.' He made as if to say more, then bit his lip, looked at his watch and began to move towards the door. 'We have sent for the police, of course. Shall I tell them when you might be ready to see them?'

'I'm ready right now,' Mark said, the deathly pallor of his face giving lie to his assertion.

'If you say so,' Lytton said, seemingly glad that he had been saved from any further accusations or cross-examination himself. He reversed his retreat and lifted a telephone to call reception.

'Yes, yes, I see,' he said, his tone becoming more clipped as he spoke to somebody who clearly ranked below him in the hierarchy. 'Yes, I suspect he can come straight up.' He held his hand over the receiver as if defending a state secret. 'It appears your wish has been granted. There's a local police inspector downstairs at this very moment. Shall I tell him to come up?'

Mark nodded. So Lytton thought his wish had been granted, did he? The only wish he had, for which he was prepared to barter everything, was that he got his daughter back in one piece and out of this country.

CHAPTER 33

There were in fact two police officers who came into the room. The apparent superior of the pair introduced himself as Inspector Clemenceau, while the other simply muttered 'Litvin' by way of introduction without any mention of title or rank. The inspector was not a large man, but there was something about him that seemed to fill the room. The first thing Mark noticed was the size of his hands. They stuck out from his jacket sleeves like table-tennis bats, whirling towards him and gripping him tightly, as if the man was trying to transfuse some of his own vitality. The rest of him seemed similarly out of proportion: a small head with a huge Gaullist nose, a thick neck set upon narrow shoulders, a paunchy midriff atop long, spindly legs.

Litvin was a mere appendage, his clothes drab by comparison to Clemenceau's light brown suit and purple waistcoat. While the inspector made all the right noises, Litvin stood apart, in the shadows of the corner, like a sulking spider who would prefer to be spinning his own web.

'My dear Mr Rossetti, what must you think of our country? You take a simple train ride to the provinces and you are brutally attacked and robbed, and then you return to find your daughter missing. My own wife was reduced to tears when I told her where I was coming and why. I left her embracing our own darling child. You must rest assured that I will not sleep until you are able to enjoy that same pleasure once again.'

'I'm grateful, Inspector...?' Mark stumbled over the

191

name, his mind unable to retain any information that was fed into it.

'Clemenceau. Yes, before you ask, it is French rather than Russian – but you must remember we are a polyglot nation and the French were here before and after Napoleon. They left behind some of their culture. One of my forefathers stayed behind at the gates of Moscow when Monsieur Bonaparte retreated. Perhaps he found something or somebody more attractive here than whatever he had left behind in Burgundy. In time my ancestors lost their identity, but they preserved their name.'

He drew up a chair which immediately appeared to be the wrong size. Despite the seriousness of the situation Patti could not help wondering how he managed to buy clothes that fitted. She poured him a cup of tea from the pot that Lytton had left behind. There was something terribly English about the gesture, and it was hard to believe that they were in the heart of Moscow.

'Now, they tell me you need some medical attention and a good long rest. So why not tell me the whole story? Tell me why you came, everything that has happened since your arrival, everybody you have met. I sense that if you omit anything then Miss Delaney here will fill in the gaps.'

He turned to her with a broad smile, made even wider by the scar at the side of his face that seemed to drag his mouth slightly towards his chin. Even as Mark told his story he could not help but think he was relating a fiction, a film he had seen long ago and far away. None of this had happened to him. His daughter was safe at home with Sally. Perhaps he had never got divorced, never suffered the indignities of false accusations that had brought his footballing career to an end. This is what it had to be like sitting on a psychiatrist's couch under hypnosis, going back to one's first memories, back to the womb and then beyond. Clemenceau did not interrupt, but merely scribbled furiously on a pad. Only when Mark had finished did he nod and turn to Patti.

'Your friend has a very analytical mind. I think he is used to investigations. Is there anything to add?'

Patti hesitated.

'Yes,' Clemenceau encouraged, 'however foolish it may seem, you must tell me.'

'Well, it is foolish. It's just as if somebody is following us, knowing exactly what we are doing, where we are going, sometimes knowing before we do ourselves. Maybe I'm paranoid.'

'No, I do not think so,' the inspector said with another lop-sided smile. 'In my experience there is no difference between paranoia and suspicion. You are suspicious, and rightly so. You have come here for four purposes. To interview and bring back Madame Murganev. To sign this player Karpov, to find some land belonging to your old friend . . . no, to you,' he corrected himself, 'and to bring your daughter on holiday. I am right?'

Mark nodded assent, the pain, that he had forgotten while telling his story, now returning.

'So one of these ventures, or perhaps a combination, or even all of them, has caused a degree of discontent amongst a group of people here, or maybe an individual. This is the mathematics of crime.' He said this with some relish, as if it were a subject that he loved to study.

'You make it sound simple,' Patti said.

'Ah, my dear, lovely young lady, crime is always simple. There are only so many permutations. It is like the lottery you have in England of which we are so envious. There are but forty-nine numbers. It is simple. You know the number of permutations, but you have to find them. It is that voyage of discovery which is not so easy. But we will work it out. I have my calculator here.' He tapped the side of his head, and as the huge hand met the small skull Patti feared that he might well knock himself over. Yet, despite his quirky appearance she felt she could trust him, could rely upon him to sort out these problems. If she had committed a crime then a man like Inspector Clemenceau was a man to be avoided.

The telephone rang and both she and Mark jumped, their nerves as taut as the high-wires upon which they seemed to be permanently walking.

Litvin moved silently and swiftly towards it and lifted the receiver like an assassin raising a knife for the kill. He answered in a monosyllable and then listened without saying a word. As the one-sided conversation ended he gestured to Clemenceau that they should go outside, and Mark wondered whether he had been mistaken in allocating the superiority to the inspector.

Left alone, Patti put her hand on Mark's. 'I'm so sorry,' she said in a tone that he could not remember hearing from her before, even during their times in bed together.

'I know. It's not your fault. I could and should have decided to stay with her – but no, I wanted to be part of the big adventure.'

'He'll get her back, this man Clemenceau. I can feel it.'

'Yes, me too,' Mark said, although he did not know whether or not the words were a mere palliative to his own fears and conscience.

The two police officers – if indeed that was what Litvin was – re-entered the room. Clemenceau looked more puzzled than worried.

'Mr Rossetti, we have some news for you of your daughter.' He lifted his hand to cut Mark short as the Englishman's mouth burst open with a dozen questions. 'Nothing bad, I assure you; perhaps from your point of view even good. I mentioned the discontent you may have caused to people here. My good friend Litvin is a specialist with regard to – how shall I put it? – groups of discontents. Such people used to be political, now they are more likely to be capitalists. It is all the same to Litvin; he is not prejudiced. He is like your English bloodhound. You put him on the scent and he is single-minded.'

'What has all this to do with me or Emma?' Mark asked impatiently.

'We think that for one reason or another you have upset our Mafia, our capitalist Mafia. They believe in free enterprise, but only up to a point. For them it is free, but everybody else has to pay the price for their freedom. It was like that before the Revolution. To quote your Shakespeare, I think, or perhaps to misquote him, "Everything comes full circle and there is nothing new under the stars." We have a department that deals solely with the activities of our Mafia. It is there that the worthy Litvin works.'

'And you think the Mafia have got hold of Emma?'

Clemenceau pursed his lips, clearly wanting to restrain himself from speaking before he had fully thought it through. 'I am not sure. That is what I meant by perhaps good news for you. We have just heard that Sonya Murganev, her daughter and your daughter – they are no longer in Russia. Two days ago, while you were travelling to Pinsk, they took a plane.'

'Took a plane?' Mark repeated in disbelief. 'To where?'

'To London,' Clemenceau replied, and even as he answered Mark knew that whatever medical treatment he might need he had to be on the next plane home.

CHAPTER 34

It was a week since Mark had got back to England, and whatever dark days he had experienced in the past seemed filled with sunshine compared to the last seven. If he had held any vague hope that Sally might be understanding, their first conversation was soon to dispel that.

'And you had the gall to argue with me when I stopped you seeing her. It's all been a game to you, a new toy to play with, and now you've lost it. What do you expect me to do, give you another one? Is that what you want, to screw me again so we get another daughter? I should never have listened to Stuart. She was never his to give! If and when she's found, and please G-d she is, you'll never see her again as long as I'm alive and have any say in the matter. Meanwhile, don't speak to me, don't try and contact me. You know the number of my solicitor.'

She hadn't cried, Mark realised, and he wondered why. He could hardly stop crying every time he thought of Emma. Immigration had a record of her arrival. The Murganevs had certainly been on the same flight, their visas had all been in order and there had been no need to raise any questions about their arrival. Emma had insisted on carrying her own passport. She'd been so proud of it. And where was she now? There was no evidence to suggest that she'd left the country, although there was no guarantee about that either. Whilst it would be difficult for Sonya Murganev and her child to leave, an English girl with her own passport could slip in and out. He

197

just hoped she was still with the player's wife. The woman was a mother; he couldn't believe she would hurt another child. Yet, it was possible she was just a runner in the relay and has now handed over the baton (in the shape of Emma Rossetti) to a more ruthless contestant in the game.

Mark had not been prepared to let things take their course with the English police and their Russian counterparts. Somehow he felt that if Emma had been still in Russia Clemenceau would have found her. However big a country it was compared to England, he, at least, seemed to know with whom he was dealing. But in this domestic millpond where could they start looking? Sonya knew nobody here apart from her husband, as far as they were aware, and he had strenuously denied that she had even tried to contact him. Indeed, he seemed as distraught as Mark over the disappearance of his wife and child.

It was to Rob Davies that Mark turned as soon as the doctors would let him do anything. He had spent the first forty-eight hours after his arrival back in England under strict medical supervision, being pumped full of penicillin to defeat the infection that had threatened to take a lethal hold on his injuries. They had wanted to keep him for a week at least, but as soon as he felt he could face the world, face up to whatever tasks he might set himself, he simply got up, dressed and walked away from Hertsmere General. The specialist in charge of his case went so far as to phone David Sinclair. He was used to the stubbornness that passed for bravery with professional footballers, but this was as close to a suicide attempt as he was likely to see.

He had phoned the wrong man. Sinclair of all people knew what it was like to lose a daughter, and therefore he knew what it was that drove Mark at a hundred miles an hour along a road that might lead to nowhere.

'He's old enough to look after himself, but I'm grateful to you for calling. I'll tell him to look after himself,' Sinclair had said. It wasn't a question of Mark looking after himself, he thought, it was more a matter of looking after anybody who happened to get in his way.

Rob Davies realised that too. Davies was the detective sergeant who'd worked with the club on the Mickey Wayne saga. He had sufficient experience of kidnappings to ensure that, with Mark and Sinclair shouting loudly enough, he could find himself allotted the case.

'Mark, what can I say? It's not that I don't want to be back at Hertsmere, it's just that I don't want to be back under those circumstances.' Davies had good reason for raising no objections to being at the ground. He was an incurable football groupie, and he was also married to Helen Archer, Hertsmere's chief executive, whom he'd met on his previous investigation. He had matured since their paths had last crossed, and it came as no surprise to Mark when he learned that Rob was up for promotion.

'Find my daughter and I'll make sure you are made Chief Constable,' Mark said.

'I don't need any incentive to find Emma,' Rob replied. 'And I will find her, don't worry.'

But he had not found her as yet. To date, all of his inquiries had met a wall of silence and ignorance.

Murganev was panic-stricken. Whatever English he had learned had been traumatised away, and through the interpreter he had screamed, 'Rossetti may have lost his daughter, but I have lost a child *and* my wife.'

There could be no doubting that his grief was genuine, and Sinclair, after discussion with the manager, had decided there was no point in having the Russian train, let alone play.

Davies sat Mark and Patti down for hours, at first together and then individually, in case one or other of them was subconsciously holding something back. He got nothing other than a list of those who had crossed their paths in Russia: Karpov, Rudi, Lydia, Jennings – there were no others to whom they could put a name, other than the two police officers.

'I can't help but feel the answer's in Russia even though the girls and the woman may be here,' Davies confided in his boss, Chief Inspector Peter Jordan.

'Fancy a holiday, do you?' Jordan said without any real attempt at humour, for he was not a man given easily to making or even appreciating jokes.

'I've spoken to my opposite number over there, a guy called Clemenceau. He seems really switched on.'

'And his boss isn't as soft as me and won't sign the chitty for a plane fare.'

'How did you guess? You know, guv, you wouldn't make a bad copper.'

'And you, son, are getting a bit cheeky. It must be married life. It doesn't do anyone any good.' He thought of his own wife, and the demands she made upon him that dragged him away from his beloved gardening. He had never understood why anybody should actually want to spend time with him, and certainly not why they should want to spend it shopping for things in which he showed not a glimmer of interest.

When Rob Davies told Mark he was going to Moscow, the distraught father had no hesitation.

'I'm coming with you.'

'In your dreams. We've no reason to think that the Murganev woman is anywhere but here. You may be needed at short notice.'

It was lame and they both knew it.

'If Sonya Murganev is here, then why do you need to go?' Mark asked.

The detective-sargeant just shrugged and Mark knew he had won.

'Anyway, you'll be glad of the company. Moscow's a dangerous city.'

'So I hear,' Davies said, 'so I hear.'

CHAPTER 35

To anybody else, David Sinclair's behaviour may have seemed heartless, but Mark knew why he had asked him to finalise the Karpov arrangements in Moscow. As soon as he had heard of Mark's intended return he had called him into his office.

'Look, Mark. We've left you alone this past week or so, but I can see you're driving yourself crazy doing nothing. We've got the work permit through for Karpov. Rather than have him come over himself, Barlucci and I think it would be a good idea for you to go and tie up the loose ends and bring him back. If you can convince yourself there's more to your trip than just looking for a daughter who's no longer there, then perhaps it'll make it easier for you.'

The Chairman was not wrong. There were odd moments when Mark could almost believe that there was a startling normality about his life. Jennings made appropriately sympathetic noises when they once more met at Moscow airport, but after that merely focused upon the work in hand, guiding Mark and the player through all the red tape that kept the native-born Russian from leaving his homeland to ply his trade abroad. The more he saw of the player the less he liked him. He was a mercenary, and Mark could not see him shedding a drop of blood for Hertsmere unless he was paid in gold for it. That didn't make him a bad footballer. Mark had been around enough dressing rooms in his time to understand that some players were motivated by loyalty, some by glory and others by mere greed. Yet it was often the greedy ones who got the results and the glory. It was always with a wry smile that he read the newspaper and magazine articles that credited them with loyalty.

For somebody who had grown up under hard-line communism, Karpov took to his new-found capitalist status with an enormous enthusiasm that suggested he, and he alone, had been responsible for its discovery. First-class air fares, the insistence on top-class hotels, a luxury car to meet him at the airport and then to be placed at his disposal – conditions that were more in keeping with a difficult pop star than a footballer who had been living in a two-roomed apartment.

'Murganev, he has problems, I hear, I think. You too, Rossetti.' Mark did not know whether the use of his surname was a linguistic failing or an establishment of the relationship between them. 'Yes, we both have problems.'

Karpov puffed out his chest like a fighting bantam cock. 'Me, I will have no problems. Murganev says he is the greatest player, but only because he is told to say that to make himself of interest. But I do not need anybody to tell me to say that. I know I am good; I know that the English public will soon realise that I am the best.'

For a moment Mark wanted him to fail, wanted the disasters that had befallen himself to hit this arrogant little bastard like a sledge-hammer. But then the footballer in him got the better of his temper, and he knew that if this man could produce on the pitch in England what he had shown him in Moscow then he would indeed take Hertsmere by storm.

Mark had persuaded Davies to stay in the same hotel they'd used during his earlier visit. He had a slim hope that anywhere Emma had been might yield up a few clues to her whereabouts. He saw little enough of Davies during the days. The policeman had taken to Clemenceau, and the admiration seemed to be mutual. As Mark sat with Rob over dinner, the detective-sergeant brought him up to date with developments.

'They're no mugs out here, I tell you. My governor could learn a thing or two from their methods, and I never thought I'd hear myself saying that.'

'So why haven't their methods found Emma yet?'

Davies poured himself another glass of his expense account wine. 'Police work isn't like that. It's not wham-bam-thank-you-ma'am stuff. You have to sift through the information you've got; but first you have to collect the information. That all takes time.'

'And why haven't we received any demands, any news?'

Davies swirled the liquid around in his glass as if seeking the inspiration to answer.

'You're assuming Emma's been kidnapped.'

'And hasn't she?'

'We don't know. We have an investigation into one missing person; the Russians are looking for three. They ask themselves a question: has Sonya Murganev got Emma Rossetti, or has she been passed on to somebody else . . .'

'Or has somebody else got the three of them?' Mark interrupted. 'I've been too caught up with Emma even to contemplate there could be other alternatives.'

'There's yet another scenario.'

Mark's mind was working more clearly than it had done since he had first learned of Emma's disappearance, and he could see exactly where Rob was heading. 'You mean that nobody has got any of them. That – for reasons we don't know – they simply got up and ran.'

'Better, Mark, much better. Now you're beginning to convince me that your journey was necessary.'

'I wish I'd been able to convince Patti. She thought I was just running away from my responsibilities again.'

'Women, eh? Who'd be with them and who'd be without them? I really do love Helen, but I didn't realise that her idea of a good time was to watch old videos of Hertsmere's triumphs when they were still in the Conference. If I have to see their winning goal against Altrincham one more time I swear I'm going to scream.'

'Maybe Patti's right. I was scared. I was scared of Sally, scared of what might have happened to Emma, so I ran with you. I didn't really expect to find anything here, but I ran all the same. And perhaps that's what Sonya Murganev did. It was just bad luck that my Emma was with her.' He paused, thinking it through even as he spoke. 'Or perhaps it wasn't bad luck for Sonya Murganev. Perhaps it was a g-dsend. She had a perfect excuse to get out of the country and into England. If anybody asked, she was taking a sick child home whilst her father was tied up with business; but it seems nobody did ask.'

'It's an interesting idea, Mark, but it leaves two questions unanswered. Why did Emma go with her tamely? And, assuming they're in England, why haven't they tried to make any contact? Your daughter's a sensible girl. She'd know that you and her mother would be worried out of their skins, so she'd try to get in touch to say that everything was all right. So if they were running when they left here that would mean that they're still running.'

'But who are they running from?'

Rob's face took on a grave expression, as if he were about to enter a new phase of their discussions, one for which he had needed a certain amount of courage. 'You were here last time, what, less than a week?'

Mark nodded.

'Well, you were certainly busy. Clemenceau tells me you made quite a few enemies.'

Mark looked puzzled. 'I keep hearing that. What did I do? I came to look for some land that I thought was mine. I came to sign a footballer. I came to bring my twelve-year-old daughter on what I thought would be the trip of a lifetime.'

Rob hesitated, not sure whether to answer, not sure, as yet, whether he could answer – but before he could say anything,

Rudi came across to them. The barman had been nothing but sympathetic to the situation.

When they had arrived he had not needed to be told that Mark's travelling companion was a policemen. 'I could smell it. A policeman is a policeman the world over. Let him do what he wants. It will not be the police who find your daughter. Since you have left I have been calling in my chips, as the Americans say.'

'And?' Mark had asked, but the barman had simply tapped his nose to indicate that the best of news was yet to come. Now, as he leaned across to Mark, he whispered into his ear confidentially so that Davies should not hear.

'So there's a phone call for me,' Mark said loudly, just to see the expression of annoyance on the Russian's face, 'so who is it?' Mark watched Rudi try to outstare Davies.

'Do you really want him to know?' Rudi asked with a nod in Rob's direction.

'Yes, I really want him to know.'

Rudi did not know when he was beaten. He slid a piece of notepaper under the edge of Mark's plate. He did not stay to see his defeat but moved swiftly back to the area of his bar where he alone ruled the domain.

'Are you going to leave me in suspense?' Rob asked.

'If Rudi had his way you'd be left in some dark alley.'

'Interesting character, your friend Rudi. Clemenceau tells me he's been held on suspicion of racketeering, pimping, forgery, not to mention a couple of charges of possession.' Rob again sounded as if he wanted to say more, and Mark was not entirely sure that Rudi was incorrect in his reluctance to speak freely in front of him. If Mark was not being told the whole story, then why should he take Davies completely into his confidence? That was part of the problem; he was living in a world of half-truths, a world where lies had taken such a hold that even honest people were sucked into the mire of deceit for whatever reasons.

All Mark said, however, was, 'Possession of what?'

'Drugs. Not even your ordinary everyday cannabis. We're talking hard stuff – heroine, coke . . .'

'So how come he's allowed to walk the streets, or in his case prowl the bars?' Mark asked. He actually liked Rudi and couldn't perceive him as a hardened criminal, living off women, living off the corruption of the young.

'Well that's the odd thing. You see, he's had no convictions. Now, they don't like drug pushers here. Prostitution, well, that's fair game and there's nobody in the establishment who's not had a go at a hooker at some time in his career. They used not to like black marketeers either. But Rudi seems to ride all these storms. It's as if he's got a charmed life or some good fairy looking after him. And what I'm asking myself as an experienced policeman is, what's he done to deserve the protection of this good fairy?'

'And what do you answer yourself, as an experienced policeman?'

'I tell myself that Rudi likes to run with the hares and the hounds. It's a dangerous game that he plays. Now, I've asked Clemenceau to tell me a bit more, and he says he's puzzled about our little barman as well – and if Clemenceau doesn't know the answers then that's a very difficult question indeed.'

Mark looked across to Rudi who, seemingly oblivious to being the subject of the conversation, was shaking a cocktail for a loud-voiced American perched on a barstool, his buttocks so fat that they threatened to draw the whole stool into the folds of his flesh. Doubtless Rudi was also practising his English. He liked to practise his English.

'So who was the message from?' Rob asked, as Mark did not seem likely to volunteer the information.

'From Lydia Karlovich. Our lawyer in Pinsk. She says she wants to see me as soon as possible. A matter of urgency that she can't discuss over the phone.'

'I'll come with you.'

'No. She says she'll see me with Jennings, but no one else.'

'Oh, yeah. That's what Rudi tells you. I don't trust him, Mark. Last time you went to see this woman you nearly got yourself killed. Talk to her yourself. You told me she speaks good English. Make sure Rudi got the message right. If not, then the offer's still there – I'll come with you.'

Mark looked at his watch. 'Her office will be closed and I don't have her home number. I'll call her first thing in the morning and then hop on the train.'

'And how do you know Mr Jennings will be available to escort you?' It was a question that had simply not occurred to Mark. Whenever he had wanted Jennings he had been available, so why should he not be available now?

'I'll give him a ring as soon as we've finished.'

Rob Davies looked down at his empty plate. 'I've finished now. Let's go find a telephone.'

As they rose to leave the dining room, Davies caught Rudi's eye. It could have been a trick of the light, but he was convinced that the barman had winked at him – not a wink of comradeship, nor one of conspiracy, but a gesture of triumph. As if to say, whatever hurdles Detective Sergeant Rob Davies of Her Majesty's Constabulary might put in the way, Mark Rossetti would tomorrow be on his way to collect his message from Lydia Karlovich.

CHAPTER 36

Not only had Alex Jennings been able to accompany Mark on the trip, but every investigative bone in Rob Davies's body told him that he had been expecting the call to invite him. Mark had tried to call Lydia, as had Alex, but the receptionist had explained to Jennings that, although she was expected in, she had not yet arrived. Yes, they could come at any time; yes, Ms Karlovich had blotted out all other appointments from her diary; no, alas, the receptionist would not be there to greet them as she would be visiting the dentist.

As the train hurtled through the countryside, Mark felt increasing regret that he had not allowed the solid Rob Davies to go with them. Perhaps Rudi had relayed the message accurately, but who would have known if three men rather than two had boarded the train? If Lydia refused to see them with Davies, then so be it – but why should she refuse to see somebody she had never met, nor indeed ever heard of?

It was hard to tell exactly where the ambush had taken place, so much of the countryside looked identical, but as they spotted a clump of bushes and a distant farmhouse, Alex and Mark exchanged a look that spoke volumes of a shared experience, a shared nightmare. Neither of them spoke, but each relived the moment when the train had screeched to a halt, the smell of gas, the sound of gunfire. Although Mark could not be certain, several of the burly men who prowled the corridors in double-breasted suits seemed to have bulges under their armpits which suggested they were armed and prepared for any new attack. This time, however, the train roared on its way without any mishap.

They were in Pinsk just after lunchtime, but the absence of taxis at the station suggested that their drivers had a longer break than the rest of the local population. Eventually a lone vehicle appeared, its colour camouflaged, one tyre noticeably bald, with a windscreen so covered in small holes and cracks that it was a miracle the driver could see anything of the road. The driver grunted to indicate that he knew where they wanted to go, then took a route so devious that Mark would not have been amazed to see the Kremlin loom up on one side of the cab. After nearly half an hour's driving, and without any sign of a meter being switched on, Jennings had finally had enough. He tapped the driver on the shoulder and began a heated argument which ended with the taxi pulling up outside Lydia's office building within thirty seconds. Alex threw a wad of notes at the cabbie, who clearly did not think the payment sufficient and drove off at a great pace, his hand giving them a one-finger gesture from the window, the bald tyre causing the vehicle to slew at an angle as it took the corner.

There was nobody in the downstairs reception area and they made their way up to the office in a silence that was a mutual decision. The building gave off a haunted feeling that seemed to require them to tiptoe through its corridors with fingers to their lips. Lydia's outer office door was closed but unlocked. The receptionist had been as good as her word. As they entered the telephone rang and was duly picked up by an answering machine, but the caller then promptly hung up.

'It's amazing how many people are still wary of talking to machines,' Alex said.

Mark was a pace or two ahead of him, and knocked politely on the door of Lydia's personal office. The bottom two-thirds were constructed of a painfully thin, cheap mock-oak, which was topped by a third of frosted glass. Lydia's name was carefully painted on the glass in fine gold lettering, both in English and Russian.

Mark knocked again and then pushed down on the handle. 'I hope she's not got a bloke in there,' he said over his shoulder to Alex. The door moved inwards and, as Mark began to speak, the words froze in the air. Lydia Karlovich's body was draped across the desk, her head flung back like an abandoned broken doll. From the angle of her neck it was clearly broken and her eyes stared upwards at the ceiling in an expression more of surprise than horror. Her dress was up above her waist, her pants pulled down to her knees and a thin trickle of blood traced the route from her vagina to her inner thigh.

Mark stood there, blocking the door, oblivious to the small frame of Jennings, who was trying to push past him to see just what had stopped him in his tracks. Then suddenly Alex was ahead of him, walking around the corpse on the desk, like a tiny bird, curious about a dead animal.

'Jesus Christ, Alex, what do we do?'

'We call the police, that's what we do.'

'How do we explain this to them?' Mark was seized by a blind panic. He had once before been accused of one crime of which he was innocent, and he had no wish to repeat the experience. This time he would not be facing a lifetime ban for corruption, but a death sentence for murder.

'We'll explain,' Jennings said confidently He did not appear to be shaken and Mark wondered how many times in the past he had been faced with the aftermath of violent death. He realised just how little he really knew about his companion, a man into whose hands he was now virtually entrusting his whole future, his whole life.

'Alex, she was waiting for us. You told me that her secretary said that she'd blotted out her whole day for us, that she'd be at the dentist herself. The only person who can say when we arrived is that taxi driver, and I can't see him going out of his way to help us.'

He could hear the terror in his voice. He needed to speak to Rob Davies, but what good would that do? The Russian authorities were not likely to be impressed by an English detective-sergeant telling them what a nice person Mark was and how he was a personal friend of his wife. His gaze was drawn back to Lydia's body. He wanted at least to pull down her skirt, to preserve her modesty, to give the body back some dignity, but Jennings seemed to anticipate his thoughts.

'Don't touch anything until the police get here, nothing – you understand? At the moment the only prints they would have of yours will be on the two door-handles. Let's make sure it stays that way. I'm going to call from inside.'

Jennings lifted the phone at the switchboard with a handkerchief, while Mark stayed rooted to the spot, feeling half-fearful, half-protective to the body. Somebody should stay with her until she began her final journey. She had been a good person, she had been loyal and trustworthy and she had paid the price. Was this the way it was to be? That everybody who showed any loyalty or affection for Mark Rossetti would be destroyed? Was this Leopold Schneider's true legacy, a gift of death and violence?

Alex was speaking on the phone, his voice tense and urgent, the meaning clear despite the fact that Mark could not understand a word. Gradually he backed out of the room, the body still in sight, the scent of death beginning to fill his nostrils. He could hear the droning of a fly, perhaps relaying the news to his comrades that they should gather around, that here was fresh food. The noise filled his ears, coming to him from all directions, out of all proportion to what the sane part of his mind told him had to be the real volume.

He felt a terrible desire to be sick, to void his stomach and at the same time void his mind of all he had seen. He conjured up a picture in his head that would not disappear. A half-naked female form, lying across a desk, dead and abused – only as his mind's eye moved up from the focus of the vicious attack, the face was not that of Lydia Karlovich, but the innocent face of his daughter.

CHAPTER 37

The senior police officer was a grizzled, grey-haired man in his mid-fifties, called Rosnik, who seemed somewhat disappointed that Stalinist interrogation tactics were no longer a part of his armoury. His squad had been at the scene of the crime within fifteen minutes of Jennings' call and now, some hour or so later, the photographers and forensic experts had done their work and the body was being taken in a bag down to a waiting ambulance. Even though there was nothing to be done for Lydia, Mark could hear the sirens wailing through the streets as if it were a matter of life and death rather then merely the latter.

'Maybe the driver just wants to get home early,' Alex said with an attempt at grim humour.

Rosnik looked disapprovingly at the use of English between them and Jennings obligingly translated. The Russian police officer was not amused, and said to Jennings, 'This is no laughing matter. A woman is dead.'

'We know she is dead. We called you,' Alex responded.

'And I know you called me,' Rosnik replied grimly. 'But what I do not know is whether or not you also killed her.' He turned to one of his aides and muttered something.

'What did he say?' Mark asked Alex.

'He said that was what comes when a Jewess starts messing about with Westerners. I get the impression that Rosnik here doesn't like us. It's a question of whom he likes least, the Jews or the English. He's really quite a warm and wonderful person at heart and he's probably kind to dogs as well.'

Rosnik virtually spat in Alex's face, but then the little man did not flinch. Instead he replied quietly and then turned to Mark. 'He says he doesn't want us talking to each other in English or else he's going to throw us in separate cells and then throw away both keys.'

'And what did you say?' Mark asked.

'I told him I had to translate for you. That you didn't speak a word of Russian. I've also told him to phone Clemenceau in Moscow. I'm quite sure that he's his superior, although this chap won't admit it and likes to think he rules the roost locally.'

'And does he?'

'Probably. He's been around a long time. I think he'll give us a hard time and then reluctantly let us go. He'll say in his report that he thought we did it, but that it wasn't deemed politically expedient to prosecute. He's off the hook. It's one more case that's closed without too much work and one less Jewish lawyer to trouble him.'

It took until nearly nine at night for Jennings' analysis of the situation to become true. Rosnik had called in a female local interpreter to enable him to question Mark on his own, but as the woman's English had been learned from books rather than practical conversation the dialogue tended to be slow, stilted and at times downright ludicrous. They had indeed taken the pair of them down to the local police station, but until seven o'clock Mark did not see the inside of a cell, merely a stark room, furnished with a rickety table, a couple of chairs and a strident strip light with an electrical fault that caused it to flash on and off an inconvenient moments. It was then that Rosnik, having gone over his story for the tenth time and finding it matched exactly with both Jennings' and the receptionist's versions, abandoned him to a small, grim cell, more out of pique than any intention of permanent punishment. Mark was almost relieved to be left alone. It had been a particularly bloody day in a bloody fortnight. He lay on the hard wooden bunk, which was merely three narrow slats across a plank, wondering how many others before him had waited, contemplating their own dark futures. What had lain in wait for them – labour camps? Exile? Death? What chances had they of a fair trial? He thought with some relief of Clemenceau liaising with Davies, of Rob causing a diplomatic storm with Anthony Lytton in the Embassy. Somehow he could not exactly see the two of them hitting it off.

The shock of seeing Lydia's body was beginning to fade, and his brain was working again. Who could have known that Jennings and he were on their way to see her, and what was it that she could not risk telling them over the phone? He hoped that whatever it was, was not the reason she had been killed. Rosnik had shown the complacency in the face of violence shared by so many of his countrymen. Who was to say that her death had been totally unconnected with his affairs in Russia? But he did not think so. Everything that happened seemed to be connected with his affairs.

Rosnik, when he came to let him out, did so with bad grace. He had Alex in tow, who could not conceal the delight on his lop-sided features at the discomfort of their would-be jailor.

'He says he doesn't believe a word that we're saying, but that he's been ordered by Moscow to let us go. He thinks that Clemenceau had gone soft on you because of the business with your daughter. If it's any consolation he classes him as French rather than Russian, and he doesn't like them either.'

'Is there anybody he does like?' Mark asked, bestowing a smile upon the subject of their discussions which elicited a snarl and a cloud of bad breath.

'Not so's you'd notice. But let's just get out of here and on the way back to Moscow, before he finds some regulation in a dusty manual that keeps us around for the next decade.'

'What about Lydia? What happened to her? Isn't anybody going to try to find out who did it and why?'

'What happened? Somebody took a crowbar and raped her with it and then when they'd finished enjoying themselves they broke her neck. That's what happened to Lydia, or at least that's the way Rosnik described it,' Alex said soberly.

If Mark's stomach had contained anything he would have been sick again, but all he said was, 'Let's just get out of this G-dforsaken place. Can we take our papers back from Lydia's office or haven't they finished checking through things? That is, if they're going to bother to check.'

Alex took Mark by the arm and began to lead him up the stairs from the cells. 'Oh, they've checked all right. They thought there'd been a robbery as well as a rape and a murder.'

'And had there?' Mark asked.

'Yes, there had. But the only thing that they took was the file on your friend Schneider's land. Now can we get the hell out of here, please?'

And this time without further argument Mark followed Alex to the door and stumbled out into the cool Russian night, gulping in deep breaths of fresh air until he thought his lungs would burst.

CHAPTER 38

Daniel Lewis had no idea why a Detective Sergeant Davies should be asking to see him without an appointment, but he had a nasty suspicion that the man had not come to buy a house. Although it had been business as normal since his last meeting with Nikolei Yevneko – indeed, business better than normal – he still found himself waking up in the middle of the night in a cold sweat. He could see the cold eyes of Yevneko's minder, the even colder eyes of Yevneko himself, and imagine himself strapped into the driver's seat of his car as it was crushed into an unidentifiable mass.

Yet the fact of the matter was that he had been asked to find more and more large houses for introductions of Yevneko, and he was eyed with envy and no little curiosity by his rivals in the trade. They could not understand how such an also-ran as Daniel Lewis had so suddenly become a major player in the game that was the residential property circus; and how, in particular, he had carved out a niche market for himself with the Russian community. He spoke no word of the language, he had never been there, and whatever relations he may have had would have emigrated to England or the States more than a century before.

'Send Mr Davies in,' he said to his secretary. She'd only recently joined him, a necessity with the volume of work, and by referring to the policeman in civilian terms he was hoping to persuade her that there was a civilian reason for his visit.

Rob came into the room, his frame filling the doorway. In

the past he had always found his size a problem with the opposite sex, but there could be no doubting its advantage when it came to a matter of questioning.

'Do have a seat, officer. Can I get you a drink?'

Rob looked around the comfortable office. Desk, chairs, plants, music system, even the decoration – all looked brand new, as did the well-stocked drinks cabinet and cooler in the corner. 'A cup of tea would be fine,' he said, although he thought a nice pint of lager would be better.

He'd arrived back in England from Moscow with a thirst and renewed vigour for all things British. He'd tried the home-brewed Russian beer and been less than impressed. If they'd tried to give that to his Sunday League football team there would have been a riot which may well have ended with the summary execution of the publican who'd had the misguided audacity to serve it.

'So what brings you to see me on this bright and sunny day?' Lewis asked, fearing the answer.

Davies was not quite sure of the response himself. His visit to Moscow had been helpful but inconclusive. He and Clemenceau had shared their information and at least now he had a better idea of the woman he was seeking, always assuming that Emma was still with her. The photograph that Murganev had given him was nothing compared to the well-rounded picture that his Russian counterpart had been able to paint for him. He was sorry that he had to cut short his trip when Mark and Jennings returned from Pinsk.

Clemenceau had been more than helpful. 'Get Mr Rossetti out of the country. I am sure he had nothing to do with the unfortunate demise of Ms Karlovich, but our local man is by no means convinced. I believe I can keep him in his place, which in this case is Pinsk, but nothing here can be regarded as a certainty. It would be safer if he is home. I do not think that Rosnik has ever had to extradite an individual from England!'

'And Jennings?'

'Mr Jennings is more familiar with our ways and well able to look after himself. Just get Mr Rossetti home.'

'And what do you suggest I do myself when I get him back there?' he'd asked, feeling confident that he could learn from this man's approach.

'Look into the Russian emigré community.'

'Are you saying that's where you think Sonya would aim, rather than her husband?'

Clemenceau had smiled enigmatically. 'You are the English detective. I am simply suggesting you look where I cannot.'

When he'd looked, he'd been pointed in the direction of Daniel Lewis as a man who knew what was happening with the Russians in London. He'd come for a chat, but something about the estate agent's attitude made him decide to ask questions that would not have crossed his mind before his arrival. He knew enough of human nature to recognise when a man had a natural nervousness in the presence of the police and when a man was nervous because he had something to hide. Lewis had something to hide. Maybe he was cheating on his tax returns, or perhaps he was just cheating on his wife, but he was a man with a secret – and one of the things that had led Rob into following a career in the police force in the first case was that he enjoyed discovering secrets.

'I'm here because I hear that you're something of an expert on all things Soviet. That they've been moving into London in a big way, and that you've been helping them move.'

'The Russians are coming, is that it?' Lewis said, giggling nervously and spilling some of the tea in Davies' saucer.

'Or have come. Tell me a little about how they operate. I hope I've not come at an inconvenient time.' He offered the escape route to see how quickly Lewis would scramble for it, and the answer was very quick indeed.

'Well, I am a bit under pressure at the moment. Maybe you could have a word with my secretary and make an appointment for next week. I think the heat will be off by then.'

And he would have had the chance to speak to Yevneko and get some guidance on how to answer, on how much he could tell this somewhat overpowering policeman. He didn't know why Davies wanted information, and he didn't particularly care, but he did know what happened to him when he last discussed Russian matters without permission. He had just taken delivery of a new car, after a prolonged battle with the insurers, and he had no intention of the same fate befalling that vehicle.

If he thought he was off the hook he was mistaken. There was a fatalistic streak about the pace with which Davies progressed his investigations, as if he alone knew where he was going and, however long it took, he would get there. 'Now I'm here this won't take long,' he said, then, without waiting for a reply, continued, 'I'm investigating the disappearance of a Russian woman, one Sonya Murganev, and her child.'

'What's that got to do with London?' Lewis asked, searching his mind to see if he had heard the name.

'Her husband plays for Hertsmere United, you may have heard of him.'

'Yes, of course I have. They're my team. But I didn't see anything about her in the papers.'

'Not everything gets into the papers. What really concerns us is that she's vanished along with a young English girl, an Emma Rossetti. I don't suppose you've heard of her, or anything about either of them?' Davies looked Lewis straight in the eye, and the estate agent dropped his gaze. He didn't like the sound of any of this, nor did he think Yevneko would be too pleased. The policeman was talking again, and he jerked his thoughts back to the here and now rather than the future possibilities that might be imposed upon him.

'I wonder if I could just look through the records you have of any Russians that may have bought properties using your good offices . . .'

Lewis could not conceal the panic. He knew he could refuse, could insist on a search warrant, but what would that tell Davies? He knew what it would tell him: that he had something to hide.

'I'd love to help you, Inspector, but—'

'Thanks for the promotion. I wish my bosses had as much faith in me. Sorry. You were saying . . . ?'

Lewis looked flustered. 'Saying?'

'Yes, you were telling me you'd love to help; so if you just leave me with the files and give me a room, then I can flip through them and you can get on with your busy schedule.'

There was no point in Lewis telling Davies that he really had very little to do, nor could he raise the issue of client-confidentiality as he doubted that the policeman would be impressed. He doubted if he would be impressed by any excuse or hurdle that he put in his way. He would brush them aside like a tank running though a straw hut. White-faced and worried, Lewis rose to his feet and pulled open the drawer of his filing cabinet in which he kept all the details of his Russian clients. He did not know what Davies was looking for, nor what he hoped to find, but as far as he, Daniel Lewis, was concerned, he felt hopelessly and irretrievably lost.

CHAPTER 39

The Park Crescent ground was packed to the rafters for the debut of Tolly Karpov. He had been signed just in time to be eligible for their next round of the European Cup-Winners' Cup, and anybody attending the run of the mill league game against Brentham was guaranteed a ticket for the home leg of the match against the star-studded Paris Olympique a fortnight later.

Another couple of weeks had passed without news of Emma Rossetti or Sonya Murganev, and Mark had passed the point of despair. 'If she was alive she'd have found a way to contact me, I know it,' Mark said to Rob Davies.

'You can't be sure of that,' Davies said, although his investigation seemed, on the face of it, to be making little or no progress. Yet he felt instinctively that there was something he had been told or discovered that was relevant. It was for him, though, to work out what it was. The case had taken on the shape of a personal crusade and his boss, Inspector Peter Jordan, had been forced to tell him to ease off, to pay at least a little attention to the other matters that were accumulating on his desk.

The last thing Mark wanted to be doing was watching football with his daughter still on the missing list, but both Patti and Rob had worked hard on him to persuade him to come to the match.

'What will you do if you don't come?' Patti had said. 'You'll sit at home on your own. You have to get a grip on things, for Emma's sake. She'll be back, I promise you, and you have to be here for her. She's going to need you.'

'You mean you hope she'll be back. So do I, Patti, but do I believe it? That's quite another question.'

But he had come. Patti had stayed over the night before, the first time they had slept together since their return from Moscow. She had cradled him in her arms like a small child, then patiently coaxed him to make love to her gently. He had cried as he climaxed, then turned away. She had pushed her body close against his back, feeling his wetness within her, wanting him to fill her again, wanting at that precise moment to be with him for ever, but knowing that she might not feel that way in the morning.

'What is it, Mark? Tell me.'

'It's stupid. I just thought to myself that with you on the pill, and my sperm dying inside you, that we'd just murdered another Emma.'

She had rolled away from him and lain on her back, peering through the dark at the ceiling. Was this the moment to tell him she loved him, that she wanted to have his child – or would that be perceived as a consolation prize for his lost little girl? For a writer there were times when she despaired of her inability to express herself, her abject failure to seize the moment.

Sitting by his side in the Directors' Box she knew that the moment had passed, was no longer there to be seized, but despite her avowed declarations of a desire for independence she fervently hoped it would come again.

Dimitri Murganev was back in training and actually in the starting line-up. David Sinclair and Claudio Barlucci had discussed the matter at length with their manager, Ray Fowler, and had formed the same view as Patti. If the two men with women missing from their lives did not work to fill the hours, they would both go crazy. They also hoped that having his fellow countryman alongside him in the team would ignite the spark that had been so sadly missing from his play to date. Not that Murganev had shown any great pleasure in having somebody with whom he could chat in Russian other than his young interpreter.

'I'm not so sure,' Ray Fowler had said in his cautious way. 'They hardly seemed to recognise that the other was there. None of this embracing and kissing like I've seen the foreigners do. Bunch of poofs.'

Sinclair had smiled. He knew that Fowler actually fined his players if they celebrated a goal with anything other than a handshake.

'The referee's not stopped the watch,' he'd say, 'so just get the ball out of the back of the net, stick it on the centre circle and start playing again. You're wasting time you could more usefully spend scoring if you're shagging each other on the field.'

Now, the crowd rose as the Hertsmere players emerged from the tunnel. Karpov ran to the middle of the pitch and turned to clap each section of the stadium, including the visiting fans, while the announcer introduced him over the tannoy system.

'Real little showman, this one,' Sinclair said to Mark.

'Oh yes, he's that all right,' he agreed glumly.

'You don't sound as if you like him.'

'I don't. You asked me to sign him, not to marry him. I must tell you, David, if I'd known Lennie Simons was going to be involved in the negotiations I think I'd have told you to back off. Or at least to leave me out of it.'

'I'm sorry about that. Did you find out how he nosed his way into the deal?' Sinclair asked, his eyes now firmly fixed on the pitch, his mind paying only minimal attention to the conversation. He was watching a football match – more importantly he was watching his team, the team he'd supported since his childhood, the team he now owned.

'I'm not sure,' Mark replied, but as the whistle signalled the

227

kick-off Sinclair was no longer listening at all.

The first Brentham attack was broken up by Stuart Macdonald, who had made a point of seeking Mark out before the match. Mark recalled their conversation.

'Forget what Sally said to you. She's hurting and she needs someone to hurt.'

'She's entitled,' Mark said, 'but I'm grateful. She must be hell to live with.'

The two men, who had shared the same woman, shared a rueful smile of understanding. It was odd the way Mark could now watch the Hertsmere captain play and wish him nothing but success, whereas once he had simply wanted him to break a leg so irretrievably that he would never play again. He had stolen his wife, his child, and he thought he had also stolen his career; but that was all in the past, and Mark clapped along with the rest of the crowd as he swept a magnificent ball forward to Karpov. The Russian cleverly chipped the ball up for Nicky Collier to nod forward and there was Karpov again, running up to sweep the ball past the Brentham keeper. Collier looked amazed at his own skill, and was still lumbering back to the half-way line when Karpov was already in the centre circle, his arms raised once again to accept the adulation of the crowd.

Sinclair, never one for the niceties of being the chairman, was standing, roaring his appreciation along with the rest of them. 'What a goal. The lad's a genius! Well done, Mark. Simons may have pushed you all the way, but he looks cheap at the price.'

Mark Rossetti picked out Murganev on the pitch. He looked anything but happy at his team's lead. Cheap at the price perhaps Karpov had been, but it was not only Hertsmere who were picking up the tab.

CHAPTER 40

Although Hertsmere had not added to their score by half-time, there had been only one team in the game. If Murganev had taken two easy chances the match would have been all but won. Each time it had been his fellow Russian who put him through, once a tantalising pass that split the two central defenders, the other a curling cross that found Murganev on the edge of the penalty area. On the first occasion Murganev fell over his own feet, and on the second, with the keeper wrong-footed, he ballooned the ball not just over the bar but also over the wall of the ground.

'I think he should take Murganev off and put him out of his misery,' Patti said.

Barlucci, who had never given up on his pursuit of Patti, took the opportunity to run the back of his hand down her cheek. 'I tell my friend David we should make you the manager,' he said.

'He couldn't afford me,' she replied.

'Ah, but I could,' Barlucci said with a wistful expression on his face. He had a guest at the match who watched the exchange with amusement. Suddenly remembering his manners, Barlucci introduced him to Patti, Mark, Rob Davies and Savvas who stood around him in a semi-circle.

'This is Nikolei Yevneko. He is going to help me with business in Russia.'

Yevneko extended his hand first to Patti and held hers just a little longer than was necessary. Then, despite his seemingly frail appearance, he firmly gripped the hands of Rob and Mark, although it was the former who seemed reluctant to let him go, staring into his eyes, trying to remember why he should know the name.

'Mr Rossetti I know of. I have a deep interest in football. And you, Mr Davies, what do you do?'

'Robby is married to the chief executive of the club, Helen Archer,' Barlucci explained. His command of English was much improved, although his accent was still thick enough to warrant a separate interpreter.

'And you also work within football, Mr Davies?' Yevneko persisted.

'It seems that way some of the time. But not exactly. I'm a policeman.'

Yevneko nodded, as if he had never met anybody from the profession before and it was a matter of all-consuming interest.

'Fascinating. You must bring your wife to eat with me sometime. Football and crime – it will make a good mix of dinner-time conversation.'

'You live in England?' Rob asked.

'I can tell you are a policeman; you ask questions. Policemen and journalists – they are very alike, is that not correct, Miss Delaney?'

Patti opened her mouth to say something, but Yevneko had already moved on.

'Yes, I live in England. I like it here, the way of life. There is something very tolerant, very restful about this country. I have a house in The Bishop's Avenue, of which I am very proud. I assume Claudio has your number. I will be in touch.'

Barlucci and Yevneko edged their way back towards the table of food and, as Mark went to follow them, Rob held him back by his arm.

'That man with Barlucci, have you seen him before?'

'No. Why?'

Davies did not answer, but continued, 'Did you know that Barlucci was doing any deals in Russia?'

'He may have mentioned it. He does deals all over the world.'

'I shouldn't really be telling you this, but treat it as a professional confidence . . .' Davies said.

'Nice to think you regard me as a fellow professional,' Mark replied.

'Perhaps. Listen, Mark, it was suggested to me by Clemenceau that I focus on the new Russian community in England. I was told to get to see one particular estate agent who seems to have got himself a cosy little number finding properties for the guys with money who want to settle over here. I've no real idea why, but he was very edgy about my visit when he knew what it was about. I made it clear that, by way of being an expert, he was helping us, but that didn't do a lot for him either. Anyway, I railroaded him into letting me look through the purchase files. I thought the name Yevneko rang a bell, and when he said he lived in The Bishop's Avenue I knew why. He'd bought a house through this agent, Danny Lewis, not in his own name, but through a company. But Lewis had his name on the file.'

'That's not a criminal offence, is it?'

'No, not yet, though it may have been in Russia at some stage. You know – property is theft and all that.'

'So what's the problem with Barlucci's pal?'

'Maybe there is no problem, but it wasn't just the fact that he'd bought an expensive house for himself. On nearly all the other sales that Lewis had in his Russian filing cabinet this man Yevneko had paid the deposits as well.'

'Maybe he's got a lot of friends. Maybe he's the only one that speaks English.'

'Maybe,' Rob said, 'but I'm not convinced. Let's go and watch some more football, then remind me to have a word with Claudio at the end of the match. I don't know where he

231

met Mr Yevneko, but I think he has to watch him carefully. Our Italian pal can be quite naive at times. He might think that he's using Yevneko to expand his business, but it may well be that Claudio is the one who's being used.'

'Can't be all bad if he invited you to dinner,' Patti chimed in.

Rob watched the man's retreating back as he returned to his seat in the Box. 'I think if we accept I'll be sure to take a couple of long spoons.' And then he turned back to the football for the next forty-five minutes, although his mind was several thousand miles away, in a much colder climate.

CHAPTER 41

If anybody was happier than David Sinclair with the final three-nil victory for Hertsmere, then it was Lennie Simons. He was back in the big time again as far as he was concerned. The bastards of the establishment could do their worst, but you couldn't keep a good man down. He'd done really well for Tolly Karpov, and Hertsmere could feel they'd not got such a bad bargain after all. He'd scored twice on his debut and set the other goal up for Nicky Collier. You had to be a special sort of player to make that donkey look talented.

And then there was Murganev as well. He didn't know why, but there was obviously a bit of bad feeling between the two of them. Now if Murganev had used him to negotiate his deal instead of that oddball amateur Alex Jennings, then he had no doubt that he could have settled in by now. Simons had convinced himself over the years that what he accomplished for the players within their contracts actually made them better footballers, which was why he described everybody who joined his stable as superstars. If it made them feel better, it cost him nothing, and he had no awareness of how the rest of those truly knowledgeable about the game regarded him. He was a joke, but he was also a particularly dangerous one.

Ray Fowler had finally taken pity on Murganev after the second miss, and his replacement by Pat Devine, the tiny Irish midfielder, had been the signal for the two goals that had buried Brentham. Murganev had gone by the time Simons got to the Players' Lounge to meet with his latest client, and to tout anybody else who might be prepared to entrust their futures to his indelicate clutches. Karpov, though, was still very much there, holding court at the bar, signing autographs, accepting drinks from the normal bunch of hangers-on and soccer groupies who wheedled their way in to be with their idols after the match.

The agent made a big show of greeting his client, throwing his arms around him in a proprietorial manner that left nobody else in the bar, rival agents included, in any doubt as to whom he belonged.

'Great stuff, superstar. I've got a bunch of journalists outside fighting to get the first exclusive interview with you. Tomorrow I start phoning the boot companies. You keep this up, and we'll be in there talking to Hertsmere at the end of the season for a new extended contract.'

Karpov listened attentively, his head held to one side as if waiting for Simons to say something of great interest. 'You told me, Lennie, that you got me a great deal, that it was the best. Why do we need to talk again so soon?'

Simons took a step back and looked at him to see if this was a show of Russian humour, but the player seemed perfectly serious.

'Yeah, well, that's the way things work in England. You push them to the brink, then you do the business and you push them a bit further, because you've not committed yourself that long to make them feel secure. That's why I said sign for the rest of the season and two more years only, not the four-year deal that wanker Rossetti wanted. Before you turn around the first year will be up; they've only got another year then, so that's when you move in for the kill and offer them another three. But for a bigger signing-on fee, bigger salary. If they don't want to know then they'll soon realise they're going to lose you. Nobody wants to keep an unhappy player. That's part of my job. Making you happy and sometimes making sure the club thinks you're unhappy.'

The answer seemed to satisfy Karpov, because he nodded intelligently. 'You know of a place I can go to? One with pretty girls.'

Simons looked around him to see who was listening, then put a finger on his lips. 'Sure, son, sure. Only this club is a bit old fashioned about things like that. They like their players tucked up in bed with their wives and a cup of cocoa.'

'I have no wife and cocoa I don't like. Business is over. We've won. I can enjoy myself. It is not against the rules?'

'No, it's not against the rules. But behave yourself. And I think there's one bit of business you've forgotten.'

'No, I don't forget. I owe you money. You do a good job and you get paid for it. You come to the hotel tomorrow night, and I have it ready for you.'

'In cash, like we discussed?' There was an eagerness about Simons' question that Karpov recognised and could deal with.

'Yes, in cash. I remember,' he said dismissively.

Simons relaxed. It was all going to work out so well. He'd already been promised his fee from another source. The player didn't know that, and the source didn't know that the player was going to pay him as well. That was the way Simons liked things to be. Play both ends against the middle and the middle is sure to gain. All he had to do was make sure that Lennie Simons remained in the middle. This time around nobody, but nobody was going to push him out again.

'I'll see you tomorrow then, Tolly. I'll just get a cab to take you where you want to go. Don't worry, I'll give him the address. You'll like it, lots of pretty girls.'

'You'll come with me?'

Simons narrowed his eyes. 'No, not really my scene. Maybe I'll join you later,' he said as an automatic response, but without any real intention.

He went out to hail a cab and then despatched his player. A few of the younger team-members were still hanging around the bar. The rest of the established agents had already left. It was time for Simons to move in. Karpov might have young women on his mind, but Simons' business was young men. To him they represented money and Lennie Simons loved money more than anything else in life. There were times when he loved the feel of the crisp new notes so much that he'd almost be prepared to die for them.

CHAPTER 42

'Tell me more about that man, the one who was with Barlucci,' Mark insisted as he, Patti, Rob and Helen sat together in a local restaurant after the match. 'We know Barlucci has had some odd business associates in the past, and nobody has ever said he was a babe in the wood, but I tend to believe this time he's firmly on the side of the angels,' Mark replied.

'It's not Barlucci I'm worried about,' Rob said. 'I tried to have a word with him after the game, but he wasn't having any of it. Said Yevneko had been introduced to him by a potential joint venture partner in Russia. That he's a serious businessman. Claudio likes serious businessmen. It's only when it comes to football that he throws the business part aside.'

His wife put her hand proudly on his arm. 'That's very astute of you.'

'Not really. I just have to listen to what you say on the rare occasions you're there to cook me a meal.'

'I'll have to be more discreet then, won't I?' Helen said, laughing.

Mark liked her. He liked them both. There was a refreshing honesty about the pair of them compared to the world in which he had found himself living.

'Do you think there could be some connection between Yevneko and Sonya Murganev?' Patti asked.

'Did I say that?' Rob said with a smile. 'That's journalistic mathematics; two and two equals five.'

'Are you going to let your husband talk to me like that?' Patti asked Helen without any real malice. 'Sometimes, Mr Clever Policeman, two and two make a story.'

Rob became suddenly serious. 'Look, Patti, if you've got any ideas of writing a story about this Nikolei Yevneko, forget it. I'm asking Clemenceau to run some checks on him tomorrow, but my gut feeling is that he's rich and he's powerful—'

'And he's bent?' Mark said. 'Rob, if there's any chance, any chance at all, that he may have something to do with Emma's kidnapping or know something about it, then we have to follow it up.'

'We?' Rob repeated. 'No, Mark, the only "we" here is the police force. No one-man kamikaze efforts. These are big boys.'

'I've taken on big boys before.'

'Yes, and they nearly got you killed. There's no real reason to think Yevneko has anything to do with our matter in hand. He's Russian, that's for sure. He helps friends buy houses. Barlucci, at least, thinks he's still well connected back home. None of that makes him the kidnapper of your daughter or the killer of Lydia Karlovich. He just happened to shove himself under my nose twice in a matter of days. Detection's not that easy. It doesn't rely upon coincidence.' Rob finished his lecture and looked at his watch. 'Time to go. I'm on early shift tomorrow and I want to get cracking. I think I'll ask our associates at the Home Office what Yevneko put down on his immigration application.'

'And you'll keep me posted, won't you?' Mark said.

Rob hesitated.

'Come on, Rob, you've got to be a friend rather than a copper.'

'And you've got to promise that you'll leave things in my hands. It's no good my finding Emma if her father's not around when I bring her back.'

'Yes, you're right, Rob. Don't worry, I'll be good.'

They had a brief argument about who should pay the bill, and although Mark and Patti were clearly in a better financial position than the other couple they compromised and split it down the middle at Rob's insistence.

Driving home in the car, Patti put her hand on Mark's knee. 'I never thought we'd be regarded as the wealthy relations,' she said.

'It's not brought us a lot of happiness. Sometimes I wonder why we couldn't have just left the Russian thing alone, settled for Leo's properties here. It was more than enough.'

'But it wasn't what Leo wanted. He was a cunning old sod – may he rest in peace. He knew the foreign challenge would bring us closer together, and that was what he wanted.'

'And he was right, but for all the wrong reasons. Patti, how tired are you?'

'Why?'

'I just wondered if you fancied a diversion through Hampstead on the way home?'

'Might that just be through The Bishop's Avenue?'

'Might you just be psychic?'

'Mark, you promised to leave the investigation to Rob.'

'No, I told him not to worry and that I'd be good. There's nothing too bad or worrying about looking for a house in a road.'

Patti sighed. She knew him well enough to realise that he wouldn't be able to rest until he'd satisfied his curiosity. 'But you don't even know which house it is. They're huge properties down there. With some of them you can't even see the front door behind the drive.'

'OK. Just one cruise up and down the road. If there's nothing to give a hint as to which house is Yevneko's we turn around and go home. Is that a deal?'

'Deal,' she said resignedly as he turned the car around and began to head south towards London.

Thirty minutes later she was accusing him of breaking the agreement. 'Mark, we've been up and down five times. We'll get arrested for loitering if you do it one more time. It's late, it's dark. What do you expect to find?'

Reluctantly, he turned the vehicle around and began to head back down the hill from Kenwood to pick up the North Circular and the route home. To their left was a house fronted by large pillars and a builder's sign that indicated there were substantial works underway somewhere on the acreage. The security gates opened as they passed and a car came out, the driver, clearly confident there would be little or no traffic about at that time of night, barely bothering to look. Mark braked and as he did so nearly swerved into a tree.

'Look at that,' he exclaimed.

'Pretty crap driving,' Patti observed, tired and just wanting to be in bed.

'No, I mean look at that. I know that number plate. LS 1. It's Lennie Simons.'

'So maybe he's visiting. There are a load more people who live in this road than Yevneko.'

'Come on, Patti. This road, this night – Simons, of all people. Barlucci hates him as much as we do. Let's assume he has been visiting Yevneko. This Russian pops up in Rob's investigations, then he surfaces at the match, having somehow or other contrived to meet Claudio and wangled an invitation, and now Simons.'

'What was it Rob was saying over dinner? Detection doesn't rely on coincidence.'

'Yes, but we're not allowed to be detectives, you heard what Rob said to me. So let's take a chance on coincidence. I think a word with my old friend Lennie Simons might be appropriate.'

'Whatever you say, Mark, only can it wait until tomorrow? I've got to get to bed.'

He put his hand on the inside of her thigh. 'That's the best offer I've had all night,' he replied, suddenly lightened by this glimpse of a breakthrough.

Purposefully and with no thought for any speed limit he drove the two of them home.

CHAPTER 43

Lennie Simons was feeling very pleased with himself. Liam O'Donnell, one of the Hertsmere players he'd chatted up after the match, had called and asked to meet him; and once Lennie got as far as a meeting, then he knew he had the player and his percentage of all future income in the bag. He'd also had a call from Mark Rossetti, which he'd taken the greatest pleasure in not returning. If he thought he was going to interfere with his business again then he had another thought coming. It would take more than a played-out ex-drunk ex-pro to keep Lennie Simons off the case.

He glanced at his watch. He prided himself on always being on time. Punctuality and reliability – his clients liked that, even if they didn't always practise those two virtues themselves. He'd never understood how grown men who only worked for a couple of hours a day in the morning found it impossible to get anywhere on time in the afternoon. He'd lost count of the number of times he'd fixed up appearances for players at local shops, interviews, picture shoots, and he'd been left prowling on his own, struggling to raise them on his mobile while trying to appease whoever had agreed to pay good money for the privilege of their presence. There was always an excuse: the wife had left them baby-sitting; they'd had to finish their snooker game and had lost track of the time; they'd suddenly felt the pressing need to test-drive a new sports car. Some days he didn't know why he was still in the game; but on days like this, when the sun shone and new

243

clients and cash beckoned, then he knew the answer to that one.

He pulled into the drive of the hotel where Karpov was staying. It was the best place for miles around, and Simons felt a sense of accomplishment in the knowledge that he'd negotiated a six-month stay into the contract with all expenses paid. Looking at the comfort of the hotel and comparing it to what he'd seen in Moscow, Karpov must have thought he'd died and gone to heaven.

He went straight up to the room, ignoring reception, and knocked on the door. The player took a few moments to answer, and when he did it looked as if he had just rolled out of bed.

'It's two already?' the Russian asked with a yawn. 'It was a late night. I like the club you sent me to. I went back. It is more fun than the club I play for. And I got up early to go to the bank for you. Then I come back and go to bed. Today there is no training. This is hard to believe for me. In Moscow we train every day. Your English footballers, they have a soft life.' Karpov laughed, to indicate he thought he had made a joke, and Simons made a strangulated noise to show he'd appreciated it.

'Yeah, they've got it cushy all right. Maybe one day you'd like to spell it out for them, tell them all the advantages of living and working in a *real* democracy.'

Karpov went to the security box that was fitted in the room, fiddled with the combination, and handed Simons a sealed package. 'Twenty thousand. And another twenty for you at the start of next year. It is what you want, yes?'

'Sure it's what I want, it's what I earn.' He shoved it into his briefcase. 'No need to count it. If it's wrong I know where you are. Now I've got you a fair bit of that back anyway. I've had an offer of a basic ten grand a year for you to wear Pila boots. Score a few goals, get your country along the path in the European Championships, and it could be worth double or treble that. How does that sound, superstar?'

'It doesn't sound a lot.'

'Look, Tolly old love, I've got to explain some of the basic facts of life. You're new here; you've had a good start, but you're not playing for a fashionable team. I explained that to you before you came. Also, you're not English. Believe me, what I've done for you is an excellent deal. Next time around you've done the business on the field, I'll do you better business off it. OK?'

Karpov shrugged. 'It has to be. And what else? I need to get back to sleep.' He nodded in the direction of the bedroom.

'You cunning little rabbit. You've got a bird in there, haven't you? Well, you find yourself a nice English rose with big knockers and I've a couple of tabloids who'll pay good money for an interview and a few pictures. Just let me know. I've also got you a car if you want it from a local garage. You only need to have a few pictures taken when they hand it over.'

As he caught a glimpse of movement through the bedroom door, Simons looked a little embarrassed. 'I'll be off and leave you to it. Don't tire yourself out too much. Save something for the next match. You've got them with their tongues hanging out begging for more. They've forgotten everything about poor old Murganev – everything except what he claimed to be when he first came here. Actions speak louder than words, that's what I always say.'

He returned to his car, shaking his head at the ingratitude of footballers. ' "It doesn't sound a lot." Who does he think he is, Lineker and Gascoigne rolled into one? Nobody else could have got that sort of money after one game.'

He turned the ignition key. Nothing happened. As he turned it again, the thought going through his mind before the explosion blew him to oblivion was that he'd treat himself to a new car with some of the money, but keep the personalised number plates.

245

CHAPTER 44

Nikolei Yevneko was not a patient man. Back home in Moscow if anybody had an appointment with him they would not be late – or at least they would not be late more than once. He had a strict code of discipline. For up to five minutes it was a personal warning, up to fifteen a warning from one of his larger associates, half an hour and they found themselves losing their watch on the way out, even if it were a Rolex. Anything more than half an hour and he made sure they would not be attending any meetings, late or not, for at least a month.

Yevneko prowled the reception room of his house and looked down the drive to where the builders were working on the site for the heated swimming pool. English workers – he almost spat out the words – they arrived at ten, had a cup of tea, then broke for lunch. They read their papers, they looked at the half-naked women, they had their tea, and then they went home. If he had control of them for just one day, he would turn them into a real workforce. Sometimes he despaired of capitalism. Perhaps that was why he had turned towards it, to show the West how it really should be done.

He picked up the glass of lemon tea and sipped it thoughtfully, his tongue oblivious to the scalding liquid, his palate well trained to withstand anything. The English even managed to ruin tea, with their milk and sugar. They still had so much to learn. There were times when he thought they needed a revolution here to teach them the lessons that his

247

parents and grandparents had been forced to endure in some of the hardest schools of all.

Eventually a car turned in at the gates and the driver emerged, looking around him as if seeking a potential escape route. Yevneko watched him walk up the drive and ring at the doorbell. He had already told his servant in which room he wanted see his visitor. He had selected the library, where he could sit at his antique mahogany desk and the other man could be perched on an uncomfortable chair, leaving him in no doubt that this was the equivalent of an interview in the headmaster's study.

He gave him time to be taken up the stairs, left him an extra few moments to sit and worry, then made his way up to the book-lined room. Yevneko liked books. Generally speaking he preferred them to people. He had dismissed employees for reading a paperback folded in half, thus breaking or creasing its spine. The only books upon his shelves which did not look brand new were the first editions he lovingly and carefully collected.

The visitor spun around in the chair and leapt to his feet as Yevneko came into the room and seated himself behind the desk.

'Sit down, sit down, Dimitri,' Yevneko said to Murganev.

The footballer did as he was told. He seemed awkward and out of place in the room, as if any unrehearsed movement might break an article of value.

'Do you read at all, Dimitri?' Yevneko asked.

The player shook his head.

'Ah, but you should. So much knowledge to be gained, and you have so much time in which to gain it. If only I were a sportsman, able to earn my living by a few hours' training in the morning, the odd game maybe twice a week. All that leisure time, all that reading time. You do not appreciate the gift that G-d gave you.'

Murganev glared sullenly at the carpet, his heel tracing a pattern in its thick green pile.

Yevneko noticed what he was doing. 'You like it? It reminds you of the turf. It costs a little more, so I should be grateful if you could refrain from marking it with what I perceive are your somewhat grimy boots.'

Murganev stopped slowly, his mind threatening opposition to the command, but knowing he would gain nothing by it. Since the very first time he had met Nikolei Yevneko his loss had been the businessman's gain. Businessman – that was how he chose to describe himself, but Murganev knew otherwise. He could dress himself in the smartest of business suits, surround himself with the finest of houses, the best of books, affect the most educated accent, but he was still a thief. He had stolen most of Murganev's signing-on fee from Hertsmere, was taking three-quarters of his wages – and for what? He had made promises, but they were merely secondary to the threats.

'Go abroad, Dimitri. We'll set it all up for you,' Yevneko had said. 'You'll earn more than you ever dreamed of, and we'll look after it for you once we've taken our commission.'

And he had been naive enough to think they might genuinely manage his affairs.

'What percentage will you take?' he had asked Yevneko back in Moscow, sitting in the man's luxurious apartment.

'Don't worry your head about such things. We'll take care of everything. We'll look after your wife and daughter as well.'

'What do you mean? They go wherever I go. I'll look after them.'

Yevneko had smiled as if he were explaining something to a child. 'That may not be possible. You will be very busy. We think it may be better if they stay in Moscow, so that we can keep an eye on them.'

They had stayed, and as Murganev had done everything he was told, he realised they were hostages and the first time he stepped out of line they would suffer. And now they were missing.

'Where's Sonya, and my Katiana?' he asked in an explosive rush of words.

Yevneko carefully took a cigar from the humidor, rolled it under his nose and clipped it with precision. 'You know, Dimitri, I was going to ask you that same question. We are not very happy with the Murganev family. There seems to be a little ingratitude being shown to us for all we have done for them. You have hardly covered yourself with glory on the field—'

Murganev began to speak. 'It was your advice to announce that I was the greatest. How can I play under those circumstances? How can I do my best when you are holding my wife and daughter as prisoners?'

'Don't ever, ever interrupt me again. I ask the questions, you answer them. Do you understand?' He leaned forward as far as he could across the desk. Murganev avoided his eyes and said nothing. In one darting movement Yevneko pushed the lit cigar hard against the player's bare forearm. Murganev squealed with pain.

'If I ask a question you answer it. I hate to repeat myself. It wastes the valuable time of which I have less than you – although if we make no progress it may suddenly transpire that you have no time at all. Now, do you understand?'

'I understand,' Murganev replied softly, holding his arm.

'So, you ask me where is your wife and child. Now, why do I think you may know the answer to that question?' Yevneko's tone was soft, and a man who knew him better than Dimitri Murganev would have recognised that as a danger signal. The quiet before the storm.

'I don't know where they are,' Murganev said defiantly.

Yevneko shook his head sadly, in a gesture of despair at the foolishness of youth. 'Your wife ran away from us, Dimitri, and she took the English brat with her. Now the first action was stupid. If she'd stayed in Russia then that would have been a little local difficulty and we could have coped with it; but she chose to come here and to involve others. To involve the British police and your friend Rossetti. It all gets complicated, and we like our affairs to be simple. We help you get a career outside Russia; you pay us. Simple?'

Murganev rose to leave.

'I asked a question. I did not say you could go. Simple?'

'Yes.'

'Well, it gets simpler. Until she gets back we take a hundred and ten per cent of what you earn. And you start performing. You earn some bonuses. Now you can go. We'll collect at the end of next week. Always assuming you and the beautiful Sonya are not reunited by then.'

Yevneko had the player shown to the door and watched him open his car. Just before he got in Murganev shot a look up at the window that was one of pure hatred. Yevneko smiled. He was sure the player had been bluffing when he asked as to the whereabouts of his wife and child; but Nikolei Yevneko had not got where he was today by ignoring possibilities rather than probabilities. And so, as he smoked his cigar and finished his tea, he began to work on the problem that, if neither he nor her husband knew where Sonya Murganev was hiding, then who the hell did?

CHAPTER 45

Mark and Patti sat soberly on the settee at her flat, his left hand idly playing with her right. There was a blank TV screen ahead of them and two half-drunk cups of tea at their side. To any casual observer it would have been a picture of domestic bliss, but the subject of their conversation was violent death.

'First the train, then Lydia, them Simons. It's as if we're leaving a trail of destruction behind us,' Mark said, his brow furrowed with worry.

'You can't be sure Simons' murder had anything to do with you,' Patti replied without conviction.

'Come on, Patti. This is me you're talking to, not an editor you're trying to put off the scent. Simons represents Karpov. Somehow or other he's got himself mixed up in Russian events. I went to Moscow to bring the little bastard back. Simons dies in the car park of the hotel where he's staying. It's all tied up, everything; and out there in the middle of it is my daughter, if she's still alive.'

'Why would anyone want to kill Emma?' Patti asked sincerely. 'And don't ask why anybody would want to kill Lennie Simons. He made enemies like you and I make cups of tea.' She took a sip, made a face and then added, 'Only a damn sight more efficiently. This is terrible. I'll put the kettle on again, unless you can live with watching me drink something a bit stronger.'

'I'm not sure how much longer I can go on without a drink myself,' he said, feeling totally lost.

'Come on. The fact that you can actually say that rather than just zip in and open the bottle means you aren't going to break the dry spell now. How long's it been?'

'I don't even need to look at the calendar. Two years, and I fell off the wagon once. That was nine months ago. I need a drink, Patti.'

'What you need is to find your daughter, that and a bit of tender loving care.' She put her arm around him and gently kissed him on the cheek. He seemed hardly to notice. He sat with his head cupped in his hands staring ahead of him, his mind working at the problem. If there was a problem then there had to be a solution. Only death was finite. He had to do something. He couldn't just leave things to drift along and rely upon the police. They were doing their best, but their best wasn't good enough. They were playing in the same game, but their stakes were different. He had to do something, to make something happen. It was a risk, but he could not continue fencing with shadows. He needed to bring them out into the open, to see their faces, the colour of their eyes. Yet, if they came out of their holes, he was certain their weaponry would out-gun his own; but were their minds capable of out-thinking him? They, them. Who were they? Did they have his daughter? Or were they looking for her too – or, perhaps of more significance, were they looking for Sonya Murganev? And if they were looking for her, was his innocent daughter about to become – or had she already become – a victim?

He said nothing for a while, tormenting himself before daring to put his thoughts into words, knowing that once it was said it had to be acted upon.

'Patti. You know, I think we've been approaching this entirely the wrong way. What if Emma's disappearance has nothing to do with her? What if she was just in the wrong place at the wrong time, with the wrong person?'

'The wrong person?'

'Yes, Sonya Murganev. Something or someone makes

Sonya run. She's got an English teenager on her hands. What does she do, abandon her?'

Patti tapped her teeth with her nails. He normally found it an irritating habit, but now he hardly noticed. 'Why not?' she said thoughtfully. 'She could have taken her back to the hotel and left her there to wait for us to get back.'

Mark hit his forehead in self-annoyance. 'Unless she didn't think we'd get back. Maybe she knew there'd be an attack on the train, knew it was aimed at us. It means she may have dangerous friends as well as dangerous enemies.'

Patti shook her head. 'Doesn't make sense. If she knew we were on the hit list she had to be involved. It's not likely she'd pick that up by way of social chit-chat. And if she was involved, then why make the grand gesture and save your daughter?'

Mark nodded slowly and reluctantly. 'Perhaps. As you've said before, she is a mother. Maybe she draws the line about killing kids, but their parents are fair game. The trouble is that we just don't know enough about her to understand what really makes her tick.'

'We could talk to her husband.'

'Dimitri? He says little enough in Russian let alone English. He's been a total misery since the day he arrived. You can't even defend him by saying it's got worse since his wife and kid vanished. That, at least, would have been understandable.'

'It has to be worth a try. The interpreter's a nice young guy.'

'Sure, why not?' Mark said without conviction. His voice slowed down. There was something there, some idea that kept slipping out of his grasp, elusive, tantalising. He had to pursue it, find it, then hold it tight.

'How easy is it to get out of Russia, Patti?'

'Certainly easier than it was, but then everything's comparable. I'm not sure anything's easy if you're a Russian.'

'But if you were a Russian travelling with your daughter

and an English child, then it has to be easier, doesn't it?'

He'd abandoned all thoughts of Emma as a young woman. She was a child again and desperately needing the help of her father.

'I suppose so,' said Patti, beginning to see where he was leading. He had come a long way since she'd first met the beaten ex-professional footballer, and she wondered just what he might have made of his life if he'd given his mind the chance to develop, rather than abandoning school for a sporting life as soon as he could.

Mark rose to his feet, his body coiled with inspiration, his hands punching the air with ideas. 'That was it! Sonya panics. She needs to get out of Russia, needs to be in the same country as her husband. And we hand her the means to get out on a plate. Now she's shepherding this English girl across, taking her back to her parents. She got out before we even knew that Emma was missing. It needn't have raised an eyebrow.'

Patti resisted the temptation to chase Mark around the room, and leaned back in her chair whilst lighting a cigarette. Just as she'd got away with the teeth-tapping rebuke, the smoke that she blew out into the air similarly escaped criticism.

'Let's assume you're right, Mark,' she said. 'Why does Sonya have to leave Russia so secretly? You said the club had told Murganev his wife could come any time she wanted to.'

'Maybe she did want. Maybe something was holding her back there.'

Patti was now warming to the theory. 'So she comes here with your Emma . . . But your daughter's not stupid. She must know we'd be worried sick about her. Why doesn't she get in touch?'

Mark was silent for a moment, freeze-framed at the window. 'I'm not sure. Could be Sonya's persuaded her that it's too dangerous. As you say she's not stupid. Quite the reverse. She's very bright, even a bit streetwise, although I've never wanted to admit it. She can balance the odds as well as the next person, better probably. What does she do, put us through a bit of misery or put the lives of two more people at risk?'

'You don't think Sonya's been in touch with her husband?'

'I don't know,' Mark replied. 'I can't see him telling us. But maybe you're right. Maybe we should try and ask him a few more questions.'

'They have to be the right questions, Mark. We don't want to panic anybody into doing anything rash.'

'You're dead right when you talk about rash. But I do want to panic them. If I'm right and Emma's not been kidnapped at all, perhaps isn't even being held against her will, then that would explain why we've had no demands, no note, no contact.'

'Yes, yes, it does,' Patti said, feeling her heart pounding. She knew Mark was not going to leave it at that, that once he had an idea he would see it through to its end.

'So,' he continued, 'that's what we need – a note. If we make it public, then whoever's looking for Sonya as well as us has to react. They come running and we're waiting.'

'Mark, it all sounds fine in principle, but we can't do this ourselves. We need to tell the police.'

He shook his head. 'No.' It was a positive negative, if that were possible. It left no room for negotiation. 'Can't you see we'd be better off if they also believe the note is genuine?' he continued. 'I've nothing to substantiate anything I've said. It's all guesswork and hunches, but I can justify it because I know my daughter. Tell this to Rob Davies and he'll start applying a Mr Plod mentality. Even if he finally comes around to the idea, it'll take him too long to get anything done.'

Patti lit yet another cigarette, looking at Mark challengingly, then took a deep draw on the nicotine before speaking. 'So let me get this straight. We write a false ransom note and give it to the police.'

'Yes.'

'I can't believe you're saying this.'

'You're a journalist. You can believe anything. And because you're a journalist you can make others believe as well. You make sure it gets maximum publicity and it's your exclusive.'

'You promised me an exclusive when we first met.'

'And you got it. This is a bonus.'

'Thanks. And what about the little matter of wasting police time, obstructing the course of justice, faking a crime you don't even know's been committed? I'm not sure of all the technicalities but it sounds to me a substantial enough list of offences to make sure we both end up behind bars.'

'I'd rather be behind bars with my daughter alive than walking the streets with her dead.'

Patti sat looking at him for some ten seconds, which seemed to them both to last much longer. The she delivered her judgement. 'You're right, you bastard. That's what I hate about you, you're always right.'

She pulled a coin out of her trouser pocket and tossed it high in the air. 'Call.'

'Heads,' he said without hesitation.

'It's tails. Get me some paper. It looks like I get to draft the note.'

As Mark moved obediently to the desk he did not think it was the right moment to ask her who would have written the note if he'd called correctly.

CHAPTER 46

Detective Sergeant Rob Davies was less than pleased with Patti Delaney. He tried to call her to tell her so, but had only got through to her answerphone. In her physical absence he'd settled for his wife.

'Look at it, Helen. Just look at it. The girl's mad. She gets a ransom demand, the first hint we've got that Emma's still alive, and she splashes it right across the front pages of this rag they call a newspaper. Doesn't she realise that we have to handle it? That's what we're trained for. She's put this kid's life at risk just for a cheap story. I thought she was different, but she's not. She's a journalist and they're all the bloody same. You can't trust any of them.'

Helen was already late for work, and with impending European Cup-Winners' matches she was really busy; but she knew her husband well enough to accept that once he began in this vein he would not be stopped until he finished. He had to talk himself out. It was the Welshman in him.

'And now she's gone on the missing list herself. She thinks she can just toss a time-bomb into the middle of a crowd and then walk away. Well, she's going to learn that she can't. I've a good mind to issue a warrant for her arrest just to show her that she's forgone the right to special privileges.'

Helen half expected him to stomp his foot like a spoilt child, but all he did was to toss the paper on the table so that it fell with a photo of Emma Rossetti staring accusingly upwards.

'I can't believe she didn't discuss this with Mark before she wrote the story,' Helen said.

'And what difference does that make? I'll pull him in as well, just to prove that he doesn't walk on water. He's a bloody footballer who fancies himself as a crime-buster just because he fell lucky once. He's not fucking Sherlock Holmes.'

'But he is Emma's father.'

'Yes, he's that all right. And he should know better, before he lets his girlfriend loose on the world.'

He picked up the paper again as in disbelief, then slammed it down once more to illustrate his point.

'And I'm off to the station. I'm going to get on with the serious business of finding this missing girl before it's too late. At least I'm going to try to do that in whatever time's been left to me.'

He stormed out of the tiny cottage that they'd bought more for the honeysuckle over the door than any practicalities. They both knew that they couldn't raise a family there. Even the ancient cat that Helen had brought with her could hardly be swung – had either of them shown an inclination to do so. But the cottage had been viewed in the early days of their whirlwind relationship, when romance still made them do things they might later live to regret. Helen watched him storm into the car and pull away at a speed that would have had any fellow member of his force who might be watching producing a ticket.

In another, far more impressive house, a man was reading the same headlines and article that had so incensed Rob Davies. Nikolei Yevneko was also less than happy with the news. He had convinced himself that Sonya Murganev was out there somewhere, deliberately hiding, but now it looked as if it might not be the case. Indeed, it appeared as if somebody was seeking to turn the situation to their advantage. It was an intrusion into what he considered to be his rights, his territory.

He idly wondered if whoever was making the demands might be Russian. If they were, then they would pay a far greater price than they might have hoped to receive. He still could not understand the delay between the disappearance and the demand – and anything he did not understand troubled him. Maybe she had gone to somebody she thought she could trust. They had waited, bided their time, and then decided that the temptation was too great, that loyalty was worth less than money. A foolish decision, Yevneko thought.

He was a careful man, meticulous in his planning. He had not got to where he was today by rushing into decisions. Any actions he took were only after lengthy consideration. He saw no reason to change his mind when it came to finding Mrs Murganev.

He rang for his butler to bring him some fresh tea, allowed it to brew a little in the English manner, and, as usual disdaining milk, chose a thin slice of lemon. He gently probed at it until its juices mixed and mingled with the steaming liquid, then took a sip. He savoured it upon his tongue as if tasting a fine wine, then expressed himself satisfied with a quiet sigh of approval. This done, he lifted the phone and dialled a number he knew by heart. A familiar voice answered and without any pleasantries Yevneko said, 'You've seen the papers?'

'I could hardly miss them.'

'Do you have any news for me? Anything that might shed some light on the situation?'

'Not really.'

Yevneko's voice became icy. 'Not really is not good enough. She's out there somewhere, like a . . .' He sought for the correct words. '. . . a loaded gun. She can go off bang and anybody can be hurt. I do not want to be hurt. You understand me.'

'Of course. I am asking questions. It's not easy.'

'When you came aboard for the ride, nobody said it would

261

be easy. Now, if you want to stay, if you want to renew your ticket, you have to work your passage. I think the little writer, Miss Delaney, she knows more than she says in her article. The father, Rossetti, he too. He must be told that if his daughter gets in the line of fire it could be dangerous, maybe even fatal. Can you get that message across?'

There was a hesitation at the other end. 'I'm not sure. I can only try. I am worried about our other friend.'

'Our other friend is my problem. Soon he will be out of the way. So try. And try hard.' A pause. 'And try today.'

Yevneko put down the phone without saying goodbye. The exchange had left him uncertain, and this was no time for uncertainty, of that at least he was sure. He did not feel he could rely upon the assurances he had been given, if indeed they were assurances at all.

He picked up the receiver in a swift, confident movement and dialled again, hammering all the digits with his stubby fingers, as if trying to teach the inanimate instrument a lesson it would not forget. This time he spoke in his native Russian, spitting out his words. They were orders, of that there would be no misunderstanding had anyone been listening. Once he had finished he felt a little better. Things were in hand; plans were underway. His whole operation in England was too delicately poised to be ruined by one hysterical woman.

Footballers. He should have known they would be trouble. Wherever they plied their trade around the world they brought trouble. Death and disaster on and off the pitch. Overpaid hooligans exciting underpaid hooligans. There was little more to it than that. Yet, like the businesses of sex, drugs and extortion, it had seemed highly lucrative. It did not do to turn one's back on any lucrative opportunities, because if one did, one could rest assured somebody else would seize the main chance. Give them the break to make some money and who was to say they would not feel sufficiently confident to step over the borders and into one's other activities?

He finished his tea and set off for a walk around the huge garden. He liked the Englishness of it: the tidy flower beds, the carefully mown lawn, the small orchard at the end with what he called his 'thinking and waiting' seat. The previous owner of the house, Daniel Lewis had told him, had it transported to the orchard from the grounds of his Scottish castle. And here it remained, dark and ancient, carved from one solid piece of oak. It had seemed to recognise him as its new owner from the first moment he had sat upon it. It seemed used to Machiavellian schemes, and the historian in him would wonder from time to time what plots and intrigues had been conceived upon it in the past. Even in winter, or what passed for winter in this country, he would walk purposefully towards it in his overcoat, then rest there until he had thought a problem through and reached a decision. Today the weather was mild, certainly by Moscow standards. He pulled on a jacket from a peg by the patio doors and began to walk down the path. He had no need for further thoughts on the subject of Sonya Murganev and Emma Rossetti. He needed only for his instructions to be obeyed. He needed to wait for Patti Delaney to be brought to him.

CHAPTER 47

Emma Rossetti knew she should have called her mother or father, but somehow she had been too entangled in the drama to have any concerns for the niceties of the situation. Moscow was now just a hazy memory. She could recall kissing her father goodbye, but piecing together what had happened after that was just as difficult as trying to recall last term's set book for English. You read it, studied it, wrote an essay or two, sat an exam, and then consigned it to the dustbin of your mind. This time, though, she had to get it straight, because someday it might be important to tell somebody exactly how it had happened.

If the phone call back in Russia had spooked Sonya, then that was nothing compared to the effect on Emma of Patti's article. It was not so much the glaring headlines – and reference to notes of which she knew nothing – it was the identity of the author. Patti Delaney, her father's lover, a woman who could easily become her step-mother, and who at times Emma desperately wanted to become a part of the family. She enjoyed being with her, felt she was almost an elder sister, eagerly anticipating the intimate girlie secrets, the shared jokes. This now felt like a betrayal, jerking her back to reality.

There had been some initial publicity when it was first realised they had disappeared, but it had all died down and Emma had slipped into the rhythm of life with Sonya and her daughter. She had not asked how the woman had found the cottage out in this remote part of the Cotswolds, between Moreton-in-Marsh and the Rollrights; indeed, there had been moments when she was actually enjoying the clandestine existence, no school, no discipline, the only routine being that there was no routine. The time passed pleasantly enough. The weather was mild for the time of year, the local scenery (what she saw of it) was quite stunning and Sonya, despite the language barrier, was surprisingly good company.

She was young for her age, and Emma began to regard her as another older sister rather than a wife and mother. In some ways she was streetwise and world-weary, but at other times she showed startling naivety. She had brought little clothing with her, and those items she had looked cheap and tawdry to Emma's comparatively sophisticated eye, but when Sonya told her what they had cost she was astonished. The girl, Katiana, was really sweet, and Emma's biggest treat was to be allowed to eat with her and then put her to bed. She realised now just what it was to be an only child, and some days the pain of her parents' separation, the brutal end to their marriage, was almost unbearable. Over the years she had thought she had become accustomed to it, not having her father there when she came home from school. Yet now all the old wounds were being re-opened, and she would tiptoe into the child's room and whisper to her while she lay sleeping, relating not fairy stories but warnings of what was to come.

She did not know whether or not Sonya was in touch with her husband. There was no phone in the cottage and, although she suspected Sonya's walks would sometimes take her to the isolated telephone box half a mile away at the end of a lane, she never asked if she had indeed made any calls. She was amazed at her own self-control. There were many question to which she longed to know the answers, yet pressing the Russian woman for information would have seemed both an intrusion and an imposition.

The problem was what to do next. Until she read Patti's

article she had not bothered to ask, and she was mildly annoyed when she visited the village shop and saw the article in the paper. Those visits in themselves were infrequent. The elderly lady behind the counter, looking like a refugee from 'The Archers', had tried to make polite conversation on the first trip. After that it was a question of waiting till the necessities ran out before stocking up again. It had to be luck rather than judgement that prevented the woman from recognising her and taking some action.

She did not feel she was being held against her will. Yet Sonya had told her when they fled that her life was in danger and that she was relying upon Emma to save her. Sonya Murganev was either a great actress or a desperately frightened woman. Desperate had to be the word to describe reliance on someone as young as Emma.

Emma had never experienced responsibility like this before. When she was very little both of her parents had been there for her, and as an only child she had been adored and spoiled. When things had turned sour between Mark and Sally they had each tried to outdo the other in their love and affection towards her, even when the money began to run out. She had tried to erase the memory of her father's drinking, day and night, the times when she had sat at the top of the stairs, hands clasped around her ears to block out the sounds of their arguments, yet drawn towards them despite herself.

But the burdens placed on the shoulders of a child whose parents' marriage was crumbling were nothing compared to the responsibility she felt now. It would have helped if Sonya had fully explained. When Emma had first been left with the Murganev family she had regarded it as a bore, but preferable to traipsing across the barren wastes of Russia in search of land that might or might not exist. Yet, in a matter of a few hours from her arrival in the apartment, she had discovered that she was actually enjoying herself in Sonya's company. This woman liked Michael Jackson, Boyz II Men, Oasis and

Blur; liked experimenting with make-up and even liked the clothes that had so horrified Emma's parents. Emma was not told to be in bed at any given hour, and had been offered the chance of being taken out to a disco for the evening. When she'd said that she did not feel physically up to it, she'd also felt inclined to offer to baby-sit.

She had actually wanted the girl to wake up so that she could hold her, cuddle her, kiss the softness of her hair and feel the child's dependence upon her.

Sonya had arrived home at two in the morning and it was shortly after that the telephone had rung, its tones sounding amplified in the stillness of the night. Sonya had said little, merely listened and then, with her whole body trembling, had turned to Emma. Her English was hardly fluent, but passable. She had made an effort to learn and seemed anxious to find someone upon whom to practise.

'We have to leave.'

Just like that. No explanation. And Emma had irrationally trusted her enough to ask no questions. We have to leave.

'What about my dad?'

'He'll have to understand. If I try to leave the country alone with Katiana I have no chance. If I travel with you I can say your father is ill and you have to return to school. That they will not expect. If we move quickly they will have no chance to make their plans.'

Emma had wanted to ask who 'they' were, but perhaps it was best not to know, best to travel hopefully. It had all gone incredibly smoothly. A brief glance at her British passport at the airport, a confident piece of acting by Sonya, a smile, a joke, any distraction that would not cause the wary officials at the airport to question the small party of travellers. She had been surprised when they had been met at Heathrow. It meant somebody apart from Sonya knew she was back in Europe, that somebody unknown to her shared their secret.

Curiously, she had not been afraid up to that point. As long as she was with Sonya and the child and they were out of Moscow the danger seemed to have passed. But seated in the back of the car, driving through the darkest night she could remember, she had begun to shiver and shake, unable to control the tears that welled up in her eyes even though she knew the behaviour was childish.

'And I have put behind me childish things and thoughts,' she misquoted to herself.

They'd driven for hours, out on the M4, then on to the M40, the driver sitting in front, upright and silent, knowing where he was going but disclosing nothing. The motorways gave way to rolling shadowy countryside, the hills a shade or two darker than the sky, the headlights catching the odd frightened rabbit in their glare. Frightened rabbits, that's what they were themselves, not knowing to whom the headlights belonged, dark anonymous shapes passing fleetingly in the night. The roads became ever narrower, until they were no more than single-track country lanes, their car forcing any vehicle they met to give way, sometimes to reverse, until they met a slight bend in the road to enable them to pass. There was something intimidating about both the driver and the car: a black Mercedes; the driver's eyes occasionally glimpsed in the mirror also coal black. He drove like an automaton, his hands mechanically moving towards the indicator, the flashing of the light on the dashboard a welcome relief to the monotony.

Eventually they had come to the cottage. He had silently handed them the keys, and then unchivalrously remained seated in the vehicle while they unloaded their own luggage. It was as if he had been threatened with some dire punishment if he overstepped the minimal boundaries of contact. Without waiting to see if they got into the property safely he had driven off into the night, his tail-lights disappearing around the bend, leaving only the spectral and hushed silence of the nocturnal countryside behind him.

The cottage itself, when revealed fully to them in the

morning, was comfortable and well stocked, the sort of place in which she could have enjoyed a family holiday under different circumstances. Had there ever been a time when they had experienced true family holidays? She could not recall it, although photographs leafed through on wet weekends told a different story. Maybe she had blotted out the good times as well as the bad from her past.

Now, with just Sonya and Katiana, she found it increasingly difficult to put her situation into perspective. There was nobody to stop her walking out of the front door, slamming it behind her, hailing a passing car and being transported to safety. Nobody and nothing except the faith placed in her by Sonya. That, and the fact that some small instinctive voice told her she was in more danger when she could be seen than when she was hidden. Not only was she in danger, but so was a mother and a child in a strange country, with enemies waiting to pounce. Emma had arrived at her decision to lie low only after careful consideration. She could have run the risk of phoning one or other of her parents and telling them she was fine, but once they had spoken she doubted her own ability not to reveal her whereabouts. All she could hope was that the circumstances of her disappearance, the absence of any demands for her return, would have reassured them at least in part as to her safety.

But now the game had moved into a different phase. Somebody was demanding money for them, somebody who did not have them to deliver. Were they friend or foe? Were they asking because they were concerned or was it simply a ruse to draw them out in the open, shouting, 'Look at me. I'm not kidnapped. Don't believe them, it's a hoax'?

It was all becoming too much for a little girl. That was how she was beginning to perceive herself, much to her own disgust. All her declarations of independence, her arguments that she was deserving of being treated as a woman, were disintegrating around her.

She lay on the bed in her room, losing the battle to keep the tears from her eyes. She could hear Sonya trying to put Katiana to sleep and knew that the evening with just the two of them lay ahead. The novelty of freedom was beginning to wear off as she realised she was not truly free. Suddenly, her mind made up, she sat bolt upright and swung her legs down to the floor. She took her jacket from the pine wardrobe, checked to ensure she had sufficient coins in her pocket, and then ran as fast as she could towards the distant telephone box. Whatever she did was a gamble, but then, even in her short twelve years, she had discovered that little of what occurred in life was not.

CHAPTER 48

The waiting was the worst. Mark Rossetti felt like the man who lights the blue touch-paper and then hesitates before returning to see why there had not been an explosion. With every moment that passed the risk rose.

He had almost forgotten about football. It was Ray Fowler who called and suggested it might be good for him to come to a match. Hertsmere had defeated Paris Olympique in the European Cup-Winners' Cup and with the next round approaching, the team's indifferent league form was temporarily forgotten. The crowd's optimism was born anew for some success to come the way of their side this season.

David Sinclair and Claudio Barlucci, the two directors who had known him the longest, were sympathy itself, as was the ever caring Savvas.

Helen Davies, on the other hand, who had caught the wrath of her husband, had been a little more brutal. 'You should have brought that note to Rob first off. He's only trying to help you, you know.'

'Yes, I do know. Soon, quite soon, I hope, he'll understand,' Mark had replied, but he could not avoid the hurt look in her eyes.

Sinclair could hardly bring himself to ask if there was any news, tears welling up in his eyes, unable to put into words the sort of world that faces men who lose their daughters.

Barlucci put his huge hands on Mark's shoulders, his frame, as ever, making the tall ex-footballer seem diminutive in comparison. 'Anything I can do, you tell me.' His grip almost hurt, but Mark did not want to insult his Italian friend by wriggling free.

'My English is good now, no?' Barlucci asked with a smile, an attempt to make Mark forget his problems and concentrate on normality.

'Better, Claudio, better – but good? No.'

The Italian looked momentarily hurt, then quickly regained his composure. 'Mark, we are friends, you and I?' The raising of the tone at the end of the sentence told Mark he was being asked a question.

'Yes, Claudio, we are friends.'

'So we have to be honest with each other. I have many contacts all over the world, much influence. I speak with Savvas. He also knows people with influence. Influence is more important than knowledge. If there is anything I can do to help with your daughter, you tell me, you understand?' He dug a finger into Mark's chest to illustrate his point.

'Thanks, Claudio. Everybody's been doing their best.'

'These *bastardos* who have the child. You tell me what you know. The *polizia*,' he spat on the floor, 'they know nothing, they do nothing. I move armies to get her back, my armies, armies nobody sees. If you have a demand for a ransom, then it's a start. Once they show themselves they can be hunted. It is like animals. Eventually they become hungry, they come for food and, boom, they are food themselves. With men like this it is greed for money that brings them out to the watering holes. Animals I can understand, but men who take children . . .' He made a gesture of slitting a throat and Mark guessed it was not his own.

Mark hesitated, then took the plunge. He needed help, needed to share the responsibility, and although he could see the dangers of unleashing the likes of Barlucci and his merry men, he had got to the stage where he was prepared to try anything.

'Claudio, listen. What I tell you may place you in danger as well. I do not have a good track record for those who get themselves involved.' He found himself speaking in Italian to ensure that Barlucci understood.

'Danger is of no concern to me. My only concern is to get your *bambina* back safe and sound.'

'I know, Claudio. Believe me, I know. Listen, whoever has Emma, and presumably Sonya and her daughter, they've not shown themselves at the watering-hole, as you put it. That note, it was to try and entice them out, but Patti and I thought the whole thing up. We wrote it ourselves. We've absolutely no idea where they are or who they are with.'

Barlucci nodded thoughtfully. 'It was a good idea. I understand. You have not told the good Rob Davies about this?'

'No. He's seriously pissed off with me as it is. I think that would give him the excuse he's looking for to toss me into jail for a night or so.'

'And Patti, where is she tonight? Would she approve of things I may have to do?'

'I'm past caring about seals of approval. All I want is my daughter back. Patti's gone out on some story or other. She got a phone call just before we were leaving. If you're a journalist then you can't resist it, can you? It's like an illness.'

'Very well. Leave it to me. We say nothing to anybody. Now we watch the match and then I make some calls.'

Again a hand on the shoulders guided Mark through to the Directors' Box. He felt like a stranger visiting an away ground for the first time. What was he doing watching football while Emma was a captive in some unknown place? He tried to rid his mind of the possibilities. Was she in a box herself, tied in the dark, terrified? Had she been hurt or, worse still, had she been abused? At that point he physically forced his head around to look at the pitch. Football, not his daughter – that had been the problem in the past. But tonight it had to help clear his mind for some answers.

There was an inordinate amount of activity on the bench, and Ray Fowler, never the calmest of people, was barking orders to his Number Two, Jimmy Townshend, the former Youth Team coach. The visitors, Radcliffe County, were already out on the field, warming up, their keeper performing athletically in front of the five hundred or so travelling supporters. Of Hertsmere, only Barry Reed, the young Welsh reserve, Aled Williams and Greg Sergovich were out, the two outfield players shooting in at the keeper, all three of them casting long glances back at the players' tunnel in the hope that they would not have to take on Radcliffe on their own.

Fowler disappeared, and the stadium clock showed seven-forty. Five minutes to kick-off. Eventually Fowler reappeared, arguing furiously with the referee, and then the tannoy system cut in and Mark began to understand what was happening.

'There are some additional team changes for Hertsmere. Tommy Wallace replaces Tolly Karpov, Aled Williams replaces Dimitri Murganev as substitute . . .'

'What the fuck's going on?' Sinclair said angrily, and received disapproving looks from the Radcliffe party, who had been somewhat frosty since they had been told that the Hertsmere Directors' Box could not accommodate all of them.

'These little teams shouldn't be in the Premiership if they can't cope with the demands.' The chairman had been heard to say.

'This little team won the Cup last year and are playing in Europe,' Sinclair had replied to nobody in particular, without adding that Radcliffe had only been safe from relegation on the penultimate Saturday of the season.

Now Sinclair lowered his voice, 'Where the hell are the two Russians now? I know Ray felt Murganev wasn't fully match-fit in his mind, but he also said he was hoping to get him on for a bit tonight. And I also know Tommy Wallace is nursing a calf injury.'

'I suppose he had to play somebody who was actually here,' Mark said.

'And then we'll get a fine for not putting our correct team-sheet in to the referee on time. I suppose that was what Ray was arguing about.'

There was no time for further discussion as the match got underway. The Hertsmere team were clearly unsettled by whatever had occurred in the dressing room immediately before the kick-off, and with Wallace operating at about three-quarters speed, the midfield was quickly surrendered to the visitors. By half-time the two-goal lead that Radcliffe had taken was scant reward for their total domination, and Sinclair grabbed hold of Mark, forgetting all of his personal problems. 'Come on, we're going down to the dressing room. I want to find out exactly what's happening to the club. We may have beaten Paris Olympique, but if we play like this against Sporting Barcelona next week I'll have to install a cricket scoreboard.'

Fowler did not appear to be in any way put out by the visit of his chairman and predecessor. 'Sorry, Boss,' he said, before Sinclair could say a word. 'One minute Karpov was here, the next he wasn't. I assumed he and Murganev were having a cosy chat outside and then when it's time to get on to the pitch they're nowhere. They didn't even leave their shirts behind. When I get my hands on them they'll think the fucking salt-mines are a soft option.'

There did not seem to be much that Mark or Sinclair could do, and they left the manager to rouse his dishevelled army and returned to the stand with barely time for a drink.

Barlucci and Savvas were waiting for them at the top of the steps. 'You explain, Mark,' Sinclair said. 'I suppose if I don't have a cup of tea with this Radcliffe mob they'll report us to the League for bad sportsmanship.'

Savvas moved aside to allow Mark to pass, but Barlucci grabbed his arm. 'What is happening, Mark?' he asked.

'I wish I knew, Claudio. But whoever you're going to have out there looking for my daughter, you'd better tell them to keep their eyes peeled for two crazy Russian footballers wearing Hertsmere shirts. I wish we'd never heard of them, never thought of visiting Russia. I wish old Leo had kept his land to himself however well he meant.' But even as he spoke he knew that whatever else could be done by Barlucci to help him, he did not have the power to turn back time.

CHAPTER 49

Emma slipped back into the house, her absence unnoticed. She could not believe her bad luck. She had tried to reach her father, but his phone had just rang out. He never forgot to turn on the answerphone. In the past he could not afford to miss any opportunity that might have come his way whilst he was out scraping together a living. She could only suppose that he was so distracted by her absence that his normal habits were being forgotten. She had tried Patti as well, but she too was out, although at least she was given the option of leaving a message. At first she hung up when she realised she was not there. She began to dial her mother's number, then guessed that she'd be at Hertsmere watching the match the radio sports news had told her was taking place that evening. Perhaps that was where her father was as well. She felt a fit of pique at the idea that he could sit and watch a football match when he had no idea of the whereabouts of his only child. Why did she feel far less angry with her mother for following the fortunes of her new husband when she had every reason to believe her only child's life was at stake?

'Bloody typical,' she muttered to herself, addressing the words in her mind to her father, then dialled Patti's number again. Having made up her mind to tell somebody she was alive and well and where she was, she had to go through with it. Relief flooded her as the answerphone clicked on.

'Patti, it's me, Emma. I'm OK. I'm with Sonya and her kid. They're fine too. We're out in a cottage near Little Rollright in Oxfordshire. I don't know the exact address, but it's called Hive Cottage, straight down a long lane from this phone box.' She gave the number and position of the box, reading from the card in front of her. 'Tell Dad. And tell him to get down here; I've just about had enough.'

Reflected in the glass she thought she saw a shadowy figure approaching the kiosk. It could well have been an innocent neighbour walking a dog, or somebody wanting to use the phone in all good faith, but she was not hanging around to find out. Ever since she had been old enough to understand, the newspapers and television had been filled with incidents of women accosted and murdered at lonely telephone boxes such as this one.

She left the phone off the hook in her confusion and ran all the way back to the cottage. She lay on the bed, panting and sobbing, hoping that Sonya was asleep and would simply leave her alone. If she could not be with her father then she wanted to be by herself. She didn't know when Patti would pick up the message, but she hoped it would not be too long. She would know what to do, and then Emma could get the responsibility for the Murganevs off her young and tender shoulders. It had all been a mistake to think she could cope with it, and she just hoped it was not too late to correct it.

Patti Delaney also felt she might have made a mistake, but the message left for her had been too intriguing not to follow up. It had been meant to intrigue, she realised now, but in the heat of excitement at following an exclusive she had not thought of that. In the world of journalism, like every other world, nothing was for nothing.

'You wrote the story about Emma Rossetti and Sonya Murganev. I think I can trust you, but we have to meet in secret. Just you and me. I know what's happened to them.'

'Like Deep Throat in Watergate,' she'd tried to joke, but the other's voice was deadly serious, and somehow that had encouraged her to believe the caller was on the level. She knew Mark would kill her for not telling him, but he'd be safe at football, and hopefully she'd be back at home by the time the match finished.

She arranged to meet her mystery caller at The Old Bull and Bush pub in Hampstead. She knew it was always full of tourists and she couldn't see how she could possibly be in danger there.

'How will I recognise you?' she'd asked.

'Don't worry about it, I know you,' he'd replied, and it was only now, as she waited impatiently, glass of wine in hand, that the tone in his voice sent a shiver down her spine. She walked down to the kerbside, looking up the hill to the left towards the Pond and then down in the direction of Golders Green. Whatever warmth there had been in the day had vanished, and she wished she'd thought to bring a coat. The high buzz of young voices congregating outside the pub and the one next door sounded like a cluster of birds in the night air, the various languages mingling in a veritable Babel of tongues. She took a few steps towards the corner of the little road at the side that ran down to a part of the Heath that was rarely visited, an area of stagnant pools, of closely entwined trees resisting the sunshine, of clandestine homosexual encounters. She had been there once before, a few years ago when she had written a feature on the Heath by day and night. It had given her the creeps and she'd been bitten to pieces by insects.

Suddenly she heard a voice so close at hand that she virtually jumped out of her skin. Then a hand held her firmly by the elbow and she realised there were two of them and her other arm was also being held tightly. The two men lifted her off the ground and skilfully manoeuvred her into the back of a car that she merely perceived to be big and black.

She should have screamed, she knew that, but would anybody have come to her aid? The foreign kids drinking just a few feet away from her would have thought it just another part of London life. If a woman could be taken at knifepoint in broad daylight in Regent's Park and raped, then what chance did she have? She couldn't believe she had fallen for this, but she had, and she knew she had to keep calm, to convince herself and her companions that she saw nothing strange about the situation.

'Where are you taking me?'

'We're taking you nowhere. You wanted to come,' one of the men said. She recognised the voice from the phone, but now she could tell at first hand that he had a slightly foreign accent. He was not a big man, but the grip he had taken on her arm told her he was strong, and the broken nose, set amid the high slavic cheekbones, suggested that at some time in his life he had boxed seriously, if not professionally. His companion was sheer bulk, well over six feet tall, wearing only a T-shirt despite the evening's chill, his muscles rippling through the thin cotton. They sat on either side of her in the back seat while a third man drove, and as she realised they could already have hurt her if they had so wanted, then her spirits rose a little. If they needed her for information then she had been at least dealt a hand in the game, and it was up to her how she was going to play it.

'If I wanted to come then where am I going?' she asked, trying to choose her most pleasant tone of voice. But even as she spoke they were already turning into the drive of a large house in what she recognised as The Bishop's Avenue, a house from which she and Mark had seen Lennie Simons drive what seemed a lifetime ago. Yet she felt oddly reassured. If they had anything unpleasant in store for her, then they would hardly be likely to take her somewhere she could instantly recognise.

And then a horrific thought occurred to her. What if it didn't matter what she saw because she was not intended to survive the encounter? She shook her head, half in anger at herself, half in a disbelieving effort to dismiss the notion. People who lived in houses like this might not be entirely honest, but they didn't kill for a living. No, she continued to herself, they didn't kill, they had others kill for them, others like the men who were now leading her politely but firmly to the front door. She had once interviewed a convicted killer on Death Row in the States. She had asked him if there was anything he regretted. He'd shrugged, 'Getting caught, I guess.'

And now she was caught, a fly in the spider's web, and as the door opened and the men stood aside to allow her to enter, she waited to come face to face with the spider.

CHAPTER 50

Hertsmere's match against Radcliffe was going from bad to worse. Pat Devine had limped off early in the second half, while Greg Sergovich, too anxious to get to a ball that had left him exposed by his defence, had handled deliberately outside his area and had been shown the red card for his troubles. Red. It was the colour of the night as far as Hertsmere were concerned. The two Russians vanished, the keeper dismissed, and then finally young Barry Reed led from the field with blood streaming from a head wound. Radcliffe grabbed the opportunity to go nap, and five goals down, with five minutes left, the crowd chose to turn their wrath on the players who were left on the field.

Stuart Macdonald, the captain, had seen it all before, and tried to rally the team for one last effort to salvage their pride, but the fight had gone out of them, youngsters and experienced professionals alike, and their opponents grabbed a sixth just before the end. They came off heads down, showered, then waited for the lash of Ray Fowler's tongue. It didn't come. Even he, fanatic that he was, could understand that this time round it had not been their fault.

'Go on home, lads, get some sleep. We're training tomorrow at ten o'clock.'

Normally one of them, probably Nicky Collier, would have complained about the loss of a day off, but tonight they all went home meekly.

Mark also wanted to go home. Sally had taken the

285

opportunity to give him another tongue-lashing. There were times when he felt sorry for Stuart Macdonald, but then, for the most part, his team-mate and his ex-wife seemed perfectly happy together. Different folks, different strokes, he guessed. He was tired, yet he hoped Patti would be in the mood to stay the night. He knew she had yet to rid herself fully of the guilty feeling caused by persuading him to leave Emma behind, but nobody could fault her efforts to remedy the situation since then.

But then Claudio Barlucci approached him, beaming, and asked him to stay. 'I don't know, but maybe I have some news tonight,' he whispered confidentially.

'How can you have made this happen so quickly when the police are getting nowhere?'

The Italian touched the side of his nose in an international gesture that required no translation. He gave the smile that had so enamoured him to Mark during the negotiations for Mickey Wayne the previous season. He was the sort of man, Mark decided, who made a bad enemy, but a better friend.

It was not the easiest of hours after the match. The Radcliffe officials were no better in victory than they had been upon their arrival. Mark longed to knock the smarmy smile off the face of the chairman and to stain his old school tie with blood from his purple-veined nose. He could see that both David Sinclair and Helen Davies wanted to do the same, but both made the effort and said, 'Well done,' in as many different ways as possible before the visiting party took off in a stream of chauffeur-driven cars.

It was nearly eleven before Barlucci beckoned Mark into the hallway.

'I think I have discovered where they are. You'll tell the police?'

Mark shook his head, half in disbelief. All that police work, all that waiting, and suddenly Barlucci called in some favours and in a matter of hours she was found. But then, since the first time they had met, Barlucci had seldom failed to amaze him.

'No, I won't tell the police. Not yet. I'm going down there to get her myself. Just give me the address, Claudio.'

Barlucci shook his head. 'I can't do that. You don't know what is there. To go on your own is madness.' He almost beat his own chest. 'I will go with you.'

Mark grasped Barlucci's hand. It took both of his hands to cover just one of the Italian's, and the touch of a man, which normally he would have abhorred, seemed perfectly natural.

'Thanks, but no again. I suppose you don't want to tell me how you got the information. I suppose you're sure it's accurate?'

'I am sure. The people who tell me, they dare not make a mistake over something that is so important to me. Mark, I worry for you. Go yourself, but if you do not call me at home by seven tomorrow morning, then I will call our dear Helen's husband, the good Detective Davies. We have a deal?'

'You were always a good negotiator, Claudio. Yes, we have a deal.'

Barlucci took Mark's hand in his. 'Then *buona fortuna*, my friend. I am waiting for your call. Tonight, Barlucci does not sleep.'

Mark looked at the address Claudio had given him. He thought at this time of night he could be there in little over an hour. He had turned down Barlucci's offer of help, refused to go to the police, but he felt he would welcome Patti's company. They had been through so much together that it would not feel right to leave her out of this latest adventure. He tried to call from the car, but was greeted by her recorded message.

'Patti, it's me. Call me in the car. I think Emma's been found. I'm on my way.'

And then his foot was down on the accelerator and he was roaring up the motorway, oblivious to any other user of the roads, uncaring as to speed restrictions, only assuring himself that every minute and every mile brought him nearer to the person he loved dearest in all the world.

CHAPTER 51

The two Russian footballers had simply walked out of Hertsmere's stadium, under the noses of fans, officials and journalists alike. On a football match day all eyes were focused on incoming pedestrian traffic, not on those leaving, who had usually completed minor manual tasks and were not remaining to see the match.

It was Karpov who had persuaded Murganev to leave. 'These people, they do not understand us. It takes a Russian to understand a Russian. You cannot play if you are sad, and you are sad.'

Murganev had at first looked at him suspiciously. He had not liked Karpov when their paths had crossed back in Russia, and he saw no reason to change his views just because fate had tossed the pair of them together in England. Yet he was beginning to think that perhaps he had pre-judged him. Since the disappearance of his wife and daughter, the man had been nothing but solicitous. It was the mention of Yevneko that convinced Murganev that Karpov was truly on his side.

'I don't know what Nikolei Yevneko is doing to you. Believe me, he is doing the same to me.' Even in his absence the power of the man commanded fear and a kind of grudging respect. Karpov would not call him just by his surname. It was as if he was in a position to overhear and oversee everything that in anyway affected him.

'I didn't realise, Tolly,' Murganev said, using his country-man's nickname for the first time. 'I thought I was alone.'

289

'We're never alone,' Karpov said. 'There is always somebody else sharing the same grief. We need to leave. You must collect your wife and go.'

Murganev looked at him, as if he had taken leave of his senses.

'I don't know where my wife is. If I knew where she was then I would have been with her. Why do you think I am not playing well? All the time I am thinking of what might be happening, of what might have already happened to my wife and my baby.'

Karpov made to say something, then changed his mind. 'It all stems from Yevneko. If he does not earn from us, then eventually he will become bored, he will look for new and easier ways to make money. If he sees that not only will we not play tonight, but so long as we see so little from our efforts we will not play at all, then we are half-way there.'

'So what do we do?' Murganev asked hesitantly.

Karpov quickly sensed he was getting through to the other man, and pressed home his point. 'We go. Now. Maybe something will happen to help you find your wife. Maybe if you too disappear she will find you.'

'But Fowler, he will be mad. He is not a bad man. He does not deserve this. How will we be able to come back to the team if we do this to him? Perhaps we can play and then think again.'

'Ach, you make me mad, Dimitri Murganev. Always you want to be nice, to be liked, to think of others. This time you must think of yourself. If not for your sake then for the sake of your wife and child. Come on.'

'Where are we going?'

As he heard the question Karpov knew he had won. He was not totally convinced that Murganev did not know the whereabouts of his family, he thought that he might not yet trust him enough to tell him. The important thing right now was to get away from the floodlights that lit up Hertsmere's pitch like the no-man's-land surrounding a prisoner of war camp. They had to get out of the light, and as the pair of them slipped away into the night he felt he had succeeded at least in achieving that.

Mark was not the only one driving at speed towards the Oxfordshire countryside. Patti was also in a car heading in the same direction, although she was a passenger and an unwilling one at that.

The spider had a face and a name – Nikolei Yevneko – although at his house, before their journey had begun, he had greeted her as a long lost friend rather than a trespasser in his web.

'My dear Miss Delaney. I am so pleased to meet you alone at last. Our brief encounter at the football was indeed too brief. I have read some of your writing with interest and indeed I think I may be described as a fan. And you have visited my country as well. If only I had known, I could have done so much more to make your visit a more pleasant one. I understand you have inherited a share in a property in my homeland. If I can be of any help in ensuring your title to the same, please, you must let me help you. Ah, but I forget the English formalities. We have brought you from your home, dragged you away from the possibility of being at the side of your friend Mr Rossetti at a football match, and I do not even offer you a drink. Some wine? I think you do not always have the chance to indulge in such vices when you are with Mr Rossetti, who has a problem in that respect.'

'You seem to know an awful lot about me,' she said, accepting the chilled white wine that was offered to her in a cut glass from a silver tray. She would have to take a chance on it not being drugged. When she saw her host take the other glass and drink she was reassured. Anyway if they had brought her here to provide information, she would be of no use to them if she was semi-conscious.

'You are of interest to us, and so we follow our noses, as I believe you say in English.'

'And ferret in the rubbish,' she couldn't resist replying.

Yevneko looked puzzled, but refused to ask for an explanation. 'I can understand you being a little concerned, but let me reassure you we will not detain you long. All we need is a little assistance, which we think you can provide, and then we will part company. Unless, as I say, we can be of help to you.'

'Is that the royal we?' Patti asked, making a vain effort to keep some humour in the situation.

Yevneko played his part and smiled politely, 'I think you are being a little unkind. Perhaps my English is not as good as it might be. If I could spend a little more time in your excellent company then I am sure it would improve.'

Patti said nothing, although the words 'fat chance' sprang to mind. She wanted to be away from this reptilian man, wanted to get under her shower at home, feel the hot clean needles of water wash away the dirt she could feel surrounding him. She glanced around the room, took in the Persian carpets on the floor, the heavy draped curtains, the gleaming silverware, the Matisse on the wall that she guessed was an original, and wondered how much blood had been spilled to amass all this wealth.

Yevneko noticed her gaze wandering. 'You like my house?'

'Not quite my taste. I'm more into original Habitat.'

Again the forced smile, and then he switched into business mode. 'Miss Delaney, you are not a stupid woman. Quite the contrary. So you will have realised that you are not invited here for a tour of my house or art collection, although if time permits I would be delighted to show you around. No, you are here because there are three people in the gravest danger and, I believe, only you can help.'

'Three people?'

'Certainly. Sonya Murganev, her daughter, and your friend Mr Rossetti's daughter.'

'And this danger, can you tell me any more about it?'

'Ah, the natural curiosity of journalists. I believe it kills.'

'Pardon?' Patti queried, despite the absurdity of the conversation.

'Curiosity. It kills.'

'Only cats, not journalists,' Patti replied.

'But there is always a first time,' the Russian said, his tone cold and chilling, the smile on his face equally icy.

'So how can I help these three souls in danger?' she asked, hoping to bring the interview to whatever conclusion Yevneko intended.

'You can tell me where they are.'

'I don't know.'

Yevneko sighed deeply. 'I was afraid you were going to say that.'

'It's true. What do you want me to say?'

Yevneko looked deep into her eyes, and as she stared back, her gaze unwavering, it was like looking down a dark, deep well, the bottom far from sight, impenetrable unless you tumbled down there to your death.

'I do not like to repeat myself. Time is money, and if you cost me time then you cost me money. I want to know where the Murganev family is hiding. I have no interest in the English girl if that is what concerns you. She has involved herself in something which is not her business and because of that she is in danger. Surely you would not wish any harm to come to her?'

'From whom are they in danger?' Patti asked ingenuously.

'People who would wish to cause them harm. Evil people.'

'Friends of yours, are they?'

'This is not a joking matter. Always the English, they treat life as a joke. That is why we are able to come here and make a success of our lives. Because you are too busy laughing to see that we are taking away your livelihoods.'

'That's very philosophical. Maybe you should run for

293

Parliament. And by the way, I'm not English. My father was Irish and my mother's Jewish.'

Yevneko was beginning to lose patience. 'Your family tree is of no concern to me. You received a note about the three of them. You wrote an article. I do not believe it ended there. I have very good instincts, and my instincts tell me that you know where they are.'

'And how do I convince you otherwise?' Patti asked, trying manfully to keep the tremor of fear from her voice.

'That, my dear, is the problem. I am not easily convinced.' He paused for a moment and looked at his watch.

'I will leave you alone for say a quarter of an hour. If you do not remember where they are by then we will have to move on to the second phase of our relationship.'

'And then the third? I do so like in-depth relationships.'

'Still joking. I am afraid there is no third stage. Fifteen minutes. Some more wine? Perhaps it will help you think more clearly.'

After that, things had moved so speedily she had some difficulty keeping them in order. They had returned, she had said nothing, and then she had found herself bundled back into the car and heading towards her own flat, some ten minutes' drive away.

'We want to give you every chance. We are not violent people. If you have something at your flat then we will find it. If we find it then we will leave you in peace.'

'And if you don't find it then you leave me in pieces,' she'd said, without any real feeling of levity.

The real mistake was playing back her messages. First Mark, then a commissioning editor from a Sunday, reminding her about a deadline, then Emma, then Mark again. Why tonight? Why did Emma choose tonight to tell where she was, and why did she choose to tell her?

Yevneko, who had accompanied his two assistants, listened carefully, his head cocked like a bird of prey. 'So, it seems you were telling the truth. A rare thing for a journalist.'

'Maybe English journalists are different from their Russian counterparts.'

'Maybe, although I doubt it.' He tapped his fingers on the table, then spoke swiftly in Russian to the two men.

'I am afraid you will have to put up with our company for a little longer. We are inviting you to take a little ride with us into the country.'

'And if I refuse?'

Yevneko ran the backs of his fingernails down the side of her cheek. 'I think maybe you are familiar with the film and the quote, but what I am making you is an offer you cannot refuse. Emma knows you; she does not know us. We would not want to scare the child.'

'And what about Sonya Murganev, does she not know you either?' Patti asked, and when Yevneko did not reply she knew the answer to her question.

CHAPTER 52

Mark knew he was getting old when he couldn't read the tiny place names on the map. His eyes were tired from the glare of headlights on the motorway, and now the dark country roads imposed a different kind of strain. He hated navigating and driving at the same time, felt the need for a companion, not just to guide him to his destination, but also to talk through the problems that were running around his mind, weaving crazy patterns.

He had tried Patti again from the car-phone, but this time the line just rang and rang. That bothered him. She must have been home to turn off the answerphone and presumably pick up his message, so why hadn't she called him? He had seen life from both sides of the law and was thinking both like a policeman and a criminal. It made him very cautious.

Finally he found the road to the Rollrights and pulled into the side of a lane in a passing cutaway. Why should he be so nervous about seeing his own daughter? The past had taught him a thing or two, one of which was that nothing was ever what it seemed. This seemed too simple. While he felt sure that his daughter was where Barlucci had been told she was, he could not be sure who was also there with her.

He trusted Barlucci, but he did not know – could not know – the source of his information. What if it were all a trap, if Barlucci had misjudged his own control of those who worked for him? Yet the Italian had seemed confident, had been prepared to accompany him, had not thought the risk so great

297

as to prevent Mark going on his own. But those crumbs of comfort did not fully satisfy Mark. He was not the same man who had gone begging to the league clubs for a job less than two years before. He had come to rely not just on his intellect, but on his intuition – and right now his intuition, every instinct in his body, told him to take care.

It was then that the phone rang, an eerie, penetrating sound in the silent car, in the midst of an even more silent night.

He answered it, expecting to hear Patti's voice, but instead he was greeted by male tones, a familiar voice, but one so out of context that he could not immediately put a name to it.

'Mark?'

'Yes.'

'Where are you?'

'Who are you?'

'It's me, Alex. Alex Jennings.'

Mark shook his head, doubting the very words he was hearing. What on earth was the man who had helped him in Moscow doing calling him on his car-phone at this time of night in this obscure part of the country, and how had he even got the car number?

'Alex. What the hell do you want?'

'Mark, just listen to me. Don't ask questions and trust me. If you value Emma's life then trust me like you've never trusted anybody else before.'

There was something about the man's voice that made Mark reply without hesitation. 'I feel as if I have to trust somebody tonight, and I guess you're as good as it's likely to get.'

'Thanks for the vote of confidence. That'll have to do. Now, where are you, did you say?'

'I didn't, but I'm just outside of Little Rollright in Oxfordshire.'

'So you're near the cottage,' Alex said, half to himself, and Mark had to resist the temptation to ask how he knew about the cottage at all. 'Stay where you are. I'm on my way. Don't go in without me. No heroics, Mark. It'll be fine, but wait. Do you hear me?'

'Yes, I hear you, but I don't know how you can expect me to sit out here in the dark when goodness knows what might be happening to my daughter.'

'I've never lied to you. I can't promise you that nothing's happening, but it has to be better to wait for the cavalry. There'll be no medals. When I'm near I'll call you on the car-phone again.' And then, as if he feared that to continue the conversation would lead to argument, the line went dead.

Mark waited for about half an hour, alone in the dark, the minutes dragging by on the car clock, the radio muted so as not to attract attention. A car passed him by, unseeing, an old man at the wheel, his wife asleep in the front seat. They were an oasis of normality in a world gone mad. Where had they been? Out for dinner, an evening at the theatre, or perhaps visiting children and grandchildren? The thought that, if he did not rescue Emma, he might never have grandchildren made him want to ignore everything that Alex had told him and go in guns blazing to get his daughter out. But then he had no guns with which to blaze, and if he were to be confronted by any opposition then the likelihood was that they would be fully armed. The most lethal weapon he had was probably the jack in the boot of the car. Not the sort of thing that anybody but Rambo could turn to advantage.

He struggled with his impatience, wondering where Alex had been when he called and how long it would take him to get there. Then a second car passed and he knew that time was most definitely no longer on his side. A driver at the front, bolt upright, eyes fixed firmly on the road, a man by his side that Mark dimly felt he had seen before, two more men at the back and, between them, the unmistakable face of Patti, her eyes wide open with fear, clearly seen even in the split second it took for the car to pass.

He waited a few moments, willing the phone to ring, to help

him avoid making a decision that he did not want to make. Nothing happened, and he turned the key in the ignition, the sound of the motor coming back to life seeming to him a disturbance that could wake the dead. Wake the dead – he did not like the sound of the phrase. What Alex Jennings had said was fine in principle, but he could not see the grim expressions on the faces of those men in the car with Patti. Patti and Emma. The two people he loved in life, about to meet face-to-face, and then face what together? He did not know, but what he did know was that whatever Jennings had said he couldn't just wait and let it happen. He slipped the car into drive and, without turning on any of the lights, drove carefully and slowly in what he assumed was the direction of the cottage.

CHAPTER 53

The walls of the cottage were closing in upon Emma Rossetti, or at least that was how it felt to her. Until now they had appeared thick and solid, built to last, the very epitome of safety. In the relatively short time she had stayed there she had grown to take comfort from the ivy that grew all along one side, the birds who had made a nest in the eaves, who woke her each morning with their song, the coolness of the interior walls when the sun shone, the warmth at night that needed no fire in the grate for comfort. But all of that had been when there had just been the three of them; there had been enough room for comfort, enabling her to be with the Murganevs when she was lonely and on her own when she needed solitude. And now the room was full of intruders, people invading her space.

It had not been so bad when Dimitri Murganev had arrived with the other Russian, who she gathered was also a footballer. She was becoming terribly weary of footballers, for they seemed to bring nothing but trouble in their wake. Her schoolfriends might envy her easy access to the good-looking heroes whose photos they pinned to the insides of their desk lids, but as far as she was concerned they were welcome to them.

Sonya had greeted her husband with surprise, then joy, followed by what Emma perceived to be fear; but was it fear for him or fear for all of them? She could not tell, but she was beginning to have feelings and awareness far beyond her tender years. Sonya and Dimitri spoke quickly in Russian, oblivious to anybody else in the room. The other man, smaller, darker, watched them closely, his eyes flitting with bird-like attention from one to the other.

When the couple went upstairs to see their child, Emma was left alone with the stranger. He switched his gaze to her and she felt as if she was being measured for size and suitability. Even at her age, she was perceptive enough to know when a member of the opposite sex was looking at her as a woman. Tolly Karpov might be doing nothing tangible to which she could take objection, but she was sure that if her father had been there he would have taken some positive action.

'How did you know where to come?' she asked Karpov, hoping that some conversation might ease the embarrassment she was beginning to feel under his gaze.

'A small bird told us. And the bird was right.'

His eyes moved from her own, down her body. Don't blush, she urged herself, don't let him think for a moment that he's getting through to you.

'Weren't you both supposed to be playing tonight?' she asked, the question involuntary as the realisation suddenly dawned upon her.

Karpov put his head to one side, and again she was reminded of a bird, only this time not a domestic garden sparrow or robin, but rather a bird of prey, biding its time.

'Ah, so this little dwelling is not so remote. Not so cut off from civilisation. You knew there was a game tonight. A true fan.' She felt he was testing her, ensuring there had been no other contact with the outside world.

'I heard about it on the radio. So, weren't you?' she persisted, feeling the urge to show she was not just a kid who could be easily diverted.

'Weren't you?' he mimicked. 'I do not understand.'

'Weren't you supposed to be playing?'

He sighed. 'Sometimes there are more important things in

life than playing football. My friend Dimitri had to make a choice between football and his family, and he took it. Do you think he was wrong? There will be other football matches. Right now, I think they are happy.' He threw his head slightly backwards in a gesture towards the upstairs bedroom.

'What happens now?' she asked.

He shrugged, made to speak, then seemed to hear something that had eluded her ears, and rose to his feet. He moved swiftly and lightly out of the small sitting room into the hall, which was really just an extension of the entrance porch. Before Emma realised what was happening he had thrown open the door and, to her astonishment, standing there was Patti Delaney. The two of them threw themselves into each other's arms and as Emma put her head on the other woman's shoulders she felt momentarily truly safe. Patti stroked her hair and held her tight, too tightly, so that she was struggling to catch her breath.

'Easy, Patti. It *is* me. We've established that. I'm so pleased you got my message. Where's Dad?'

Patti eased her gently away and Emma, looking up into her face, realised that something was wrong.

'Is it Dad? Is he OK?'

'Your father is fine . . . for the moment.'

Emma spun round at the sound of a man's voice, a voice that sent an immediate shiver down her spine. There, now, filling the doorway, was the thin form of Nikolei Yevneko, and behind him three other bulky figures to tell her that Patti Delaney had not come unescorted.

Yevneko looked at Karpov who, with a jerk of his hand, indicated that Murganev was upstairs. Two of the three men came from the shadows behind him. They did not appear to need to be told what to do, and moved menacingly towards the foot of the small staircase. They seemed so large in the small cottage that Emma felt as though she had slipped into some nightmarish fairy-story land inhabited by giants and ogres. In a moment they would take the stairs in one giant stride and, with a fiery breath, reduce the walls to smouldering matchwood. She opened her mouth to call out a warning to the Murganevs, although how they could have escaped she had no idea. Yevneko, however, was taking no chances, and anticipating her action, clamped his hand across her mouth.

'Leave it be, little girl. You have already interfered enough in things that do not concern you. It must run in the family. Your father, Miss Delaney here, and now you. All making life very difficult for me, when all I wanted was to ensure that the Murganevs were together again . . .'

'Together again under your control, you mean,' Patti said, then immediately wished she had kept her counsel.

'So, not just a pretty face.' Yevneko's eyes bored into those of the journalist. She wanted to turn away, to look anywhere but into those cold depths, yet he magnetised her gaze.

'And how much else do you know or have you guessed?' the Russian continued, half to himself.

'She doesn't know anything,' Emma said in a small hopeless voice, attuned to the threat.

'Such loyalty. It deserves reward. Perhaps another day you will get a candy for your troubles – but not today,' Yevneko said, with a slight smile on his face that Emma longed to remove with her bitten-down fingernails.

'Who are you?' she insisted, struggling to restrain herself.

'Does it matter? I suspect we will not be acquainted a sufficient length of time to make introductions relevant.'

It was then that Emma felt fear, real fear, the stomach-churning knot of fear that would in the past have seen her screaming out for her mother or her father, or even her teddy bear.

Patti saw the look of horror on the girl's face and instinctively moved in closer to her, a protective arm around her trembling shoulders. 'Don't let the bastards get to you, Emma. That's what they want. They may be wearing suits, but they're still monkeys underneath.'

A flicker of annoyance crossed Yevneko's face, a rare show of emotion, and then, just as quickly as it had come, it was gone. 'As a writer you have a way with words, Miss Delaney, but I do not respect you for using a swear-word in front of the child.'

'I'm not a child,' Emma said swiftly. 'I'm old enough.'

'Old enough for what?' Yevneko interrupted.

'Old enough to look after myself, to think for myself.'

Yevneko nodded, as if a particularly troublesome problem had been resolved.

'Good, good. Old enough to look after yourself, old enough to think for yourself, and perhaps, therefore, old enough for a few other things . . .'

And that was the last Emma remembered, as the room suddenly began to spin around her and she collapsed upon the floor in a tidy heap.

CHAPTER 54

The curtains were not quite drawn, and Mark could just see his daughter when she moved across the room. He had already decided that if anybody laid a finger on her then he'd be through the window, through the wall if necessary, irrespective of the prospects of success, oblivious to his own safety.

He was still trying to piece it all together in his mind, trying to understand why Yevneko, his daughter, Patti and goodness knew who else had all assembled in this remote country cottage. He was also trying to decide who were the good guys. Life had moved along since his youth, when John Wayne always wore a white hat and Lee Van Cleef was forever dressed in black. Nothing that was in any way connected to Russia seemed to be so clear-cut. It was a country of shades, a kaleidoscope of colours, forever shifting, as politics shifted, boundaries shifted, as the very earth beneath the feet seemed to be constantly moving in some seismic rhythm. He did not pretend to understand. Some ideas had crossed his mind as he drove, but whatever clarity had come had now sunk back into confusion.

When it finally happened, it happened so quickly that all thoughts of caution, all of Jennings' warnings were tossed aside. One moment Emma was there, the next she was not. From his viewpoint he could not tell if she had been struck, shot or stabbed. All he could see was that his daughter had collapsed, and he needed to see no more. He leapt out of the car, leaving the door open to avoid any noise and racing over

307

the flowerbeds instead of the gravelled path, instinctive acts of caution, for cautious was the last thing he felt. Distances were hard to judge, but it seemed that he reached the cottage in two strides. Although it was self-evident from the confusing drama within the room that he had neither been heard nor seen, he still shrank back against the ancient stone wall, pressing his body so hard against it that he feared it might give way beneath the weight. Stage one, he whispered to himself, hoping that the fact he could hear his own voice might give him some comfort, some sense of accomplishment. But as yet he had accomplished nothing. He had arrived unseen, he had moved from the car to the exterior of the cottage; his daughter and his lover, though, were still inside, still at the mercy of one he perceived to be ruthless.

He tried with a great effort to slow it down. If he could only understand what was going on inside, what had brought this motley band together from the cold of Moscow to this lonely spot in the English countryside, then he had a better chance of being able to deal with it.

First the Murganevs. He had the distinct feeling that Emma had gone willingly with Sonya. Just a casual glance at this cottage was enough to tell him there was no way she could have been kept here for the past few weeks against her will. So maybe that put Sonya on the side of the angels, wherever and whoever Sonya was. He'd not caught a glimpse of any female in the room other than Patti and Emma, so he couldn't rely on any appearance, innocent or otherwise. He had to rely on the facts. The facts, man, just the facts. It was an echo from an old television series. He sought the name. Dragnet.

Crazy, that's what he was. Trying to conjure up the name of a cop show from an era before he was born while the lives of everybody near and dear to him were on the line. Marshal the facts, get all the pretty ducks in a row, Sonya Murganev, probably good. Dimitri Murganev? He catalogued all his meetings with him. Difficult really to fault him from what he'd seen. Maybe with too high an opinion of himself, but hardly a capital offence. He couldn't believe he had anything to do with his wife's disappearance, Emma's danger – or at least not deliberately. Yet, Sonya had run. Run from whom? To protect her daughter, to protect her husband. The running. That's what had triggered off everything. Running from whom? From the smartly dressed Russian who seemed to be in charge, he'd presumed. He'd seen him before, he recalled, met him just the once at Hertsmere. He'd seen his house as well. With Murganev and Karpov in the squad there had been no shortage of soviet visitors, from the Russian Ambassador down. Yes he remembered this man, although his name eluded him. They all had such complicated surnames. He thought of John Motson, commentating on Russia against Yugoslavia in an International match. He almost smiled at the memory, forgetting for that split instant where he was. He chanced a glance through the window. Emma was lying on a couch, then sitting up slightly, and he could see even in that brief glance that the colour was edging back into her face.

Temporarily reassured, he felt he had gained a little breathing space. He couldn't see them gathering solicitously around the teenager and then shooting her immediately afterwards. But then there was such a thing as fattening the turkey for Christmas.

Force yourself back, Mark. Who *is* he? Nick, Nicky, Old Nick, the devil himself, Nikolei. Come on, you're supposed to have been a private eye. What good were you if you can't remember names? Maybe you're not hungry enough any more. But are you hungry enough to want to save your daughter? Names, car numbers, faces. The first things you're taught in the beginner's guide to sleuthing. Yevneko. That was it, and it wasn't just once. They'd met somewhere else, not at a match, but something to do with football. Perhaps not even met, but just seen him across a room. Some enchanted evening, a stranger across a crowded room. Stop it, stop it

309

right there; you're getting hysterical. A picture in his mind. Yevneko talking to Claudio, sitting next to Claudio. Was that how Claudio had discovered where Emma was? If that was the source then they knew he was coming. And if they knew he was coming then there'd have been a welcoming committee; but the group inside the room seemed to be finite. There were no guards posted; if there had been he assumed he would have been aware of it by now. So probably not Barlucci's little birdie. But if not anybody here now, then who?

Another glance through the window. He was becoming increasingly voyeuristic. Tolly Karpov. He had never liked the man. He had found it very hard to like anybody who seemed that close to Lennie Simons. And Simons was dead. A bit player, like Rosencrantz and Guildenstern. But what part had he played? Had he tried to grab a role for which he wasn't earmarked, for which he simply wasn't cut out? That would have been fairly typical. When it came to not speaking ill of the dead, Mark found it easy to make an exception for Lennie Simons. Now he could see that Karpov was on the side of Yevneko. He was relaxed in his company, physically moving away from Emma and Patti as if to say, whatever happens to you, I shall survive.

He could hear a little, but Yevneko and Karpov spoke in Russian, the tones of the two men clearly demonstrating which of them was in charge, which was deferential. Mark realised with a growing sense of panic that even the most basic of weapons that had occurred to him – the car jack – he had left in the vehicle. He could hardly knock at the door, put his hand in his pocket and tell them he had a concealed, loaded gun and that they were under arrest.

He balanced the risk of getting to the car and back again unseen against the suicidal notion of going into the room totally unarmed. Yevneko, Karpov, and a large man who looked as if he might be the driver. There was no sign of the two heavies that had sat either side of Patti in Yevneko's car.

So if that was all there was between him and his daughter, then he had a chance if he had the element of surprise on his side; but he'd have to crash into the room almost without thinking, because if he took time to think, then they would take time to react. If he went in with just his fists, he'd stand no chance, but the jack could cause real damage. The whereabouts of Yevneko's thugs worried him, but he had to take a chance. Still without his shoes he got back to the car. Somewhere behind the clouds there was a moon which at least enabled him to locate the boot.

He had never changed a tyre in his life. An odd admission, but he was not the most technical of men, and the array of screws, spanners and other equipment challenged his capabilities beyond their limits. All he knew was that tucked into the side of the boot was a rolled bundle that was heavy enough to make an irritating sound if it were not properly secured. He opened the trunk and left it raised high. The car with its door and rear now open gave the impression of being vandalised, but that was the least of his worries. It had made quite enough noise going up, without him taking the risk of banging it down. Instead, he took the metal bar that he assumed was the jack in his right hand and gripped it tightly.

He had, by now, at last an idea of what he was going to do. It was by no means a great idea, but it was better than no idea at all. He moved silently back to the house, this time with more purpose, more discipline. Somebody had readjusted the curtains in his absence and his view was even more restricted.

Yet he did not hesitate, could not hesitate. He wrapped his jacket around his arm to avoid the shattering glass and crashed the jack through the window, quickly moving to the side of the front door in traditional B-movie fashion. What would they do? Now that he'd actually done something he couldn't believe they'd just fall for it. It had been a foolish gesture, a stupid effort. He should have listened to Jennings and waited for the cavalry. Trust me, he'd said, but why trust him more than

311

anybody else on this night of madness?

As the door opened all thoughts of Jennings were abandoned. He felt only a thrill of exhilaration; it had worked. The big man he'd guessed to be the driver took one step outside and Mark hit him hard. The man turned with the momentum of the blow, then his eyes glazed over and he fell to the floor. Mark jumped over him and was virtually in the room before his feet hit the ground.

'Dad.'

'Mark.'

The cries of recognition were simultaneous. Yevneko stood stock still, his arms opened wide in what at first appeared to be a gesture of welcome, then an intimation of surrender.

It was Emma's fault, but afterwards he could not find it in his heart to blame her. In another split second he would have hit Yevneko, swung the full force of the weapon into his face, but his daughter launched herself into his arms and he was lost. Then, as he turned round and saw Dimitri Murganev and a woman he dimly recognised being pushed down the stairs by Yevneko's two heavies, he knew he was lost beyond recall.

CHAPTER 55

'You are a very lucky man, Mr Rossetti,' Yevneko said, slowly and clearly, as if to demonstrate that not for a moment had he believed he was in any danger. 'You have given Yuri out there a headache; but had you laid so much as a finger on me, then these two –' he pointed to the couple posed menacingly at the foot of the stairs – 'would literally have torn you limb from limb.' His voice had dropped to a whisper, as if he did not wish to offend the susceptibilities of one as young as Emma.

'That's me, Lucky Rossetti. I've been called that all my life.' Mark attempted the joke to see if he could work his old magic and bring a smile to the tearful face of his daughter. Yet even as he spoke the humour drained out of him as he realised the hopelessness of the task. His eyes then met those of the woman with Dimitri Murganev, and the recognition became complete. Her expression begged him to say nothing, to reveal nothing to her husband, but he found it hard to stifle the memory of her as the prostitute in leather boots who had come to his hotel room in Moscow.

Mind reading without undue difficulty, Yevneko broke the awkward silence. 'Ah, I see that you two know each other. A nice touch, I thought at the time, sending you the player's wife to give you comfort through the night when you are there to sign the player himself. I thought this couple here would understand that as a warning, would know for certain that we had complete power over them to make them do as we say, but no, it proved not to be the case. And now the penalties must

313

be paid. Penalties, my dear Dimitri. You understand the footballing turn of phrase.'

Murganev said something in Russian which was obviously an oath, and took an aggressive step forward as Sonya Murganev blushed a deep shade of red. One of the bulky men who had escorted them down the stairs immediately restrained him. The player continued to yell in his native tongue at Yevneko, who smiled the same calm smile that had dwelled upon his features virtually without pause since Mark's arrival.

'Dimitri, Dimitri,' Yevneko said wearily. 'It is rude to say things aloud that our friends here do not understand. I will translate. He is cursing me for turning his wife into a whore; but at the end of the day I have found nobody does anything totally out of character. The lawyer may not take a penny from the blind man's hat, but offer him a million for a larcenous act and he will do it. And so when he passes the blind man and tosses him a penny he believes himself to be honest and moral; but he is no better than the drunken tramp who follows him by, knocks the blind man to the floor and steals all, including the blind man's penny. A long, roundabout story, but then that is ever the case with we Russians. Nothing is ever directly to the point; nothing, and nobody, is quite what it or they appear. So, Dimitri, to return to that point I mentioned, I did not make your wife a whore, she was one already.'

Murganev could control himself no longer, and pushed forward towards Yevneko with his fists raised. One of the guards was too quick, even for the trained athlete, and knocked him to the ground with a casual blow. Sonya fell on top of him, kissing him, cradling his head in her arms.

Mark felt he had to do something, to keep talking, for as long as there was dialogue there was life. 'Dimitri, don't worry. Don't listen to him. Nothing happened between your wife and me.' He half turned to Yevneko, slowly, so as not to suggest a hostile movement and attract a blow. 'And you, Mr Yevneko, so that is how you make your money. Players go abroad when you decide it's time, you put the frighteners on their families, even hold them hostage to make bloody sure that the lure of the west doesn't get too strong to encourage them to misbehave. Then you just sit back and watch the money roll in. What do you take? Ten per cent, like an agent?'

'No, ninety per cent, like a thief,' Dimitri said from the ground, even in pain struggling to find the words in English, and receiving another blow for his troubles.

A shadow flitted across Yevneko's face like a swiftly passing cloud. Mark guessed that like most crooks he regarded himself as a semi-legitimate businessman, a businessman who made his own rules and ignored those that were made for others.

'Whatever we take is no concern of yours. Whatever they are left with here and in Europe is far more than they can earn at home. Tolly understood that. He played the game according to our rules and nobody has been hurt.'

'Except Lennie Simons.'

Yevneko's eyes bored into him, plumbing the depths of his mind. 'Lennie Simons. Now why should you think his unfortunate demise was anything to do with me? Or do you know something more about us?' Yevneko hesitated, like a buyer weighing fruit in his hands, deciding which to acquire. 'I think, perhaps, we shall have to discover exactly what it is that you do know.'

He turned to look at Emma. 'Or maybe we should demonstrate on your little girl the power that we have.'

'Is it just with Russian players that you work this way?' Mark asked.

Yevneko signalled imperceptibly to the man who had knocked Murganev to the ground. He lashed out with the back of his hand and caught Mark a stinging blow across the face. Emma cried out, but Mark held up his arm in the sort of gesture he had used on the field to claim off-side, but on this occasion to signal that he was not hurt.

315

'I ask the questions, Mr Rossetti. You answer them.'

Mark nodded, realising he had bought a few precious moments, but anxious to gain a little further ground without pushing so far that he put everybody else in danger. 'That's fine. You've told me.' Mark summarised. 'So you do operate that way. What, footballers, tennis players, scientists? Writers? A right little agency you've got for yourselves. Only nobody leaves to go elsewhere, do they, nobody looks for alternative management; and if they do then you get peeved, don't you?'

'We have a contract. We perform our part. It was the Murganevs who tried to break it,' Yevneko replied, being drawn into the conversation and, despite his position of strength, feeling the need to fight his corner.

'In England we take people to court for breach of contract, we don't threaten them with guns,' Mark persisted.

'I do not think English law applies to my contracts. I am afraid, Mr Rossetti, that there is so little you understand about us, though there is so much you think you know. I have, perhaps, underestimated you a little. Not too much – because otherwise you and I would have our positions reversed. I believed from what I heard that you were just another footballer, whose brains were in your feet. Although one who was indeed fortunate to have found a woman as smart as Miss Delaney.'

Patti opened her mouth to say something. Mark could not recall her ever remaining silent for so long, but Yevneko put up his hand, palm towards her, and to Mark's surprise, and perhaps her own as well, she cut herself off without a word. Mark just hoped she was putting her silent time to good advantage in conceiving a plan, because his mind was a total blank. He could only hope and pray that Jennings would arrive in time. Even then, he could not be sure that he might not be leaping from the frying pan into the fire. However, if Jennings were to prove not to be on the side of the angels, Mark could not help thinking that he would rather be at his mercy than that of Yevneko.

What did he know that he had not already told Yevneko? The football stuff was all clear to him now. Hertsmere had been set up, if not twice then at least once, with the Karpov transfer. That's why Simons had become involved. They'd heard that with him on the team they were sure to succeed. His greed would drive the transfer home – and then what happened? Had he got a little too greedy?

So was Yevneko also involved in the other events that had befallen Mark and Patti since they'd inherited Leopold Schneider's land, or was that all coincidence? Lydia Karlovich, poor sweet Lydia, poor dead Lydia. It seemed to him now that she too had been a victim. Yes, if Yevneko wanted to discuss what he knew then he would also have to put that on the agenda, but not yet. Some things were better left unsaid for the moment. Not that Mark felt he had a great chance of survival, but if his nuisance was limited to football, and if Yevneko was going to withdraw gracefully, or ungracefully, from that particular field, then he had some chance. If the Russian realised he was in the frame for the domestic matter then Mark might as well say his prayers, and quickly at that.

Leo, did you know what you were getting us into when you gifted us that land? he thought to himself, and immediately answered, Certainly not.

The gentle old Jew had regarded it as a kindness, a way of pulling together two people of whom he was exceptionally fond. Well, he'd done that all right. Here they both were, and here they were likely to stay, until death did them part. Only in this case, death was not going to part them, death was going to unite them far more permanently than Leo could ever have anticipated.

Mark keened his ears like an animal, straining to hear the distant sound of a car, or any form of life that might in turn grant him life. If Jennings was coming then he assumed he was coming mob-handed, and they were hardly likely to walk up to the front door and knock. He took a sharp breath as he sensed rather than heard the sound of a vehicle. It was probably a false hope, anybody could be driving, and at that time of night every sound travelled huge distances. That time of night. He realised he had lost all track of time. A quick glance at his watch told him it was past one in the morning. That rather ruled out the casual passing motorist, although it could be somebody totally unrelated to their drama returning from a restaurant or a party.

Keep talking. If you can hear it so can he, he thought to himself, but Patti saved him the trouble. She had a protective arm around Emma, and the three of them seemed to have moved closer together, excluding everybody else in the room.

'So where do we go from here? I'm not sure I can take much more of the suspense. You've got your player back – and his wife. We've done nothing to harm you permanently, just a little inconvenience. Why not let us go?'

Yevneko smiled, that by-now familiar smile that had no humour, no tolerance, no pity, the smile of the snake about to pounce, the smile of the sadist taking pleasure from pain.

'Why not indeed?' he echoed.

Emma, more naive than Patti or her father, exhaled the breath she seemed to have been holding for hours.

'Why not?' Yevneko continued. 'I tell you why not. Because you are honest people and your honesty will make you lie to save yourselves. What are you going to tell me? What assurances are you going to give me? That you will say nothing, that you will erase this whole experience from your memories? I think not. I think that you will go straight to the police. I am many things, but I am neither gullible nor stupid.'

'You never intended this to end this way, did you?' Patti asked angrily, furious with herself for any falsely optimistic thoughts she might have harboured.

'The road to hell is paved with good intentions – is that not

318

an English proverb, or have I got it wrong? But to be perfectly honest, although I suspect it will be small consolation, no, I did not intend it to end this way. You must understand, I am not a sole entrepreneur. I have commitments to others.' He sighed. 'To so many others.'

It was at that moment that the door quite literally exploded. Mark instinctively grabbed Emma with one arm and Patti with the other, pulling them down to the floor with one continuous motion. He did not even look to see what had happened to Yevneko, but merely waited for a moment or two before raising his head, expecting to see Jennings, hoping to see the comforting bulk of Davies. In fact what he saw filled him with astonishment.

'Claudio, you old bastard. I thought you were going to give me until morning.'

Barlucci shot him an apologetic grin, a grin that was perhaps more lop-sided than usual, a grin that suggested to Mark that all was not quite well in the large, wide world of Claudio Barlucci.

Yevneko scrambled to his feet.

'Barlucci.'

'Nikolei.'

Mark looked from man to man as if he were watching a tennis match. He suddenly remembered again just who Yevneko had sat next to at Hertsmere. It was all becoming too confusing. Barlucci and Yevneko knew each other. Barlucci was good; Yevneko was bad. Barlucci had pointed him in the direction of this cottage, but had he known Yevneko would form a welcoming committee, and if so then why had he been sent to put himself and his loved ones in danger? He began to put his thoughts into words.

'Not that I'm ungrateful, Claudio, but if you knew what I was in for then you took your time to organise the rescue.'

He saw the smile was back on Yevneko's face and wondered what it would take to wipe it off once and for all.

'Rescue,' Yevneko said slowly, savouring the word as if it were new to him. 'No, I do not think so. Once again, Mr Rossetti you find yourself in the way. I think you call it the meat in the sandwich. Your friend Claudio Barlucci has come for me, but I do not think he will be taking you with him. I fear you are again cast as the man who understands too little, but knows too much.'

Mark got to his feet and automatically dusted himself down. 'Is that right, Claudio? Tell me this bastard's lying through his teeth.'

Barlucci gave him a long regretful look, and as he did so Mark knew with a terrible certainty that Yevneko was telling the truth.

CHAPTER 56

Now Mark Rossetti was really angry. He was angry with himself for being fooled, for wanting to trust Claudio Barlucci because he liked him, for ignoring the first rules of self-preservation he had taught himself – never to take anybody at face value. He was angry with himself for not thinking it through, for eliminating the likes of Barlucci from suspicion because he regarded them as friends. Yet when it all came down to it, how much did he really know about the Italian, how much had he been permitted to know?

He had looked at him through rose-coloured glasses because of the available comparisons. Barlucci and Versace, his old rival in Rome; Versace bad and therefore Barlucci good. He had made the same instinctive mistakes when his old friend had burst into this room. Yevneko bad, Barlucci good. Too many Westerns with men in white and black stetsons. It had never occurred to him that there could be two types of bad guy. Yet, listening to Yevneko and Barlucci talking, it was quite clear that this was indeed the case.

Had he been wrong to trust anybody? He felt an increasing despondency at pinning his hopes on Alex Jennings, a man he knew even less about than Barlucci. He was just a pawn in a game and he did not even know who was moving the pieces, had no real idea whose game it was. All the others – Sinclair, Savvas, the Russian policeman, Clemenceau, Ray, even Patti – he felt he had to rethink his relationship with them, to try and see if he was being used or even abused. If only he'd done that earlier he might well not have been fooled by Barlucci. Yet, how much time did he have left to readjust his perspective? Not very much, he feared.

He'd always known the Italian had sailed close to the wind, but that had been part of his attraction. It all began to fall into place – his sudden abandonment of his home team and his move to London, not to be near to Hertsmere, his adopted love, but to be close to Yevneko, his mafioso partner. Thinking back, it had almost certainly been Barlucci who had urged Sinclair to look abroad, and Mark was equally sure that Karpov had been his man, his target. So much he recalled – so much, so late.

Barlucci seemed to have no compunction at all about talking freely to Yevneko, and that did not augur well. Mark tried to make Emma meet her 'Uncle' Claudio's eye, to shame him into saving them from harm, into granting them a reprieve that he felt sure was within his power, but it was to no avail. This was not the avuncular bear of a man who had so amused him with his tales of how he had bucked authority. This was a hard, ruthless stranger who had come to take vengeance on a man he perceived as having wronged him; and Mark had merely been a diversionary tactic. Bucking authority – that was one way of putting it; another was simply breaking the law, although he had not seen it in that light at the time. So much he had not seen.

There was no other explanation as to why Barlucci had turned up at the cottage with three men armed to the teeth. He simply had to pick up the strands of the story from what he could hear. The Russian mafia seemed to have branches in New York and Tel Aviv, that much was clear. Barlucci had personally negotiated a tripartite pact between the Italian mafia representatives in Rome and the respective Russian groups in the States and Israel. After that meeting it had been decided that Yevneko could be put in charge of London, with its increasing ties with Moscow. That, it appeared, had been fine; it had worked well and profitably. The only problem was that Yevneko was directly responsible to Barlucci. And that had not been fine, that had not worked well. Yevneko had never been able to see beyond the face that Barlucci showed to the world, the laughing clown, the apologetic villain, who seemed to rejoice in the role of Robin Hood. He had considered it an insult that someone like Barlucci should rise above him in the hierarchy. The Russian mafia in Tel Aviv and New York was run by the Jews. Why did they put a Catholic into the game, who had no manners, no taste, no veneer, no culture and probably no intellect?

Though Yevneko was certainly wrong on the final count, there had come a breaking point, which appeared to have been Lennie Simons. Yes, he had got greedy, but Barlucci had only wanted to scare him. Simons had a value whilst alive. He was their man, their contact with the players, their only contact. He could do things they could not do and with him dead there would be a need to find another agent. That would take time and money. They would have to put up a new bond for two hundred thousand Swiss francs to get this new agent a FIFA licence. It would be a learning process, learning of the new man's weakness, tempting him into the net with whatever kind of honey it might take. Yevneko had thought otherwise. Simons had broken the rules, and in his book for that sort of breach there was only one punishment. It had been duly exacted and Yevneko could not see he had done anything wrong. Barlucci tended to think otherwise. There were further matters. Alleged accounting deficiencies, hirings and firings not approved from above, a certain profile that was not to the liking of Tel Aviv. Tel Aviv did not want a profile. Tel Aviv had enough to cope with domestically, with the vast influx of Russian Jewry that had not yet been absorbed. Israel, privately, regarded them as a liability, but a liability they had to welcome publicly under the law of return that gave every Jew the absolute right to come to live in his homeland, a liability that pushed the population of the tiny country to bursting.

The Mafia, however, clearly saw them as an asset, another means to a profitable end, Mark surmised. They spoke the same language, and Russian mafia demands were no surprise to them. They'd not yet started to move into Israeli footballers, but that was tomorrow's plan. It wasn't as easy in Israel as in Moscow – the native-born sabras were tough cookies who'd fought for every inch of their land – but the mafia knew that if you tried hard enough, if you hit people where it really hurt, then nothing was impossible. When they finally moved into that business then England, Italy and Israel were going to be good markets, and they weren't about to let Yevneko screw up for them with his blind ambition for power.

All this Mark gathered as Barlucci and Yevneko argued in their mutual foreign language of English, in the now ominous stillness of the Cotswold night. And then he gathered that Barlucci the negotiator had been turned into Barlucci the avenger by the powers to which even he was subject. Yet, somewhere along that road to vengeance, the Rossettis and Patti had got in the way. Presumably the Murganevs would be retained, brought to heel, like disobedient dogs. Karpov was anybody's, but Mark could not envisage that Barlucci would rely on his past friendship with him to ensure he kept silent. Claudio knew Patti too well to underestimate her as a journalist. There was a story here, a major story, and if she stayed alive it was not one she was likely to let get away. Even if they promised to ignore the night's events there was too great a risk – it was not worth trying to open negotiations in that respect.

Suddenly Barlucci was all business, and what happened next occurred so swiftly that it seemed to be a whole series of scenes from a Tarantino movie shown in rapid motion. A gesture to his armed men, and one of them grabbed Emma, the other Patti, and they hustled them outside. Yevneko and Karpov, sensing danger, moved behind Barlucci into the corner of the room. The third of Barlucci's men fitted a silencer to one of his weapons and, to Mark's horror, methodically raked Yevneko's men with gunfire, almost cutting them in half. When he'd finished, Barlucci looked at Mark as if to say, At least I have saved your daughter from the sight of this carnage. But the Englishman saw no other sign of pity or remorse in his eyes.

'Now, Marco, I am afraid we have to go. I think your friend Jennings will be here soon and there are good reasons why I do not wish to be here to make him a nice cup of English tea.'

'My friend Jennings,' Mark mocked. 'I thought it was my friend Claudio.'

Barlucci made the now familiar gesture of extending his hands while shrugging. 'It could have stayed that way, but I too have masters. I am sorry. I will be sure to make it quick and painless – for all of you.'

'Then don't drag out the agony. Do it here and be done with.' Mark could barely believe what he was saying – it was almost as if he too were playing a part. But 'all of you' meant his daughter too.

Barlucci shook his head. 'Alas, it is not possible. The English police find three dead Russians, it is a puzzle but it is not a problem. Gang warfare. They give names to the authorities in Moscow, and your Mr Clemenceau tells them they are all criminals, all murderers. So the courts and the executioner have been saved a job, the mother country has been spared the expense. But they find an Englishman, his daughter and a journalist with a reputation, we have a manhunt. Much better, I think, if you disappear, slip quietly away. You are not dead, you are not alive – you are just missing. And after a while you are all forgotten. Yes, much better I think. Now come.'

Mark moved slowly towards the door, his feet leaden as if weighed down by heavy shackles. So Barlucci knew that Jennings was coming. But how? Another case of nobody telling Mark Rossetti what was going on. What a fool he'd been taken for – and his foolishness was going to kill Emma and Patti.

'Marco, I really take no pleasure in this, but I am not an idiot, and I know that you can move faster than that. If you do not do so then I will have to ask my man here to help you.'

Mark's eyes took in the devastation they were leaving behind. However remote the cottage, however effective the silencers, surely somebody must have heard something. Yet, as he took his first step out into the night air, there was no indication that anyone but the animals was aware of their presence. An owl hooted in the trees, a night-hawk rose into the sky, a small furry creature scuttled across the road, its eyes little jewels of light. Emma and Patti were standing limply in front of their captors. The Murganevs seemed to have lost all sense of purpose, all sense of time and place. Yevneko stared into space, as if whatever was happening was beneath his dignity to acknowledge. Tolly Karpov just wanted to talk to anybody who would listen, and in particular Barlucci, who would not.

'If he says another word,' the Italian said to the man who stood behind Emma, 'hit him with your gun. He's giving me a headache. If he says anything after that, then cut his tongue out and stuff it down his throat.'

Karpov immediately paled and fell silent.

'Now,' Barlucci continued, 'quickly into the cars.'

He gestured towards the two saloons that could now be seen in dim silhouette by the roadside, their shapes gradually becoming clearer as a cloud passed in front of the moon. Hunter's moon, Mark thought. Only they were the prey, and somewhere, sometime soon, it would all end as the pack had its way with them.

He had to do something and he had to do it before they got into the cars. In the open there was a chance, a slim one, but a chance that he could use the countryside to his advantage.

Barlucci and his men had the guns, Barlucci was confident he was in control, and because of that he had not even bothered to tie them up. The Murganevs clung to each other for comfort, she holding the child who, incredibly, was still fast asleep, having been fetched from the upstairs bedroom by one of Barlucci's men. Emma and Patti stood in front of his men, guns at their backs. Karpov was dispensable, Yevneko aloof, waiting with a calm sense of destiny for whatever his erstwhile superior had in store.

It was all going to work so easily. Jennings, when he arrived, would be left with three dead men within and a group of missing persons, some of whom would remain missing and others who would remain silent.

Mark looked at his daughter, trying desperately to think of a sign she would understand, a signal from her childhood that would give her some indication that something was going to happen even if she did not know exactly what. He closed his eyes, transporting himself back in time to the nursery, to days when he'd come back from training to play with his wife and infant daughter. She'd always so looked forward to her daddy coming home, even before she was really old enough to know who he was. Just a big man who returned smelling of shower gel, his hair still wet and plastered to his head, the man who came into the room and stuck out his tongue at her. Stuck out his tongue. Was she close enough to see the gesture in the dark? And even if she did, how quickly could Patti react? It was all going to be a massive gamble, but he had no other cards to play or dice to roll. He felt a rough push in his back and knew it had to be now, right now, or never. It was that moment on the high diving board when if you don't jump you know you'll never get up there again, the second before you push off on your skis down the black run.

When it happened it was like a chain reaction. Mark jabbed Barlucci as hard as he could in the paunch that passed for his stomach, then, instead of running, which he assumed the armed men would have expected, he fell to the ground and rolled over and over towards the road. Before Barlucci could draw his breath there were lights everywhere and a voice he recognised was telling everybody (to no avail) to stay exactly where they were. The blow, his dive, the lights – they were all part of a sequence and there was order in them; but after that all was chaos, and later he was unable to reconstruct the scene with any accuracy. Perhaps Emma followed his lead, fell forward and made progress along the ground, perhaps Yevneko seized the moment and perhaps it was Barlucci's men who fired the first shot. Whatever might be the case, there was a sudden hail of bullets flying above Mark and Emma. Mark somehow found himself by her side and covered her body with his own. One part of him wanted to bury his face into the ground, the other wanted to see what was going on, wanted to record it for all time.

As he peered up anxiously he saw Yevneko leap into the air like a small stag in flight. Only as he landed in the full beam of the arc-light did Mark realise he'd been hit by bullets in his front and back. The Russian stood for a moment, looked in disbelief at the blood pouring on to his immaculate grey suit, then fell to the ground, still with that look of distant amusement on his face.

Barlucci tried to make it to the first car – did in fact get as far as the door, pulling it half-open– and then took two bullets in his back and slid down the paintwork, his nails making a rasping sound that would echo in Mark's mind long after the noise and smell of the firing had ceased. At the sight, one of the Italian's men tossed down his gun and raised his hands in the air. It did him no good. A bullet hit his neck and blood spurted out in a red fountain that he feebly tried to staunch. The others saw the fate of the surrendering man and decided to make a fight of it. One let off a round that brought a figure crashing out of a tree, then went down himself, still firing. The other got to the side of the second car, shot carefully and accurately, then actually got inside and turned the key. As he began to pull away he failed to notice the tossed grenade that fell directly in his path and blew him and the vehicle into oblivion.

It was a strange sight as silence fell over the night once again. The shell of the car crackled and burned, a woman sobbed – Sonya Murganev – and men dressed in traditional SAS dark roll-neck sweaters and woollen caps began to appear from the clump of trees opposite the cottage. They moved cautiously, as they had been trained, not to assume the enemy was dead just because he seemed to be. Some locals had been drawn to the scene by the noise but they found themselves met by a cordon and then expertly ushered away by more men.

Two familiar figures emerged into the light – Alex Jennings and, by his side, Rob Davies, who seemed to be the only representative of the civilian police force.

'Nice touch, Mark, to distract them like that. I'm not sure we could have done it so cleanly without you,' Jennings said by way of a greeting, his lop-sided, gnome-like features looking grave despite the levity of the words.

It was then that Mark realised that Jennings, whoever Jennings might be, was wrong. It hadn't gone cleanly, with or without him. Everybody who could had risen to their feet, but Patti was still lying on the ground, her red jacket splayed out about her like a cloak. Only she hadn't been wearing a red jacket, it had been white, and the still spreading stain was her life blood, a life that Mark knew at the moment he desperately wanted to share for ever.

CHAPTER 57

It had been a hard struggle to be allowed to sit by her bed. No, he was not her husband; no, he was not family . . . It had taken the intervention of Rob Davies to gain him permission, and now, by her side in the Oxford hospital, he had mixed feelings. If only he had waited, if only he had listened to Jennings; but life could not proceed upon the basis of 'if onlys'. If, indeed, he had stayed outside then who was to say what Yevneko might have done to Patti and Emma anyway? There were moments when he felt a sense of elation that at least Emma was safe, whisked back to London to the tender care of her mother who, he had little doubt, was cursing his name at this very minute.

The Murganevs were probably tucked into bed by now, under a strict police guard. Yevneko might be dead, but from what Davies had told him there was a reasonable chance Barlucci would live – and so long as he was alive, with the chance of a trial, any witnesses were going to be in danger. Karpov, too, was in police custody, with every possibility of a kidnapping charge against him.

'I don't know if it'll stick, but it'll enable us to keep a hold of him for a while. If I had my way he'd be on the first Aeroflot plane back, with Clemenceau arranging to meet him with handcuffs and leg-chains. I get the impression that they don't have the same legal niceties there about innocent until proven guilty. A shaven head and a few years in the current version of a gulag would do him the world of good. I'm sure he'd be a great asset to the camp football team.'

Davies patted Mark's arm, giving him a reassuring smile, and told him he had to go. 'Hey, she'll pull through, Mark. She wouldn't die without writing her own obituary. I can't believe she'd let anybody else have the last word about her life.'

A white-coated doctor came in, older than the fresh-faced young man in casualty who'd admitted her in a flurry of tubes and wires. This one looked every inch the prototype professional, silver-grey hair swept back, severe, functional steel-rimmed spectacles, a long narrow face with calm grey eyes.

'I'm terribly sorry, Mr Rossetti, but I'm afraid that at this stage we will have to ask you to leave.'

Mark was impressed by the fact that at least the man had taken the trouble to learn his name.

'How is she?'

'Stable. But that could change. We have to operate to remove some of the pressure building up in her brain. That's why you need to go, while we deal with the pre-med. She's young, she's tough, and I'm told she's very stubborn. There's every reason to be hopeful, but right now you have to let us get on with it. Believe me, there's nothing you can do. I'm not a particularly religious man myself, but I'm sure that if you want to hedge your bets the odd prayer won't come amiss. As soon as we've any news –' he hesitated, then decided Mark could take the truth – 'either way, you'll be the first to know; and as soon as we can let you back in, then we will. In post-recovery I often find it helpful to have a familiar voice easing the patient back to the world.'

'So you think she'll get back to the world?'

The doctor smiled gently. 'I'm not G-d. I just do my job and let him do his.'

Mark leaned forward and moved a stray lock of hair from Patti's face, then, scared he might break down, left rapidly without a backward glance. He began to pace the corridor, the endless white corridor, remembering the day Emma had been

332

born. Sally's waters had broken on the way to the hospital and he'd thought it would be quick and easy; but four hours of waiting had felt like twenty-four, and then he'd been told it was going to be a Caesarian. But he hadn't panicked; he'd still had the anticipation of fatherhood. This was different. Same white pictureless walls, but an anticipation of death rather than life.

He didn't see Jennings at first. The small figure could have been watching him through the glass or could have just arrived; he had that ability of seeming to materialise.

'Mark. I'm so sorry.'

Mark looked at him oddly, as if trying to place him, yet all the while his thoughts were beginning to crystallise, his mind was beginning to focus on something other than Patti's survival.

'Sorry? Yeah.'

Mark's voice sounded distant, bouncing back at him off the walls. He looked down at Jennings' shoes – brown, scuffed, in need of a polish – then very slowly began to speak.

'Why are you apologising, Alex? Who *are* you?'

'Let's get a coffee. I'll explain.' He put his hand on Mark's elbow to guide him down to the cafeteria, but the other man angrily shook it off.

'You know, Alex, all of a sudden I get the feeling that I'm not going to like the explanation. That once I've heard it I may not even like you.'

'Liking has nothing to do with it—'

'Oh, doesn't it? Well, maybe not in your world, whatever that world is, but in my world you do have caring relationships. Some are good, some are bad, and sometimes you like the wrong people. I liked Barlucci. And I liked you. He let me down – I'm beginning to think maybe you did as well.'

'Coffee? Come on, it's been a long night. There's nothing you can do up here. They'll take Patti down for her operation quite soon. You may just as well be sat with a cup between your hands as pacing the hell out of their linoleum. After the coffee, after we talk, you may hate me, you may want to hit me – but we have to talk.'

For the moment the fight went out of Mark and he followed the diminutive figure down a couple of flights of stairs, like a large boat being towed into harbour by a small tug.

Jennings found them a seat in the corner and brought Mark a polystyrene cup of hot, steaming coffee. 'The china's not up to much, but what's in it smells good. Have a sip.'

Mark obeyed and felt the scalding liquid hit the back of his throat, then course its way down into his bloodstream. It was like an injection straight into the heart; once more the adrenaline was pounding and he could appear in control of his own exhausted body, a fighter doused by a bucket of water, coming out for the final round.

Jennings stirred his own drink, his head to one side, seeking a way, a place to start, deciding just how much he would tell. 'OK. I guess we owe you some kind of explanation, although if you ever repeat a word of this I'll deny it, even assuming you can find me. If last night happened at all, then I wasn't there, and you'll not unearth anybody who'll say any different, not even your good friend Rob Davies. I was simply another Robin Goodfellow passing through, somebody who came into your mid-winter dream. Do I make myself clear?'

'I think you mean my nightmare, but yes, it's clear.'

'I am, I suppose, a civil servant. I work for a government department with special responsibilities for that part of the Eastern bloc that was Russia. Until Glasnost, our activities and interest were political, but now we're more concerned with the criminal forces that our liberal, reformist friends over there have unleashed – greed, corruption, protection, drugs, prostitution. I thought I'd seen it all. What's come out of the woodwork over there is really something special.'

'How long have you worked in Russia?' Mark asked, the

question banal, the polite conversation instinctive rather than of any great interest in the answer.

'Worked, or been there?' mused Jennings. 'A lifetime – at least it seems a lifetime. I went at first to a different country, but then I was different man.'

He took a sip of his coffee, reflected, then continued. 'I found it easy to get to know the Murganevs. We'd been watching Yevneko for a long time. He was into everything in Moscow; nothing was out of bounds for him as long as it made money. He had a whole band of hookers working for him, some of them just kids – ten, eleven, maybe even nine. Your Emma was almost past it by their standards. Believe me, wherever Yevneko is now, it's not going to be pleasant for him.'

'I didn't think you were the believing type, Alex,' Mark said.

'Some days I'm not. Some things I've seen . . .' His voice trailed off and his eyes momentarily became clouded and distant. 'Anyway, Yevneko seemed to have no problem with my involvement with the Murganevs. He was taking a slice of their income. If Dimitri had somebody helping him with his contract he was likely to get more money. The more he got, the more Yevneko took. I had to take a tough line so as not to arouse suspicion and he was delighted with the deal I negotiated, delighted when the flow of players began out of Russia. What they earned over there was peanuts compared to the riches on offer in Europe. All he needed was to ensure that nobody left without his consent, and for that he had to be sure they were sufficiently scared to go nowhere unless he said so. Even then if he wasn't one hundred per cent sure he kept someone behind as his insurance policy.'

'And he wasn't sure about Murganev?'

'No, he wasn't sure; but he was even less sure about Sonya. That's why he put her on the game.'

Mark shook his head in disbelief, even though he knew more than anybody that what Jennings was saying was the cold hard truth. 'How did he make her do that?'

'Simple. She had a child. She loved her. He said if she didn't do as he asked then she would no longer have a child to love. Nice guy, hey? It was a particularly unpleasant touch to send her to you. Weren't you tempted?'

'No, Alex, I wasn't tempted,' Mark replied, thinking how he'd thought about Patti as he'd refused Sonya's advances. The aching began again, the panic began again. Even now the surgeon's knife was poised over her body, cutting through her flesh, finding its way through the maze of arteries and nerves.

'So how did Sonya get away?' Mark asked.

'Simple. I arranged it. We waited till Murganev was safely in England, then I called and told her to get the hell out. By then Yevneko was up and running in London. We had to spook him.'

'So you used Sonya.'

'Used. Helped. You pays your money, you takes your choice. In my world semantics are just another tool of the trade. Whatever. I got them out, had them met, rented the cottage.'

'And Emma went too.' There was a hard edge coming into Mark's voice.

'What could I do? I could hardly leave her there. At first she wasn't part of the escape plan, but then it was perfect. We'd paid off a few individuals at the airport, but having Emma along for the ride made it so much easier.'

'I'm pleased she could oblige.'

Jennings leaned across and touched Mark's hand. 'It wasn't like that, my friend, I promise you. I really thought she'd just fly over, stay a night or two, then come home; but it began to get nasty and the cottage was the safest place for her. We thought of having somebody guard the house, but decided it would attract too much attention in a sleepy little place. We thought that if we had any kind of problem we could react quickly enough.'

'And was it the safest place for Patti as well?'

Jennings said nothing. He could see two red spots appearing on Mark's stubbled cheeks and knew that nothing he could say would ease the pain or assuage the anger that was rising like a volcano in the man seated opposite him.

'Go on,' Mark said grimly.

Jennings neatly changed the subject, although what he had to say did nothing to calm the man seated opposite him. 'And then there was Leopold Schneider's Russian land.'

'Don't tell me. Yevneko wanted it for a theme park of Cossack fairy stories.'

'No. Close, but somehow I don't think Yevneko was into fairy stories. He did indeed want the land. More than that, he actually had it. He was planning a department store filled with all the Western goods that he knew he could lay his hands on. Then you came along with your title deed and your claims and, worse than that, you find the one lawyer in the neighbourhood who's not scared of the big bad wolf. And so he huffed and he puffed and he blew her house down.'

'Lydia.'

'Yes, Lydia.'

'Another innocent who got in the way,' Mark said, and Jennings nodded sadly. 'Why wasn't she scared of Yevneko?' Mark continued. 'She seemed to me to be the sort of woman who would do what was necessary for her clients, but not to the point of martyrdom, at least not where her family was involved.'

'You don't miss a lot, do you?' Jennings said.

'That's not what the fans said when I used to play football,' Mark responded with a wry smile, which he immediately switched off, irritated with himself for allowing Jennings' charm to get to him once again.

'I'll tell you why Lydia wasn't scared of Yevneko. He was her husband, the father of her child. Whatever he'd done to others she couldn't bring herself to believe he would do anything to the family. She was wrong. When it came down to it he'd do anything to anybody.'

'Yevneko, Lydia's husband? You have to be kidding. Why should she have got involved with scum like that?'

'She was young. He must have been quite striking until you got to know him. She was attractive and he had the money to attract despite his less than impressive physical charms. He could be cultured; I guess under certain circumstances he could be entertaining. Everybody's entitled to one mistake in their life. Lydia made three: she married him, she had his child and then she underestimated him. When it came down to it, he had her killed for the land – your land. So all in all it was no great coincidence that led you to Lydia.'

'Couldn't you have avoided it? Shouldn't you have realised that she was putting herself in danger?'

'I think you give us too much credit. We're not divine. There's an element of free will in all human behaviour. When Lydia took on your case, she took on her own husband – and he had her killed. We didn't want it that way, she didn't want it that way, but it happened.'

Thinking back, Mark recalled her mentioning a husband, a husband in England. But even if she had told him his name was Yevneko, it would have meant nothing to him at that time, and there would have been no change in his plans. Was that what Jennings meant by free will? Mark waited for a moment to let the information about Lydia and Yevneko sink in. He would not – could not – let it go just like that; there was the child to think of. But right now he had to plough on with his search for the truth.

'So tell me about Barlucci,' Mark continued, his tone less than friendly, but now determined to learn the whole story before he exploded. 'Are you going to reveal that he also had some secret spouse that I know? Maybe he'd married Patti behind my back. These Russians and Italians have an odd way of dealing with their ladies.'

'Claudio. Your friend, my friend, everybody's friend. An odd man, yet in his way more frightening, more dangerous than Yevneko. The Russian was all bad, but Claudio—' Jennings shrugged in a subconscious mimicry of Barlucci.

'So what was good about Claudio?' Mark persisted.

Jennings paused: 'I'm not sure I can tell you.'

Mark leaned across the table and grabbed Jennings by the neck, oblivious to the gaze of the other occupants of the cafeteria. 'Alex, you've put me through a living nightmare with my daughter, you've got Patti upstairs fighting for her life without any guarantee she'll ever be the same woman even if she survives, and you say you can't *tell* me? Fuck your official secrets. We're talking people here. Have you got so far away from reality that you can't understand that? Or is there so very little difference between you and Barlucci?'

Jennings' mouth made a little sideways jerk, as if he had not had to focus on that particular question before. 'Maybe not.'

'So how was Barlucci able to find out where you'd hidden Emma and the Murganevs?'

'That was easy. Your phony story about the note had put the cat amongst the pigeons. We needed some action ourselves. So we told him. He told you. He also told Yevneko. By then we were almost sure that he'd been turned and was playing a double game. Once he'd pointed you in the direction of the cottage and was on his way himself, then we were sure.'

'So let me get this right. You deliberately got me to go down there, along with half the murderous bandits in Europe, just so you could get them tidily in one net.'

'Not quite right. It was all a bit unfortunate. Your Emma took it upon herself to leave a message on Patti's answerphone. Yevneko heard the message. He was on his way before we intended. That was when all the timing went out of synch. That, and you not listening to me when I told you to wait. I guess we were lucky in the end that only one of my men got hurt – and Patti, of course. It could have been much worse.

Look, Mark, I've been totally open with you, too open. I have to say this yet again. If anybody ever asks about all this, it never happened. I wasn't there last night, and if you claim I was nobody will ever believe you. Nobody will admit to knowing who I am. You understand that, don't you?'

Mark looked at him long and hard, wondering what it was about paid patriots that gave them the right to risk the lives of others in the name of their country. It was just a job, so did that make him a patriot or a mercenary? Suddenly he didn't care any more. All that he knew was that this man sitting so calmly, drinking his coffee in this dull cafeteria, had put his daughter's life in jeopardy. However indirectly, his actions had led to a bullet blasting its way into Patti's body. And despite all that, the man thought he was right and justified, that to stop the likes of Yevneko and Barlucci the risks had been worth the taking.

Mark pushed his chair back with a scraping noise that once again got the attention of everybody else in the room. His tall frame overhung the seated Jennings like the shadow of doom. He searched for the right words and found they were beyond him.

'Jennings, you and your pack of guard dogs, you're real cunts,' was all he said, then he hit him once and walked out of the room, leaving the prone body on the floor behind him.

CHAPTER 58

As he ran up the stairs towards the floor that contained Patti's empty room he felt a terrible sense of weariness, of waste, of disappointment. Barlucci and Jennings – he'd liked them both and they'd both used him, deceived him. Had it all been an act, or had there ever been any genuine affection on their parts? He tried to find a way through the maze of memory that was the past, but it was hopeless. Too many lies, too many deaths.

That damned Russian land. Leo dead. Lydia dead. Simons, Yevneko – all gone. And under this very roof, Patti and Barlucci, the latter under the closest of police guards, fighting for survival. Mark sat on the floor of the corridor, his long legs splayed in front of him, his back against the wall, both physically and metaphorically. There was nothing left to do, as exhaustion gave way to despair and he began to cry. It was a useless gesture, like the punch he had thrown at Jennings, but it made him feel better, and it was time he did something for himself.

The nurse who'd administered to Patti bustled by in a whirlwind of starch and efficiency.

'You can't stay here, Mr Rossetti, you're making the place look untidy and somebody's going to fall over you. I've just heard all our beds arc full, so we can't let that happen can we?'

It was all said with a gentle smile, a smile that made Mark see the absurdity of his position.

'Yes, of course, you're right. I'm sorry.'

He got to his feet, his frame unwinding like a snake entranced by its charmer.

The nurse must have been at least a foot shorter than him, yet she succeeded in total domination of the man who towered over her. 'Right, come along with you. We've a waiting room at the end of the corridor. There's nobody there at the moment. I'll put the telly on and bring you a nice, strong cup of tea. I'm on duty for another hour yet and I promise as soon as there's any news from theatre I'll be up to tell you.'

She spotted a hint of doubt in his eyes. 'Good news or bad news – I'll tell you, I promise.'

'Thanks.'

He allowed himself to be led along the corridor in a much calmer frame of mind, and placed in a well-worn armchair in the corner. The hospital administration had done their best with the room. Three prints of waterfalls and mountains, relaxing and easy on the eye, pale lilac paint on the walls in stark contrast to the bleak white outside, a coffee and tea maker, a magazine rack, and even some optimistic music from a machine in the corner.

'Music or TV?' the nurse asked.

'Music, please.'

'Any preference?'

'Your call.'

'I'm a nurse, not a disc-jockey,' she grumbled, but without any real conviction. She pressed a couple of buttons and some Mozart came quietly from the speakers on the wall.

'OK?'

'Fine.'

'Good. You just stay there and I'll get your drink from the machine. It's outwitted minds in better condition than yours. Tea or coffee?'

'I think you prescribed tea.'

'I did indeed. Just the medicine.' She hit a few buttons, there was a series of threatening noises, a hiss of hot water and the drink appeared.

'There you are. Now just stay here. Don't move until I get

back. If you need the loo it's the second door on the right, but apart from that nothing and nowhere. No pacing, mind, the carpet's new. Just sit there, close your eyes and think nice thoughts. Everything's going to be fine.'

She said the final words with the confidence of someone who'd said it all before and knew it to be true. She had to be totally genuine or else a great actress. Either way, Mark was willing to believe. He was willing to believe in Santa Claus as well, if only he would bring him Patti as a present, Patti in good health, Patti back to normal with her moods, her temper, her laughter, her love.

Whether it was the music, exhaustion, or whether the nurse had actually slipped something into the tea, he had no idea, but he awoke with a start, feeling disorientated, dirty, in need of a shave, a shower and a change of clothing. A glance at his watch told him it was ten in the morning. It must have been two by the time they'd got here and three or four when he'd returned to this floor. Six hours. The nurse must have broken her promise and gone off duty by now without talking to him. Six hours. Anything could have happened to Patti in that time, anything at all.

He rose creakily to his feet. It had been a while since he'd run every morning, but part of him almost wanted to take off now. Fresh air in his lungs, clear sky, empty streets, the chance to be alone to think, adrenaline pounding through his bloodstream. Instead of the run, however, he took a few unsteady steps in the direction of Patti's room, terrified by what he might find, or not find, as the case might be. If she wasn't there he could only think the worst. He'd seen it in a hundred movies, the sheet pulled over the face, the body removed, the bed stripped down, blankets rolled, all ready for the next occupant.

The first human being he saw was the nurse, Patti's nurse, as he perceived her to be. Now he saw that she had a name pinned to her uniform, Theresa Kelly. He felt he had known her a long time.

'I thought you'd abandoned me. How is she?' The two sentences were scrambled together.

'She's not in there,' Theresa said, without realising the effect of her words on Mark. She saw his face drop and gave him the same smile that had relaxed him in the small hours of the morning.

'They've moved her down a floor, into intensive care.'

'Intensive care?' he repeated in a tone that one might save for the word 'cancer'.

'Sure,' Theresa said breezily. 'She's had a long and serious operation. It's intensive care that she needs. You can hardly expect to see her sitting up and asking for an extra egg and the morning paper.'

'Can I see her?'

'See her, yes. Be with her, no. Come on. I'm supposed to have been off duty hours ago, but I couldn't bring myself to wake up Sleeping Beauty. Has anybody ever told you how sweet you look when you're asleep?'

'Only my mother.'

Theresa laughed. 'Then all the others don't know what they're missing.'

Again he followed her blindly, down a flight of stairs and through swing doors that opened on to a series of glass-fronted rooms.

'We have to be able to keep our eyes on them,' she said in whisper, 'but there you are, she's sleeping like a lamb.'

Patti lay still on the bed, her breathing regular, the equipment to which she was attached looking simpler and less alarming than the pre-operation array.

'Are you sure I can't touch her?'

'Sure. If you want to hang around I'll tell the staff down here where you are, because I'm off to my well-earned rest. I must say that you look as if you could do with the same in some comfortable hotel. Preferably one with a bath,' she added, holding her nose.

'That bad?'

'Worse.'

'I'll go and have a proper wash. But apart from that I'll wait. I'm fine really.'

'Sure, and I'm the Blessed Virgin.'

He wasn't fine, and he knew it. He also knew that the waiting would be an agony, but he had nothing else to do. He had no job, no need of a job any more; yet without work to do, somewhere to go, he felt incomplete. When this was all over, when he and Patti had the chance to take stock of the situation, then there would have to be some decisions made. He made his way back to the room where he'd spent the night, via the gents, where he did his best to tidy himself up. He knocked a disposable pack of washing things out of a machine that looked as if it might have been stolen from an airport, then shaved unsteadily with a wobbly razor and cleaned his teeth. He felt and looked marginally better and was grateful for the time he'd managed to absorb in the simple tasks.

As he pushed open the door he was annoyed to find the waiting room occupied. He'd come to regard it as his exclusive territory and the last thing he wanted was company or conversation. His annoyance turned to surprise when he realised that the man in dark glasses seated in an armchair with his back to the door was Alex Jennings.

'Morning, Mark. Sleep well? I did. That was quite a punch.'

'I hope you're not expecting me to apologise.'

'No. I deserved it.'

'So why are you here?' he asked, without any show of regret or contrition.

'To finish my story.'

'I'm not sure I really want to hear it.'

'Oh, I think you do,' Jennings replied, with a calm certainty that Mark found even more annoying, largely because he was right. 'From what I gather it'll be a good few hours before Patti comes round. It'll help to pass the time. And the story affects her as well. Have a seat, have a cup of tea.'

'Why is it everybody is trying to pour tea down my throat?'

'Probably a sense of triumph because they've got the hang of this machine.' Jennings nodded in the direction of the debris in the waste-bin which attested to some half a dozen abortive efforts to make a drink.

Despite himself Mark managed a laugh. 'The nurse warned me.'

'And she was right. A perceptive lady. She even got my eye seen to in casualty with a minimum of time and form-filling. I told you I wasn't at the cottage and I sure as hell don't want to have been involved in a punch-up here either.'

He removed the dark glasses and Mark looked with horror at the puffy eye sheltered beneath a swelling and a bruise of rainbow hues.

'I'm not usually a violent person.'

'I know.' Jennings handed him a cup of tea. 'You ready for that story?'

Mark nodded. It had been a long night and it threatened to be a longer day. He was too tired to talk. He might as well listen. He walked over to the window before he sat down, just to convince himself it was daylight, just to get back his time bearings, that his own wrist-watch could not supply. He saw a car he thought he recognised, but then he was so exhausted he could have been hallucinating. He rubbed his eyes in disbelief, then looked again. When he was sure of what he was seeing then he knew that whatever Jennings had to say would have to wait. It was time for action, not for words.

CHAPTER 59

He didn't know why he said nothing to Jennings. He merely dashed from the room like a man possessed. Perhaps it was because too much had been happening around him, too much had occurred which had been out of his control – and this time he had a chance of doing something about it himself.

The top floor was where Jennings had said they were keeping Barlucci, the top floor, under armed guard, until he was well enough to move. He took the steps two at a time and burst through the door at the top of the final flight. There was no evidence that any security was there at all.

In fact, there was an eerie silence along the whole corridor. Obviously all other patients had been moved off the floor to accommodate Barlucci's arrival, causing the area to seem totally removed from the rest of the hospital. Mark's mind recalled a science fiction story he had read in his youth about a high-rise building without a thirteenth floor, built by a superstitious developer. And then, mysteriously, the elevator had once stopped on that floor, stopped in that void, never to move again. That was how he felt. Whatever dangers were ahead of him he would have to face them on his own.

Have to? No, that wasn't right. He could turn around right then, and go back to Jennings to tell him what had aroused his suspicions. Yes, he could do that, but he didn't want to. He felt foolishly indestructible, as if his survival from the events at the cottage had meant that nothing could touch him again.

Then he saw the guard and felt reassured. Whatever was

347

happening was only about to happen. He had got there in time and now he could pass the responsibility on. He'd got on to the floor because it had been intended that he should be allowed on to the floor. He'd now show his credentials and be allowed to leave in peace, and anybody who meant harm to Barlucci would get no further. He didn't know why he wanted no harm to come to Barlucci either. Surely it would be better all round if he were to be blotted out, if there were to be no trial, no involvement of frightened, innocent people. But he could not convince himself of that. There had to be justice, and justice had to be seen to be done. All of the victims deserved that, and at once he knew precisely why he was there, despite all the grief that Barlucci had caused him and his family.

He moved swiftly towards the guard. He could see that he was wearing the same outfit that had been worn by the rescuers at the cottage – dark roll-neck sweater, dark baggy trousers. The man's hair was fair and close-cropped. Mark was virtually on top of the guard before he realised why he had not been stopped, why the man even now made no movement. There, in the middle of his forehead, was a single bullet wound, so neatly drilled that it looked like some kind of birthmark, as if it could not possibly have done so much damage to have snuffed out this young man's life. Another nameless victim.

Mark hesitated before going into the room that the dead man had been guarding, not so much worried for his own safety, but scared as to what grisly sight might meet his eyes. But the door was already open, and he had only to push it a little wider. There were three bodies inside, none of them remotely resembling Barlucci's huge bulk. All of them were young, all of them wore the SAS-type clothing, and all of them had been disposed of with one shot. It was the work of consummate professionals, but Mark knew that now was not the time to stand and admire their handiwork. Quite how they had managed to take out four highly trained guards he could not for the moment begin to imagine, but they had, and for the moment he had only to deal with realities.

The man in the car downstairs. The fact that he was still there surely meant that Barlucci's removal had not been completed. Mark forced himself to touch one of the bodies. Sure enough, the man felt warm and alive to his fingers. Whatever had happened, however it had happened, it had only just taken place – of that he was sure. Once again, he had been saved by a matter of moments. He had little doubt that if he had arrived fractionally earlier he too would be lying sightless and dead by a single bullet wound.

It only added to his sense of inviolability as he looked around desperately for the route that must have been taken by Barlucci's rescuers, if indeed they had come to rescue him. His mind raced through the possibilities, the chance that he was being removed not for his own good, but for the good of those at whom he might point the finger. If half of what Jennings had told him about Barlucci was correct, then surely he would not hesitate to do anything within his power to save his own skin, whoever he had to destroy to achieve that aim.

There was something missing from Barlucci's room, something so obvious that it was easy to miss. It was a hospital room, like any other, intended, it would seem, for private use. The decor was of a higher standard than anywhere else he had seen in the building, and there was a bathroom off it. The television was still playing on a satellite channel, urging him to buy a new breakfast cereal. There was a fitted hanging wardrobe and a matching bedside table – but there was no bed. Whoever had carried out this raid, whoever had taken Barlucci, had wheeled him out on the bed.

There was only one way they could have gone with that encumberance, and that was the largest lift at the opposite end of the corridor from where he had arrived, the lift that led down to the operating theatres at one level and the rear car park at the other, the same car park where he had seen the car with the familiar occupant.

He moved swiftly towards the stairs that would take him down, glancing out of the window as he ran, noting that the car was still there – but now there was an ambulance next to it, its rear doors open and the ramp down, all ready to receive a patient on a bed, all ready to receive Claudio Barlucci, who, he felt with increasing certainty, was about to make his final journey.

His knee was beginning to hurt him, as he leapt down the stairs, and he hoped it would last him long enough to make it to the ground. He was working on automatic, and the auto-pilot did not permit him to ask the question of how he was going to deal with the armed marauders who had easily taken out the four expertly trained men who now lay dead above him.

He came out into the fresh air cautiously. There were other people around and there was no reason to draw any attention to himself. They had the bed on the ramp. He could see the form beneath the blankets, which he guessed from its size had to be Barlucci. To his surprise there were only three of them. One man, who seemed to be guiding the bed into the back of the ambulance, was not only dressed as a doctor, but seemed to have some kind of medical skills. They wanted Barlucci alive, it seemed, to learn all he knew – otherwise there was no reason why a bullet should not have ended things for him also on the top floor of this Oxford hospital.

The Mini with the number-plate SAV 1 started up. Savvas Constantinou, the banking saviour of Hertsmere, had seen the man who threatened his life and livelihood safely ensconced in the ambulance, and it was time for him to go, to follow them wherever they planned to take Barlucci, and presumably to take charge of the interrogation. Without hesitation, Mark went for the car rather than the ambulance, and jumped at the driver's door, gambling on it not being locked. It flew open in his hand, and the Cypriot's eyes showed their absolute surprise. Instead of accelerating, he made the mistake of taking a hand off the wheel and fumbling in the glove compartment, presumably for a weapon.

That was all Mark needed. He pulled hard at Savvas's neck and had him half out of his seat before the men completing the loading operation could see what was going on. One more effort and Savvas was out of the car completely. With a muscle-wrenching leap, Mark was in his place and driving the car straight for the ramp that led into the back of the ambulance, without any real thought as to what might happen when he finally made impact.

CHAPTER 60

'Well, well, if it isn't our own little 007,' Jennings said, in a mixture of sarcasm and admiration. 'We were all terribly impressed by that audition for a Bond movie, not to mention your experiment to prove that a Mini can fit quite tidily into the back of an Oxfordshire Health Authority ambulance.'

The hospital had promoted them from the waiting room to one of the administrative offices. Rob Davies had departed with his assistant, Jennings had speedily supervised the cleaning-up operation, and Mark was left with the feeling that Alex had seen worse in his time. That was not to say that he was letting Mark off lightly.

'You know you really seem to attract trouble. Why the hell couldn't you have told me what you'd seen, what you were going to do?'

'You mean like you let me into your whole game plan? At least this time it was only my life on the line.'

'Was it, Mark? And what if those goons had started shooting up the hospital? Just because you decide you're going to be a hero . . . Jesus, I hate amateurs.'

Mark gave him a quizzical look, trying to decide whether or not he was serious, but with Jennings it was never easy to tell.

He was just coming down from the buzz of it all. Savvas had been running after the car and his shouts had attracted the attention of the two hit men, but it had been in vain because Mark and the Mini were on them before they could do anything about it. Mark had braced himself for the collision, knowing he had not had time to put on the seat belt, knowing that whether it was to be metal on metal or metal on flesh it was going to hurt.

In fact the anticipation had been worse than the deed. The bed was already up the ramp, but the first man turned and was caught a crushing blow by the front bumper of the car and that in itself protected Mark from the worst of the crash. The second man was pinned between the passenger door and the interior of the ambulance, and it was only as Mark reversed that he realised he had crushed the killer's chest on first impact. The doctor crouched behind Barlucci's bed, which was slightly bent but otherwise unharmed.

After that it was a case of Jennings picking up the pieces. He may have lost four men on the wards, but he had some back-up positioned at the front of the building and they speedily arrested Savvas and had him winging his way back to London before the local media arrived. The bodies of Jennings' men and their assassins were treated like any other natural death in a hospital and, having momentarily over-crowded the morgue, went to their respective rests, their deaths unreported, their names concealed. They were taking no chances with Barlucci and he too was despatched, this time in a prison ambulance with an armed motorcycle escort, down the M40 towards the top-security wing of Wandsworth Prison.

Rob Davies had been summoned back to smooth things over with the local constabulary, but now it was only Mark and Jennings left to talk.

'I suppose you think you've been very clever, that you qualify as a real private investigator now, don't you?'

'I didn't do it to be clever.'

'So why did you?'

'Hard to say. I saw his car out of the window and suddenly it all seemed so obvious. He arrives at Hertsmere shortly after Barlucci. He's a banker. His bank is based in Cyprus. Cyprus is near Israel. I remembered what you'd been telling me and it all clicked into place. I assume Barlucci needed an amenable banker who wouldn't ask too many questions. When Savvas realised what had happened to Barlucci and presumably learned he was also still alive, he also realised that he was going to point the finger in his direction, so he had to do something about it, and quickly at that.'

Jenning leaned back in his chair and applauded. 'Very good. I guess we would have got him eventually.'

'Sure, with Barlucci's help. Without Barlucci . . . ?'

'This isn't some sort of competition, you know, Mark.'

'It is, Alex. You made it one. Is there any more news of Patti?'

Jennings shook his head. 'They know where we are. They've promised to call us as soon as she comes out of it.'

'And if she doesn't?'

'They've promised to call then as well.'

Mark tapped his fingers on the arm of his chair. His actions had taken so brief a period of time, yet they seemed to have taken for ever, and he found it hard to accept that Patti had slept through it all. If and when – no, when she could talk, all of this was going to take some explaining.

'So that's all the loose ends tied up, is it?'

'Not quite. We have to unravel their corporate structure. They used Cyprus for that as well. Savvas brought quite a lot to the party. Russians forming offshore companies weren't too welcome in the Channel Islands. It should be an interesting exercise. Then, of course, there's the end of my story. That is, if you can keep still for long enough. I didn't think I was that boring.'

'Believe me, Alex, boring is exactly what I'd like at the moment. Can you promise me that?'

Jennings made a pyramid of his fingers and looked at them closely, as if they might give him the solution to a particular problem.

'No, Mark. I'm sorry, I can't promise you that – but I'll tell it like it is anyway.'

CHAPTER 61

There was something both hypnotic and calming about Alex Jennings' voice. He could have been an actor; perhaps, indeed, he was. Mark had given up on placing people into pigeon holes. All of his anger seemed to have drained from him with his onslaught on Savvas. Crime and punishment. Both had been concluded. He somehow felt far more hopeful about Patti's recovery. She had survived this long, and he could not believe that so much effort could have gone into a wasted struggle.

He no longer believed Jennings to be a bad man, just someone who was motivated only by his work, focused on what he set out to achieve, oblivious to anybody who might be a bystander on the paths he took.

'You liked Schneider, didn't you?' Jennings asked with some certainty.

Mark looked up from yet another cup of tea in surprise. There had been many subjects of conversation he'd expected, but the old man had not been one of them.

'Yes, I liked him. He was good to me when I was down, believed in me when nobody else did.'

'So you weren't surprised when he left you and Patti everything?'

'Yes, I was surprised. If he'd given us something to remember him by in his will, then I'd have expected that, but everything – well, no.'

'And the Russian land?'

357

'Neither Patti nor I even knew he had any land in Russia. We both thought he was Austrian – at least that's what he had told us. Maybe he thought of himself as Austrian. Obviously I was aware of all the English properties – I lived in one for long enough. And I was actually his rent collector on the odd occasion. Leo wasn't a great one for talking about the past in any detail. He always liked to look forward.'

'Yes, he did,' Jennings said.

'What, you knew him?' Mark asked in astonishment.

Jennings nodded. 'He was helpful to us from time to time. He had no love for the old guard in Russia. They'd done things to his family which were almost as bad as the things the Nazis did to him.'

Mark stared blankly in bewilderment. 'Is there anybody, or anything, that you don't control?'

Jennings gave a reluctant smile. 'You. Although if you ever want a job in the future, I think we might be able to find you an opening.'

'I don't need your job,' Mark said, a hard edge of bitterness returning to his voice.

'No, I forgot. You're a man of independent means, courtesy of Leopold Schneider.'

'You said he helped you from time to time. How?'

Jennings hesitated as if he regretted going down that particular road. A flicker of annoyance crossed his face, simply because he should have anticipated that Mark would not permit him to tell the story in his own way without any diversion, without any cross-examination. 'He's dead, so I suppose it can't hurt now. He was still in touch with a whole crowd of people from the "old countries", as he put it. Some of them he'd met in the camps, some of them went back even further than that. They had a weekly drinking session. They drank vodka, some schnapps, but for the most part it was lemon tea. I saw them once, sitting in a café in the Finchley Road. They were wearing clothes that went out with the ark,

looking like characters from a Chekhov play. I guess they felt
they were dressing up for an occasion and that was the best
they had to offer. Schneider would listen—'

'Yes, he was a good listener,' Mark interrupted with a lump
in his throat.

'He *was* a good listener, and from time to time he'd pass on
what he thought was information. Usually it was either stuff
we knew already or the dreams of old men, but just
occasionally there was a gold nugget amongst it all. It was
from him that we first heard the name Yevneko. The first time,'
he paused, lost in reverie. 'But not the last,' he concluded
grimly.

He drained his coffee and made to pour himself another
from the percolator that had been thoughtfully provided. Mark
waved away the offer of another tea from the flask on the table.
It was all becoming fantastic. Was there anybody in his life
who was what they appeared to be? Leo with his huge
greatcoat, amiable Leo, some kind of spy. As he pondered on
the idea, suddenly it no longer seemed so odd. It would all
have been a game as far as Leo was concerned, another game
like bringing Mark and Patti together.

Leo had cause to be grateful to England, to a country that
had taken him in. Leo loved gossip, loved to help, but shied
away from gratitude and publicity. Apart from avarice, weren't
they the best attributes of a spy? Solitude and secrecy. There
could be no question of greed. Leo would never have done it
for the money.

Jennings fidgeted with the polystyrene cup, twirling it
around with the tips of his fingers as if it were too hot to
handle.

Mark looked into his eyes, seeking the ultimate truth.
'There's still more, isn't there, Alex? Come on, you've come
so far, you have to tell me everything.'

'Have to? We should have you on our interrogation team.
You know how to play the guilt card.'

'Guilty? You, Alex? I don't think so. I don't know why you're telling me all this, but I don't believe it's out of guilt.'

'I gave up on motives a long time ago, Mark. Better to accept reality at its face value than wonder why or how it's real.'

He took a deep breath, then continued. 'Anyway, it doesn't really matter . . .'

A nurse peered in through the frosted glass in the top half of the door and Mark looked up, anxiously anticipating some news of Patti, but the woman went quickly away, intent on some other task.

'Relax, Mark, she'll be fine.'

'How do you know?'

'They tell me more than they tell you.'

'Why? Because if she died it would be down to you? Because you have to make sure you put all the right information in your report?'

Again a shadow flitted across Jennings' odd features. 'You were wasted as a footballer. They did you a favour getting you out of the game.' He rewound the conversation to the question Mark had asked several moments before. 'Yes, there's more. The land, Lydia Karlovich, her death – are you sure you really want to hear it all?'

Mark nodded grimly. Patti was still at the back of his mind, but as long as he was listening to Jennings the time passed in minutes rather than seconds.

'Very well.' Jennings was deadly serious now, leaving Mark in no doubt that the time for any sort of teasing, any kind of levity, was past. 'We pointed you in the direction of Lydia. I have to confess we're not sure ourselves just how much she knew or didn't know, but she was intelligent . . .'

'I can't believe you can talk about her so calmly.'

'You're not going to hit me again, are you?' Mark could tell he wasn't joking.

'No, Alex, I'm not going to hit you. I just can't come to

terms with the fact that she was brutally murdered because you decided to involve her in one of your games. She had a little girl, for Christ's sake. Don't your people care about anything or anybody?'

'Don't moralise at me, Mark. My people, your people. What's the difference? We have a job to do, just like you had once. You thought it was important to score goals, we think it's important to save lives. Sometimes there are casualties along the way. You may think they're innocent, that's your prerogative. You may think you've been hard done by and that's your prerogative too. But believe me, Mark, nobody's innocent, nobody can be a by-stander in our game as you like to call it. We're into the business of rooting out absolute evil. That doesn't mean that our side is absolutely good, it just means that we have some standards, some codes of conduct, some rules in our game. We try to play percentages. I had Rudi at both hotels to try and look out for you, and he did his best. That, at least, was how we knew Yevneko had tried to get Sonya into your bed. At the end his best wasn't good enough; maybe we miscalculated the percentages. Sure, I'm sorry about Lydia, but she didn't necessarily die because of us. She, at least, knew the rules. She knew about the forces of evil and they knew about her long before Mark Rossetti and his Merrie Men came into her life.'

Mark saw he had pushed too far. He did not want to apologise, did not think any apology was merited, but found himself mumbling 'Sorry' in any event. He wanted to hear all that Jennings had to say, and without some kind of apology there was a chance the man would simply get up and leave.

Jennings appeared mollified, and continued as if nothing had happened to halt him in his stride. He spoke more rapidly, as if his tale were coming to an end and he wanted it to be over, wanted to be away from this hospital, wanted to be out of Mark Rossetti's life for ever.

'Lydia knew all about Yevneko. He had a power base in

Pinsk. When there was nothing to sell he found things to sell – at his own price. As Russia began to move into a consumer society that threatened his operation. Yevneko was never one to let the grass grow under his feet. He had to be a step ahead. If there were goods to be sold then there had to be a supermarket in which to sell them. Your land, Schneider's land, was a perfect site. He had it already earmarked, had everything in place to build, and then you came along. You find a lawyer who's already taken him on, a lawyer who can't be bought. She proves the land's yours and he's facing a long fight through the courts. Believe me, Yevneko's killed for far less than that.'

'So he takes Lydia out. Another victim, nobody to fight her corner.'

'That's where he was wrong. Lydia genuinely believed her mother had been the sole survivor of her family, but she was wrong. Someone else came through the camps, made his way to England. Lydia Karlovich was Leo's great-niece, and neither of them knew it.'

'But you did, so why didn't you tell them?'

'We only discovered it after Leo died, otherwise we would have done. We're not totally heartless, despite what you might think. You asked me before about Lydia's daughter. Well, we've looked after her so far, but so can you from now on. Whatever Leo may have said in his will, under Russian law our lawyers say that Lydia should have inherited at least the Russian land. And after her death it would all have gone to the child.'

'So, the land's really hers,' Mark mused. 'Funny, it never really felt as if it belonged to us.'

Jennings shrugged. 'Your call, Mark. You do nothing, we say nothing. The girl never knows. Make no mistake, this is valuable real estate we're talking about, even out there. Yevneko might not be around to be building supermarkets but there'll be others who'll want to. So you see, we're not the only ones who have to make moral decisions.'

'Did you really think I'd have a problem with this? And nor will Patti. Of course, we'll make sure the land goes to the child. Maybe we'll do more, Patti and I. Perhaps we can adopt her.'

Patti and I. The sound of her name, rolling off his tongue, knee-jerked him back from the remoteness of Russia to the stark truth of here and now. As if at a signal, a nurse came hurriedly into the room.

'Mr Rossetti,' she said, her voice carefully controlled and trained to give no sign of any panic, 'it's Miss Delaney. Can you come with me, right now?'

And, oblivious to Alex Jennings, without saying goodbye, uncaring as to whether or not he ever saw him again, Mark followed meekly and blindly. As the door closed behind that part of his life he was too frightened even to ask why she had come for him just at that moment.

CHAPTER 62

It was warm in Amsterdam for early May, and the crowd gathered to see the final of the European Cup-Winners' Cup between Hertsmere and Lokomotiv Moscow, the very side from which Murganev and Karpov had been purchased, were largely in shirtsleeves.

Once again David Sinclair was amazed by the sheer number of Hertsmere supporters who came out of the woodwork on these occasions. The demand for replica blue and white shirts, Barlucci's legacy, had exceeded supply, and the chairman could not help but think that if only this level of support could have been maintained for the whole of the season he would have had no need for Italian directors and Cypriot bankers bearing gifts.

It was just after half-time and the game was still goalless. They needed to win this, needed it desperately after such a traumatic and disappointing season. It had been just a week before that they had assured themselves of Premier League safety, with a narrow victory over their old rivals Thamesmead. But for the fans that wouldn't be enough. For too many years they'd endured the taunt from the fans of Liverpool, Arsenal and Manchester United of 'Silverware, no silverware, you ain't got no silverware. From Park Crescent to anywhere, you ain't got no silverware.' And last season, against all odds, they'd gone and won the cup. And now, somehow or other, more perhaps by luck than judgement, they'd struggled through to this final.

His mind went back to the semi-final against Turin, when, in a penalty shoot-out after a goalless draw, Greg Sergovich had thrown his huge frame to the left to palm the decisive shot away, and almost before he had landed on the goal-line he had disappeared beneath a scrimmage of his jubilant team-mates. It was Sergovich, again, who had kept them in this match so far, with two magnificent saves, one of which he'd tipped over the bar after the ball had taken a wicked deflection, and the other he had plucked out of the air with a clean catch when the Moscow striker was already turning away to celebrate a goal.

At the other end Hertsmere had been almost invisible in the first half. One speculative effort from Nicky Collier, who had already made it clear that this would be his last match in a Hertsmere shirt by refusing to sign a new contract, had ballooned over the bar, and the Moscow keeper could hardly have experienced a more restful forty-five minutes.

Sinclair could not envisage what Ray Fowler had said to them in the interval, but he could not believe it to have been polite. He'd been tempted to go down there himself, but it was enough that Mark Rossetti had joined the manager. It was good to have Mark back with them, scarred though he might be by his experiences; the players seemed to respect him even more than they feared Fowler. It was a shame he had made it quite clear that he had no intention of any permanent managerial position at any level, but after all he had been through because of his involvement with the club, then Sinclair could understand and respect that decision.

Suddenly, Dimitri Murganev collected the ball midway in his own half. He saw the young Welshman, Aled Williams, make a diagonal run to the left, whilst Collier ploughed on through the centre. The Russian defence expected a pass from their former player, but Murganev saw the gap open and just too late the opposition realised what he was going to do. With incredible speed of thought he made straight for goal, covering the ground in strides that suggested a much taller man. The ball appeared to be affixed to his boots by some invisible string as he switched it from one foot to the other without any noticeable let up in his pace. The Moscow sweeper, their last line of defence, moved across confidently to cover, to take him out, then was left mesmerised as Murganev cut past him on the inside. One stride later his right foot lifted back, hardly enough to cause any damage, and then the Moscow keeper was rooted to the spot as the ball sped by him into the net.

Immediately, the Hertsmere fans who had been so silent during the first half, after an initial burst of enthusiasm, came to life. As a man they rose to their feet, ignoring the efforts of the Dutch stewards to keep them seated, and began to chant their Russian player's name as if he had been a favourite from the very beginning of his career with the team. In the VIP box, David Sinclair also leapt out of his seat, ignoring the black looks he got from the various European officials and visiting dignitaries. He simply didn't care; he was just another fan and he knew more about football than they would learn if they were invited guests at a hundred such finals.

It had taken a long time, but only tonight, as he had entered this neutral stadium for the most important match ever in Hertsmere's history, did he sense that matters at the club he loved so much were returning to any semblance of normality. It had been difficult for him to accept that Barlucci had done half of what Mark had told him, even more difficult to accept that he, personally – he who had regarded the Italian as both friend and saviour – had been used. It had been far easier to cope with the truth about Savvas. They had not shared all the traumas of the Mickey Wayne situation together, had not grieved together for the loss of a child. He had kept an empty seat at his side at Hertsmere's ground all season. It had spoken of treachery, as well as a sense of loss. Once his daughter had filled that seat, then Claudio Barlucci, and although one was still alive and awaiting trial, they were both dead to him.

It had been nearly five months since the night that both

Karpov and Murganev had disappeared, with all the tragic consequences. Apart from the European run the club had experienced little success on the field, but enormous publicity off it. The press had enjoyed a field day. Simons, Barlucci, Karpov, Savvas – they'd put out their sniffer dogs and come up with enough to fill their pages every day for a month, although the names of Yevneko and Jennings had never appeared. Simons had been involved in many deals as an agent, but the poison pens decided to focus on those at Hertsmere, until Sinclair himself began believing almost everything he read.

They'd loved it even more when the team, as holders, had exited from the FA Cup to a team of third-division giant killers. They had been quick to write the obituaries for the club who'd risen to glory against all odds, who'd always been despised by the huge, successful clubs, the old money in the game, the clubs who'd hated to go to their tiny ground and then look for excuses for their defeat. Yet here they were, a goal up in a European Final, and if they could only hold on, then perhaps the ghosts of the last year or so could finally be exorcised.

The man by his side had his ghosts to exorcise as well. Mark Rossetti was living every second of the match, a man who had been reborn, a man who had learned to live again, just as Patti Delaney had also miraculously learned to live again. In the darkness of the stand her face shone with a pale transluscence and, despite the warmth of the night, she was cossetted in a huge coat, her lap covered with a blanket. She looked more like an elderly invalid than the young vibrant journalist he had first met. Yet her recovery had been remarkable – unbelievable, according to Rossetti.

Mark had left Jennings in mid-sentence when the nurse had arrived, and taken the steps to the ward in twos and threes, until only a hatchet-faced staff nurse had barred his entry into her room while they had him gowned and masked.

Relenting a little, the woman had given him the reassurance

he'd been awaiting. 'Don't be frightened by how she looks; you don't look so great yourself.'

He picked up the Irish cadence in her voice and wondered why such a small nation should produce so many sisters of mercy. Perhaps it was just an acceptable alternative to the actual sisterhood itself. He had walked slowly into the room, realising after a few steps he was on tip-toe, and had stood looking down at Patti's supine figure. Although it was less than twenty-four hours since he'd seen her, spoken with her, touched her, she seemed smaller than he remembered, as if she had curled up within herself to withdraw from the terrible events that had encircled her like a whirlwind. She'd opened her eyes and, as he saw her trying to focus, feebly lifted her hand in salute.

'Hi,' she had mouthed, and he fought back the tears, frightened that he might in turn scare her into a belief that she might not pull through. He took her hand in his and was surprised by how fragile it felt, the bones like twigs between his fingers that could snap like the branches on the winter trees outside the window.

They'd sat there for some fifteen minutes without talking further, his eyes never leaving her face, oblivious to the maze of wires and tubes that linked her up to the life-supporting system. Finally, on his hand, she'd scratched her secret message with her nails, the bitten nails about which he'd teased her so often. 'I . . . love . . . you . . .'

'I love you too,' he had said, feeling the banality of the words, yet also knowing they were taking on a new significance. He'd said them before, of course, said them a hundred times as a youngster, just to get a girl to remove her knickers; and then to Sally, his ex-wife; but he'd never meant them like he meant them at that particular moment.

He stroked her fingers, and put his own gently over her mouth, recalling how she'd annoyed him by trying to bite his nails when she had nothing left to chew on her own. She'd even been able to bite her own toenails. He couldn't believe it at the time, but then there was so much he couldn't believe about Patti Delaney; and even the unbelievable, the unpalatable, became so much a part of him that he could not envisage life without it.

It was then that the nurse had re-entered, had taken one look at Patti's racing pulse and sent him packing. But by then he'd known with absolute certainty that everything was going to be fine, that not only would she survive, but that they would survive together.

It was nearly two months before they would let her out of hospital. Mark had visited her every day, even moving himself into a hotel on the outskirts of Oxford. Some days Emma would join him, and now he always made sure someone responsible brought her on the train and took her back to Sally's doorstep. He still feared that the aftermath of Yevneko was out there somewhere, still gunning for him and his little family. But by the time he took her home he and Patti could almost see the funny side of what so nearly had been a tragedy.

'It took the Gunfight at the OK Corral to bring us together,' she joked, and as she smiled he could almost erase for the moment the memory of the gunfire illuminating the dark – almost, but not quite.

She'd insisted on coming to this match against all the doctors' advice. 'Hertsmere's first European Final. They can bury me on the half-way line at the end, but just try and keep me away.'

And they hadn't, although Mark could see her begin to shiver as the night wore on.

'Are you all right?' he asked.

'We're winning; I'm fine,' she replied, showing slight irritation at having her concentration interrupted. It was only when she took her mind off the game that she realised how weak and ill she still felt. Patti, Mark and Sinclair all leaned forward in their seats as Moscow attacked yet again, now throwing caution to the winds as the clock began to wind down inexorably against them. The rest of the Hertsmere contingent – Helen Davies, accompanied by her husband Rob, who'd actually got leave for once to be there with her; old Ben Porter, well into his eighties, but sitting up as straight as a ramrod, staying fully awake; Jonathon Black, a survivor also in his disapproving way; Sonya Murganev, now feeling safe at last – the rest of the reconstructed board, were strung together by the tension, like telephone poles, all conducting the same message. If they could will Hertsmere to victory from the stands then they would.

Wave after wave of attack was launched against the Hertsmere defence, but Darren Braithwaite, Liam O'Donnell and Stuart Macdonald cleared everything with an unnerving calm. A minute left. Macdonald, playing his captain's role to perfection, hoisted a long ball upfield. Pat Devine, the tiny Irishman in midfield, played the ball wide to Barry Reed, now playing wide on the left wing, he switched the play brilliantly with a twenty-yard crossfield pass and found Aled Williams. Williams took only one touch and instinctively knew that Murganev had made a run into the channel of uncertainty on the right flank, flicking it on with a single movement. Murganev was on it like a greyhound out of the traps; a couple of paces took him into the penalty area, the keeper came out flailing, tried to bring him down, risking a penalty and instant dismissal – but Murganev was having none of it. Arrogantly he feinted, leaving the keeper sprawled on the grass, and had time to glance at him in pity before he found the net. Two-nil. This time there was no holding the Hertsmere contingent. They were on their feet, arms raised in triumph, copying the very gesture that their player had shown to them after he had scored. David Sinclair hugged Mark and Patti. The two men supported the girl to her feet and stood there laughing and singing right until the final whistle.

The players ran to their fans and applauded them,

seemingly without end, until finally Dimitri Murganev alone peeled himself away and ran to the Russian fans. He gave them a wave and, to their credit, they sportingly cheered him in defeat. Finally he trotted over to where the Hertsmere officials were leaning over the edge of the front row of the stand. Mark saw Sonya hanging back, as if she wanted to leave the limelight to her husband and the rest of his team-mates. He took her gently by the arm, realising that, despite the fact this woman had once offered him her body, it was the first time he had actually touched her. Patti moved along slightly to allow the player's wife in beside her. Sonya gave her a sidelong look, a shy smile, that belied the knowledge of what the two women had endured together. Dimitri looked up, holding a bouquet of flowers that had been thrust upon him by the delighted English supporters. He stood for a moment, his whole face illuminated by a smile brighter than the floodlights themselves, and then tossed them up to his wife. They rose in the air and then landed from a perfect arc into her arms.

'Everything's falling into place,' Patti said, then, taking her gaze away from the Russians whose eyes were locked on each other, she fell in contented exhaustion into Mark Rossetti's waiting embrace.

EPILOGUE

Daniel Lewis was not too sure who had instructed him to sell the house in The Bishop's Avenue. He had no idea what had really happened to Yevneko. Yes, he had read all about the scandals that had engulfed his own Hertsmere football team, but the Russian's name had not appeared in any of the articles, and he had not connected the events with the fact that his Russian connection had dried up completely.

In a way he was relieved. He remembered all too clearly Yevneko telling him he was 'back on the team', and then the use, or abuse, of his client account for monies to come pouring in. Money-laundering. Nothing clean about it. He shivered, still not finally convinced, even at this late stage, that he was free from the threat of any prosecution.

Contemporaneously with his downturn in fortunes, Elaine, his wife, had also taken it into her head to withold any conjugal rights. She had been less than pleased over the cancellation of their Spring cruise and the BMW convertible for which Daniel had placed an order, and which was to have been her birthday present.

Then the phone call came from the lawyer.

'Mr Lewis? You won't know me. My name is George Carson. I represent the estate of the late Nikolei Yevneko.'

'Late?'

'Oh, you didn't know? My client met with a fatal accident earlier this year. Amongst his assets were some shares in a company called Marshland Properties Ltd, which in turn owned his property in North London, with which I believe you are familiar.'

'Yes, I introduced it. But at that time I dealt with a solicitor called Nicholas Spence.'

'I am afraid the man is unknown to me,' Carson said, in a tone that suggested that the man was unknown to anybody and that he would not welcome any further mention of his name. He belonged with a living Yevneko in the past, and this was now the present.

'Anyway,' Carson continued, 'we have established that you are familiar with the property and therefore it is only natural for us to tell you to sell it.'

'Us?'

'My firm.' The response was just a little too hasty, and Lewis felt a tremor of nerves course through his body. Business may have been slack, but despite his wife's complaints he had welcomed the absence of pressure in his life. Now, he had a nasty feeling that although he would earn a substantial amount of commission from the sale there might well be an additional price to pay.

He could, of course, always say no. He should have said no to Yevneko at the beginning, but somehow he had not been the sort of man to deny. Yet the quiet, cultured voice at the other end of the phone sounded quintessentially English, a far cry from the Russian who had so brutally ordered the destruction of his car and who knew what else. He tried to blot out of his mind the visit of the detective sergeant. He had done nothing wrong. Surely it was not the legal or moral duty of an estate agent to question the source of funds of his clients.

'So, you'll be happy to accept our instructions?' Carson persisted.

There was a pause. Lewis thought of his wife, thought of telling her the holiday and car were back on the agenda, thought of her naked body once more lying against his bare chest.

'Yes,' he said eventually, sensing even as he spoke that he had made the wrong decision.

There was a barely audible intake of breath from the lawyer. 'Very good. I'll send you a letter of confirmation. How quickly can you get round there to do a valuation?'

'Tomorrow.'

'Fine. I'll have the keys delivered.'

Carson seemed reluctant to end the conversation. 'There is one thing more.'

'Yes,' Lewis replied resignedly.

'In due course, once the sale is completed . . . you see how much confidence we place in your abilities . . . we shall require you to buy some other properties.'

'Other properties?' Lewis did not know why he felt the need to repeat everything that was being said to him, but for somebody who was usually so loquacious he was lost for words.

'Yes. There will be other purchases. Discreet purchases.'

'For who?' Lewis asked, although he had the distinctly unpleasant feeling that he already knew.

'Certain foreign clients.'

'Foreign?' Again the parrot-like repetition.

'Is that a problem? My clients have not had the impression in the past that you are xenophobic.'

'No, it's not a problem.' Lewis hesitated before asking the next question. 'Am I allowed to ask the nationality of these clients?' The word 'discreet' was still fresh in his mind.

'You are indeed allowed to ask,' Carson replied, and when the lawyer told him they would be Russian it came as no surprise at all.